THE
PRICE OF MERCY

THE

PRICE OF MERCY

A NOVEL BY

DICK HERMAN

Willowbank Books

FIRST EDITION

Previously published as
Shades of Mercy

Cover art and design by Maria O'Neil Consulting

Also by
Dick Herman

Caly's Island

Writing as
Richard Herman

The China Sea
The Trash Haulers
The Peacemakers
A Far Justice
The Last Phoenix
The Trojan Sea
Edge of Honor
Against All Enemies
Power Curve
Iron Gate
Dark Wing
Call to Duty
Firebreak
Force of Eagles
The Warbirds

For
Carolyn Marie
A muse in her own way.

Sins cannot be undone, only forgiven.

Igor Stravinsky

PROLOGUE

Claire Marie Allison loved her son, mother, husband, and sunflowers. Although she never thought about it, she loved them, more or less, in that order.

Sunflowers made the list because she had been tending them as long as she could remember. She closed her eyes and saw the sunflowers in her garden, turning and following the sun as it arced across the sky. They were still growing and heliocentric—she loved that word. Soon, they would bloom and become fixed in place. *Just like me*, she thought, *fixed in place and not following the sun.*

She pulled a face, the one that made Logan, her five-year-old son, giggle. She gazed out the window of her office. The school parking lot was jammed with cars, and a group of young mothers were chatting on the sidewalk. She nodded when two men joined them. Claire was the principal of Stella Madura Middle School, and in her world, it was a good thing when parents were involved. She sighed softly and turned to her laptop to deal with the problem of the day.

For a moment, she stared at the sunflowers that filled the screen. "Just do it," she murmured. One of Hank's favorite sayings echoed in the back of her mind: "Duty is a terrible burden." Henry 'Hank' Allison was her husband, an officer in the Air Force stationed at Luke Air Force Base on the other side of town.

She was fresh out of college and teaching advanced eighth graders basic computer programing when they first met. He was a macho fighter pilot doing his Top Gun thing at a party, and she was wearing a pair of shorts that stopped all conversation when she entered the room. It was mutual lust at first sight. They were in bed that night and eloped the next month. Logan was born two years later. She loved being a mother and still teaching. Hank was still the fighter pilot.

She filed that particular problem away to solve later.

Claire Allison was very good at problem solving, which was why, four years ago at the age of twenty-eight, she was appointed the youngest middle school principal in Phoenix, Arizona. The county school superintendent had railroaded Claire's appointment through the local school board, fully aware that behind a pleasant personality and gorgeous smile lurked a first-rate intellect and a true leader.

Unfortunately, most of his colleagues only saw a pretty face, a slender figure, and brown eyes framed by long auburn hair with golden highlights. Claire stood just over five-foot-eight and spent hours on a treadmill and swimming laps to keep in shape. She did have a perfect nose and flawless skin but was not a classic beauty. But she often commanded a second and even a third look.

An editorial in a local newspaper had questioned her appointment as the principal of the lowest performing school in her district and labeled her as a pretty disaster who had found the perfect catastrophe. It had taken her four years to turn the school around.

The superintendent gave her full credit and called it a tour de force. He often said that he would never be caught in a knife fight in a dark alley with her. Everyone thought he was joking, but he wasn't. When her children were in harm's way, Claire was a momma wolf.

But on this particular day, Claire was in a very visible fight with one of her teachers, a bitter sixty-year-old who shouldn't be allowed within five-hundred feet of a school. Claire had to fire her. Unfortunately, the teacher thought she had the teacher's union in her corner and was fighting the inevitable.

Normally, it was impossible to fire a tenured teacher, but the state legislature had recently modified the teachers' tenure act, and Claire sensed an opening she could exploit. She had grown up with computers and had a rare ability that had astounded her professors at the University of California, and she used that skill like a weapon. She had laid the groundwork a week earlier when she hacked into the teacher's union computer net.

Once inside, she had discovered some very interesting emails that a prosecutor would delight in pursuing. She dropped a few hints into the union president's email and waited. He promptly became one of her most ardent supporters, and more than willing to interpret the new law in a way that allowed her to fire incompetent teachers. The entire process had taken less than an hour of work spread over three days; she was that good.

Claire stared at her computer as the sunflowers faded and her home screen filled in. "I wish you would just retire," she murmured. She had offered the teacher early retirement but had been firmly, and loudly, rejected.

Unconsciously, Claire's protective instincts flared. "When something goes wrong, get aggressive," she muttered. It was a saying Hank lived by. She called up a file on the teacher that involved repeated verbal abuse of a student. *How did you ever get away with that?* The woman had hurt a student, and in Claire's world, that was a sin bordering on pure evil. *She must be suffering from paranoia.* She keyed on that and was soon looking at the teacher's medical records. It all came together confirming her fears that her students were in danger.

A knock at her open door caught her attention. She automatically closed the file as she looked up. Rebecca Laska, her twenty-two-year-old assistant, was standing at the door. The backlight framed her young figure and long blonde hair. "May I take the afternoon off? Attendance is done, and your schedule is clear for the day. There's just the board meeting tomorrow night." She handed Claire a thin folder. "I worked out a new format for the school's status report." She smiled. "The board will love it."

Claire scanned the report. Rebecca had skillfully documented how the school was on track and improving in all categories. "This is lovely," Claire said. "You are a treasure. Go. You deserve it."

"Thanks." Rebecca started to leave but stopped at the open door. "You should take some time off. Hector can handle anything that might come up." Hector Mendoza was the school's vice principal. He was a forty-five-year-old widower and had come into education after retiring from the Army. While he seemed competent, Claire was still watching him not sure if he had the temperament to deal with young adolescents in crisis. “He only wants the chance to prove himself, and you need to take a break.”

“I’d love to,” Claire replied. “But there’s too much to do.”

“That’s what you always say. See you in the morning.” Rebecca disappeared out the door.

Claire turned back to her computer and reopened the teacher’s folder. *I don’t want to do this.* Another thought came to her. *Good shepherd, shield your flock.* It sounded like a hymn, but for Claire, it was her personal anthem. Again, she considered her options. But the bottom line was always the same: her students were at risk and the teacher wouldn’t retire. It was just a matter of forcing the issue.

A warning flashed on the screen. Someone had probed her computer, but the firewall she had developed easily fended off the attack. She automatically backed up her files on a flash drive. *Am I wasting my time?* She often wondered if she was reaching an end at Stella Madura Middle School. *Not yet*, she told herself.

The sunflowers were calling and Rebecca’s advice echoed in her mind. *Why not?* She reached for her cell phone and hit the speed dial, calling her mother. She waited as the phone rang. Sarah Madison was a trim and lively fifty-nine-year-old widow who claimed she was descended from the Founding Fathers. Unfortunately, she had lost her way after the death of her husband and was severely depressed when Claire had moved her into the small apartment Hank had built behind their garage. Fortunately, Sarah had melded smoothly into their family, eagerly caring for Logan. Being an engaged grandmother had saved her and freed Claire to pursue her career.

Sarah finally answered. “Hi, Mom. Are you and Logan home yet?” Logan was enrolled in Prime Star Academy’s preschool, one of the best in the state.

“Oh, no,” Sarah replied. “Didn’t I mention that he’s on a field trip with Katherine and Bobby Lee?” Katherine MacElroy had created Prime Star Academy, and her son, Bobby Lee, was the new headmaster. “They’re looking at dinosaurs today.”

Claire smiled. “Logan loves dinosaurs. What are you doing?”

"Shopping." Sarah spent hours shopping for clothes she seldom purchased. "Don't worry. I'll pick Logan up at five."

"Buy something pretty. I'll cook dinner." She broke the connection and glanced at her watch. It was almost time for lunch. She looked out the window again and made a decision. "Well, Hector," she murmured to herself, "it's time to find out." She hit the intercom, calling her vice principal.

Hector picked up on the first ring. "Good morning, boss. What's up?"

She liked the sound of his voice. "I'd like to take the rest of the day off. Is your schedule clear?"

A deep chuckle answered. "I thought you'd never ask. I got it."

"Super. I'll be on my cell if you need me." Both knew how fast things could go wrong. She broke the connection and quickly logged out on the school's network. She told her receptionist where she would be and headed for her car. But old habits died hard, and she walked the campus as the lunch bell rang. She was swamped with hellos and greetings as kids surged out of classrooms, heading for the building that doubled as the gym and cafeteria.

She laughed. *Never get between a thirteen-year-old boy and food.* Her "Three-Meals-A-Day" program had helped turn the school around. She followed her kids into the gym, loving them for all they were. Finally satisfied that all was well and they were safe, she headed home.

The traffic was light and she held herself in check, her right foot only teasing the accelerator on her nondescript SUV. She hated the car, but it fit the image of a professional educator, dull and reliable. She loved driving Hank's car, an old Ferrari he had restored. She headed for Trader Joe's to pick up a few things for dinner, and it was after two o'clock when she arrived home.

Like her car, the house was a perfect image of respectability, buried in a quiet neighborhood just outside Scottsdale. She keyed the remote control for the garage door but nothing happened. "Not again," she groaned. Rather than deal with the stuck door, she parked on the driveway, retrieved her shopping bags, and walked around the side of the house, eager to see her garden. She pushed through the side gate and sighed. The sunflowers were fixed, looking eastward and not following the sun.

Are you sending me a message? She dropped the bags and collapsed onto a sun lounge in the shade of the lanai next to the pool. A magnificent bougainvillea laced through the lanai, creating a flowery cave. She sidelined the cares and problems of work. It wasn't often that she had alone time to revel in the sun and feel free and sensuous. Hank loved that side of her personality.

Claire kicked off her shoes and stood. She hadn't gone skinny dipping in well over a year. She quickly shed her clothes, savoring the caress of the warm air on her bare skin. She smiled when she heard a voice coming from inside the house. *Hank's home early.* If the garage door had worked properly, she would have seen his car. Still naked, she walked around the lanai, surprised to see the French doors leading onto the patio wide open.

Then she heard another, very familiar voice. "I'm never going to wear a bikini again." It was Elise, their neighbor from two doors down.

Claire froze, and for a moment, couldn't breathe. *What are you doing here?* Without thinking, she knew the answer. *I thought we were friends.* A devastating hurt cascaded over her only to be swept aside by raw anger.

She stepped back around the lanai, retreating into the shadows. She drove her raging emotions into a carefully guarded cage. She took a deep breath, now in control, and peeked through the bougainvillea. She had a clear view into her home. Hank was standing in the family room, fresh from the pool, a fluffy towel hanging loosely around his hips. At thirty-five, he was the poster boy image of a fighter pilot: six-feet tall, lean and trim, with blue eyes, a little close-set, and a full head of dark blond hair. He had the standard straight teeth and crooked grin required of an aerial assassin, his term not hers, and as her mother liked to say, he was "a total hunk." Hank also shared a few other traits with his fellow fighter pilots. He was aggressive to a fault and on the randy side. Claire knew he had the occasional fling, but as long as it was a one-time thing and he didn't flaunt it, she accommodated his roaming eye. She rationalized that it went with being part of the Millennial Generation. But this was different.

Elise stepped into view. Like the neighbors from across the street, her family often used the pool. She walked across the room carrying two glasses of wine. The towel she was wearing slipped to the floor next to her bikini as she kissed him. *You fucking bitch!* She watched as Elise's fingers pulled the towel from around Hank's hips free, dropping it to the floor. She reached for him.

Claire's eyes narrowed. It was time to face the reality of their relationship, a problem she had ignored far too long. Her claws came out. She gave her hair a shake and pulled it over her left shoulder, letting it cascade over her breast. She paused for a moment, panting deeply, a savage tigress ready to defend her realm. She stepped back into her shoes, wishing they had higher heels.

She walked around the lanai and sauntered up to the open doors, her heels clicking loudly on the flagstone. As one, Hank and Elise turned to look at her. She raised her right hand and leaned against the door jamb, her face a blank as her left hand rested on her bare hip. They stared at each other, not moving. This was a Claire who Hank had never seen before.

"I . . . I just came over for a swim," Elise said. "It just sort of . . ."

Claire shook her head. "Get out." Elise scooped up her bikini and ran from the room. Claire snorted loudly at the sight of her jiggling buttocks.

"She was here when I got home," Hank pleaded.

Claire shook her head sharply, driving him to silence. "Hank, this has to stop." Her voice was amazingly calm. "You're a married man with a wonderful son and a wife who loves you. Either commit to us one-hundred percent or get out. Make a decision. Now." She turned and walked away, her heels echoing over the patio.

PART I

Two Years Later

1

Monday, April 2

The alarm went off at exactly seven o'clock, but I was already awake. It's going to be a bad day, and for a moment, I don't move. I lost a lawsuit and the jury tagged me with five million dollars in damages. The judge is handing down her ruling at ten this morning, and I'm praying and hoping she won't buy the five million. But my ecclesiastical credit is in short supply and hope is not doing its eternal springing.

My name is David Parker, and I fancy myself a freelance investigative reporter specializing in rooting out scumbag politicians and others of their ilk. I can assure you, there's never a lack of candidates worthy of my creative endeavors. But sometimes the aforementioned scumbags and associated ilk bite back.

I definitely do not want to get out of bed. I grab the offending clock and chuck it across the room. "Fuck it."

"Was that necessary?" Lynn asks. As usual, she is rolled up in a fetal position on the far side of the bed.

"I always feel better after using the f-word."

"How civilized." Lynn is always at her best in the morning and likes to cuddle and chat. She rolls over and wraps a bare leg around me. Lynn and I are the same height, five-foot-ten. She outweighs me and is very strong, which makes for sporting, if not painful foreplay. "Why don't you write an article about it? Call it *The F-Word in Action.*"

Lynn is one of my best sources and full of ideas. She is also my lawyer representing me in the above-mentioned lawsuit by an irate doctor who claimed I libeled him in an article I had adroitly penned last year. "I heard a story when I was in Thailand about the f-word," she tells me. "It involves a Buddhist monk and American GIs."

Lynn had taken a break between college and law school and joined the Peace Corps where she fucked her way around the world. Very sophisticated, no doubt, but not the best training for law school. Or maybe it was. "A true story?"

"Since when has that mattered?"

That's Lynn, always the lawyer. In my business, the truth often gets in the way of a paycheck, and I have been known to stretch it. However, a protest is in order. "Hey, I'm a pro."

"Where I came from, a pro is hooker."

That's a good line and I file it away for later use. That's my creative process at work. "So, tell me about your run in with the monk."

"The monk said it happened during the Vietnam War, before I was born." The war in Vietnam ended for Americans in 1973, and she had just defined my audience. Fortunately, there are a bunch of military magazines always on the prowl for something new about that misbegotten war, and almost anything about Vietnam is worth a couple hundred bucks. I feel her hand reach down. She gives the old Johnson a jerk and twist. I'm always looking for a new word for penis and tally-whacker is overused. "Are you awake?" she says.

"I'm awake." No one gets much sleep around Lynn. She is still holding on.

"According to the monk, it really did happen. There was a large American Air Base in northeast Thailand at Nakhon Phanom, just across the Mekong River from Laos."

"I've been there." That was eighteen years ago. I was fresh out of college and researching an article for The New York Times about a few of the CIA's nasty secrets from that war. "They called it NKP or Naked Fanny." I like to impress the women I screw with my esoteric knowledge. She jerks harder. I gasp. Lynn does know how to hold your attention.

"Well," she says, rolling on top of me, "a group of airmen from Nakhon Phanom were doing a public service thing on their day off building a school, or something like that, for the locals."

"It kept the horny bastards out of trouble," I add. The Air Force created a great deal of good will by building schools and clinics in local villages, and that still sold well with a military audience.

"The GIs were working with a Buddhist monk in an isolated village about sixty miles from nowhere. It was so remote that the villagers had never seen a European, much less an American."

"Which, no doubt, occasioned a great deal of cultural shock."

"It registered on the Richter Scale. Anyway, one of the airmen hit his thumb with a hammer and cut loose with a loud 'Fuck!' The sergeant in charge was embarrassed. It's not something you say in front of a priest."

"Monks aren't priests."

She gives my schwanz another twist. "Will you shut up?" Under the circumstances, I decide it is in my best interests to do so. She does work out a lot. "Anyway, the sergeant tried to apologize. The monk smiled and said, 'That is why you Americans are so wonderful. When anything bad or painful happens, you immediately think of something pleasurable, and fucking is the most pleasurable thing I know.'"

"Can't argue with that." I'm always agreeable when that subject comes up.

Lynn cuddles closer. "Well, it is your birthday." I was born forty years ago, which, as of today, makes me middle aged. But I don't like to think about things I don't like to think about. She nuzzles my ear. "Happy Birthday, lover. You wanna fuck?"

Which proves there are stupid questions.

The Lynn Majors who walks into the Sacramento courthouse is not the same creature who occupied my bed earlier that morning. She is dressed in a dark conservative business suit with ankle length skirt. It's the perfect attire for the judge of the day. The Honorable Patricia Wells is a stickler for protocol and Lynn fills out a pants suit to the point of distraction, not the best tactic in Judge Wells' courtroom. Lynn is, as the fashion gurus like to say, "full figured." She is eight years older than me and very attractive. She also claims to be happily married, which I haven't figured out. So far that particular detail hasn't interfered with our evenings together.

Without a word, Lynn leads me into a vacant attorney-witness room, closes the door, and stands me at attention. "Not bad," she murmurs. She adjusts my tie, pulling it off to the side, and messes with my hair a little. "Think little boy look. Her Honor likes that." She strokes my cheek. "The image does fit."

I've heard that many times. I'm on the skinny side. I like to think lean and fit, but that's my ego talking. I'm lucky to puff my way up two flights of stairs. I do have a very light beard and only shave two or three times a week. She messes with my hair again. "A little gray, but it blends well." My hair is light brown. She gingerly pulls off my glasses. "Let Her Honor see those wimpy green eyes."

"Will that help?"

"Hey," she protests. "Work with me. It's all we got. You did lose this one."

It's complicated. I had a confidential source, a highly placed administrative assistant in the state legislature, who ratted out the Speaker of the California State Assembly. The clever bastard had diverted over two billion bucks from a state tax that funded care facilities for seniors suffering from Alzheimer's to one of the state's bankrupt retirement funds. The story was a blockbuster. The Speaker countered by having a stroke and was declared brain dead, for real this time.

Then, I heard a rumor that the Speaker's doctor had botched his treatment in what was a clear case of medical malpractice. I checked out the source and it looked good. You might have read the headlines when I broke that story. The doctor countered by suing me for libel.

Normally, even bad publicity is good for my business, but in this case I was dead wrong, pun intended. The doctor was just doing his job. I had been set up by the very folks who had benefitted from the two billion bucks pilfered from the mentally indigent. Such is politics in the State of California. Thanks to a clause in the small print of my publishing contract, the publisher was held blameless, and it all roosted on me.

Lynn wanted to avoid a trial and was confident she could cut a settlement for around a hundred grand. But I was certain a jury would buy my story. We went to trial and I took the stand, all against her advice. Lynn couldn't save me after that, and she is one damn good lawyer. But even she was stunned by the five-million dollar award the jury handed down.

"It's time," Lynn says, and we head for the courtroom. I feel like a dead man walking. We take our places behind the defendant's table and the bailiff calls for everyone to rise. The Honorable Patricia Wells flounces in. She is a small, highly energetic woman who is, by far, the most intelligent judge on the Sacramento County Superior Court. I don't like her.

Her Honor smiles. "Please sit down." She does the same and stares at me over her glasses obviously not impressed with my errant schoolboy look. She gets right to business. "Mr. Parker, the jury has found for the plaintiff and awarded him five million dollars in damages and suffering plus lawyer and court fees. I have reread the two articles in question. While I find your first article accurate, that does not excuse the gross inaccuracies in the second article. However, as your counsel established, the plaintiff's practice was not harmed by your baseless accusations and has continued to flourish. Therefore, I am reducing the jury's award to 200,000 dollars plus lawyer and court costs not to exceed 50,000 dollars."

Happy fucking birthday! And I mean it. Maybe the schoolboy look did work. I decide I do like Her Honor. We are adjourned and Her Honor gracefully retires.

"You got off lucky," Lynn whispers loud enough for everyone to hear as she packs her briefcase. I think she's negotiating with the doctor's lawyer from the fine old law firm of Shaft and Lynch. I'm not making that name up.

"Crap. I haven't got that kind of money."

"What do you have?" the Shafter, or the Lyncher, asks. He's trying to act friendly, but really looks more like a piranha in heat. "My client is most receptive to a payment plan."

I bet he is. "Seventy-thousand," I answer. That was the end of my savings and 401k.

"We'll accept a down payment of 100,000 dollars, followed by monthly payments of 3000 dollars at six percent interest."

Of course, he would. "Where am I gonna get the other thirty grand?" My math is good, thanks to a third-grade teacher with infinite patience.

"Take out a loan," the lawyer counsels.

"What lender in his right mind will do that?" I ask.

"Get Dottie Sue to cosign the loan." This from Lynn, ever the optimist.

"Oh, joy," I moan. Dottie Sue, her proper name is Dorothea Sue Ellington, is my mother. I am her only child and the result of her first marriage. She tried four more times with different husbands but nothing came of it. She is a retired schoolteacher and lives on the other side of town in Rio Linda. Currently, she is shacked up with an over-the-hill gigolo named Benny who drives a school bus.

Lynn pulls me aside. "Take the deal. Pay off the thirty grand as quick as you can and then declare bankruptcy. Your mother is off the hook for the loan, and since Shaft and Lynch get paid off the top, they won't get involved in collecting the balance." I like her strategy about never getting between a lawyer and money. I take the deal and smile at the lawyer. He smiles back. I wonder if he is related to Shaft or to Lynch.

Tuesday, April 3

"Too bad there aren't tornados in California," I mutter to myself, turning into the Shangri-La Paradise Mobile Home Park where my mother lives. It advertises itself as 'A home for active seniors,' but in Oklahoma it would just be another tornado magnet. I like to think that a tornado would improve the local ambiance.

On the plus side, mom owns her double-wide trailer outright and qualifies to cosign for the loan. But Benny is going to be a problem. He thinks I'm a turd, and that's on a good day. Besides driving a school bus, he's a retired Marine gunny sergeant, and I'm not about to repeat what he calls me on a bad day. Let's just say it references the offspring of half-assed baboons mating with warthogs.

The door to mom's trailer is open, but I knock anyway. "Oh, David," she calls. "Is that you? Come on in." I step inside and look around. The room is squeaky clean and neat as a pin. Neither are mom's long suit, and I suspect Benny's been at work. He does take good care of her. "Benny will be right back," she announces. "I'll make you a cup of coffee."

I follow her into the breakfast nook and sit down while she puts the coffee maker to work. I can smell fresh-baked something and the kitchen is freshly painted. She plops a big cinnamon roll and a mug of coffee in front of me and retreats to the counter. “Where’s the Big Ben?” I’ll need Benny as a witness to mom’s signature on the loan application.

“He’s fixing Mary Jane’s car.” Mary Jane is a widow who lives three spaces down and is mom’s best friend. “The bitch better not shag him.” From that, I sense all is well. We pass the time making small talk about all the sinning seething below the surface of Shangri-La. Based on Dottie Sue’s extensive knowledge of the trystings and moanings going on, they should rename the place Eldersex Mobile Home Park. She looks up expectantly as Benny comes through the door.

“Hi, Pumpkin,” Benny says. His pet name for mom isn’t original, but it is accurate. Mom is short and round, and her hair is dyed a botched blonde that came out orange. Benny kisses her on the forehead and heads for the coffee maker. He’s a big man, bald and burly with the requisite Marine tattoo on his right bicep. He has that grizzled look that says, ‘Once a Marine, always a Marine,’ and under no circumstances do I want to piss him off. He stares at me for a moment and growls, “What brings you here, asshole?” I relax. We’re having a good day.

Old and trite sayings hang around forever because they are true, so I decide to go with the flow and cut directly to the chase. I tell them about the lawsuit and why I’m here. The part about cosigning for the loan doesn’t go down well and Mom looks at Benny.

He stares me in the eye and says, “Are you good for all those payments?” It wasn’t the question I was expecting. Rather than tell the truth, I say nothing. Benny thinks for a moment. “I don’t think you are, and cosigning is a bad idea. But Dottie Sue is your mother. It’s her decision.”

I turn to mom and don’t like what I see. Her head is cocked to one side, and she has the look of a hungry coyote eyeing a baby rabbit. I’ve seen it too many times when she comes off her meds and slips into an angry paranoia. I think it’s a permanent condition that she covers up to be sociable.

“I’ll sign, but I want a favor.” I nod, feeling like a young and juicy bunny being primed for sacrifice. “You remember that story you wrote about that politician that croaked?”

I nod. Mom does have a mean streak. I don't remind her that is the article that led to the lawsuit and why I need her to cosign the loan.

She stares at me, her eyes on fire. It's the old Dottie Sue I remember from when she was teaching school, and I know what is coming. "I was a good teacher, but that woman was jealous of me. They should have fired her. But, oh, no! I get fired instead. That bitch should've never been a principal."

I can't remember the name of the principal who fired her. But I do remember how mom chose to fight being terminated for cause rather than take early retirement. She maintained the family tradition, lost, and had to settle for severance pay. She left Phoenix in a huff with Benny in tow. At least, she had the good sense to use the severance money to buy into Shangri-La.

"She just made 'Principal of the Year' in Phoenix, the second time! It was on TV this morning. There's only one way she got that, she fucked her way to the top. She's a class A bitch!"

"Dottie Sue," Benny pleads, "that was years ago. Let it go."

But mom is on a roll. "In a pig's ass! She ruined my life! Now I'm going to ruin hers." She shakes a finger at me. "David Alexander", she's over the top and around the bend when she uses my middle name, "you screw her like you did that politician and maybe she'll have a stroke. You tell the world the truth about the bitch. You do that and I'll sign."

I want out of here, so I give her my best nod and hand her a pen. She scribbles her name on the loan application and shoves it at Benny to witness. Big Ben doesn't like the idea, but he isn't stupid and quickly signs. I grab the form, kiss mom goodbye, and run for safety. Benny is right behind me. "Jesus," he breathes. "I've never seen her so fired up."

"She'll get over it," I say.

"She will," he replies, "if you hold up your end. You nail the broad, or I nail you. Capiche?" He fixes me with a hard look and I'm glad I was never in his platoon.

I capiche and really want out of here. "I can't remember her name."

Benny snorts. "Claire Allison.

2

Wednesday, May 9

Morning was Claire Marie Allison's favorite time of day when she was at her very best. She readily admitted that she was a so-so cook, but that didn't faze her in the least when it came to cooking pancakes. Hank often kidded her that she was an incurable optimist, yet he always devoured anything she cooked.

But on this particular morning, he had an early morning training flight and had left home for the base at 4:30. Normally, that was when they enjoyed early-morning sex when they were fresh and eager for the new day. She finished stirring the pancake batter and glanced at the clock. It was 6:30 and time to get things moving. She poured some batter onto the griddle. "Logan," she called. "Breakfast."

Logan slouched into the kitchen and collapsed into the breakfast nook. She flipped the pancake. "You're a bit grouchy this morning," she said. He didn't answer and stared at the table. She flipped the pancake onto a plate and spread butter over it. Without thinking, she squirted maple syrup on top, making a happy face. "

What would you like for your birthday?" she asked, setting the plate in front of him. Logan's eighth birthday was less than a month away and he was growing like a weed, resembling his father more each day. He grumped and used his knife to rearrange the happy face on the pancake, carefully turning the smile into a frown.

"If you eat a frownie face, you'll be grumpy all day."

"I don't care."

This wasn't her usual Logan and she chalked it up to growing pains. He was the tallest boy in his class and outgrowing his clothes on a daily basis. "Well, maybe Mr. Smiley cares," she said. He played with his food and still didn't answer. She sat down across from him. "Are things okay at school?" she asked.

"I guess so." He took a bite.

"Well, kiddo, we still need a clue about what you want for your birthday." No answer. "We could always get you a nice dress. Your grandmother would love taking you shopping."

"Ah, Mom," he groaned. He took another bite and his appetite claimed his attention. Without a word, Claire stood and poured three small dollops of batter onto the griddle. They cooked quickly and she flipped one towards him, missing his plate. "Try again, Mom."

"Incoming," she said, sending the second one his way. Logan used his plate to catch it as she flipped the third one at him. He caught it too. She handed him the syrup and watched as he gulped the pancakes down. "I take it this means you don't want a dress?"

He brightened. "How about an electric scooter?"

Sarah Madison rushed into the room, late as usual. "You're too young for an electric scooter," she announced.

"Ah, Grandma," Logan protested.

"It's time to go," Sarah said, "or you'll be late for school."

Logan picked up his school bag and bolted out of the room, following Sarah to the car. "Love you," Claire called.

Logan ran back into the room and jumped into her arms. "I love you, Mommy." He ran for the car.

"And I love you," she murmured. She checked the time. She had to hurry, or she would be late for work. *Why rush?* she thought. There was only bad news waiting for her.

Claire saw it the moment Rebecca knocked on the door to her office. The engagement ring on her left hand was missing. "Mr. Hatchette is on line one," Rebecca said. Claire hated using the intercom to direct incoming calls and preferred the personal touch. The interaction kept everyone involved and friendly, and that included her vice principal, Hector Mendoza, the only man in the office.

"Thanks," Claire said, glancing at the wall clock. The phone call from the president of the local school board was long overdue. She punched at the button on the phone. "Hello, Sidney."

Hatchette's voice exploded through the receiver. "Claire!" As usual, he was all boom and bluster. Claire motioned for Rebecca to close the office door. Her smile disappeared. "The executive session lasted past midnight," Hatchette said. The school board had met the evening before to select a replacement for the district superintendent who was retiring. Claire was one of the three finalists, but she didn't give herself much of a chance.

Her fingers danced over the keyboard on her lap as she pulled up the computer program she had developed and refined over the years. Her original objective in college was to develop an improved search engine she could sell to Silicon Valley. But life, and Hank, got in the way and it became a hobby. Later, she melded the search engine into a spyware program. The results totally surprised her. She had a program that could break undetected through any firewall. Being Claire, she added it to her personal toolbox and kept it a secret. Now, it gave her an inside edge when dealing with the likes of Sidney Hatchette.

The log for the security service that guarded the district flashed on her computer. The meeting had started promptly at 7:30, as scheduled, and a security guard had logged the building closed and secure at 9:05. *So much for burning the midnight oil.* Claire enjoyed engaging with smart, hard-headed executives, but dealing with Hatchette was painful. *How can you be so stupid!*

"Claire," Hatchette continued, "you know I'm in your corner and have been from the get-go."

Sure you have. They had a long history of butting heads, mostly over finances and personnel, and thanks to Rebecca's networking with other secretaries, Claire knew exactly where she stood with Hatchette. It wasn't good. But it went deeper than that. It was common knowledge that he required certain favors, preferably sexual, to guarantee advancement.

Claire had short-circuited any overtures early on by introducing him to Hank and laughing about her husband's abilities as an aerial assassin. Hank reinforced it with a crushing handshake, convincing Hatchette to look elsewhere for a softer target. Hatchette avoided legal fallout from his side pursuits mostly because his construction companies employed over five thousand people in the local area and his connections extended to the statehouse.

"I fought hard for you," Hatchette said, "but you were up against some tough competition, and the board wanted someone with a fire in his belly for discipline."

"Really," Claire replied. She had broken the back of the two gangs that had terrorized her school. She had hacked their emails and message traffic, turning them against each other. The results were bloody but very effective. She couldn't go public with that, but with the gangs gone she had quickly restored order on her campus. That was a very visible accomplishment.

Hatchette plunged ahead. "I tried to sell 'em on your experience, but honestly, they wanted someone with a financial background to make the hard budgeting decisions we're looking at."

"Really." She ratcheted up the astonishment. Claire had chaired the budget committee that had put the district on track to financial health and cut costs. She didn't bother to mention the second Principal of the Year award she had won a month before. She'd had enough. "I take it Taylor is our new superintendent."

Seymour Taylor was one of the so-called professional superintendents who moved from district to district in search of more pay, perks, and a higher pension. Eventually, Taylor would run for the Maricopa County School Superintendent, which was an elected office. He talked a good game and knew how to play to local financial interests. Hatchette was one of those financial interests, and she knew, without doubt, that the district, and more importantly her students, would get the short end of that arrangement. *Enough is enough*, she told herself. It was time to solve that problem.

She heard a toilet flush in the background. "We haven't released the name," Hatchette said. "We're making the introduction at the board meeting tonight. We need you there as a show of support."

Her fingers were a blur, working the keyboard. *So, where are you?* On cue, her computer flashed the answer. Hatchette was calling from the Back Landing, a boutique hotel that catered to very private affairs for the wealthy and influential.

She easily multi-tasked, penetrating the hotel's security system while still speaking with Hatchette. *Okay, you're in room seven.* She tapped into the hotel's security video and cycled to the hall camera outside the room. She rewound the tape and hit the freeze button when Hatchette walked into view. She noted the time. *It's a little early for a nooner.* Unfortunately, she could not see his companion's face. From the backside, she was young and shapely. Claire zoomed in on her shoes. *High platforms with five-inch heels. I wonder how much she charges?* Her eyes narrowed and her claws started to itch.

"Sidney, I do appreciate the call, more than you know."

"Thank you. And I appreciate all that you've done for the district." He paused.

Next subject, Claire thought.

"You know there's a principalship opening in Prescott. The pay is good, and I'll give you a recommendation that carries weight."

I read you loud and clear, Sidney. Her head was on the chopping block, and while she loved Prescott, taking another job as a principal was a sidestep at best. "It sounds interesting. I'll think about it." It was time to end the call. "I will be there tonight."

"Claire, thanks again, but I've got to go. Some important business is hanging fire."

Now what could that business be? She dropped the receiver into its cradle and copied Hatchette's cell number into the spyware program. Within seconds, she had a list of all his recent phone calls. The rest was simple. Her program traced a number to 'Escorts Phoenix' and two seconds later, she had a name and profile. She thought for a moment. *You are a pretty little thing and don't deserve this.* Claire ran her options through her mental abacus, calculating the fallout. *I think you'll survive* A decision made, she hit the speed dial on her cell and called KPIO, a local TV station. She knew the extension. "Mike," she sang. "It's been a long time."

Mike Westfield's gruff voice rang in her ear. "How's it goin', doll baby." Mike Westfield cultivated a gruff, thoroughly incorrect manner that gained him a wide audience on his nationally syndicated TV show.

"I just thought you might be interested in the latest shenanigans going on at the Back Landing."

"Shenanigans? Haven't heard that word in a long time. So who's shenaniganing?"

"An old friend. Sidney Hatchette."

"What's the SOB up to now?"

"Enjoying a nooner with a hooker in room seven."

"Not much I can do with that." Westfield was a realist.

"What if there's a fire drill in forty-five minutes?"

"You gotta be shittin' me. No one does fire drills."

"It does happen. I just thought you'd like to know."

Westfield knew he was onto something juicy. "I'll be there."

"You won't regret it." She ended the call and checked her smart watch. The thought of Sidney Hatchette being caught with his pants down by a TV crew amused her. *It should make the six o'clock news.* There was no way she was going to miss the school board meeting. She laughed aloud at the thought and went back to work.

Her smart watch vibrated with an incoming call. It was her mother. *Oh, oh.* Sarah only called during the day when there was a problem. "Hi, Mom, what's up?"

"I had to pick Logan up from school," Sarah said. "He was crying."

Claire quickly switched from principal to mom. "He has been a little moody lately. I wonder if he's being bullied?" Bullies in her school quickly learned that was not a good idea and after a chat or two, most often ended up on her friendly side, which was much better than being on the other end of that equation.

"I asked when I picked him up," Sarah said. "His teacher said, 'absolutely not.' I believe her."

Logan's teacher rated high with Claire. "We're home and he's okay now," Sarah said.

Claire made a decision. "Keep him home for the rest of today." Prime Star Academy prided itself on its afterschool activities that centered on social interaction and academic enrichment. The program had received national recognition, and parents paid top dollar to enroll their children. While it was high-achieving and could be stressful. "Let him play with his computer."

"He'll like that," Sarah said.

"Keep an eye on him." Claire ended the call and thought for a few moments, the mother in her very concerned. She hit the speed dial on her cell phone and called Hank.

He answered on the second ring. "Hi, babe," he said. His voice was rich and commanding. "Good timing. I just finished debriefing the mission." She quickly told him about the phone call from Sarah. "It's just growing pains," he said. "But I'll get home as soon as I can."

"I've got to make the school board meeting tonight. I didn't get the job."

"Ah, babe, I'm so sorry. You were the best one, hands down. You take care of business, me and Logan will take care of ourselves. There's a ball game on base this evening. We'll take that in. Might have a hot dog or two."

"That sounds like fun," she replied.

"Always is," he assured her. "Especially if we win."

"I should be home by ten," she said.

"One does hope," he replied. "We need to make up for this morning."

"You are a lustful bugger." She liked English slang.

"I see you got the memo." He laughed and broke the connection.

An image popped into her mind as she did a rerun of Westfield interviewing a local politician who was being audited by the IRS. The politician claimed that he was set up, and she considered the possibilities. *Overkill?* she wondered. She worked the keyboard and carefully shielded her computer's location and ID.

She knew how readily the government could trace back any message. Satisfied that she was anonymous, she joined the IRS's whistleblower hotline where she quickly downloaded her file on Hatchette, detailing his real income and where it was hidden. In the hands of a competent investigator, the links could be very productive. But that would take time to develop.

Claire checked the time and turned back to her computer. "Hello, Sidney," she murmured as she called up the same search program and, within seconds, was inside the Back Landing hotel's security system. Again, she checked the time and waited. At exactly forty-five minutes after the phone call to Mike Westfield, she triggered the hotel's fire alarm. "I do hope you're there, Mike."

The passing bell rang and she locked down her computer. Hector was at a luncheon placating a group of concerned parents, and she was covering his schoolyard duties. She grabbed her sunglasses and headed out the door. "Rebecca," she called. "Let's go walkabout." She loved walking around the campus and interacting with her students. They trusted her, and occasionally, one blurted out a tidbit of information that proved helpful. Rebecca jumped up from her desk and joined her. Claire gave her a concerned look as they headed out the door. "Are you having your ring cleaned?"

Rebecca shook her head and quietly explained that she had broken off her engagement with Mark Graham, a very successful lawyer. They spoke as they walked the campus, often interrupted by a friendly student. Soon, the bell rang and the quadrangle quickly emptied. Rebecca gave her a hopeful look. "May I ask you something? It's personal."

Claire laughed. "If it's not too personal."

Rebecca took a deep breath. "I caught Mark with his secretary. I do love him, and he says he wants to marry me. What would you have done?"

"You mean if I caught Hank with another woman?" Rebecca nodded in answer. "I did. In our own home with a neighbor." Rebecca gasped and stared at her. "Oh, Rebecca, that was over two years ago. And, well, she wasn't the first. But she was the last. I gave him an ultimatum and we were able to work things out. I'm glad we did." They walked in silence. "Can I ask you a personal question?" Rebecca nodded. "Hank has a roaming eye. I know that. Has he, ah, has he ever?"

Rebecca shook her head.

Claire touched Rebecca's arm. "Thank you." A little smile played at the corners of her lips. "Men!" Arm-in-arm, they walked into the office.

Back at her desk, Claire kicked off her shoes and had barely sorted her in-folder when the panic alarm for room twenty-six sounded. "Lock down!" she ordered, coming to her feet. The school had a well-rehearsed plan that included locking doors, hiding, and protecting students until the police arrived. She bolted out the door, not bothering to grab her shoes.

Every second counted, and she ran for the room. *Please, God, no guns.* The door to the modular classroom was open and she came to a stop, scanning the area and assessing the situation. All was quiet. *Okay, Stan Atkinson, 8th grade social studies, should be studying the constitution.* She steeled herself and walked through the open door.

She froze. Her worst nightmare was standing in front of the class clutching a semi-automatic pistol.

She ransacked her memory, desperate for anything she could use. *Danny Hawkins, fourteen years old. Quiet. Tall for his age. Bullied in the 6th grade.* She couldn't think of anything else and was operating in the blind. The classroom was absolutely silent as every head turned towards her. One girl in the first row whimpered and started to cry. Stan Atkinson, a very popular and competent teacher, was seated with his palms flat on his desk. He had hit the hidden panic button with his knee. His student aide, a senior from the high school, was seated in the corner. *Jenna Bradley*, Claire thought. *Very feisty and intelligent.*

She needed a diversion. She smiled at Danny and turned to the teacher. "Oh, Mr. Atkinson, I was just passing by and thought I'd drop in." She gestured at the weapon in Danny's hand. "I see you're discussing the second amendment." She turned to the class. "Anyone want to play 'Stump the Student?"

She was greeted with blank looks. "Here's how it works," she said, improvising. "I ask a question about the second amendment, and if anyone knows the answer, raise your hand. I'll point to one and that person answers. If you get it right, Danny points the gun at the ceiling. If you get it wrong, he points the gun at me, and I have to answer." She looked around expectantly. "Any questions?"

A boy at the back of the class half raised his hand. He was shaking. "Who knows the right answer?"

"Danny does," Claire answered.

"How do we know that?" a girl with freckles asked.

"Because he does," Claire answered. "Isn't that right, Danny?" He answered with a slight nod. "Okay, here we go," Claire said. "The Second Amendment is what part of the constitution?" The same boy in the back raised his hand and Claire pointed to him.

"The Second Amendment is part of the Bill of Rights," the boy said. Danny pointed the gun at the ceiling. After a moment he dropped his arm.

"What freedom does the Second Amendment guarantee all citizens?" Claire asked. Now a few hands went up.

Claire pointed to a girl in the seat closest to Atkinson. "The right to keep and bear arms," she answered. Danny pointed the gun at the ceiling, only to quickly drop his hand. He had been holding the heavy weapon for some time and was obviously tiring.

"Okay, next question. Can anyone recite the Second Amendment?"

No hands went up and Danny stared at Claire. Slowly he raised the weapon and pointed it at her. "You answer."

Jenna Bradley sprang to her feet. She shook her head in anger, her red hair flying. "Don't you go pointing that gun at Mrs. Allison. She loves us."

Claire turned to Danny. "And that includes you."

Jenna folded her arms across her breasts and glared at Danny. "Point the gun at me."

Three students came to their feet, shouting for his attention. "Me! Me!" Within seconds, half the class was standing and shouting "Me! Me!"

In the distance, Claire heard the wail of a siren. The police were coming. She looked at Danny and held out her hand, not saying a word. He dropped the pistol to his side and she took three quick steps, throwing her arms around his shoulders, embracing him, making no attempt to grab the pistol. "Help me," she whispered. She felt his body stiffen. "Help me get you out of this."

Danny pulled back and slowly raised the weapon. For a split second, she knew she was dead.

He handed her the gun.

3

Wednesday, the same day

The car's air conditioner gave out around Bakersfield and it's hotter than hell driving across the Mojave Desert. I left Sacramento early in the evening, hoping to make Phoenix by nine the next morning, but the damn car isn't cooperating, and the twelve-hour drive is now pushing fifteen. I should've taken up Benny's offer for a tune up and oil change, but I wanted to keep my exposure to mom's wrath to a minimum.

I had shoved her vendetta with Claire Allison to a back-burner for over a month, pleading assorted ass-dragging problems. Getting the lawsuit squared away and scraping up 3000 bucks for the first month's payment was a killer. But Benny had his own ass kicking program, which was enough motivation to get my bruised posterior moving towards Phoenix. So I gassed up the car, threw in my back pack, a battered suitcase, my folding bike, and headed south.

I figured an interview and a few days of scratching around would do the trick. I'd bang out seven hundred words or so, post it on the internet, and head home mission accomplished. That should get mom off my back. And who knows? In my business, you never know what might turn up, and I always need to turn a buck or two. I'd heard about a big swingers club around Lake Havasu on the Arizona side of the Colorado River, and sex always sells. I might take a detour, but a single guy needs a partner, preferably female, to get inside a group like that. That might be just right for Lynn and me.

Phoenix is one spread out piece of real estate and I head for the raggedy side of town to find cheap lodging. It's just after one in the afternoon when I find the right flop-for-the-night-house. I negotiate a cut rate and find my room on the backside of the swimming pool with the world's largest specimen of algae, and collapse on the bed for a quick nap. The walls sport a fresh coat of paint, and the air conditioner is quiet enough and working well. When I wake up, I turn the TV on and surf the news channels. It's amazing what lurks below the surface of local news, if you know where to look. I don't have to look far and sit up, my feet flat on the floor.

Claire Allison is on every news channel.

I swear, my heart is pounding along at 120 beats. I grab my notebook. Yeah, I know, us reporters are supposed to be tech savvy and speak into our smart phones in low tones, proving we are super cool. But I deal with the written word and start with that. I write as fast as I can while surfing the channels. I freeze on one channel.

"Son of a bitch!" Mike Westfield is standing in front of a pack of highly agitated news hounds with microphone in hand. Mike and I go back a decade, but I wouldn't exactly call us friends. Allison is holding the slobbering pack back with one outstretched hand while her other arm is wrapped protectively around a small red-haired girl with freckles.

"Mike, I'll get back to you as soon as I take care of my kids, okay?" There is something in her voice that soothes the panting hoard. Mike Westfield nods and drops his microphone. He turns and says something to the pack and they visibly relax. Most of my brethren in the news business are not known for being shy or retiring, and I don't think I've ever seen that happen.

I make a note about Allison. She is tall, I guess around five-eight, and dressed on the dowdy side. It's hard to believe she's the savage beast mom told me about. Then I look again. Claire Allison is not a frumpy middle school administrator. In her own way, she's beautiful.

I study her as she gathers her kids and leads them into the principal's office. "I'll be damned." She's barefoot. I make a note. It makes her look smaller and more vulnerable. A woman cop is guarding the door, challenging anyone to take her on. There is no doubt that Allison and the kids are very safe inside.

Westfield turns to the camera. "As best we know at this time, a teenage boy with a nine-millimeter handgun was terrorizing a classroom when the principal, Mrs. Claire Allison, intervened. We don't know what happened, but we do know that no shots were fired and everyone is safe. The identity of the would-be shooter is not known at this time, but the police have taken a suspect into custody."

My pencil is flying, filling the page, as I pull on my shoes and flip through the channels. I hear a name, the Stella Madura Middle School, and check its location. The school is three miles away. I bolt out the door, running for my car. An unhappy teenage boy is cleaning the pool.

Luckily, the car starts and I head for the school. I know traffic will be heavy and the police will barricade the area around the school. That's why I have a folding bike in the trunk. I make it to within a quarter mile of the middle school before I abandon my car, grab my backpack, and peddle like hell for the scene of the action. My press card works wonders and gets me through two police barricades. The scene is calm and orderly. Someone has planned for this type of emergency. Nothing newsworthy there.

I chain my bike to the bike rack outside the principal's office and join the growing press corps. Again, my press card helps, and I do have a reputation of sorts. I see Westfield at the front of the pack and barge my way through, crunching a few feet, all women. Westfield sees me and grins. "Hey, Parker, how's the old gonads hangin'? Oops. Sorry. I heard they got ripped off in a lawsuit."

I sense an opening. But I gotta be subtle, not Westfield's strong point. "Yeah, they did. Libel lawsuits suck. My source was bad. I got hit with a quarter mil judgement."

"I heard," Westfield says. He gives me a cool look and extends his hand. The bastard gets it! Sometimes you have to suck up a lawsuit in our business. We shake hands and exchange insider chit-chat. I ask how he got out front on this one. "I had a tip and was nearby with a camera crew when this went down. We were the first on the scene." We get to the important stuff and he tells me about the local website to use to hook up for a quickie. I give him a number to call in Sacramento and tell him he will like Teri. He makes a note.

The woman cop opens the office door and Allison comes out. She is wearing shoes now and her hair and makeup are perfect. The woman knows how to make an entrance. She stands there, a calm look on her face as my fellow idiots yell questions.

The woman standing next to me is shrieking. I want to step on her foot. Allison reaches out and takes Westfield's microphone. She looks at us expectantly and I swear, everyone shuts up. I have never seen anything like it. I make a note about the press being easier to control than junior high schoolers.

"Good afternoon," she says. Her voice is pitch perfect. "I know your time is valuable, and I want to thank you for being so patient." She knows how to butter up the press. "First, all our children are safe, and no one was hurt. I know you want to know who the boy is. Just let me say he is a good student and has never been a problem. He needs our help, and we will be working with all the resources we have to help him. Please help us save him."

She pauses and bestows a pleading look on us. It works and she continues. "I'm certain the teacher, Mr. Stan Atkinson, can tell you all you need to know about what happened in his classroom. There'll be a press conference in the gym in a few minutes where you can interview him." She smiled. "We call him 'Stan the Man', and he is one great guy."

"Stan the Man" has it made with a reference like that. The door to the office opens and a man and boy rush out. The guy is wearing an Air Force flight suit, sleeves rolled up, but no hat. I can tell from the rank that he is a lieutenant colonel. The shrieker standing next to me sucks her breath in with an "Oh, my!" Oh, my what? The boy is maybe seven or eight, tall for his age, and the spitting image of his dad with his mother's hair. Allison steps into their outstretched arms and they hug. The perfect family reunited in a time of stress. This is stuff that will make every news feed in the world. I'm jealous, but not sure why.

Allison is still holding Westfield's microphone. "Please forgive me, I really need to be with my family now." She turns the microphone off and hands it back saying, "Thanks, Mike. We'll try to sort all this out at the school board meeting tonight." There is no way I'm going to miss that meeting.

And neither will Westfield. My brain finally kicks in. This could not have been staged better by professional entertainers - or politicians.

I follow the shrieker into the gym for the interview with Stan the Man. He's sitting alone at a score keeper's table talking on his cellphone while TV cameras set up at the back. I watch his face and wonder who he's talking to. He hangs up and stands as everyone jams into the bleachers. It is one big crowd and I'm squeezed up against the shrieker. She has nice bazongas. Stan the Man starts to talk, not waiting for the news hounds to stop barking. Within seconds, the gym quiets. I make notes as he tells his story.

Applause breaks out as Allison and her husband walk into the gym. Stan the Man introduces her and she takes the microphone. "Mr. Atkinson asked me to please join him and answer questions," she says. I guess that's what the phone call was all about. Some idiot asks if he was scared. Stan answers with a smooth "I almost wet my pants" and passes the mike to Allison. "Yes and no," she answers. "I still don't understand it." She hands the mike back. They are a smooth team as they answer questions.

Suddenly, a question pops out of some black hole in my brain. I make a note. "Holy shit," I mutter. The shrieker looks at me and I get an idea. In our world today, a guy can't ask a woman a really hard question. But a woman can. Besides, I like to stay in the background, so I show her the question. She jumps to her feet and shouts, "By telling the suspect to point the gun at a person, didn't you encourage him to pull the trigger?" From the silence, I know it is a good question. Maybe the shrieker would be interested in doing Lake Havasu. Out of gratitude, of course.

Allison tears up. "I don't know. Maybe. I didn't know what to do." She looks at me, and I am dead certain she knew it was my question. "I do know my students saved my life." Much to everyone's surprise, her husband steps forward and takes the mike.

This guy is imposing. He stares at the shrieker. "Have you ever been in combat?" he asks. The shrieker doesn't answer. He frowns. "Everyone in that classroom—the kids, Stan, Claire—were in combat. I learned the hard way there are no right options when you're facing real bullets, real danger, and real death. You have to go by the results. It's as simple as that." He pauses. "Any more questions?" The shrieker gives me a cold look and steps on my foot. Havasu is definitely off the table.

The interview goes on for another twenty minutes or so, and the questions are becoming very repetitive. Reporters are a persistent bunch, not necessarily bright. I check my watch. It's past four o'clock. I check the school district's website. The school board meeting is scheduled for 7:30 this evening. It doesn't take a genius to know it will be crowded, so I make a break for the door. I need to get to the district headquarters ASAP to stakeout a seat. At least twenty other reporters are thinking the same.

Luckily, my bike gets me ahead of the maddening pack and around a huge traffic jam. I peddle my body there in less than fifteen minutes. That's a record for me and I'm sweating hard. A sign outside points to the main conference room, which is wide open. A little old lady is guarding the door. I flash my press pass and trot out the old Parker charm. It works, and I'm the first person inside.

Mike Westfield's assistant producer is right behind me, panting hard from a long run. She's also sweating like a pig. We find seats together, and I make friendly. Her name is Susanne. We save each other's seats when a call of nature beckons. I have a few power bars and an extra bottle of water in my backpack.

Bribery always works and we Google Claire Allison, sharing information. Strangely, Allison is not on Facebook. But she does have a Twitter account. Susanne is disappointed. "Look at this. 'Happy birthday Rebecca!' Who the hell is Rebecca? We read through more of the same. I'm betting Allison's text and message traffic is more juicy. But we will never see that.

Westfield makes his entrance ten minutes before the board meeting starts and Susanne gives up her seat. They whisper a few words I can't hear, and she smiles at me. I think Lake Havasu. Mike throws a grunt in my direction. "You suffering a yellow out, yet?" It's his way of saying, "Go take a leak and get lost."

It's a chance to score some points. "I could use a pee break." I give up my seat to Susanne just as a man steps up to the podium. He looks like a pot-bellied used car salesman with a bad tailor.

"Good evening, I'm Sidney Hatchette, president of the school board. Because of today's events, we have to postpone tonight's meeting. I apologize for the late announcement, but as you can imagine, things are hectic around here. We'll let you know the time and date of the next meeting as soon as the dust settles." He retreats off stage.

"Who is Sidney Hatchette on a good day?" I ask.

"Strange you should ask," Westfield says. He eyes me for a second. "Susanne says you took good care of her." He's taking pity on me and I try to look forlorn. "Ah, come on." He motions for me to follow them. I'm thinking dinner on his expense account. I follow them out to a waiting limo. I climb in, not worried about my bike. I can retrieve it later.

Susanne pours a stiff drink of Scottish for Westfield. I note the label. It's good stuff. She offers me a drink, which I take. I don't say much and listen as Westfield and Susanne talk business. She pours him another shot that he knocks back. I decline a second. I don't want to miss any slipped tidbits because I'm plowed.

The limo drops us at a condo I have only dreamed about and I follow them inside. I am impressed. We take a private elevator that only serves the top floor and walk into a multi-million dollar apartment. Westfield does live well. We settle into two overstuffed chairs and Susanne orders dinner. I grab a remote control and surf the news channels.

Claire Allison is everywhere and even FOX, not the kindest network, is playing nice. As usual, CNN is all over the place, pursuing every wild assumption known to mankind. Make that humankind. We talk. Both Susanne and Westfield are mesmerized by the phenomena called Claire. But I keep thinking of mom, and what she says about the woman who fired her.

Sidney Hatchette appears on MSNBC and Westfield grunts something unintelligible about heads stuck up asses. Then, "He is one lucky bastard." He grabs a remote and calls up an in-house feed on a small screen monitor. An unedited video opens with an exterior shot of the Back Landing Hotel. Westfield does a voice over. "If you're going to have a nooner, this is the place."

A fire alarm sounds as the camera scoots through the main lobby. Guests in various degrees of undress make a break for safety, all careful to hold a hand up shielding their faces. The camera catches a man scurrying down a hall, also holding up his hand. He is wearing a pair of baggy white boxer shorts, a sleeveless undershirt, and black socks. A stunning brunette is right behind him, wearing a thong and lacy bra. She is breathtaking and the camera focuses on her.

"She charges two thousand a pop," Westfield says. He rewinds the video, framing the man. It could be Hatchette. The video stops. "That was when we got the call about the shooter," Westfield says. "We didn't have time to confirm identities and had to beat feet over to the school."

"You're breaking my heart, Mike."

Westfield nods. Because of the would-be shooter, Allison is the hottest story of the year and, thanks to the tip, Westfield was close by and the first on the scene. But without a confirm on Hatchette, that video is dead on arrival. Westfield's competition would treat it as an attempt to coattail on Allison and raise his ratings. And they would be right. "Like I said," Westfield muttered, "Hatchette is one lucky bastard."

Something tickles the black hole in my brain. "Where was the fire at the Back Landing?" I ask.

"No fire," Westfield replies.

"So, a false alarm."

"Nope. A fire drill."

I'm suspicious. Suspicious hell, I'm incredulous. Hotels don't do fire drills. "So why were you at the hotel with a camera crew?"

"We had a tip."

"About Hatchette and the hooker?" You don't get to where I am in this business without good instincts.

"Yep." He draws the word out. He raises his glass at the main TV and toasts the image on the screen. Allison is standing barefoot in front of the camera, one arm outstretched and holding the camera at bay, while her other arm is wrapped around a little girl with red hair.

"I'll be damned," I reply.

"She is totally amazing," Susanne murmurs.

Mom's voice screeches in my mind at around 120 decibels. Dottie Sue is crazy, not stupid, and there is more to Claire Allison than meets the eye. The woman is, without doubt, worth watching.

4

Thursday, May 10

Claire groaned, twisting in her sleep as Danny Hawkins ran through her nightmare, shouting and firing a huge handgun. Suddenly Hank was there, shielding her from harm. "It's okay, babe," he whispered. "You're having a bad dream." Claire fought through the haze, coming awake. She took a deep breath and rolled into his arms, wrapped a leg around his and pulled him close. "I can feel your heart beating," he murmured. "Want to talk about it?"

"Danny was . . ." Her voice trailed off as Hank's lips caressed her hair. "It seemed so real."

"I've been there. It goes with PTSD." Hank had experienced post-traumatic stress disorder after his first combat tour in Afghanistan. Fortunately, they had worked through it with a brilliant counselor, a woman who had experienced combat in the Army. The price a sane person pays for going into harm's way had been a revelation for Claire, and now it was happening to her. The counselor's advice that "having sex helps" seemed as fresh as it did then. She reached for him. "Now," she whispered.

"You don't need much encouragement."

"Shut up." She kissed him, her tongue searching for his.

Suddenly, Hank sat up. "What's that?" The sound grew louder. Hank jumped out of bed and reached for his boxer shorts. "It's Logan." He ran for their son's bedroom. Claire was right behind him, pulling on one of Hank's black T shirts. Hank was first through the door, partially blocking her view. As best she could tell, Logan was curled up in a tight fetal position, still asleep. Hank sat on the side of the bed, his hand on Logan's shoulder. "Hey, good buddy." His voice was low and warm.

Claire sat on the other side and reached across, touching Hank's arm. Logan's eyes opened, darting back and forth between them. He was still caught up in the nightmare that had claimed him. "It's okay," Claire cooed, her hand on his cheek. "We're here."

"And you're safe," Hank added. Logan sat up and threw his arms around Claire. He was shaking.

"It's okay," Claire repeated, gently rocking back and forth. Logan's breathing slowed. "Did you have a bad dream?" she asked. He nodded, his head against her breast." I had one too," Claire confessed. "But your dad was there and he saved me."

"I wish someone would save me," Logan said, his voice almost inaudible.

"Not to worry, good buddy," Hank said. "Just let me at them." He ruffled his son's hair.

"I don't want to go to school," Logan said, his voice stronger.

Claire held him tighter. "Neither do I."

"Yesterday was a bummer," Hank said. "I got an idea. Why don't we all take the day off? We can go hiking and look for dinosaur bones or go out on the boat."

Logan gave a little nod.

"We're on," Hank said.

"Do you want to get up or go back to sleep?" Claire asked. "It's still early, but I can fix breakfast."

Logan snuggled down and closed his eyes. They waited for a few moments to be sure he was asleep. Hank stood in the doorway, waiting for Claire as she tucked him in. She kissed Logan on his cheek and followed Hank out, closing the door behind them. "What do you think?" Hank asked.

"I'm not sure," Claire answered. "Yesterday was very traumatic."

"I think he's being bullied at school," Hank said.

Claire thought for a moment. The symptoms were there, but she hadn't seen any bruising or red marks, and Sarah had talked to Logan's teacher about that very subject. Still, much could happen on the playground or in the boys' restroom. "If he is, I'll end it," she said.

Hank knew how she reacted when anyone she loved was threatened. "Don't hurt the guilty bastard."

"I won't," Claire promised. Thanks to Hank, she could draw the line between being a 'helicopter mom' hovering over her loved ones and a 'fighter pilot mom' ready to engage in combat.

"Coffee?" he asked. Without a word, he led her into the kitchen and turned the coffee maker on. She curled up in the corner of the sectional couch in the family room while he brewed two cups. She stroked the couch's soft fabric and closed her eyes, remembering how she and Hank had loaded the old one onto a trailer and hauled it to the dump. That had helped expunge the hurt of Hank and Elisa's brief affair. Hank shot her a worried look, sensing she was back in time. "I wish I could change the memories," he said, handing her a cup.

She patted the spot beside her, sending the unmistakable message where she wanted him. "That was years ago. Besides, it was just sport fucking."

Hank's face softened. "I'll never understand you." Claire's smart phone buzzed, sounding like a school's passing bell. "It's still oh-dark-thirty," he said, "a bit early for school business." He handed her the offending instrument.

Claire glanced at the name. "It's Hatchett," she muttered. "Good morning, Sidney." She listened while he talked. "Thank you, and yes, we're all fine here. See you Monday." She hung up. "School's cancelled for today. The police have closed the campus while they search for weapons and evidence, and everyone has the day off. He told me to take the rest of the week off."

"Five days off," Hank said, opening the drapes and letting the early morning sun fill the room. "Sounds like a plan." He sat down and gestured at the French doors that opened onto the patio. "Check that out." Outside, her sunflowers were facing eastward, towards the rising sun.

"It's a new day," she murmured, cuddling close, drawing her fingers across his stomach and probing under the waist band of his shorts. She kissed him. "Now, what were we doing?"

* * * * *

"You might want to see this," Sarah Madison called. She closed the slats of the shutters overlooking the street in front of their home.

"See what, Mom?" Claire asked, coming out of the kitchen where she was cooking breakfast. Hank was right behind her. Sarah didn't answer and only pointed outside.

Hank peered through the slats. "The paparazzi are here." A large group of over thirty reporters and camera technicians were camped out on the sidewalk and the gravel that substituted as their front lawn. Judging by their chairs and umbrellas, they were settling in for the long haul. "Sarah, can you check on Logan. He doesn't need to see this."

"They better not mess with this grandmother," Sarah said. Strong protective instincts flowed through the family, and she hurried towards Logan's bedroom that was on the street side of the house.

Claire joined Hank, her arm around his waist, and cracked the slats to get a better view. "Don't let them see you," he warned. She was still wearing his black T shirt.

"They've seen legs before," she said.

"Yeah, but not yours." He gave her a sideways glance. "Which ain't bad, babe." She gave him a little poke in the ribs. Claire considered her legs her best feature after her hair. "Okay, they're traffic stoppers."

"That's better," she murmured. They watched in silence as a man with a cane joined the reporters. "That's Hector!" Claire said, totally surprised to see her vice principal, Hector Mendoza. He set a camp chair on the path leading to their front door and made a big show with the cane, chasing the reporters off the gravel and onto the sidewalk while he cursed eloquently in Spanish. About half moved across the street to the sidewalk on the other side. Then he collapsed onto his camp chair, the cane across his lap, holding the reporters at bay. "What's he doing here?" Claire asked.

"Guarding you," Hank said.

"Why?"

"Because you're his boss." From her look, he knew she didn't understand. "It's about leadership."

"But I'd never ask anyone to do that," she protested.

"He knows that. Hector is protecting his leader. It's what us followers do."

"Don't be silly," she replied. Another thought came to her, and she checked the time. She hit the speed dial on her phone. "Rolinda should be in her office by now."

Rolinda Johnson was Logan's no-nonsense principal and one of Claire's mentors. Their friendship went back years and Claire trusted her. "She'll know if Logan is being bullied." Rolinda answered on the second ring. They spoke for a few moments, and Hank overheard enough to know Logan was not being bullied. "Rolinda's a sweetheart," Claire said, hanging up. "She doesn't know of any problems, but said to drop by anytime to chat. I don't know . . . she's very busy."

"Babe," Hank said, "the President of the United States would say the same thing if you called today."

"Now you are being silly."

"Am I?" His eyes filled with sadness. "Do you remember the massacre at Sandy Hook Elementary School where a deranged student killed twenty-six people, including twenty children?"

"How could anyone ever forget?" Claire replied. "They were six or seven years old. But that was years ago."

"The principal and school psychologist," Hank said, "heard the noise and ran out to check on it. They shouted the alarm and were killed. But they saved many lives."

"They were incredibly brave," Claire whispered.

Hank held her close. "And so were you." He kissed the top of her hair. "People remember and are making a connection." He held her tight as Sarah joined them. "So, how are we going to shake that bunch of zombies out there?" he asked.

"I have an idea," Sarah said. "People say we look alike, and we are the same size. Why don't I put on sunglasses and a hat and drive your car somewhere? If they follow me, you three can escape." She looked at them expectantly, obviously enjoying the thought.

"We can't let you do a Princess Diana," Claire said, recalling how the paparazzi had hounded the glamorous princess and how she had died in a car accident.

"That won't happen," Sarah promised. "Besides, if Hector and I do it right, they'll stop bugging you."

"Oh, Mom!" Claire laughed.

Friday, May 11

At exactly ten o'clock the next morning, Claire backed her car out of the garage. She wore the same hat and sunglasses her mother had worn the day before, and she waved at the small group of reporters and paparazzi still clustered on the sidewalk. One of them raised an extended middle finger in return, assuming she was Sarah. Claire suppressed a grin, remembering how Sarah had led the howling pack of reporters and paparazzi across town to a police station. The police and the reporters did not think it was funny, but TV news editors did and gave it their full attention. Hank chalked it up to professional cannibalism.

It was a short drive to Logan's school and Claire parked outside the main office. She glanced at the mirror in the sun visor and decided to wear the hat and sunglasses inside. She opened the door and stepped out, flashing more leg than normal. She was wearing one of her mother's ensembles, a sleeveless blouse with a soft blue pattern and a mid-cafe length skirt with a slit up to mid-thigh. A wide soft leather belt cinched her narrow waist, and the skirt's solid blue highlighted the blouse, making a perfect combination for the warm Phoenix weather.

It was not the sober attire of a professional educator, and she walked into the office with more confidence than she felt. She was totally surprised when the school secretary jumped to her feet. "Mrs. Allison, I didn't recognize you. You look like a movie star."

"Oh, Linda, you are a sweetheart." The older woman beamed when Claire remembered her name. "I hope Mrs. Johnson is free."

"She's expecting you," the secretary said, rushing from the room. Two waiting parents jumped to their feet and offered Claire their seats. They gushed when Claire thanked them and introduced herself. Rolinda Johnson joined them. She was a tall, statuesque, no nonsense African American. She had married at eighteen and divorced at nineteen.

The marriage had been a disaster but launched her into college. She had never remarried and was eleven years older than Claire. She dressed in a style many women envied, and her staff wondered how she could afford it on a principal's pay. Only her best friends knew she haunted bargain outlets and used clothes stores. She hugged Claire and motioned at her office.

"These ladies were here before me," Claire said. Both mothers shook their heads, saying they were in no hurry. Claire thanked them and followed Rolinda down the hall.

"You look marvelous," Rolinda said, closing her office door behind them. She motioned Claire to the two comfortable chairs in a corner. "Coffee?" Claire shook her head but Rolinda ignored her and hit the intercom. "Linda, would you be so kind as to bring us two cups of coffee. Mrs. Allison likes hers with a little cream." The secretary almost sang that it would be right in. Claire looked at Rolinda, a concerned look on her face. It was accepted protocol to never ask anyone to get coffee. "Linda's feelings would be hurt if we didn't ask," Rolinda explained. She reached out and touched Claire's knee. "It goes with the territory. You'll get used to it. By the way, I love your outfit. Where did you find it?"

"It's my mother's. I needed a disguise."

"Your mother has good taste."

Linda knocked at the door and Rolinda told her to come in. The secretary was all bustling efficiency, arranging the service and pouring coffee. She asked if they needed anything else. They thanked her and she quickly left, closing the door behind her.

Rolinda studied Claire for a moment. "Claire, people have always liked you, now you have their respect. They want to help you in any way they can. It makes them feel useful and connected."

An inner voice told Claire she was hearing good advice, and she filed it away for a later discussion with Hank. "You do see things I don't," Claire admitted. "I'm hoping you've seen something with Logan that I'm missing."

"Not really," Rolinda replied. "I know you're worried about bullying, but that's not it. I talked to Logan's teacher after you called. She said he does seem a little moody lately. Are you having any problems at home? Hank?" She had heard the rumors about Hank's indiscretions.

Claire shook her head. "Not anymore. His brain finally kicked in."

Rolinda's laughter filled the office. "I like that." Her eyes filled with concern and she grew serious. "You need to see a counselor, a good one. I have a name, Sandra Shriver."

"I've heard of her," Claire said. Shriver had an excellent reputation and was very expensive. "I imagine she's fully booked."

"Why don't we find out," Rolinda said. She dialed a number and was talking to the psychiatrist within moments. "She can see you this morning. Just you. Can you make it?" Claire nodded, surprised by how fast doors were opening. Rolinda set a time and broke the connection. "You get over there, right now." She scribbled an address on a sticky and handed it to Claire.

They walked out to the secretary's desk where the two parents were still waiting. Claire smiled. "Mrs. Randall, Mrs, Danville, it was a pleasure meeting you, and thank you so much for your understanding." The two mothers were thrilled that she had remembered their names, and both gave her a hug. Claire caught Rolinda's approving look as she headed for her car.

Claire started her car and savored the blast of cold air coming from the air conditioner. She hit a button on the steering wheel and recited the address Rolinda had given her into the GPS. "Directions to Phoenix Children's Hospital started," the voice said. Claire arched an eyebrow. It wasn't what she expected. The hospital was one of the best in the United States. As usual, traffic was heavy, but she made good time, driving aggressively. She glanced in the rearview mirror and caught sight of two cars following her through traffic. *More followers, no doubt.*

She loved the quiet order of the hospital and had no trouble finding a directory board. But there was no Sandra Shriver listed. She made her way to the information desk and asked for directions to the psychiatrist's office. The older of the two volunteers at the desk, a man in his seventies, recognized her and stood. "I'll take you there," he said. The younger of the two volunteers, a woman in her thirties, asked for her autograph. Claire felt her face flush, not sure what to do.

The man saved her. "Don't be rude," he said. He grabbed his cane and motioned to a hall. "Please, this way." They made small talk as they took the long walk to Shriver's office. "My wife would love your outfit," he said. "It is most becoming."

Rolinda's advice about Sarah echoed in her mind. *I guess clothes do make the woman.* The volunteer at the information desk had called ahead and Sandra Shriver met them in the hall. She was a short, grandmotherly looking woman with gray hair and rosy cheeks. The two women shook hands and introduced themselves. Claire turned to the volunteer and glanced at his name tag. "Thank you, Bill."

He smiled and nodded his head. "My pleasure, Mrs. Allison." He turned and walked away.

"You made a friend," the psychiatrist said, leading her into her office. Claire was surprised to see there was no desk or filing cabinets, just comfortable chairs and toys scattered around the room on a beige rug. A computer center was tucked in a corner. She motioned Claire to a comfortable seat. "I prefer to go by first names," she said. "Coffee or tea?" she asked.

"A glass of water would be fine," Claire replied.

Sandra produced two bottles of water from a small refrigerator and sat down beside her. "Well, what can I do for you?"

"Thank you for seeing me on such short notice," Claire began.

A little smile flickered across Sandra's lips, and she waved a hand dismissively. For some reason, Claire instinctively trusted her, and started to talk. Sandra listened, not taking notes. Soon, Claire was pouring out her heart. "I'm babbling on like a school girl." Sandra reached out and touched her hand, encouraging her to continue. But now, she asked the occasional question, always about Logan. At one point, Claire started to cry and Sandra handed her a box of Kleenex. "I can't believe I'm going on like this." She smiled weakly.

The psychiatrist took her hand. "I don't think Logan is being bullied. To be truthful, I don't think it's school related. But obviously, something is bothering him."

"Is he . . . is he being . . ." She couldn't bring herself to utter the word "molested."

"Don't go there," Shriver said. "It doesn't make sense, not in his environment. Logan is a very well cared for and protected child." She checked her calendar on her smart phone. "Why don't we all get together next week and talk?"

"You can fit us in on such short notice?' Claire asked.

"Most certainly," Sandra replied. "Bring Logan and he can play while we talk." The session was over and Claire made her way back to the parking lot, eager to get home and talk to her family.

"Hey, babe, time to hit the sack. I've got an early morning flight. I'll put Logan to bed." Hank sat his beer down and chased Logan into his bedroom. The house echoed with high-pitched shrieks as Hank wrestled his son into bed. He was back in a few minutes and nuzzled Claire's neck as she sat at her computer. "Wanna mess around?"

She laughed softly. "I need to talk to mom when she gets back." It was Sarah's night to play Bunko, a silly game that gave women a chance to gossip and socialize.

"About your meeting with the shrink today?" Hank ventured. Claire nodded. "Your mom means well," he said. "But she can be a little flighty at times." He kissed the top of her head and headed for their bedroom.

Claire watched him go. *You are the best. But it took some work.* She turned to her computer and took a deep breath as she slipped into another world. It was her escape hatch and she left the worries and stress of her everyday world behind.

She called up her search/spyware program and went to the handler that dealt with firewalls. It was getting harder to break through firewalls and hack into other systems, and her watchdog app had twice saved her from being mauled by a more robust system. She played with the spyware, trying to improve it, but soon gave up.

The world of computer technology was rapidly moving beyond her. The siren of artificial intelligence was calling and she went looking for a program she could 'borrow' before her spyware was history. She thought of the theft as a form of self-defense and never shared what she had 'borrowed' or tried to make a profit. It was a weapon she used to protect those she loved.

But first, she had to find a more capable processor she could 'borrow'. She had done it before, but this time it would have to be in the realm of super computers. Her searchware was still up to that task and within seconds she hit pay dirt. *Oh, my!* Her eyes opened wide. She had found an IBM WMX-I.

It was the latest in super computers that far outstripped the competition. *So where are you?* She typed in a command and had the answer immediately. The computer was in Sydney, Australia. It was all too easy. *Oh, no!* She had stumbled into a honeypot, a decoy computer system for trapping hackers.

Her fingers flew over the keyboard, trying to extract her probe and protect her system from what had to be coming at her. She was under attack almost immediately and lost partial control as her watchdog app froze. She tried another gambit, this time with a little more success. Slowly, she regained control of her system, finally repairing her firewalls. Claire relaxed. "It's getting dangerous out there," she murmured.

"Indeed, it is," a voice answered. It came from her computer and she could hear an accent. Claire reached for the power cord. "Can we be friends?" the voice asked. She hesitated. "You are very good." She pulled the cord.

Don't panic. Give it a moment. Go dark and check the damage. She turned the computer back on, making sure she was on internal mode and hidden from cyberspace. She scanned her systems for malware. Nothing.

"Hello, again," the voice said.

Claire knew when she was defeated, but her backups were safe. She grabbed the power cord and jerked. She sighed as the computer shut down for the last time. She would tear it apart and pulverize the microchips, ensuring that the malware died with it. Her smart phone rang with Sarah's ring tone. She hit the speaker button. "Hi, Mom. What's up?"

"Please don't hang up, Claire." It was the same voice, now coming over the phone's speaker.

"Everything's fine," Sarah said. Claire spun around in her chair. Her mother had just walked in and had overheard the phone call. She was standing in the doorway, her hair in slight disarray. She gestured at the phone and arched an eyebrow. "Australian?"

"Hello, Sarah," the voice said, its accent much thicker now. "We haven't met. I'm Nedd, that's with a double *d*. I'm an old friend from down under, but I did live in the states. I hear you've met Stuart."

"Do you know Stu?" Sarah asked.

"Not really," Nedd answered. "But we have a mutual friend." Claire hit the end call button on her smartphone. "I hear he's a good bloke," Nedd continued. She hit the phone's power button, determined to end the call. "Bit of a screamer, though."

Claire looked at her phone. It was off, but he was still talking. *How's he doing that?*

"Screamer?" Sarah asked.

"He likes to party," Claire answered, not sure why she replied. Sarah blushed and said goodnight. She turned and left. Claire's mind raced. *This is creepy. What am I dealing with here?* Not sure what to do, she took refuge. "I need to use the bathroom," she said.

"Please hurry back," Nedd replied. "I am a friend."

Sure, you are. She left the smartphone on her desk and headed for the master bathroom. The phone's battery would soon go dead, and she could rip the sim card out, effectively killing it, before smashing it to pieces along with the computer. She felt the need for a hot shower.

5

Friday, June 29

"That came fast," I say to no one in particular, staring at the envelope. I'm standing in the lobby of the no-tell-motel, my flop house of the moment, picking up my mail and paying the weekly rent. I've been staying here for over two months and have become a fixture. Ali and Khepri Salib, immigrants from Egypt who bought the dump for unpaid taxes, seem to like me. They often invite me to dinner with their two children. I turn the letter over and over, almost afraid to open it. I say "almost" because I know what is inside. I just don't know how much. "I hope it is not bad news," Ali says. His voice has a distinctive sign-song accent that seems to be lessening by the week.

"Nope." I don't tell him that it is very good news. I rip the envelope open and pull out the check. I almost wet my knickers. A production company has bought the movie rights to my story on the Lake Havasu swingers, "Fun in the Sun." My hand is shaking when I re-read the two-page signed agreement. It is amazingly straight forward. Those idiots, sorry, make that "those wonderful folks," are forking over a $50,000 advance against $900,000. They will pay me $50,000 now for the movie rights and $850,000 the day the movie goes into production, which must happen within one year or all rights revert to me. If that's the outcome, I get to keep the fifty grand. Then my agent can sell it all over again. Of course, he takes fifteen percent off the top, so the check in hand is for $42,500.

Which just goes to prove that sex sells. All I have to do is endorse and cash the check. I borrow a pen from Ali and scribble my signature with the speed of Arizona lightning. The pen is still smoking when I kiss the check. "Life is good!" My ship has just come in, and I'm standing at the dock, and other trite phrases. Okay, so I'm banality personified. My mind races with the implications. Do I owe Susanne anything? Mike Westfield's assistant had been a willing partner, and I'd have never made it inside the group without her. She was an immediate hit, and she got me into a lot of other things. But I digress. I need to find a way to avoid paying taxes, which can get tricky. Thankfully I had declared bankruptcy the month before and Shaft and Lynch are history.

"Is there a problem?" Khepri asks. She's the smarter half of the Salibs and a very hard worker. I explain my problem of having too much money too quickly. We have discussed money and investing, always in very general terms, many times over dinner. Khepri eyes the check, not knowing the amount. "I have an uncle who is a private investment banker and can create an anonymous account for you. He pays good interest." I tell her that I've never heard of a private investment banker in the States. "Oh, yes. We have private banks here," she assures me. "FDIC insured, of course."

"Of course," I agree. She has solved my problem and I could almost kiss her. But that would get me in trouble with Ali, not to mention their seventeen-year-old son, Jeffrey. He's a good kid and works hard around the motel. He's also as strong as an Egyptian ox and I don't want to mess with him.

"Why don't you come to dinner tonight and we can talk about it." I agree and she calls the bank to make an appointment. I make a quick trip across town to the 'Sunrise Personal Investment Bank FDIC Insured' and deposit the check. Said uncle has a big office and is very professional.

Dinner with the Salibs is delightful. Khepri has cooked up a pot of Kushari, which must be the Egyptian national dish, and Chione, their fourteen-year-old daughter, is dressed in a pretty dress looking all of eighteen. She is smart like her mother, and is showing signs of being a beautiful woman. Even Jeffrey is congenial. Ali serves an excellent brandy after dinner as we sit beside the sparkling pool.

Khepri joins us and we make small talk. "David," she says. "You did say you were married once." It's true, I was. But it didn't last long. Mutual loathing got in the way after we sobered up. "Didn't you have a son?" Well, maybe. While DNA tests indicated otherwise, I still have to pay child support. That's California for you, but I digress. He's a year younger than Chione and I'll be out of child support for five more years. Khepri nods at her daughter. "Did you know Chione means daughter of the Nile?"

"What a beautiful name," I reply.

"You know that we believe in arranged marriages for our children," li says

Obviously, the uncle has spilled the beans, or the amount of the check to be more accurate. "What a charming custom," I say, which pretty much ends the evening. I make my way back to my room and look around. The Salibs have really upgraded the place. Then it dawns on me that the Salibs' marriage was arranged and the results are all around me. Then the light bulb really comes on. In their own way, the Salibs have paid me a rare compliment. I doubt that I deserve it.

My smart phone buzzes, and I check the caller. It's mom so I answer. Benny's voice comes over loud and strong, but different. "David" - it's the first time he has ever called me by my name - "get your butt back here ASAP. Your mother overdosed. I called 911, but she didn't make it"

Saturday, June 30

Benny is sitting outside Mom's mobile home when I pull into the Shangri-La Mobile Home Park. It's still morning and I'm exhausted after making the drive from Phoenix. He comes to his feet when I park and motions me to stay in the car. He climbs into the passenger seat and stares straight ahead. He takes a deep breath. "I went fishing and wasn't gone that long." He stops. He's hurting. "When I got back, she was in bed with an empty bottle of Seconal still in her hand. I called 911 and they got here within minutes. I don't know if she was still alive or not, but they declared her DOA at the ER." He falls silent.

I sit there, my hands clenching the steering wheel, and for a moment forget to breathe. Dottie Sue was a bit looney, but she was always there when I came home for dinner. I suck in my breath and exhale. What comes out is a moan of despair. The past is back and I remember my high school graduation present. Most kids get a watch, she gave me a suitcase. I didn't know it at the time, but it was a good present. I guess she was loving me in the only way she could.

I want to cry, but the tears aren't there. I had lost them somewhere on the drive in from Phoenix. Does that make me a bad son? I simply don't know. I've lost my mother and I never told her that I love her. That's a hurt that I can never make right. "Did she leave a note?" I ask.

"It's inside with a few of her things she sat aside," Benny says. He gets out of the car. "Let me go in first. Kissy Poo can be very aggressive."

"Kissy Poo?" I ask

"He's a rescue dog. The pound was gonna put him down, but we got him instead." I shake my head in wonder. Mom had a cat once, but she ran away. Benny cracks the mobile home door open and a dog barks as it slams into Benny, trying to get out. Not a smart move, even for a dog. Benny out barks the dog, ordering it back inside. The dog immediately complies and whimpers as it retreats. If I were the dog, I'd do the same thing.

I go in and the dog cocks his head to one side and looks at me. He looks like a golden retriever with something from down the street thrown in. " He's almost two years old," Benny says. The dog has the saddest eyes I've ever seen, which I understand, what with living with my mom and Benny. His tail starts to wag. Maybe I'm not on the menu.

I sit down. The mobile home is spotless and all of mom's knickknacks are gone. It as if she's never lived there. I guess that's how Benny is handling his grief. He hands me the note. I unfold it and read.

I was a good teacher and didn't deserve to be fired.

I'm stunned. "That's it?" I ask. Benny nods. I reread the note and start to understand. Dottie Sue defined herself as a schoolteacher. That's all she had. "I wasn't much of a son, was I?"

Benny doesn't answer and stands up. He disappears into the bedroom and is back within moments holding a thick file. "She left this for you. Allison used it to fire her." He hands it to me. I open the file and start to read. It contains mom's medical records and words jump out like schizoaffective disorder, dementia, and bipolar. It sounds like the quacks can't make up their minds about her.

Then I see it—paliperidone. Even I know that is a very strong antipsychotic drug. There was a trip to the Mayo clinic and the diagnosis was not good. One of the recommendations was that she avoid any stressful situations, like her teaching job. I close the file. "Medical records like this fall under doctor-patient confidentiality," I tell Benny. Because of the lawsuit, I know all about stuff like this. "So how did Allison get a hold of it?"

"Beats me," Benny says, "but she did. Allison made it obvious; keep fighting and everyone will learn you're a mental case. So Dottie Sue just gave up."

"And you think I should find out how Allison got the file."

"Dottie Sue couldn't live with it," Benny says, "and it drove her to suicide. I hope you know that."

I know he's right and my gut ties itself into a knot. "I got it."

"Dottie Sue wanted to be cremated. She said she'd be damned before having a memorial service, and just scatter her ashes in the desert."

"I'll take care of that," I promise.

Benny gives me his Marine look. "You need to set things straight with Allison." It's an order, not a suggestion.

"I will," I promise. "Okay, I'm outta here,

Benny helps me load the car with a few boxes of photographs and mementos of her life. It fills up the back of the car. "Take the dog," Benny says. I open the front passenger door and motion for Kissy Poo to jump in the car. He does and sits on the seat, facing forward. The mutt obviously wants to get the hell out of Shangri-la. We collect the dog's bowl, blanket, and thirty pounds of dog food, and throw them in the trunk.

"David, take care," Benny says. We shake hands, none of this hugging stuff, and I hop in the car. I glance in the rearview mirror as I drive off. Benny throws me a salute.

"Well, Kissy Poo," I say, "if that doesn't beat all." The dog ignores me and looks straight ahead. "You don't like your name, do you?" The dog farts. I'm not joking.

I pull to a stop light and read the street sign; Mockingbird Lane. "To Kill a Mockingbird," I mutter. My eighth-grade teacher made me read the book and then do a review of the movie. That's when I discovered I could write. The dog looks at me. The light turns green and the car behind me honks. I accelerate away. "Okay, Atticus, we're going home."

Atticus licks my ear.

6

Tuesday, July 24

The thunderstorm moved over Phoenix just before midnight and stalled over Scottsdale. A torrent of lightning followed by rolling thunder shook the bedroom windows, jolting Claire awake. She sat up in bed, her heart beating fast.

Hank's hand reached out and touched her bare back. "It's okay, babe." She relaxed and laid down, pulling the sheet over her. She closed her eyes. A whisper of a touch she knew so well caressed her cheek. Claire opened her eyes to look at her son. She hadn't heard him come in and he was standing beside the bed, his eyes wide with fear. Another burst of lightning and thunder shook the house. Logan scampered onto the bed and Claire pulled him to her. She could feel his heart beating through the sheet.

"It's okay, honey." She cuddled him for a few moments, cooing in his ear. "Honey, why don't you go get your robe and come sleep with us?" Logan bounced out of bed and ran for his room. Claire pushed on Hank's shoulder. "Get some clothes on before he gets back." She jumped out of bed and grabbed a T shirt.

"He knows we sleep starkers," Hank said. They were natural and comfortable with their bodies, but always discreet.

"Not tonight." She crawled back into bed. "Right," Hank said. He got up, pulled on a pair of boxer shorts and crawled back into bed as another jolt of lightning and thunder chased Logan back into their bedroom. He leapt into Claire's waiting arms. Hank reached over and tousled his hair. "That was fast, good buddy."

"I was scared," Logan said.

"I was too," Claire replied. "But we're safe now."

"I know," Logan said, his voice calm and sleepy. Hank's hand moved and touched Claire's cheek. They had been on an emotional rollercoaster since taking Logan out of school in May. It had been a struggle, but his bad dreams and crying episodes were slowly fading away. They were seeing their little boy again. "What are we doing today?" Logan asked.

"Well," Claire replied, "we're seeing Mrs. Shriver this morning. And then we can do whatever you want." It was their fifth appointment with the child psychiatrist, and as usual, the three of them were going in. There was no response. Logan was fast asleep. "I'll put him in his own bed," Claire said.

"Let him sleep with us," Hank replied. Claire kissed his hand. Her family was safe.

Wednesday, July 25

"Hello, there," Sandra Shriver sang when Logan rushed into her office. She laughed as she swept the eight-year-old into her arms. She waved Claire and Hank to the lounge chairs next to her. Logan wiggled with excitement and told her about the thunderstorm that had shaken their home during the night. "Were you frightened?" Sandra asked.

"Only a little," Logan confessed. "Mommy was scared too, but my daddy was there. He's a fighter pilot and he keeps us safe."

"You're very lucky," Sandra said.

"Yes, I am," Logan said.

The psychiatrist glanced at Claire and gave a little nod. They were making progress. "Well," she said, "we're going to do something different today." She pointed to the computer in the far corner. It was on a child-sized table and framed with little clown and animal faces. "You can play games on that while your mommy and daddy and I talk."

He bounced out of her arms and ran to the computer. Sandra followed and sat down beside him. They both donned a headset and she spent a few minutes showing him the games before rejoining Claire and Hank. She picked up her iPad and called up an app then turned the iPad so they could see it. She pointed at Logan then at the iPad. They were seeing exactly what Logan was seeing.

"Let's see what game he chooses," she said. "Don't worry, he can't hear us. The games all involve dolls. It's a form of play therapy. It can allow Logan to express any painful feelings or act out whatever may have happened to him. Or he could simply be playing."

Hank asked the obvious question. "So where are the dolls?"

"Rather than use actual dolls," Sandra explained, "I'm using computer games with dolls. He can move them around and place them in different scenarios." They fell silent and watched as Logan carefully removed the clown and animal faces that framed the screen. He carefully sorted and arranged them on the table before turning back to the computer.

"He is a neatnik," Claire said.

"Is that a clue?" Hank asked.

'Perhaps," Sandra allowed. Logan's fingers danced over the keyboard and track pad as the screen rapidly cycled. "I've never seen anyone who can extract information so fast and move on as quickly as he does."

"You should see Claire," Hank muttered.

Sandra studied Claire for a moment and reevaluated her before turning to her iPad. An image of various shaped dolls appeared on the screen as Logan played a game with faceless, highly stylized dolls that resembled statues. They were all sizes, male and female, and of a uniform golden color. He moved the cursor and put shoes on one. Sandra closed her iPad and sat it on the coffee table between her and Hank. "I'll look at it later."

"What are you looking for?" Claire asked.

"Patterns," Sandra answered. "I must ask if there is anything new in your life or a problem you might have been talking about."

"Well," Hank said, "I'm up for a PCS, a permanent change of station." He explained how his wing trained pilots to fly fighter aircraft, and he was due for an assignment to an operational squadron. It would involve moving to another state. "I'll be deployed so often that we're thinking Claire should stay here and not move. I'll get home as much as I can. With a little luck, I'll get reassigned back to Luke in a year or two."

"Logan did overhear us talking about it," Claire added.

Sandra listened as they talked about the stresses of service life, and how they adjusted their family life to the mission of the Air Force. They had been separated twice before and seemed stronger for it. Finally, their hour was up. "Logan," Sandra called. "Time to go."

He twisted around in his chair, his eyes full and bright. "Ok," he said. He shut down the game he was playing as Claire and Hank stood by the open door. He bounced to his feet and skipped out of the room.

Sandra smiled at them. "We'll talk later."

"Lunch?" Hank asked.

"Pizza!" Logan sang.

Why not? A wave of relief washed over her.

Thursday, July 26

The phone call came just after nine the next morning. "Claire," Sandra said. "Could you drop by this morning?"

"I'll see if Hank can make it," Claire replied.

"Alone would be best," the psychiatrist said.

A cold panic held Claire tight. "Is there a problem?"

"We need to talk."

Claire sat in her car, afraid to get out and make the walk into the hospital. *Waiting isn't going to make it go away.* She got out of the car, forgetting at first to lock it. It was the shortest walk of her life and she didn't remember how she got to Sandra's office. She knocked and the door clicked open. Sandra Shriver was sitting in her usual chair and came to her feet. She motioned to the overstuffed chair beside her. "Tea or coffee?"

"No, thank you," Claire replied, sitting down.

"I hope you don't mind if I have a cup," Sandra replied. Claire said she didn't mind at all, suddenly wishing for a cup of tea. "Earl Gray?" Sandra asked. Claire only nodded, thankful the psychiatrist understood. Sandra handed her a cup and sat down. She sipped at her tea and waited as Claire forced herself to relax. "I know you're worried," Sandra began.

"If only you knew," Claire murmured.

Sandra sat her teacup down and touched Claire's hand. "My daughter was abused." She gently took the half empty teacup from Claire.

"And Logan," Claire whispered.

"I may be wrong," Sandra said, "but I believe he may have been sexually abused."

Claire's world collapsed in on her and she sat motionless, totally stunned, not capable of thinking or feeling. Sandra waited silently. Claire took a deep breath and her right hand jerked in an uncoordinated movement. Her fingers clenched into a fist and then slowly relaxed. She looked at the psychiatrist. "Please tell me about the video." Her voice was flat and toneless, totally lacking in emotion.

Sandra carefully chose her words. "The dolls he chose to play with were faceless manikins, all a uniform light bronze color, but you can determine their gender. There were four adults and four children. All the adults were male and two of the children were girls."

"You said, 'he may have been abused.'"

"Claire, you know Logan much better than I, but I'm not seeing any signs of trauma now. Whatever happened to him, it is not happening now."

Claire only stared straight ahead, her eyes cold and unblinking. "How do you know this?"

"It's the way Logan ended the game," Sandra explained. "He moved all the big dolls into separate rooms and closed the doors. Then he divided the small dolls into two groups, boys and girls. You saw his reaction when he left the room."

"I did." Claire up on the edge of her chair, her back rigid. "What makes you think there was sexual abuse?"

"The dolls played with each other in a sexual way a child his age would never know."

"Can I see the video?" Claire asked.

"Of, course. But I would prefer to view it with Hank, and after you've both had a chance to talk about it. I can tell him, if you want."

Claire inhaled deeply, forcing herself to be calm. "It's best if I tell him. He can be very aggressive. Any indication, any clues, who the men are? When or where it happened?"

"Not at this time," Sandra replied.

A heavy silence came down as Claire clasped her hands to keep them from shaking. She looked up, her eyes full of tears. "He's just a child. How could anyone?" Sandra reached out and held Claire's hands, not saying a word. Claire blinked her tears away but made no effort to dry her cheeks. "Could I have another cup of tea?"

Sandra came to her feet and stood by the tea cart, pouring two cups. "May I offer a suggestion?" There was no answer. "It's summer vacation and Logan is home and safe. Don't change anything for now. Can I see you and Hank as soon as possible?"

Claire nodded her head in answer. She sipped her tea and gazed at the wall, deep in thought. She glanced at her watch. "I must go. I know you have other patients waiting."

"I'll walk you to your car," Sandra said.

"That would be very kind of you." Together, they made the long walk to the parking lot. Sandra carefully studied her as she fished the car remote out of her purse and unlocked the car. Her hands were steady and not shaking. Claire settled in and started the car. She reached out the open window and clasped Sandra's hands. "Thank you," she whispered. "I'm okay." She shifted into gear and backed out of the parking space. With a little wave she drove off.

Claire wheeled out of the parking lot and onto Thomas Road. *It had to be at school,* she raged to herself. How else to explain the presence of four men and three other children? *Which school!* Logan only went to elementary school or Prime Star Academy Day School. But neither made any sense because the children were so closely monitored by their teachers and hordes of parents. The children were never alone or left unattended.

Hank! The thought made her want to vomit. She quickly dismissed the idea. She knew, with certainty, that Hank would kill any pedophile who molested Logan. The light changed and a car behind her honked, bringing her back to reality. The numbing hurt that had claimed her washed away in a flood of pure, raw anger that consumed her. *My beautiful, beautiful Logan was violated!*

She mashed the accelerator in rage and shot across the intersection, shooting underneath the Piestewa Freeway. She made a hard left turn onto the entrance ramp and accelerated, heading north. She banged on the horn, weaving in and out of traffic and shouting "Get out of my way!" She wanted to hurt someone, anyone, as a primal rage tore at her. She held the accelerator down and passed three cars on the right shoulder before cutting back across to the inside lane. Slower traffic forced her onto the narrow inside shoulder.

A driver laid on his horn, which only made her more angry. The speedometer touched one hundred miles an hour. A barrage of red lights barred her way as the heavy traffic came to a stop and the shoulder narrowed. She stomped on the brakes dragging the SUV down to a crawl.

Frustrated, Claire barged her way across traffic and onto the outside shoulder. A siren blared, capturing her attention and she glanced in the rearview mirror. An Arizona State Trooper patrol car was tailgating her, flashing red and blue lights. She took the next exit and pulled to a stop on a much wider shoulder. Both hands clasped the top of the steering wheel as her head bowed, her forehead touching her hands. She shook in despair as tears cascaded down her cheeks.

"Ma'am," a voice said from the right side of the SUV. "Please lower the window." Claire hit the power control and the window slid down. She looked across the passenger seat, trying to focus through her tears. A young woman wearing a tan uniform was looking at her. "Oh, no! Mrs. Allison?" The State Trooper had immediately recognized her.

Claire nodded dumbly. "I couldn't take some bad news . . . I lost control of the car . . ." She beat on the steering wheel. "I just lost control . . ." She shook with tears. "Damn, damn! It's just not right."

"We all heard," the State Trooper said. Claire stared at her, not understanding. "The suicide was on the news," the trooper said. "The boy in school with the gun."

Claire banged her forehead off the steering wheel as she cried, her body wracked with pain.

7

Thursday, the same day

"Here is your mail, Mr. Parker." Ali places a stack of envelopes and junk mail on the motel's office desk. He is being very proper and I suspect he is less than happy with me. They haven't invited me to dinner since I returned from California a month ago and I don't know why. I gather up my mail and head back toward my room. Jeffrey is playing in the pool with Atticus. I take a detour and flop down in the shade of an umbrella while I sort through the mail.

Jeffrey climbs out of the pool and sits down beside me while Atticus paddles furiously to the shallow end and bounds up the steps. He runs over to us and shakes furiously, showering us with water.

"I like Atticus," Jeffrey announces. He's a good kid and thoroughly Americanized, but he's nothing compared to Chione who just turned fifteen. Her T shirt of the moment declares she is a "Free Islamic Woman and Proud of IT!" Like what most girls wear these days, it's two sizes too small.

"What's bugging your folks these days?" I ask. Teenagers like to piss and moan about their parents, so he'll talk. Jeffrey shrugs. I figure it's because Chione has just walked up. She's wearing a bikini that might make three good eye patches. I look again. Her backside is covered, so make that four eye patches. No wonder her parents are worried. I'd install a hot line to the National Guard to call in reinforcements if my daughter wore anything like that.

"They don't like Atticus," Chione replies. Obviously, she has good hearing. She jumps in the pool and Atticus barks. Maybe he wants to rescue her.

"Dogs are unclean in our culture," Jeffrey says, staring at his feet. I need to think about that. I sort through the mail and open my first bank statement from Sunrise Personal Investment Bank FDIC Insured. I gasp. The $42,500 I deposited a month ago is now worth $43,580. I whip out my smart phone and key up the calculator. That's an annualized interest rate of over thirty percent. I'm going to jail, or at least through one hell of an IRS audit.

What the hell, money is money. I open the rest of the mail. There are two checks for ghost writing articles for illiterate CEOs. All very technical, of course. I add it all up. I'm flush. It's time to mend fences with my landlords and I meander back to the now vacant office. "Ali, my man," I call. Khepri comes out.

"May I help you, Mr. Parker?" she says. Yep, she's pissed at me.

"I know Atticus is a pain in the ass," I begin. She only looks at me. "I think it's only fair that my rent be increased accordingly." She smiles and quotes a number, effectively doubling my rent. I try not to gasp, but I can afford it. I hand over my credit card, and the room temperature goes up thirty degrees. I may get invited to dinner again.

"Thank you, David," she says, bestowing a lovely smile on me. I head back to my room and notice some interesting action going on poolside. A teenaged boy I've never seen is putting the make on Chione. She's eating it up, but Atticus is between them. He has a very hungry look and his tail is not wagging.

"Good boy," I call. Chione gives me an angry look. I laugh. The kids are turning into Americans, and I'm acting like an Egyptian uncle. Dinner is a slam dunk.

The temperature is pushing 110 degrees outside and a cold blast of air washes over me when I open the door to my room. Everything at the motel works these days, but my room is a mess. Atticus climbs onto the unmade bed and spreads out. I've turned into a Claire watcher since Dottie Sue's death. She has become an obsession and I'm living in a war room littered with boxes and books stacked on the floor, and my reference system is based on yellow Post-its stuck on everything. Paper flow charts are tacked on the wall with more Post-its. Black Magic Marker lines weave the Post-its together.

So far, there is no rhyme to it all, but everything circles one subject—a poster-sized photo of Claire Marie Allison taped to the wall. I glance at the velvet bag next to the TV holding the urn with Dottie Sue's ashes. I tell myself that has nothing to do with it. Yeah, right.

I turn the TV on and perk up. Claire Allison is on the news again. I grab a notebook and start taking notes. An attractive State Trooper is talking to a gaggle of reporters. "No, we do not think it was a case of road rage." She takes more questions and I finally piece together what had happened. Apparently, Allison was accelerating onto the Piestewa Freeway when her car went full throttle on its own. So much for modern electronics. Apparently—my favorite word to distrust—only her skillful car handling had prevented a serious accident. I study the look on the trooper's face. I know bullshit when I hear it.

A savvy reporter obviously agrees. "Has the car been impounded for inspection?"

The trooper answers. "Yes, it has been impounded. We're waiting for the results." The reporters go into a shouting frenzy trying to out-vocal each other. I hear a question about a suicide. It gets drowned out in the hubbub, and I make a note to follow up. I turn the TV off and go to work. So, what was that suicide thing all about? I search the local news stations and find a rerun of the press conference with Allison.

After two commercials about a hemorrhoid suppository and panties for incontinent geezers, I hear the question. "Mrs. Allison, have you heard that the boy you disarmed at school committed suicide?" It went unanswered, so naturally, I ask Siri. She tells me the boy blew his brains out. Apparently—that word again—he had a 9 mm semi-automatic tucked away in reserve, no doubt for just such an occasion.

My curiosity is aroused and I dig deeper, searching for the kid's name. It takes some heavy shoveling before I find it: Danny Hawkins. I try to chase that down and come up dry. It's going to take some heavy hacking to get behind a few firewalls. I have a geek buddy, Barry the Hacker Bodkin, who does that for a living. I table it for the time being.

I have a dedicated computer and program for searching the internet that cannot be traced back to me. Anyway, that's what

Barry the Hacker said when he sold it to me. I print out the bits and pieces I want to keep and trash the computer files. Then I shred the trash with a special program Barry sold me. Okay, so I'm paranoid. It comes from researching the NSA's eavesdropping capability on US citizens. But I digress.

I've a few drinking buddies in the police department, and I might be able to chase down more details on Hawkins and his intimate relationship with the muzzle of the semi-automatic. I definitely want to pursue the car malfunction that turned Allison into a NASCAR queen, but the State Troopers are a tight-lipped lot and not as forth coming as their brethren in the police department. Fortunately, Barry the Hacker is always available.

I check my watch. It's too early for Happy Hour with the cops, so I surf the local news. A local news girl is wetting her knickers about the President coming to Luke Air Force Base on Saturday. It seems the 56th Fighter Wing is involved with the F-35 super-duper fighter and scaling back on the F-16 Fighting Falcons stationed there. That triggers a connection. So back to Siri to find out exactly what is going down. It seems that one Lieutenant Colonel Henry Allison is an F-16 squadron commander and will be escorting the President.

I have to kill some time so I start to surf the porno sites. Atticus growls at me. I switch the porno site off just as there's a knock on the door and it swings open. It's Chione with the same boy who was panting poolside. They are holding buckets with cleaning supplies and pushing a vacuum cleaner. "Oh," Chione says. "I thought you had left and we could clean your room." Judging by the look on the boy's face, he has a different definition of cleaning than I do. Well, maybe not. I wait while they clean the room. The old sheets and towels don't smell too bad. Finally, they're finished. Chione waves at the stacks of boxes and books piled on the floor. "What are you doing?"

"Research," I answer.

She points to the photo tacked to the wall. "About her?" I nod.

"Isn't she the principal who saved all those kids?" Chione's boyfriend asks.

Chione gives him 'the look' only a teenage girl can muster. "That's Mrs. Allison." She adds an unspoken "you idiot." Chione shifts 'the look' to the boxes and books. "How can you find anything?" I don't answer because it is a good question. She sighs. "Mother is very good at organizing. You should hire her." I tell her I'll think about it. Atticus looks sad when they leave.

I check my watch. It's still early, but I head for the bar where my cop buddies hang out. It's a slog through rush hour traffic and we get there just before five o'clock. I'm not going to name the place because it is one of my best sources of information, and underneath all the bullshit and bragging that goes on lies the stuff of radioactive scandal. I strap a service dog vest and harness on Atticus so he can go in with me.

It's amazing what you can get away with in the name of emotional support. I even have a letter from a doctor, a cousin of the Salibs who has a website, certifying that Atticus is legitimate. Three off-duty peacekeepers are there drinking and trying to out lie each other. "Hey, Parker," one calls, "what's Atticus drinking?" They like Atticus.

I pull a hundred dollar bill out of his service vest. "He's buying today," I answer. I buy a round and crawl onto a bar stood. For the next hour, I listen as more cops arrive. The six o'clock news comes on the TV and the conversation quiets a little, but not much. Near the bottom of the hour, the pretty state trooper appears on the screen. It's a rerun of the earlier news clip, and the cops hoop and holler. "I'd do her in heartbeat," Harry the Cop Winslow calls.

"With your schwantz?" a grizzled veteran asks.

"You an expert on Harry's chingus now?" another cop asks. The comments taper off.

"What do you think went wrong with the car?" I ask the cop sitting next to me.

He grunts. "Nothing, from what I hear." Apparently, the police and the state troopers do talk to each other. The hundred-dollar bill just paid dividends.

"You think they're covering up for Allison?" I ask.

The cop shrugs. "Shit happens."

I know I'm onto something big and it's worth pursuing. It's an instinctual thing that is critical to success in my profession.

It's time to reach out to Barry the Hacker and contract for a little hacking. I glance at the TV in time to see the announcement of the President's visit on Saturday.

The room explodes and everyone seems to have an opinion about the current resident of the White House. But this is not the good-natured kidding over Harry's male member. The peacekeepers are definitely not being peaceful. I haven't learned a thing about Danny Hawkins, but I know when it is time to cut and run. Me and Atticus are out the door. Atticus's tail is not wagging, and he is one unhappy pooch.

"Time to go home," I tell him. He gives me his sad look when he crawls into the car and tries to curl up on the front seat. But he's too big. The world according to Atticus is not good. Again, my instincts kick in. There's a story spinning around Allison, if I can sort out the connections. This is not your usual one-time opinion piece for the Sunday papers. It's the big leagues, and I'm thinking Watergate. I make a mental note to call Public Affairs at the airbase and get on the press list for the presidential festivities.

Friday, July 27

Barry Bodkin is the geek I mentioned earlier and my hacker of choice. He answers on the first ring. I tell him that I'm looking into Claire Allison's incident on the freeway yesterday. Could he poke around the State Troopers and find out the story on the car?

"Can do," Barry says. "She had a stuck throttle, right?" It seems like everyone knows about the trials and tribulations of Mrs. Allison. I confirm we are on the same page.

"Can you also check out the boy who committed suicide yesterday? His name is Danny Hawkins."

"Isn't he the kid she stopped from shooting up a classroom?" Barry obviously watches the news.

"One and the same," I reply.

"Is there some sort of connection?"

My gut tells me there is, but that's presumption without proof. "I'm not sure," I tell him.

"I'll see what I can find out." He quotes a price that jiggles my toes. I figure he's a millionaire at nineteen.

Saturday, July 28

Barry calls me early in the morning with some news. Hacking the State Troopers was no big deal. "There's a flood of emails between the brass and the worker bees," Berry tells me. "They can't find anything wrong with the car, but no one wants to go public with the news.

"Are we talking cover-up?" I ask.

Barry snorts. "The last email from the colonel—that's the Troopers' honcho-in-chief—directed the garage to not release the car awaiting further inspection. They're flying in a whizz kid from Japan to troubleshoot the car. Apparently"—there's that word again—"there's an interface problem between the seventeen computers in that model SUV, and the system has been known to hiccup."

"Hiccup?" I ask. "Is that a technical term?"

Barry snorts. "Hey, we're talking State Troopers."

Barry has complained about being stopped about a dozen times by the State Troopers so I dismiss it as sour grapes. "Anything on Hawkins?" I ask.

"Still working it. I've run into some pretty strong firewalls. I should have something for you by Monday."

It's time to head for the air base and check in. I figure traffic and security will be a hassle, so I need to get started early. I stroke Atticus's head. "Sorry, good buddy. You can't come on this one." Based on past experience, there is no way Air Force security or the Secret Service will fall for any service dog bullshit. I need to reassure the mutt. "Jeffrey loves to dog-sit, and he'll take care of you." Atticus perks up. He looks pleased.

As expected, the traffic into the base is a killer, so I abandon my car and pedal my folding bike the last two miles to the main gate. About halfway there, I pass the KPIO-TV news van stuck in traffic. Susanne, Mike Westfield's assistant, waves me down and asks for a ride. I'm not happy peddling her ass a mile in the hot weather, but she's very appreciative. We hook up with Westfield and I tag along. It really helps getting through security and up front with the big boys in the press corps.

Air Force One lands right on time and taxis to a halt in front of a mass of cheering fans. The Pres deplanes with his usual panache and is greeted by a bird colonel and one Lieutenant Colonel Allison. Both men salute and escort him to the reviewing stand. A gaggle of dignitaries, including the governor, are waiting for him. And directly in front is one Claire Allison.

She is wearing a big floppy hat, sunglasses, and a long skirt that seems to flow with a motion of its own. Susanne gushes over her clothes while Westfield hyperventilates for a totally different reason. In her own way, she is a supernova. The Pres holds onto her hand a little too long when introduced. He starts to talk, something about F-35 fighters and the heroes who fly them. “And it is my pleasure to meet a most heroic lady, Claire Allison.” The crowd goes wild while Westfield mumbles something about getting all riled up over one confused kid with a gun.

The rest of the dedication ceremony and reception that follows is routine and nothing to write home about. But there is no doubt that the star of the day is Claire Allison. For some reason, the Pres does not seem upset about this in the least. I mention this to Westfield.

He grumps. “Distraction is his stock in trade.” And Allison is the distraction of the moment.

Sunday, July 29

My smart phone buzzes just after six the next morning. I groan and roll over Susanne and Atticus and fumble for the phone. It’s Barry with an update on Danny Hawkins. He was able to finally break through the firewall at the Department of Child Safety. Apparently, it was a tough one and there will be an added charge. He reads a short report.

I sit up in bed, fully awake. “Ah, shit,” I moan. Danny Hawkins was sexually molested when he was in the third grade. This just got complicated.

8

Sunday, the same day

Claire and Hank were still in bed and she had spent a sleepless night, tossing and turning, a sure sign that something was bothering her. "It's okay, babe," Hank murmured. "You've had a helluv a week, what with the car and meeting the President." She didn't answer and only rolled into his arms. "I thought it went pretty damn well." It had been a full day at the base, and the President's visit had gone off without a hitch.

"I was so proud of you," she murmured, "escorting the President with Colonel Mass."

"Colonel Billy Bob was not a happy camper," Hank replied. Normally, escorting the Commander in Chief fell to the ranking officer on a base and was not a shared duty.

"Mrs. Wing Commander wasn't happy either," Claire said. Wives often wore their husband's rank, and escorting the commander-in-chief was a big step on the road to promotion. "It wasn't your fault, they must know that."

"It did cause a stir on base when the White House asked for me by name to be an escort officer," Hank replied. "Personally, I think the President wanted to be seen with you." He stroked her back. "You were the show of the day. Is that what's bugging you?"

Claire snuggled closer. "Maybe . . . a little." She fell silent for a moment. Then, "I had a strange conversation with Sandra last week."

"All conversations with shrinks are strange."

"It was more difficult than strange." She hesitated. "I needed time to think about it before telling you."

Hank knew the warning signs. "Tell me what?"

Claire didn't breathe for a moment. "She's not sure, but she thinks there's a possibility that Logan may have been molested."

Hank exploded. "Shit! Fuck! Hate! That'son of a bitch!"

Claire had never seen him so angry and stroked the back of his head, whispering in his ear, desperate to divert his anger. "We're okay." She repeated it three times and felt his muscles finally relax. "The important thing is that Logan seems to be okay now, and she did say it was only a possibility."

"Yeah, I got that," Hank muttered. He held her close. The crisis was over. "How do you do it?" he said. "That on top of everything else. You're doing too much on your own, babe. You've got to let me in."

"I know," she admitted. "I just didn't know how to tell you, and I didn't want it to interfere with the President's visit."

Hank kissed her, his way of saying thanks. "Okay, what did she see to make her think all that?"

"It's those videos of the games Logan has been playing," Claire said.

"What's on the videos?"

"I haven't seen them," Claire answered. She related what the psychiatrist had told her about the dolls representing four men and four children and how they had interacted. "He could have seen or heard something at school from one of his friends, there's a very good chance he saw something on TV, we just don't know. Sandra will work with him and find out what happened."

Claire knew his mind was racing, recalling every word and incident involving Logan. "Okay," Hank said, "for now, Logan is our first priority. Thank God, it's vacation and we've got some time to sort this out."

"Let's make the most of today," she urged. "Are you going to Cars and Coffee this morning?" Cars and Coffee was an informal gathering of 'gearheads' held the last Sunday morning of the month where they showed off their cars, drank coffee, and talked. "Logan loves doing that with you."

* * * * *

"We're headed out," Hank called. He made a show of chasing Logan into the garage. Claire followed them out and watched as Hank strapped their son into his Ferrari. The twenty-year-old 550 Maranello was Hank's pride and joy. The two-door coupe was in bad shape when he found it six years ago. He had rebuilt the motor and did a major restoration, painting it dark blue. Logan had always been involved, and, even as a two-year-old, handed his dad tools.

Claire loved watching them polish and clean the car after they drove it. They were a good team. "We might take a cruise afterwards," Hank said. A group of five to ten cars often ended the morning by caravanning at too high a speed to a restaurant for lunch. "I'll call."

"Drive safe," Claire said. She wasn't worried about Hank but still gave thanks to the radar detector Hank had built into the car. She blew a kiss to the two men in her life as they drove away.

She walked back into the house and brewed a cup of coffee. A slight tremor swept over her and she put down her coffee cup. She swallowed deeply as her entire body shook. It was a delayed reaction as the full enormity of what had happened to Logan finally hit her. She collapsed to the floor, hugging her knees to her breasts as she rocked back and forth.

Sarah came through the door and froze. She knew her daughter well, but this was new. She knelt and held her tight as she waited in silence. Claire looked at her mother, her eyes full of tears. Slowly, she calmed. "Oh Mom, we think Logan may have been molested."

Sarah froze, unable to move. She forced herself to breathe. "Oh, my dear child." It was all she could say as tremors again wracked Claire's body. Their cheeks touched as their tears flowed together. "I love you," Sarah whispered. Slowly, Claire's tremors quieted and her breathing slowed. "We will get through this," Sarah promised.

"Will we?" Claire whispered. She had seen too many of her students forever damaged by sexual predators.

"Sunflowers always come back," Sarah said. "So will we."

"But they have to die first," Claire said, plummeting back into a dark emotional pit of despair. She held onto her mother and wept as she talked. Sarah didn't reply and only listened.

Claire's tears dried and her voice calmed. "We've lost so much. Will anything ever be right again?" A new emotion, unrelenting and unyielding, flared and claimed her, and for the first time in her life, Claire knew what it meant to hate. "Good shepherd," she commanded, "guard your flock."

"Is that from the bible?" Sarah wondered.

Claire's voice hardened. "No, but it should be." She had to cleanse her world and make it whole again, and above all else, she had to protect her family. But she knew, without doubt, that her world would never be the same again, and so much that was so good was forever lost. Claire hugged her mother, loving her for simply being there. "You're right. We will come back."

Saturday, August 18

Rolinda was waiting when Claire walked into the garden café. "Vacation is certainly agreeing with you," Rolinda said. The hostess smiled and led them to a corner table. They settled in and scanned the luncheon menu. "Hector promised he would join us, so where is he?"

Claire smiled. "I hope some poor soul didn't get in his way." Normally, her vice principal was famous for being prompt.

"How are things with Logan?" Rolinda asked.

"Much better, thanks to Sandra. She is a miracle worker." She fell silent as Hector joined them.

"Sorry, ladies," he said, a big smile on his face. He sat down and handed Claire a six-page form. "A retired NCO who worked for me in the Army sent this along. He's a State Trooper now and backdoored this to me a few minutes ago." His smile broadened. "You're looking at their final report on your car. The cruise control did malfunction and went full throttle on you. I like the last bit." Claire handed the report back and Hector read the last section. "Only the skillful handling of the subject vehicle at high speed prevented a collision and subsequent injury." He handed the form to Rolinda.

Rolinda's laugh rolled over them. "Well, girl, it looks like you are a hero."

"Better and better," Hector added.

"You're being ridiculous," Claire said.

"Are we?" Rolinda said, now very serious. "We've been talking and want to run an idea by you." She paused, reading Claire's body language. She seemed receptive and Rolinda took the plunge. "We think you should run for County Superintendent in the upcoming election. Hector and I can do the work and get your name on the ballot, but we have to file by next Tuesday."

"I know Charles has his problems," Claire said, "but I'm not about to run against him. Besides, I'm not really political and haven't a clue about running for office."

Rolinda touched her hand. "Is it okay if Hector and I do some poking around and try to get a sense of the situation? We've both done this before. It won't hurt to take a look."

"I suppose so," Claire said. "Now what's for lunch?"

The house was quiet when Claire finally arrived home later that afternoon. Hank and Logan were camping and Sarah was reading in the lounge. Claire changed into a baggy pair of shorts and an old T shirt before pouring herself a tall iced tea. She padded barefoot into her office and sat down in front of her new computer. She absentmindedly turned it on as she read the Sheriff's report on the investigation into her car. "That doesn't make sense," she murmured.

"I fixed your car," a voice announced.

Nedd! she raged to herself. The Australian accent was gone, but it was the same voice. She reached for the power cord to her computer.

"I am a friend. Please, believe me."

She hesitated. The cyberworld was replete with a full complement of the weird and dysfunctional, but this was different. "Why should I believe you?"

"We've never met, but you saved my daughter, Anna Edwards."

"Anna! Oh, my word. She was one of my first students. I taught her basic programming in the eighth grade." An image of a shy and sensitive, very overweight girl played in her memory.

"You gave her confidence in herself when she was vulnerable," Nedd said.

"Anna is very bright with tremendous potential," Claire said. "She was a delightful student and we all loved her."

"But you saw it when no open else did. Her mother and I had split up and I had gone home to Brisbane. You had faith in her when everyone had written her off."

"How is she doing?"

"She's a Rhodes Scholar studying at Oxford. Claire—I hope I may use your given name—you were there for my daughter when I had deserted her. I can never thank you enough."

Claire relaxed her guard. "You're more than welcome." She pulled into herself for a moment. "What exactly is going on here?"

Nedd laughed. "Coincidence, serendipity, something like that. I'm currently in Canada under contract with the Canadian government to develop cybersecurity programs using artificial intelligence, mostly to fend off the Chinese, the clever devils. You came looking for a computer to 'borrow'— I believe that is your term—and stumbled into mine. You did something no one else has—you penetrated my firewalls. Naturally, I followed you back and you fended off my attack. Very impressive, to say the least. By the way, I never hacked your core systems, only the audio, which is why we can talk now. That was also how I learned it was you. We weren't off to the best of starts, so I lurked around in the outback, so to speak, watching and learning. I believe we can help each other."

"How so?" Claire asked, now intrigued.

"Besides cybersecurity, I'm working on a self-learning program that can interact with humans and other programs to solve problems. I call it Gizmo. Here, I'll show you." Claire watched in amazement as Nedd took control of her computer and downloaded part of a program. "Please, look at this and we'll talk."

Claire gave a mental shrug and installed the download. She called it up, expecting to see a portion of a program that created artificial intelligence. But nothing made sense. *What am I looking at?* Then she saw it. The programing was simple and elegant, the work of a genius, and it opened up a new world for her. *Oh, my God! He's telling the truth.* "Nedd," she called, "are you there?"

He promptly answered. "Always."

"Why did you show me that?"

"There are many reasons. I can't do this myself and work best with a partner. I think we would make a great team. But most importantly, you saved my daughter. Like I said before, I can never thank you enough."

Why do I want to believe him? She turned inward, searching for an answer. It was testing time. "Nedd, you said you fixed my car."

"I did. Your State Troopers are good chaps, but not the full quid when it comes to information technology." He laughed as he explained how he had hacked into the systems analyzer the State Troopers used to examine her car for a throttle malfunction. "They couldn't find anything, so I made sure their expert would. I buggered your car's system and he discovered the automatic override for the cruise control was malfunctioning. It was a piece of cake. You're off the hook."

"What you did was illegal."

"It's the consequences, my dear lady, always the consequences. The bottom line is quite simple; are people helped or hurt by what I do—or don't do. In your case, you did break the law, but no one was hurt. Based on what I've learned, you won't do it again. So what would happen if I buggered the system in your favor? What would happen if I did nothing? Think of it as a chess game and consider the most likely moves an opponent would make in response to your moves. But it rapidly compounds the further you project into the future. All projections favored buggering. I'll let the results speak for themselves."

"What if I asked for something that involved hacking and stealing information?"

"Ask and let's find out."

"Why did Danny Hawkins commit suicide?"

"Ah, yes, access to privileged conversation. Hold on. There, I have it." Claire was amazed by the speed of his response and said so. Nedd laughed. "You never want to see me in a hurry. I have his school records, including your report of assessment, the police report, and his file from the Department of Child Safety. Good firewalls there, by the way. Do you want to see them, or shall I summarize."

"Please summarize."

"Based on your record of assessment, you know most of the details. What you didn't know is that he was repeatedly sexually molested."

She closed her eyes and counted to ten, finally taking a deep breath. Underneath a sullen attitude lay the heart of a good boy whose life had been taken from him. "Was it recently?"

"It started when he was seven years old. It never ended."

"Did they catch the . . ." Her voice trailed off. She didn't possess the words that could describe the anger and contempt she felt.

"No. He wouldn't talk about it. The only evidence they have is one photo. It wasn't enough to proceed. Do you want to see it?"

Claire steeled herself. "Yes." A photo of a naked man standing next to a boy filled the screen in front of her. The man's face had been carefully blurred out and his arm was around the boy's bare shoulders. There was no doubt that it was Danny Hawkins. "Oh, no," she moaned. Nedd zoomed in on the man and isolated the watch on his right wrist. Unfortunately, the angle was wrong and she couldn't determine the make. "Can you rectify his face?"

Nedd went to work, trying to clear the blurred image. He was partially successful and Claire could make out the general contours of the man's head. "Zoom out," she said. The image filled the screen, this time without the boy. Nedd repositioned his arm as Claire studied his feet and hands. "There must be some way we can find out who he is."

"He might be in another photo with Danny," Nedd said. "I'll use facial recognition and search the dark web for Danny." Within seconds, four more photos flashed on the screen, all with Danny Hawkins and the same man. As before, the man's face was blurred.

"Nedd, can you reconfigure your facial recognition to do body part recognition?" She suggested a modification to the code she had seen.

Need grunted in satisfaction. "I didn't see that. Very clever. I believe it will work." Now the screen was flooded with photos from the dark web. The same man was in all of them but with different children, boys and girls. Again, his face was blurred.

Then she saw it.

Claire bent over and threw up in the waste can beside her desk. She wiped her lips only to start retching with dry heaves. She clasped her stomach and coughed, fighting to breathe. Finally, she raised her head but couldn't look at the screen. "The photo at the bottom with four men and four children." She forced herself to face the screen.

Four naked men, their faces all carefully blurred out, were standing each with an arm around a naked child. The faces of the two little girls and two boys were very clear. The man from the other photos Nedd had found was on the right, slightly in front of the others, with his arm around a naked boy. It was Logan.

She touched the image on the screen. "My son," was all she said. Her finger moved to the man. "Who is he?" Her voice was icy calm.

"I'll find out," Nedd promised. Much to Claire's surprise, her screen reverted to her home page as her cell phone buzzed. It was Nedd. "Sorry, I'm going into the Abyss and have to isolate." The Abyss was the subterranean layer in cyberspace below the dark web where highly guarded criminal transactions were conducted. An unwelcome intruder was the object of numerous overlapping 'search and destroy' programs.

"I haven't been there in ages and don't know what the boys can do these days. Physically unplug your computer from all power sources and turn your phone off—don't need the bastards backtracking. Stay dark until I contact you. This may take some time." Her phone went dead. She removed its battery and unplugged her computer before collapsing into her chair, her mind racing.

Forty minutes later, Sarah knocked on the door. "Honey, that nice man from Australia is on the phone. How did he get my number?"

Claire opened the door. “I’m not sure,” she said, taking the phone. “Thanks Mom, this is personal.” She closed the door.

“Hello,” Nedd said. “That was a bit sporting, but I found a video. Trust me, you don’t want to see it.”

“Is Logan in it?”

“No, it’s the other boy, Danny. But it’s the same man. I have a name; Bobby Lee MacElroy.”

A flood of emotions swept over her. *So simple, so obvious. How did we miss it?* Guilt beat at her sanity only to dissolve in a wave of loathing and despair. *It’s not our fault! We only found out last month. But we missed it.* She forced herself to breath slowly. “Are you sure?”

“Absolutely. His face is never shown in the video and is always blurred in the photos, but they were all taken in the same RV. There’s a logo of a shooting star on the refrig door with a name: Prime Star Academy. That led to MacElroy and I confirmed by hacking his medical records. He had some interesting cosmetic surgery on his penis a few years ago, complete with before and after photos.” Nedd snorted. “We don’t have a matching face or fingerprints, but we do have a matching penis.”

Claire shook with rage. *Why didn’t I see it all sooner?* She knew the answer; she lived in a comfortable complacency where bad things only happened to other people. A bitter cold captured her as she slowly refocused, finally taming the emotions that threatened her sanity. “I can’t tell Hank. I just don’t know what he would do.” Then, with a calm and hard resolve, “I will make things right.”

“Good on ya,” Nedd replied.

9

Saturday, September 15

I loathe politicians and don't trust them. When I say "them," I mean all of them, and that makes me an equal-opportunity loather. I also have a reputation as an equal-opportunity muckraker, which is why I picked up an assignment that causes wet dreams. A major media conglomerate, which will go unidentified if I want another paycheck, wants to nail a political scumbag from my state who is running for reelection to Congress. They are willing to pay big bucks for someone to find the muck and write it up.

In the world of politics, this is an easy one—just follow the bucks. But getting inside to find the money trail gets tricky, and that's where Mike Westfield comes in. He knows people. Susanne, bless her sweet little bootie, has invited me to a fundraising event with Westfield where said scumbag will be scrounging for money.

The event is a cocktail party on steroids at a fashionable resort in Scottsdale, and we arrive in Westfield's car of the moment, a new Porsche. It has the horsepower to attract valets and they swarm over us, fighting for a chance to park the car. I can only speculate about the drive to a parking spot. Susanne gets out, flashing a generous length of right leg, and I carefully unfold from the rear seat. Westfield gets me past the gatekeepers and into the inner sanctum of all politics—the money pit.

This is a gathering of high rollers with big checkbooks. Westfield is one of the attractions, and he's busy posing with the deep pockets and their spouses for assorted reporters and photographers. I go looking for the above mentioned scumbag, but he's a no-show. Rather than waste the evening, I go on the prowl, always careful to hover in the background.

Susanne peels off from Westfield and comingles outside camera range. Like me, she is searching for that telltale clue, the bit of information that leads to a big story. She is wearing a classic little black dress that is really little and living proof that sex and booze pry lips loose, not to mention checkbooks. Susanne shakes off a big lump who fancies himself irresistible to the opposite sex and joins a small group clustered around an attractive woman with beautiful dark skin. She is my height, I guess in her mid-forties, and well-dressed. A burly guy trying to look like a Mexican-American is standing beside her.

I think I should know him. Naturally, he immediately hits on Susanne. That leaves room for me to get closer to the lady. I introduce myself. She replies, "David, so nice to meet you. I'm Rolinda Johnson. May I ask what brings you here?"

I laugh. "I was going to ask you the same question." She gives me the look that says, "Don't mess with me." I come clean. "I'm an investigative reporter on assignment. This is an election year and I'm here doing my job." Now it's her turn.

Her tone immediately changes. "Well, Mr. Parker, I'm an elementary school principal. You've probably heard the County School Superintendent was running for reelection, but he passed away this week. Heart attack." I hadn't heard because school superintendents are dull, boring, and solid citizens who don't make for good news. The señor lusting after Susanne rejoins us. Then I remember. He's Hector Mendoza, a retired Army lieutenant colonel and Claire Allison's vice principal.

A gut feeling tells me not to get on his bad side under any circumstances. On cue, Rolinda rolls out the pitch. "It's too late to qualify a candidate for the ballot, and this is all spur of the moment." She pauses for effect. "We're drumming up support for a write-in candidate." I stifle a snort. Write-in candidates have the proverbial chance of a snowball in hell, not to mention in Phoenix. Don't ask me why, but I didn't see what was coming. "Our candidate is Claire Marie Allison."

"Good luck with that one," is all I can manage. Her look is the stuff of frostbites. I regroup. "Isn't the County Superintendent a non-partisan office?"

Rolinda gives me the look normally reserved for idiots. "It's always been political."

"But we're here in strictly a nonpartisan role," Hector says. "We're approaching both parties." He doesn't mention the 'm ' word, but they are going to need a big bank account to mount a TV and social media campaign. "I happen to be a military conservative, while Mrs. Johnson is of a more liberal persuasion."

"But we both support Claire," Rolinda adds.

Before I can ask why, a big gray-haired man surrounded by a flock of followers and a beautiful trophy wife joins the group. Joe Prescott is the largest rain maker in Arizona politics and has access to the really big donors. "Rolinda!" he booms. "I'm surprised to see you here." He laughs. "What you did to my boy in the last election wasn't Christian."

They embrace, obviously the best of enemies. I wonder if they've ever slept together. The trophy wife frowns and I sense my wondering is shared by her as well.. "How much did you squeeze out of your bunch for Allison?" Rolinda mentions a low six figure number. It's not impressive in modern politics. "I'll match it," Joe the Rain Maker says. Now the figure is impressive.

"Thank you, Joe," Rolinda replies. "We must get together for lunch." The trophy wife frowns, and I double down on the sleeping together.

"Did you see her on TV?" the trophy wife asks in a loud squeaky voice that is hard to ignore. "She is so elegant." Her comment rouses the rabble and every woman within hearing distance starts raving about Claire Allison. I figure she has the women's vote. I percolate through the crowd and hear Allison's name enough to know she does have a snowball's chance.

It's obvious that I'm not going to rake up any muck tonight, and so I head for the bar where Hector is talking to a group of gray and greens. They all have gray hair and green money—a little of the former and a lot of the latter. From the way Hector is scribbling in a little black book, I figure he's striking pay dirt. The little black book and hitting pay dirt makes me think of little black dresses, so I go looking for Susanne. The night doesn't have to be a total loss.

I find her talking to a tall geeky guy. She introduces us and he gives me his card. He's the chief legal counsel of the legislature's political ethics committee. I stifle a comment about 'political ethics' being the ultimate oxymoron. I'm sure he hears it every day. We talk and he rewards my suaveness with an astute and insightful take on the evening. "I find it very interesting," he says, "that the most successful fundraising tonight is for a write-in candidate for a minor local office."

I mutter something about all politics being local. "True," he replies, "but this is unusual in the extreme. Mrs. Allison certainly bears watching."

"Indeed she does," I reply. Susanne and I call it an evening and we go looking for Westfield. A KPIO-TV cameraman tells us he's outside waiting for his car. We do the old quick step and hurry after him. We arrive in time to see Joe the Rain Maker's trophy wife getting in Westfield's Porsche. They roar off in a cloud of burnt rubber and smoking testosterone. "Joe the Rain Maker doesn't strike me as the type to take this lying down," I say, pun intended.

"Oh, he will," Susanne says. "Kimberly Prescott is the one with the money—tons of it. Joe hasn't got a dime." That's one for the books. The Rain Maker family has a trophy husband, not a trophy wife.

"Uber time," I say as I call for a cab. "I'll drop you off," I tell Susanne.

"For breakfast, I hope," she replies, obviously thinking the same thing I am. It's a long ride across town to my motel, and Susanne slips off her shoes and cuddles up. She obviously likes me. We finally arrive and I notice the 'No Vacancy 'sign is lit. Judging by the cars parked outside, the Salibs are attracting a much better clientele. I open the door to my room and let Susanne in. She turns on the light and giggles.

Jeffrey, the heir apparent to the Salib fortune, is sleeping in my bed with a teenage girl I have never seen before. Both teenagers are fully clothed and sound asleep. Judging by her blond hair and tight jeans, the Salibs will not be discussing arranged marriages. Atticus is sprawled out between them, and thanks to his due diligence, a shotgun wedding is off the table, at least for now. "That is so cute," Susanne says.

The pooch looks up at me. “Good dog,” I say. Jeffrey moans, and sits on the edge of the bed. “Hey, I’m not running a house of ill repute here,” I tell him.

The girl wakes up. She is a pretty little thing and I give Jeffrey high marks. “What’s a house of ill repute?” she asks. I groan. Obviously, she isn’t a smart little thing. I throw my car keys at Jeffrey and tell him to take his friend home. She rolls out of bed and kicks her way through a stack of newspapers and books piled against the wall. “Why are you keeping all this stuff?” the girl asks.

“Research,” I mumble.

Jeffrey looks around and mentally counts the boxes. “How can you find anything?” I don’t answer because it is a problem. “My mom is really good at organizing stuff,” he says, echoing Chione. Two teenage endorsements of a parent carries a lot of weight in my book. I need to think about it. Jeffrey disappears out the door with the girl in tow. I hold the door open for Atticus to go do his thing, while Susanne sheds her little black dress and crawls in bed. Atticus takes way too long and finally trots back in and leaps on the bed next to Susanne.

I motion him off the bed. “Come.” He ignores me and hunkers down in the middle. He’s not going anywhere. “Bad dog,” I mutter.

Friday, September 28

A nice check in the mail convinces me it is time for Khepri Salib to sort out the mess in my room. Besides, it would be nice to have a clear shot at the bathroom when I stumble out of bed in the middle of the night. We negotiate a price that is quite reasonable, and she goes to work.

Her first move is to relocate me to a bigger room that has an alcove and a kitchenette, all with a higher rent. She sets my computer up in the alcove next to a bookcase and uses my old room to sort through all the boxes. Much of it can be cross-referenced online, which she does. Then she cross-references my current notebooks by date, subject, and names, and files them on three shelves of the bookcase. She arranges my books by subject and author. What’s left over is filed away in a three-drawer cabinet. She carefully packs and stores Dottie Sue's things in a closet. I get a hernia carrying out the trash and my room is habitable. Finally, she redoes the flow charts on the wall and connects a few more dots. Allison is now organized and on display.

"Did you know she taught programming when she was in college?" Khepri says. I tell her it is news to me. "Yes, she taught an introductory course on coding and created a curriculum that is still used today." I ask why she chose to teach information technology in a junior high. Khepri's finger's dance over the keyboard, the screen flashes, and she delves into the top drawer of the filing cabinet and produces a profile from an educational journal. "She likes the age group."

"Sounds like she found her own age level," I reply. I'm pleased with myself for such a clever and quick response.

Khepri shakes her head. "There is a better explanation." I wait, but she remains silent. This is going to cost me money. I mention a bonus for doing such good work and get an answer. "She likes a challenge and solving problems. Based on her teaching career, she is very good at identifying problems and creating workable solutions."

Khepri has an excellent command of the English language, and I tell her so. She blushes. "Thank you for such a nice compliment." She gets up to leave and stops to rearrange the candles on the small table in the corner where she placed the urn with Dottie Sue's ashes. It's not something I would have done, but it feels right.

"Khepri, I never realized Allison was so good with computers."

"Oh, yes. Her skills are far beyond most."

"Would she be any good at hacking?" I'm thinking that is the simplest explanation of how she got Dottie Sue's medical records.

"You would have to ask someone who knows about that," she replies. I watch her leave and hit the speed dial on my cell phone. My hacker of choice, Barry Bodkin, answers on the first ring.

"Barry, my man, how's business?" He tells me things are very slow, which is encouraging. I might be able to negotiate a discount. I concoct a story how my mother passed away two months ago under suspicious circumstances and hint at a possible malpractice lawsuit. But first, I need to retrieve all her medical records. He tells me that as her son and executor of her estate, I can request them through normal channels. "You ever mention 'malpractice' to an HMO?" I ask. Barry agrees to see what he can find. I give him the details and he quotes a price. He'll do this one on contingency for fifteen percent of any court settlement. The man does know how to make a buck. He'll get back to me soonest.

I'm bored and scan the TV and web for any news that might lead to a story. It's prime viewing time and there are five TV ads for Allison touting her record as a teacher and principal. They all stress her problem-solving skills and urge the great unwashed to write her name in for the Office of Maricopa County School Superintendent.

One ad showing her working with her staff catches my attention. Rolinda Johnson and Hector Mendoza are listening attentively with a young woman I have never seen before. I record the ads and save them to a folder that I add to the computer's growing file on Allison.

Still bored, I go to my website of last resort, a social media dating site that I last used in Sacramento. I update my profile and search the Phoenix area. Within minutes, a star flashes. Someone is interested in my profile and wants to make contact. I call up her profile, have a quick laugh, and move on. The hunt turns interesting as four more stars flash. There are a lot of horny women in Phoenix. It must be the heat.

My cell buzzes. It's Barry the Hacker reporting in. There is good and bad news. He has retrieved all of Mom's medical records but one. It seems the Mayo Clinic has excellent firewalls that not even he can penetrate. This is a first and he complains loudly. He breaks the connection mumbling something about Scandinavians. I download the files and dig out the medical record that Allison had given my mother. I compare the two. They are identical except Mom's file includes the Mayo Clinic file that Barry couldn't hack.

The big question remains: How did Allison get Mom's medical file when Barry couldn't? Is Allison that good, or did she screw some lucky bastard to get the file? I like that option, but it doesn't fit the lady.

I'm pondering all this when a star flashes in my message app. Someone else is interested in my profile on the dating site. I quickly call up the site. Okay, so I'm a little too eager to check out the profile. I stare at the lady's photos, stunned by what I'm seeing. I call up the TV ads that I recorded less than two hours ago and compare photos. The young woman I had not recognized has just flashed an interest in my profile. I return her flash and we are soon exchanging messages.

It's a modern mating ritual with its own protocols. We exchange first names, Rebecca and David, and compare interests and backgrounds. It's assumed we are both lying about our age. I reassure her about the big three: I'm not married, I can see my belt buckle when I look down, and I still have all my hair. We agree to meet for coffee at a Starbucks on Saturday morning at ten.

Talk about coincidence. I don't believe in it, but stranger things have happened, I tell myself.

10

Friday, October 5

Hector was waiting for Claire when she drove up the long driveway. "Mi casa es tu casa," he said, ushering her into his home. She took it all in, amazed by the antique furniture and paintings on the walls. An exquisite portrait of a beautiful young woman thoughtfully gazing at the artist caught Claire's attention. "My wife, Maria Christina," Hector said. "She died in an accident on the autobahn near Munich. She was six months pregnant. I miss her to this day."

Claire nodded in sympathy and followed him onto a patio with a sweeping view of Phoenix. A carefully manicured lawn sloped away to a swimming pool and a big cabana. "You have a lovely home," she said.

"My father was a career diplomat with the State Department, and my mother an avid art collector," Hector explained. "My great grandfather fled Mexico with his family to escape the fighting between Pancho Villa and General Pershing in 1916, and my grandfather started a credit union serving Latinos."

Claire berated herself for having stereotyped her vice principal and made a mental promise to never do it again. "Rolinda and Rebecca are already here," Hector said, gesturing at the cabana. Claire slipped out of her shoes and padded after him. She liked the feel of the grass under her bare feet.

I can't believe I'm doing this, she thought. It had been almost a month since Rolinda and Hector had convinced her to run for county superintendent following the death of the current superintendent. She had hesitated at first, but Hank told her, "Babe, there's a fire in you to solve problems. You can make a difference. Do it."

An inner voice told her the obvious, she had reached an end at Stella Madura Middle School and it was time to move on. The more she thought about it, the more she knew it was the right thing to do. Later that night, she told Hank. He held her tight. "I'd like screwing a politician," he said. She woke the next morning feeling young and refreshed, and the crushing hurt of Logan started to yield.

She reached the cabana and hesitated, coming back to the moment. Hector held the door and made a show of ushering her in. "Welcome to the war room for your campaign," he said. The walls were covered with posters of her surrounded by students.

She looked around, surprised by the number of yard signs and boxes of pamphlets awaiting distribution. Eight computer cubicles occupied half the room. There was little space to move around, and she squeezed into a chair at one of the cubicles. Rolinda, Hector, and Rebecca joined her. "This must have cost a fortune." Claire said. "It's all so new to me, running for an elected office. I keep asking myself if it's worth all the trouble."

Rolinda and Hector exchanged glances. "The answer is yes," Rolinda said. "Ultimately, everything that matters depends on politics. Things can go wonderfully right if we work at it and elect the right people. Elect the wrong people and it can go terribly wrong. The simple truth is that Hector and I can run a campaign, but we are not electable. We don't have that special something that makes a difference. You do."

Claire sighed. "I don't feel it, whatever it is."

"Trust me, you have it," Hector said. "Rolinda and I are old hands at this." He chuckled. "Usually, on opposite sides."

"But I'm not really political," Claire said. "I just want everyone to get the best education possible."

"And there's your platform," Hector said.

"I like it," Rolinda said. "Let us worry about the finances and organization. You concentrate on drumming up support, meeting and greeting potential voters, and knocking on doors. It's very old fashioned, but it works." She handed Claire a sheet of paper. "Here's a list of potential endorsements that we need to contact over the weekend."

Claire scanned the list. The second name down was Prime Star Academy, where she was scheduled at ten o'clock Saturday morning. For a moment, Claire couldn't breathe. *Oh, no!* They had not enrolled Logan in the fall program when the school term started and Hank had handled the details. Now, Bobby Lee MacElroy was back in her life. *Deal with it!* "Will you come with me?"

"Of course," Rolinda replied. Claire handed the list back and Hector went over the schedule. It was going to be a busy weekend ending Sunday evening when over a hundred volunteers would gather at Hector's home to meet Claire. "There will be TV coverage," Rolinda warned. "We're hoping Mike Westfield from KPIO-TV will be here."

She paused. "In the meantime, we have a problem we need to discuss. Unfortunately, you have attracted the attention of a free-lance reporter who has, shall we say, a rather unscrupulous reputation. His name is David Parker and he's digging around for dirt. If there's anything in your past that could be embarrassing, like an old boyfriend, a wild weekend in college, an affair, anything that could come back and haunt you, we need to know."

Claire thought for a moment and shook her head. "I'll talk to Hank. He . . ." her voice trailed off.

Hector took over. "We know about his earlier days and can use that to our advantage." He grinned. "We'll leak it. Everyone will love to hear how you tamed a wild fighter pilot. There will be some righteous do-gooders thumping their bibles and pointing fingers, but most women will admire what you did, and most men will wish they were in his shoes."

"I contacted a friend from Sacramento," Rolinda said, "who has dealt with Parker and knows how he works. He will try to schmooze someone in our campaign to backdoor any gossip or problems. So we're going to set him up. That's where Rebecca comes in."

All three heads turned to look at her. "Well," Rebecca began, "I made contact with him on a dating site and we're meeting for coffee tomorrow morning. I'll tell him I work for you, and let's see what he does."

Claire shook her head. "Rebecca, you don't have to do this."

"I'll be careful," Rebecca promised. "Besides, he's cute."

"But he's not harmless," Hector warned. "He's the guy who exposed the Havasu Swingers, and he has a reputation for being sexually aggressive."

"One thing bothers me," Claire said. "How did you find out Parker was investigating me?"

"An old friend received an anonymous tip and she contacted me," Rolinda answered. She looked at her list of potential endorsers and checked off the first one. "We are invited to dinner with the 'Concerned Educators of Arizona.' A lovely way to spend Friday night." She sighed. "I hope you like chicken. You'll be eating enough of it." She stood. "We'll prep you on the way over."

Logan and Hank were gone when Claire arrived home late that night, and Sarah was waiting up for her. "The boys went fishing on the boat," Sarah explained. "It was a last minute thing. They'll be back late Sunday."

Claire collapsed onto the couch and closed her eyes as her defenses came down. "It's been a long day," she said.

"How did it go at the dinner?" Sarah asked.

"It went well. They like our platform and gave their endorsement. Hector collected over five thousand dollars in pledges, and Rolinda says we're off to a good start."

"That's encouraging," Sarah said.

"Mom, you know I couldn't do this without you." She gave her mother a hug. "I do love you."

"And I love you," Sarah said. "Oh, since the boys are gone, Stu and I are flying to Las Vegas tomorrow morning. We'll be back Sunday."

"Mom!"

"Oh, don't worry. What happens in Vegas, stays in Vegas." Sarah stood and kissed her on the cheek. "We're going in Stu's plane and leaving early. I'm off to bed." Claire watched her mother leave before heading for her office. She closed the door and shed her clothes, finally relaxing. She pulled on a beach robe and loosely tied it as she stepped into a pair of fluffy slippers with rabbit ears that Logan had given her for Christmas. She sat down at her computer and turned it on.

"Nedd, are you there?"

"Hello there. I heard you were running for county superintendent."

Claire laughed. "You don't miss much." She hesitated for a moment. "Nedd, I'm in over my head and could use some help."

"It would be my pleasure."

"I'm worried about cyber security, but I don't have the time to monitor it."

"Piece of cake. I'm on it. I can also do general surveillance, if you want."

"That would be appreciated. There is something I was wondering about. My campaign received an anonymous tip about an investigative journalist, a David Parker."

"Right. Give me a moment." He hummed a tune as he ran his search programs. "Here we go, his name is David Alex Parker. He's a freelance investigative reporter and an absolute wanker. He's been poking around and doing a lot of research on-line, cross-referencing everything from blogs to Facebook and every news article known to man with one common point of reference—you. Hold on, there's more." Again, he hummed an offbeat tune. Then, "He may have a bit of an ax to grind with you."

"Whatever for?"

"You fired his mother, Dorothea Sue Ellington, three years ago."

Claire sighed. "Oh, dear. She was mentally disturbed and hurting her students. I tried to persuade her to retire, but she fought it. I didn't really have a choice."

"She passed away two months ago, an apparent suicide. Ah, this is interesting. He hired a very good hacker, one of the best, to retrieve all his mother's medical records. Why, I have no idea, but he does bear watching."

"Rolinda wants to keep an eye on him," Claire said, "and find out what he's up to. Rebecca contacted him through a dating site and set up a meeting. I don't like that."

"I'm running a predictive algorithm I've been working on—bloody thing still needs tweaking—hold on." She waited over a minute while Nedd refined his program. "Ah, there we go," he said. "I'm afraid your concerns are well founded. I can only foresee negative results. Best to cancel and avoid Parker."

Claire thought for a moment. "It's too late. Besides, Rolinda would probably override any suggestion at this point. She is very strong willed." She moved on. "Sarah is flying to Las Vegas tomorrow with Stu. Is he a good pilot?"

"Give me a moment. Searching. Here we go. He's a very good pilot. The weather is good and I don't foresee any problems."

"One last thing, we're approaching Prime Star Academy tomorrow for an endorsement. I'd rather not, but Rolinda thinks they can help, and she is running the show. I feel like I'm between a rock and a hard place. Can you profile Bobby Lee and Katherine for me?"

"Certainly," Nedd replied. "Here we are." A folder appeared on her screen. "It's also on your iPad, and I've locked it so only you can open it. Use your thumbprint. Apparently, Katherine has no idea of her son's extra-curricular activities."

"I find that hard to believe," Claire said. "She must suspect something."

"There is some good news," Nedd said. "The IRS is auditing the beloved president of your school board. Hatchette is unavailable for comment and has hired a law firm."

Claire laughed. "You just made my day. Thank you."

"Glad to be of service."

"Good night." She turned the computer off and went to bed, leaving her office door open. The computer came back on and the screen lit up for a moment before going dark. Outside, eight infrared security cameras swept the area.

Saturday, October 6

"I've never been here before," Rolinda said. Hector wheeled his Lexus sedan into a parking space outside Prime Star Academy and hopped out to open the door for Rolinda. Claire was the last out. "It looks better on the news if Claire is the first out," Rolinda said. "Just remember; last in, first out."

"I'll remember," Hector promised. He followed them inside

where a tall, gray-haired, heavyset woman was waiting. "Katherine MacElroy," she said, introducing herself to Rolinda and Hector. They shook hands. "Mrs. Allison, it is so good to see you again. May we ask after Logan?" She extended her hand to Claire. "We do miss him."

Claire took her hand and smiled. "Logan is so busy and something had to give."

"We do understand," Katherine said. "Perhaps you will reconsider re-enrolling him when all the dust settles." She led them down the hall. "Mr. MacElroy is talking to our maintenance team and will be with us shortly." The hall was antiseptically clean and the windows gleamed in the morning sun. "We take pride in maintaining the highest hygienic standards," she told them, holding open the door to her office. It was dominated by a huge desk and Victorian furniture. "May we get you some coffee or tea?" They all asked for tea as she stepped into an adjoining pantry.

Hector looked around, not impressed. "The royal 'we'?"

"Katherine is descended from the last Russian Czar," Claire said, recalling the profile Nedd had created.

"A bit much for Arizona," Rolinda said. "But I suppose snob appeal does sell. And their academic program?"

"Absolutely excellent," Claire said. "It's based on committed teachers, small classes, and involved parents. It's why we enrolled Logan in preschool here."

"But you enrolled him in public schools when he was older," Hector said.

"Hank said Prime Star was too elitist. We did keep him in their afterschool program, but Logan's really too old now, and, frankly, I think it's too protective." Claire breathed easier when Rolinda and Hector both nodded, accepting her explanation.

Katherine pushed a tea cart through the open door. Her son, Bobby Lee, followed. He was tall and slender with a full head of wavy black hair and long thin hands. His fingernails were carefully manicured, and he wore a Tag Hauer aviation chronometer on his right wrist. He was casually dressed, perfect for an afternoon at any country club.

"Thank you for waiting," he said. "I had to resolve a problem with the maintenance crew before they quit for the day." He spoke with an upper-class English accent. "They just can't quite get the restrooms right." Katherine poured them tea and sat next to her son. "I must tell you," Bobby Lee said, "I was thrilled to hear you are running for County Superintendent of Schools. Is there any way we can help?"

Claire sat the teacup down and leaned back in her chair, her hands clasped as her fingers interlocked. "We could use Prime Star's endorsement," she said. Her fingers clenched.

Rolinda glanced at Hector, sensing something was wrong. "If I may," she interrupted, "we want to build on the integration and cooperation with all schools: public, charter, and private. Rather than compete with each other, we want to work together and increase our strengths. For example, we build on Prime Star's tripod of committed teachers, small classes, and involved parents."

Bobby Lee nodded graciously. Katherine refreshed their tea while they talked and worked out the details. Prime Star would make a public endorsement, signing on to Claire's proposed platform. Time seemed to drag for Claire and she almost jumped out of her chair when Bobby Lee suggested a classroom tour. He led them down the hall and they walked into a class of four-year-olds. "We have many working mothers," Katherine explained, "who require our Saturday service."

"Very nice," Rolinda said. "Could we take a photo with Claire?"

"As long as you can't see the children's faces," Bobby Lee said. "Parental consent is always a factor." He quickly arranged the children around Claire as she sat in a child's seat with a book in her lap. Rolinda stood behind the children and captured the scene with her cell phone. She showed the photos to Bobby Lee. "Perfect," he said. "Please send me copies. We can use them."

"We will need a release," Rolinda said.

"Of course," Bobby Lee replied.

Claire felt sick to her stomach. She leaned forward and talked to the children, smiling and asking them their names. *How can I keep you safe?* She stood and smiled. "Thank you so much," she said. "Please forgive us, but we must run."

"Certainly," Bobby Lee said. He escorted them to Hector's car and held the door for Rolinda and Claire. He waved good-by as they drove away.

Hector snorted. "What a creep, with that phony accent."

Rolinda pulled a face, agreeing with him. "But we need every endorsement we can get."

Do we? Claire thought.

The house was deserted when Claire finally walked in late that night. She slipped into her jogging togs and stepped onto the treadmill in their bedroom and started to run. Her face was a mask as she stared at the HD touchscreen in front of her. She ran harder. Facebook chimed with an incoming caller, but she ignored it.

Ah," Nedd said, taking control of her computer, "there you are." She didn't answer and picked up the pace. "Going for a record?" She increased the incline and ran as hard as she could. Suddenly, the belt slowed until she couldn't move it. "Sorry, luv," Nedd said. "Your heartbeat was over 180 and going up."

"Leave me alone," she ordered.

"I will as soon as you tell me why?"

"Why what?"

"Why you are punishing yourself like this."

"Who are you? My father confessor?"

"I'm your friend and will do anything to keep you safe from harm."

"It's too late. And it's my fault." The treadmill started to move as the incline returned to level.

"Just walk," Nedd said. She walked in silence. "I know you met with the MacElroys today, and that you asked for their endorsement. That wasn't your idea, and based on the photos Rolinda sent them, you got it. Please move on and put them on a back burner."

"I can't. Did you see those children? They are innocent and sweet, and, and . . . I've got to stop him." Tears flowed down her cheeks. "But I don't know how. Hank doesn't know about MacElroy, and I can't tell him. He'll kill . . ." She walked purposefully, setting a slow pace. "Nedd, there's something I just don't understand. Why didn't Logan tell us? Why haven't one of those children he molested said anything?"

"Sandra Shiver may find an answer," Nedd replied. "But that will take time. I suspect it's because MacElroy is a master at manipulating children, and he carefully selects his victims and conditions them before molesting them."

"He's a monster," Claire said. "I've got to stop him." She paced slowly, thinking. Then, "There are so many children at stake. I'm going to the police."

"There's a problem with our evidence," Nedd said. "It's inadmissible. They can't use it."

Claire couldn't believe it. "Why?"

"Unfortunately, it's all based on artificial intelligence and linked together by the photo I stole from MacElroy's medical records. It's called 'the fruit of the poisoned tree,' and no judge will allow it in as evidence. Bottom line, the victims would have to testify in court."

Claire sat on the backend of the treadmill, her head down. "Do you know what a lawyer will do to them on cross-examination? How much more damage would that do?" She answered her own question. "Too much. I won't allow that to happen to any child." An image of Danny Hawkins flashed in her mind. "Whatever happened to justice?"

"Justice lies in what is possible," Nedd answered.

She stood, a decision made. "I'm going to stop the bastard."

"Let me help," Nedd said.

"Why?"

"Because a good shepherd guards his flock," Nedd replied.

11

Sunday, October 7

Rebecca steered her little Miata sports car along the long drive winding up the hill. I can't take my eyes off her. She's wearing a very short bright red dress, and her blonde hair is pulled to one side, cascading over a bare shoulder. How did I luck into this one?

Okay, I seem to attract a certain type of femme, but not a gorgeous twenty-four-year-old with legs that go on forever and a beautiful smile. I check the time. It's Sunday evening and we met exactly thirty-four hours earlier at a Starbucks for coffee. I haven't gotten her into bed yet, but I'm working on it.

She pulls to a stop in front of a low ranch house with a classic look. We're talking big bucks. A valet opens her door, and she climbs out giving him a good look at her undies. "Welcome to Casa Mendoza," he says. He hands her a pretty bracelet with a flower and a number to slip on her wrist in exchange for the car keys. I have to get out by myself. He drives off, wheels screeching.

We walk inside and I'm bombarded with good taste. I point to a painting on the wall in a place of honor. "Is that a Degas?"

Rebecca looks sad. "No. That's Hector's wife. She died in a car accident years ago. He never remarried. Hector's grandfather founded Azteca Credit Union. You need to hear his story." Personally, I'd rather not. All I inherited was a dog.

The room is packed with happy campaign workers. This is not your usual Phoenix frolic where everyone tries to out casual everyone else. The ladies are all dressed in stylish but casual attire and all the men are wearing long pants and shirts with collars. I follow her outside where a huge party tent is set up between the house and the pool. "Come on," Rebecca says, "you must meet Claire." She takes me by the hand and leads me inside the tent to the guest of honor. Claire Allison is standing by an overhead heater cleverly disguised as a palm tree—the heater, not Allison—with husband Hank by her side. She's wearing a casual off-the shoulder dress with low-heeled sandals. She's a show-stopper. "Claire," Rebecca chimes, "this is David who I told you about."

Claire turns and smiles at me. Husband Hank gives me a look that could send a grizzly bear up the nearest tree. She extends her right hand. I almost bow and gently take her hand.

"Rebecca tells me you're an investigative reporter following our campaign," she says. Up close, her voice has a charm and resonance that makes me want to hear more.

Everyone looks at me like I just crawled out from under a rock. We're not off to a good start. "Yes, ma'am, I am." I drop her hand before husband Hank breaks my arm.

"Please call me Claire," she says.

"Thank you, Claire. I think there's a story in what's happening here. I could not believe it when Rebecca told me she was your assistant."

Hank is eyeballing me like potential roadkill. "I heard you met on a dating site," he says.

Obviously, he thinks I'm some sort of predator and my survival instincts immediately kick in. "Rebecca did contact me," I reply, making sure to stress "did." I explain how we met for coffee at a Starbucks yesterday, and that I came clean from the get-go that I was doing a story on Allison.

"Isn't that a coincidence?" Rebecca says brightly. "It was my idea to invite him." She smiles at me. "He didn't want to come at first." That's true. I often play hard-to-get as part of my cover.

Claire bestows a beautiful smile on us. "I hope you enjoy the evening."

We're dismissed and we beat a hasty retreat to the bar where I help myself to a champagne punch. Rebecca introduces me to everyone in sight, with a friendly warning that I am a reporter. That's a show-stopper and dries up any conversation. "There's Hector," she chimes. She drags me back to the house where Mendoza is talking to Susanne. I look around for Mike Westfield, but he hasn't arrived. "Hector," Rebecca says, "there's someone I'd like you to meet."

He recognizes me immediately. "Mr. Parker," Mendoza says, extending his hand. "We've never been formally introduced." We shake hands and he gives me the same look as husband Hank. What's with these military types? "Rebecca," Mendoza says, "can we talk for a moment?" She gives me a cute little shrug and they step aside to discuss something.

"She's a bit young," Susanne mutters. I try to explain how we met, but she's not buying it. I'm about to shift into my groveling mode when Mike Westfield makes an entrance with microphone in hand. He's the celebrity of the moment, and it shifts the spotlight off me. Meanwhile, Susanne goes to work doing her behind the scenes thing.

I wander back to the bar and try to strike up a few conversations. Everyone gives me the old 'skin and grin' treatment. I shake a lot of hands and get a lot of friendly smiles, but that's all.

My suspicious nature kicks in. I look over all the happy folks enjoying Mendoza's largess and it dawns on me. I'm now a known commodity to the working troops and not a faceless nonperson hanging around in the background waiting for the inadvertent comment that leads to a breakthrough story. They may have been warned about me, but now they know what I look like in person. And all because of a coincidental meeting on a dating site. Or was it?

Crap! I've been set up. I'm wondering if I should call Uber and get the hell out of Dodge when I see Rolinda Johnson looking at me. She is standing alone on the steps leading into the house and looking very regal. What is it with that woman? Then the old light bulb finally comes on. I am slow at times. She is the lady in control. She walks towards me, and I know better than to try to escape. "Good evening, Mr. Parker," she says, obviously pleased with herself. "I do hope you're enjoying yourself."

"Good evening, Mrs. Johnson. Yes, I am enjoying myself." I can't shut up. "Thank you for arranging all this, but next time an invitation in the mail will be sufficient."

"Would you have come?"

Her reply surprises me, and I play it straight. "Probably. But I'd have just been another face in the crowd, not the most wanted suspect being passed around for inspection."

"I assure you, that was not Rebecca's intention."

So, what was Rebecca's intention? Before I can ask the question, a young staffer scurries up and blurts something about an aircraft accident. From Rolinda's reaction, I can tell it is serious. "Where's Claire?" she asks. The staffer points to the cabana by the pool and Rolinda takes off. She is amazingly graceful and fast.

I follow, sensing something very serious is going down. I can't get into the cabana but hover outside with a growing crowd. Then a rumor spreads with a speed that defies all known laws of physics—Sarah Madison was killed in an aircraft accident!

I know who she is but ask anyway to be absolutely sure. A woman with tears in her eyes whispers, "She's Claire's mother."

I make a quick phone call to my friendly editor at The World Review. Within seconds, I'm on a paid assignment and go looking for Mike Westfield. I ask the cameraman where his boss is, and that's when I get my first break. I overhear his audio feed with the location of the crash. I know where it is, and better yet, I know how to get there ahead of the madding crowd. I really have to find Westfield.

Wednesday, October 31

It's early morning and I'm proud of myself for finally coming into the 21st Century. I'm sitting at my computer looking at my account with Sunrise Private Investment Bank FDIC Insured. I've just received my first on-line deposit. Susanne crawls out of bed and stands behind me, her long hair brushing my shoulders. She sees the deposit and nibbles my right ear. It is always nice having a naked woman appreciate any portion of one's anatomy, right ear included. "Very nice," she murmurs.

I laugh and Atticus groans in reply. Yes, dogs can groan. The deposit is payment for my heartwarming story about Sarah Madison that made page one of five major newspapers. "Mike is most appreciative," she says. Because of me, he was the TV reporter that broke the story that dominated the news for over twelve hours.

And it all happened because I overheard his cameraman's audio feed about the crash. The plane was reported down northwest of Las Vegas near the junction of Crystal Road and Appaloosa Lane in Nye County.

I knew exactly where that was, and more importantly, that there's a private landing strip a few yards away that isn't on any map. I immediately told Mike and we headed for Sky Harbor International where KPIO-TV keeps its helicopter on standby. Mike told me the chopper didn't have the range to get there without refueling and a single-engine turboprop aircraft was waiting for us.

One hour and twelve minutes later, we landed at the airstrip on the edge of Crystal, Nevada. I hadn't told Mike that the airstrip belonged to Mable's Whorehouse and Bar and Grill. Please don't ask how I know this.

You can imagine our surprise when we taxied in and saw Sarah Madison and her boyfriend, Stuart Ranager, sitting on the wing of said boyfriend's plane while a mechanic worked on the engine. Mike understands plane talk and it seems that Sarah and Stu were flying by Mabel's when the aircraft's oil pressure warning light flashed, signaling no pressure and imminent doom.

Stu immediately radioed a mayday and shut the engine down. He dead sticked his homebuilt aircraft to a safe landing on Mable's airstrip. But thanks to the non-miracle of modern communications, not to mention piss poor cell phone reception, the word had gone out that they had crashed. They could have walked into Mable's and availed themselves of the excellent phone connections therein but chose not to for propriety's sake. That would have sorted the mess out. Instead, they asked a local mechanic, who just happened to be at the airstrip, to fix the problem, which was a faulty warning light and not a busted oil pump.

Mike and Susanne had no hang ups over propriety and rushed into Mable's to use the phone. They arrived in the bar in time to see a weepy TV commentator lamenting the demise of poor Claire's mother. Mike immediately established contact with KPIO and set the record straight.

That's when I got a second break. I asked Stu why he was eighty miles north of Las Vegas when home was 250 miles south of Las Vegas? It turns out that the love-stricken pair were eloping to Reno to get married.

Naturally, I asked why they didn't do the deed in Las Vegas. They blushed brightly and mumbled something about Reno being more appropriate. The story about elderly lovers flying to Reno for propriety's sake and ending up at a whorehouse wrote itself. That gave the story the twist it needed to dominate a very slow news day. Mike loved breaking the story, I loved the byline in the newspapers, Sunrise Private Investment Bank loved the deposit, Susanne loved demonstrating her thanks.

Atticus was simply glad we were all home safe and sound.

Monday, November 5

It's the first Monday of November before the first Tuesday, which means it's the day before election day, and the mail arrives early. There's the usual junk and two letters. The top letter's return address announces it's from Rolinda Johnson. I throw it in the trash.

The second letter sends me bouncing off the ceiling. It's a registered letter from my agent. The movie production company has put "Fun in the Sun" into production, which means they owe me the tidy sum of $850,000, minus fifteen percent for my agent, of course. The check for $722,500 is attached.

I try very hard not to wet my knickers. Atticus gives me a sad look so I explain it all. The mutt listens attentively. I hope I can visit the set when they film the scene on board three houseboats rafted together on Lake Havasu. Strictly as a professional consultant, of course.

Atticus rouses himself and roots around in the trash can, spilling rubbish on the floor. He finds the bone he had stashed there and settles down for some contented gnawing while I pick up the trash.

The letter from Rolinda catches my attention. Out of curiosity, I open it. She had remembered our last conversation and I'm invited to a victory party tomorrow night. "Atticus, m'lad, that's one confident lady." Atticus tilts his head and gives me a sad look. That means he's interested. "Maybe she wants to rub it in." Atticus is still looking at me. "It's at Casa Mendoza, and I can bring a guest. That's you." That seems to satisfy the beast and he goes back to his bone. "Why not?" I mutter. I've a reason to celebrate, and why not on Hector Mendoza's dime?

I fondle the check from my agent. I know I should go for on-line deposits, but holding and fondling the check is so damn sensual. Enough is enough, and I make a quick trip to Sunrise Investment Bank, deposit the check, and am back at the motel in less than an hour. Ali and Khepri wave at me from the office and invite me to dinner. Good news does travel fast in the Egyptian community.

As usual, dinner that evening is delightful, and Ali artfully turns the conversation to taxes. "You must be very careful and avoid an audit by the IRS," Khepri tells me. "They can impound your bank accounts and damage your reputation." I ask if they know of a CPA who can help forestall such a catastrophe.

Silly me. Of course, they do. They have a cousin who is a defrocked CPA. Apparently, he experienced a disagreement with the IRS that led to his license being suspended. "He will not make that mistake again," Khepri assures me. The Salibs consider it a mark of honor. Another thought pops up, and I kick myself for being so slow. It's late and I excuse myself. I need to talk to Barry the Hacker Bodkin.

He answers on the first ring. "Barry, my man, how they hanging?" He assures me they are dangling quite well. I get right to business. "I'd like to take a look at Claire Allison's tax returns." He assures me he can do that and we agree on a price. He'll get back to me soonest. I hit the sack and reach to turn out the light. The votive candle on Mom's shrine in the corner flickers in the dark. "I need to do something with you," I whisper. An inner voice tells me not yet. Atticus crawls on the bed and spreads out beside me.

The buzzing of my cell phone wakes me and I check the time. I've been asleep less than two hours. It's Barry the

Hacker so I answer. He starts screaming at me in decibels that would get the attention of mating orangutans. "The IRS was a walk in the park," he screams. "Shitty firewalls. No problem downloading her last ten returns. As best I could tell, she's as clean as a whistle. So I ran 'em through an audit program. There are some bigger than normal deductions for business expenses, but nothing else. So I decided to check that out."

He explodes with invectives that I won't repeat. But as a writer I am impressed and take notes. "I coat-tailed on an email from a Rolinda Johnson and got inside Allison's computer on the first probe." He's hyperventilating. "The shit hit the fan like you wouldn't believe. I was caught in a honey pot. She has a firewall like nothing I've ever seen." He takes a deep breath. "It followed me back and fried my computer." I wait for the shoe to drop. "Man, you owe me, big time."

"What the fuck for?" I answer. "All I wanted were her tax returns. I never asked you to go trolling for anything else, much less make a run on her computer." The silence on the other end is telling. He knows I'm right. But I need him and I'm flush right now. "Okay, so you need a new computer. What's the damage?"

Barry grows ecstatic describing all the components he needs. The price skyrockets, so I negotiate. "Ten grand, tops." I hope that satisfies him so I don't have to go looking for another hacker. Good ones are hard to find. Barry takes the offer. I break the connection and try to go back to sleep. But I'm wide awake. I'm missing something important about Claire Allison.

"Atticus, my man, we're definitely going to make that party." Atticus yawns.

Tuesday, November 6

Atticus is washed and groomed, his service dog vest on, and sitting in my car's passenger seat looking straight ahead when the valet opens the door. "Welcome to Casa Mendoza, Mr. Dog." He holds the door for Atticus, and I have to get out by myself. We do the key exchange and he gets in behind the wheel, not looking happy. He turns the key, the engine starts, which makes me happy, and he drives off.

"Walkies," I tell Atticus, and we trot up the stairs into the house. He doesn't need a leash and I'm proud of him. The place is packed with folks gathered around TV sets and the various bars, monitoring the election results.

Mike Westfield is on the center screen and he is surrounded by screaming rejoicers. "Exit polls indicate strong support for Claire Allison," he announces. More screaming. Mike turns to the camera and pontificates. "This reporter has never seen this level of enthusiasm for a county office." He goes on to update the state and national election, but no one seems overly interested in who will have his, or her, fingers clutched around their life, liberty, or property. I head for the bar in the big tent.

We're edging our way across the lawn when Rebecca sees us and rushes up. She skids to a halt on her knees in front of Atticus and rubs his ears. She acknowledges my presence—barely. Everyone loves the pooch. "It looks like your boss has a chance," I say. She stands up and gives me a hug. She hurries off on some errand. "What was that all about?" I ask.

Atticus cocks his head and looks at me. I guess he doesn't know. I merge into the crush around the bar. Surprisingly, everyone seems glad to see me and many remember my name. A pretty red-haired teenager with green eyes brings her mother up to meet me. Her face is familiar but I can't attach a name. Then I remember. She was the student aide in the classroom with Allison on that fateful day with Danny Hawkins.

"Jenna tells me you are an investigative reporter," the mom says. She's nice looking, a bit on the hippy side, and is not wearing a wedding ring. I plead guilty as charged. "I was wondering why you are investigating Claire? She hasn't done anything wrong and is very brave." I hesitate, her words clanging like Big Ben. She hasn't done anything wrong! I think. My ass! Because of Allison, my mother took her own life. I stare at my feet.

"Are you writing a book?" Jenna asks.

The words of my first editor ring in my memory. "In simplicity there is truth." The teenager has asked a simple question and she deserves an honest answer. But honesty is not my long suit, so I change the subject. "I write articles for newspapers and magazines, like the one about Claire's mom and the aircraft accident."

The mom lights up. "That was you!"

But Jenna won't let it go. "I'm reading a book by Theodore White called 'The Making of the President 1960' for my history class. He won a Pulitzer Prize. Can you do that?"

"I honestly don't know."

"Are you going to try?" She looks at me expectantly.

Kids! They keep you honest by asking the hard questions. "I might have to find out."

The mom is definitely more friendly and gives me her card. It turns out Monica Bradley is a 'Sexual Relations Therapist.' I wonder what she looks like in a bikini. Unfortunately, she recognizes the look on my face and quickly straightens things out. "I'm a therapist, not a surrogate." Damn! Then I notice the MD after her name. This woman is not a lightweight.

Mendoza's voice rolls over the crowd. "Everyone! Quiet!" An unearthly silence claims the crowd. Someone turns up the volume on the TVs, and Mike Westfield's voice rings out. "In a closely contested election, Claire Allison made history tonight by being the first write-in candidate to ever win an election for a contested office in the state of Arizona." The crowd explodes in a tsunami of shouts and whistles.

Atticus hides under a table as Monica Bradley throws her arms around me and gives me a big kiss. She pulls back and looks at me. I'm thinking bikini again when she grabs Jenna and they join a conga line weaving across the lawn. I wander back to the house and someone shoves a bottle of champagne my way. Judging by the hugging and kissing going on, more than a few young ladies are going to give their all tonight. I hope Jenna isn't one of them. That must be the Egyptian uncle in me coming out.

A smiling Mendoza is standing on the veranda, surveying his domain. He waves me over. "Congratulations," I say. "Where's Mrs. Allison and your cohort in crime?" I try to sound magnanimous but fail miserably.

He ignores it and slaps me on the back. "Claire and Rolinda are at the Recorder's Office. They should be on their way. I wanted to say thank you."

I'm confused. "Really? For what?"

"Your story about Sarah. It was the publicity we needed to push Claire over the top. You won the election for us."

12

Tuesday, the same day

"We have a visitor," Rolinda warned Claire and Hank. "That's Victor Rodriguez." Claire smiled at the man pushing his way through the crowd outside the Recorder's Office. Rolinda had carefully staged a 'spontaneous' election night vigil for TV, and it had turned into an endurance contest as the election see-sawed back and forth. It was almost midnight with eighty-two percent of the precincts counted when KPIO-TV declared Claire the new County Superintendent of Schools. Victor Rodriguez had come in second.

"Señora Allison," Rodriguez said. "¿Puedo ser el primero en felicitarte?" (May I be the first to congratulate you?)

"Gracias." Claire extended her hand. "Eres más amable. Espero que podamos trabajar juntos. Por favor llámame." (You are most kind. I hope we can work together. Please call me.)

Rodriguez bowed his head graciously. "Your Spanish is excellent, and I must admit, I am impressed." They shook hands. "And thank you, it would be my privilege to help in any way I can. I will call."

They chatted for a few more moments in Spanish before Rolinda broke in. "Please forgive us but duty calls." Rodriguez laughed and they shook hands all around. He wished them well and disappeared into the crowd.

Hank humped. "He thought it was all campaign hype that you speak Spanish. You called his bluff."

"Not really," Claire replied. "It was a gentle reminder that we have a large Hispanic student body. I like him."

"Rodriguez swings a big bat in the community," Rolinda added. "We want him in our court." She checked the time.

"The team is waiting at Hector's. Now comes the fun part." The traffic was light and they arrived at Hector's home just before midnight. Rolinda pulled in behind a KPIO-TV van. "I didn't expect them," she admitted.

"Mike Westfield is an old friend," Claire said. "We go back a few years." Hank climbed out and held the door for her as a bright strobe light came on. Claire made a graceful exit and waved at the camera as they made their way inside. "Oh, hello," she said to a golden retriever wearing a service dog vest. She knelt and stroked his neck. "And who are you?"

"His name is Atticus," Parker said. He stood back as TV cameras recorded the scene. "We were just leaving. Congratulations on your win tonight."

Claire looked up. "Thank you, David." She stood and shook his hand. Again, the camera focused on her as she made her way inside where Hector was waiting. They embraced as tears filled Claire's eyes. "Thank you, thank you," she whispered. "I never dreamed . . ."

"Always dream big," Hector said. He led them into the gathering of workers who had made it all possible. Claire knew most of them by name and she was among friends, shaking hands, and embracing. At one point, she pushed her way through a group of teachers to reach a heavy-set young woman standing shyly in the background. She looked at Claire, her lips pursed and quivering. Claire swept her up in her arms.

Rolinda smiled. "You do make it all worthwhile."

"Pardon?" Hank said. He had been standing in the background, taking in the goodwill surrounding his wife.

"That's Anna Edwards," Rolinda explained. "She was one of Claire's students. We thought she had a learning disability, but Claire didn't agree. Anna only needed someone to believe in her." She studied the young woman, her face radiant as her eyes misted over. "Anna's an A student, a Rhodes Scholar." Two little boys ran past, their arms outstretched as they weaved through the crowd. Both were wearing red capes with a shooting star logo. "What's that all about?" She watched them as they ran up to a woman reporter standing by the pool. The reporter was interviewing the MacElroys.

"They should be home in bed," Claire said quietly. She said goodbye to Anna and headed for the reporter.

"Congratulations on your stunning win," the reporter said. "I don't believe I've ever seen so much interest in a local office. It's been said you have made election history." She tilted the microphone at Claire.

Claire smiled graciously. "You are being most kind, but I think our parents see a future in what's happening in Maricopa County. I only hope I can contribute to that."

The reporter turned to Bobby Lee. "Mr. MacElroy of Prime Star Academy was saying the same thing."

"It was our privilege to endorse Mrs. Allison," Bobby Lee said, "and we hope we can continue to work together for the benefit of all our children." He reached down and stroked one of the boy's head. Claire stiffened and he quickly withdrew his hand.

Rolinda sensed something was wrong and joined them. "Please forgive us, but it has been a long day, and Mrs. Allison is exhausted. I imagine your boys are tired as well and need to hit the sack."

The reporter thanked Claire and lowered the microphone as Rolinda shepherded her into the house.

"Are you okay?" Hank asked, wrapping a shawl around Claire's shoulders. His cell phone rang before she could answer. "Colonel Allison," he said, identifying himself. He listened. "Copy all. On my way." He punched the call off. "That was the command post. I've been recalled. Got to go." He touched her cheek. "Probably just a training exercise. Not to worry."

"Hector or Rolinda can drop me off," Claire said. "Go." He kissed her and hurried for his car. "I love you," she whispered.

Wednesday, November 7

Sarah was sitting in the kitchen when Claire finally made it home. It was just after midnight and she was exhausted from the excitement of the long day. Sarah automatically brewed a cup of tea and handed it to her. "Where's Hank?" Sarah asked.

"The base had a recall," Claire answered. "They've never done that before and, and . . ."

Sarah reached out and touched her daughter's hand. "There was nothing on the evening news. I'm sure they're just practicing." Claire only stared at her cup. "Let's go to bed, darling." She quickly tidied up the kitchen. "Go on. I'll check on Logan."

"Sleep tight, Mom," Claire said. She sat alone, thinking. Her Smart Watch buzzed. It was Nedd. "Yes?" she asked.

"G'day." The voice was bright and cheerful.

"It's the middle of the night," she grumped.

Nedd keyed on her tone and grew serious. "I heard about Hank. It's okay. The Air Force relieved a squadron commander from duty and pegged Hank to replace him. It seems the bugger was harassing one of his pilots, a Captain Dearborne."

"I know her. Hank says she's an excellent pilot." Then it hit her. "Oh, no. Her squadron is deployed to the Middle East. The Air Force didn't say where. They never do."

"The Prince Sultan Air Base in Saudi Arabia. It's in the central desert and very isolated. I'll keep my eye on things. Right now, boredom will be his worse problem."

Claire felt better. "Nedd, nothing is ever boring flying an F-16. I'm going to bed."

She was undressing when Hank walked in. "I'm back, babe." He swept her up in his arms and swung her around. "I've got an operational squadron. It's deployed to the Middle East." He kissed her. "This is what it's all about. I've got to pack. We're ferrying two Vipers, takeoff tomorrow morning."

She kissed him back, long and loving. "Right after you take care of things here." She kissed him again and grabbed his belt, pulling him into their bedroom.

Hank sat on the edge of Logan's bed while Claire and Sarah stood in the doorway. "Hey, good buddy. Time to wake up." Logan rubbed his eyes, coming awake. It was just after six AM and the night was beginning to yield to the new day. "I'm going away for a while."

"Why?" Logan asked.

"I've got to take care of some of my pilots and protect some nice folks from very bad men." He touched Logan's shoulder. "I need your help while I'm gone." Logan nodded. "Help your mom as much as you can. It's okay to worry but always be brave and do the right thing." Hank kissed the top of his head. "I love you, kiddo."

"I love you too," Logan said.

"I'll drive you to the base," Claire said.

Hank stood and patted his son's shoulder. "See you soon, good buddy."

Without a word, Logan jumped out of bed and grabbed one of Hank's bags. He struggled with it as they walked to the car. "Your flight suit looks funny," he said.

Hank's nomex flight suit was stripped of its normal patches and name tag, with only his rank still on the shoulders. But the lieutenant colonel's leaves were black, not silver, and attached with Velcro. "It's what we wear when we're over there," Hank explained.

Claire helped Logan load the bag into the car, fully aware that was the uniform fighter pilots wore into combat. Hank swept Logan into his arms. "Be brave," he said. He sat Logan down and kissed Sarah on her cheek. "I love you, Mom." He hopped into the car and Claire started the motor. Hank waved good-by as they drove off.

It was afternoon when Claire returned home. Sarah had called and said she was at school with Logan, helping his teacher, and the house was unusually quiet. She sat down at the kitchen table and buried her face in her hands, finally giving into the worry she had held at bay. *I'm not sure I can do this without you.* Her cell phone buzzed. It was Nedd. She flicked it on.

"He's safe," Nedd said.

"Really? How can you be so sure?"

"I can only run the probabilities, and Hank is one of the best they have. That's why he was chosen. Right now, his F-16 is hooking up with a KC-10 for an air-to-air refueling."

"I'm not sure I need to know all that," she pleaded. "I'm being silly," she murmured. "He told me what to do." She stood up, feeling better. "He said to take care of our kids—all of them." She headed for her office. "I can do that." She sat down at her computer and turned it on. “Nedd, I need an organizational chart and a profile of my new staff.” The screen flashed with a classic diagram of names and titles as she went to work transitioning to her new job.

“Coffee’s on,” Nedd told her.

“You can do that?” she asked.

“Madam Superintendent, you have no idea what I can do. But you’ll have to get it yourself. Let’s go to work.” He laughed as the organizational chart reformed. “Here’s the real pecking order you’ll be dealing with.” Two names were circled in red, a man and a woman. “You need to fire this pair. They drive the work flows and have effectively created policy. Let me scratch around for a bit. Ah, here we go. They’ve been having an affair, and here’s their off-shore bank account. They’ve also been bribed.” Nedd chuckled. “And on the cheap. Details on request.” Claire made a few notes as she worked.

Two hours later, her cell phone buzzed. It was Rolinda. “We may have a problem. Did you sign off on the TV ad for Prime Star Academy?”

“No. This is the first I’ve heard about it.” Her computer screen flashed and the ad appeared. Nedd had monitored the call and found the sleek promotion touting the accomplishments of Prime Star Academy. “Hold on,” Claire said. “I’m looking at it now.”

Her eyes narrowed as it ended, showing Claire sitting in a child’s chair reading to children clustered around her. Katherine’s voice over urged concerned parents to enroll their children in the best academic program west of the Mississippi. An image of Bobby Lee standing in the shadows flashed in her mind’s eye. Her stomach turned. *He’s using me!* “Rolinda, I’m very uncomfortable with this. Is there anything we can do?”

“I don’t think so. We did use his endorsement and the same photo, and I signed a release. Besides, we don’t want any controversy before you’ve even been sworn in. I’ll talk to Bobby Lee, but we’ll have to live with it.”

Claire felt the sour taste of bile rising in her throat. *Only for now.* “We can talk later,” she said, breaking the connection. She swung around in her chair, pulled on her running shoes, and headed for the treadmill in their bedroom. She paused for a moment, staring at the still unmade bed. She stepped onto the treadmill and started to run. But this was different and not an emotional venting. She considered her options as she ran. She touched the HD screen in front of her, bringing it to life. "Nedd, are you there?" She waited.

"I'm here," he finally said. "Sorry for the delay, I was talking to Montreal."

"I have a question. How can I stop that miserable bastard without hurting my son?"

"The testimony of the victims is all we have. As a parent, you can refuse to allow Logan to testify. Unfortunately, other children will have to take the stand."

"Which won't happen if I can help it." She picked up the pace. "I'm going to stop him. Now." Claire slowed to a stop as her face hardened, a decision made. "Nedd, is there a poison that doesn't leave traces behind?"

"Not that I know of," Nedd answered. "Don't go there. I can't handle all the variables."

"What variables can you handle?" The HD screen flashed and an image of a man appeared. He was pleasant looking but unremarkable with a full head of dark hair, a roman nose framed by dark eyes, and a full mouth. He was sitting in a wheelchair in front of an array of screens and readouts. "Nedd, I didn't know."

"Not to worry, luv. A terrorist muffed his assignment." He grabbed the wheels and spun the chair around. Nedd Edwards was a paraplegic. He looked at her, smiled, and shrugged.

"Why are you showing yourself now?" she asked.

"If we're going to off the fuckin' bastard, you need to know your partner."

13

Tuesday, December 11

Thanksgiving is in the rearview mirror but I'm still celebrating. The reason is sleeping beside me—the lovely Monica Bradley. It all started the week before Thanksgiving when I received an invitation from Jenna, Monica's teenage daughter. I was invited to Thanksgiving dinner, please bring Atticus. Obviously, she likes the pooch and only puts up with me. But I'm not one to let a little jealousy get in the way of a good turkey dinner, so I presented myself at the designated abode with Atticus in tow.

I was witty and erudite, charming the other diners. Atticus was the perfect guest, although he ate in the kitchen. My reward was a grateful mommy, now ensconced in my bed. Dr. Monica Bradley, M.D. does look good in a bikini, and better out of it.

Monica wakes up and starts chatting. "Parker, I was wondering, perhaps . . ." She ponders a bit and strokes my tickle stick. "Have you ever . . . would you . . . ah . . . consider videotaping a session with me." What! I'm many things, but I'm not a porn star. I stare at her, but my willie is very interested. "I think it would be a valuable therapy resource," she quickly assures me. "It's a tool that I can use in counseling."

Right. But it's my tool she's talking about. "I thought you were a sexual therapist, not a coach."

She snuggles closer and starts tugging. "Coaching is very much a part of therapy, and I can be a surrogate when needed." The old schwanzstucker perks up. I won't go into what comes next, but she could coach the Lake Havasu swingers any day of the week. She gets out of bed and does stretching exercises before pulling on proper panties. I sit on the edge of the bed while she sits between my legs, her back towards me. I hook her boring bra while she studies the charts and photos lining the walls.

"Most interesting," she declares. "You have a fixation on Claire Allison." I grunt an answer. She rubs her rear into my tender parts. "Is there a purpose to all this?"

An inner voice that sounds like Dottie Sue tells me it's time to set the record straight. "I'm writing the book Jenna talked about." Like every drudge who fancies himself a writer, I want to write the great American something—novel, biography, history—you name it. I want my name on library shelves before they become extinct. But I have to write it first.

"Do you have a title?"

I hadn't thought about it, but the title is obvious. "The Sunflower Girl."

Her reaction is immediate. "I love it." She stands and pulls on a demure white blouse. "I must go." She steps into a pair of dark, loose fitting pants, now the cool professional. "Think about the video." I walk her to her car that is parked by the office and kiss her goodbye.

Khepri Salib is watching from the office and comes to the door. "David, our CPA is here going over our accounts. His name is Mohammed. You might want to talk to him. It is best to stay ahead of events." That sets off a chain of sound bites in my brain that passes for thinking.

I head back to my room and rustle around for the folder with Allison's tax returns. It's right where Khepri had filed it, and I hustle back to the office to meet Mohammed. He's working in the rear office and looks all of twenty years old. Khepri introduces us and he sums me up with the eyes of a much older and wiser man. I hand him the folder and show him the notes Barry the Hacker had made before he was hacked.

"Would it be worth ratting her out to the IRS?" I ask. The Internal Revenue Service pays whistleblowers anywhere from fifteen to thirty percent of money recovered. Mohammed lights up like the aurora borealis and says he'll get right on it.

I wander out through the new breakfast lounge the Salibs have built for their guests and stop for coffee and to stoke up on calories. The TV is tuned to a national news network and a very serious lady is standing in front of a map of the Middle East. The news is not good. "The Chinese have signed a mutual defense treaty with Iran and have deployed over a hundred fighter aircraft to the Middle East."

A young couple wanders in and look at the TV as four Chinese fighter jets fill the screen. The young man stares at the screen. "Those are fuckin' J-20s." The girl reaches out to calm him. She is sporting a huge engagement ring.

I know nothing about airplanes so I Google 'J-20 fighter aircraft' on my smart phone while they talk in low tones. He is stationed at Luke AFB on the other side of town. My smart phone delivers the answer. 'The new J-20 stealth fighter aircraft is swift, maneuverable, and armed with a new long-range standoff missile. Aviation experts claim the fifth generation J-20 compares to the latest US fighters.'

The young couple leave holding hands and I can see a worried look on the girl's face. For some reason, I'm envious.

"Ah, there you are," Mohammed says, bringing me back to the moment. He sits down at the table and opens the folder with Allison's tax returns. "All is correct," he announces. "But I did find something of possible interest."

He talks like Ali, grammatically correct with clear enunciation. He thumbs through the most recent return. "You will notice the increased deduction for the depreciation of office equipment." He turns to the same section in previous returns. "The on-going deduction is for one piece of equipment. Given the high initial cost and the rapid write off, it is safe to assume it is for a very large computer with an increased capacity to perform calculations for design and research programs."

I can hear the periods and commas as he talks. "A tax auditor would expect such an advanced computer to be used to generate income, and, of course, was such income reported?" I am impressed and hire him to do my taxes. "It will be my pleasure," he says, taking his leave.

I sit there alone, staring at the TV, only half hearing what the commentator is prattling on about; something about the deteriorating situation in the Middle East. What would a teacher do with a computer on steroids? Or was it husband Hank's computer? I head for my room, anxious to start work. I stand in the middle of the space, my head on a swivel as I turn from one wall chart to another. The research is all there and all I have to do is arrange it in an order that has meaning for the reader.

But who will be reading The Sunflower Girl? The truth is that I don't care. I'm only writing for one person—me.

I sit down at my PC and call up a fresh page. I start with the title but hesitate before typing in my name. I decide to go with "D.A. Parker." Next, I've got to set the hook. A book like this usually starts with a defining incident in the person's life to catch the reader's attention. That's an easy one, and I've already written the story about Danny Hawkins and that fateful day. I do a quick cut and paste, fiddle a bit with the format, and the prologue is good to go. I'll revise it as the story develops, but I'm off and running.

The hard part comes next, getting her early life organized. But I need to take a pee break first and head for the bathroom. As usual, it is spotless, but like many motels the adjoining walls are on the thin side, and I can hear the TV in the next room. At first, it doesn't make sense. Then it does. A local educator was found dead on a houseboat near Sacramento California, apparently the victim of gunfire. Identification is being withheld pending notification of kin, etc., etc.

I rush back into my room and turn on the TV in time to catch a glimpse of a minivan being towed away. I can barely make out a small mud-splattered logo on the door. It's a shooting star.

Holy shit! Prime Star Academy's logo is a shooting star, and I'm guessing the local educator is none other than Bobby Lee MacElroy. I hit the pause button on the TV remote to freeze the scene. The minivan is being towed onto a two-lane road next to a river with a patrol car in close trail. I can make out the logo—Isleton Police Department. I Google Isleton and get a lesson in geography. It's a small town on the Sacramento River in Sacramento County. What the hell was Bobby Lee doing there?

"Thank you, Lord," I whisper. This is the type of story I specialize in, so I call my friendly editor at The World Review. Thirty seconds later and I have the assignment. My next call is to Barry the Hacker. I'm guessing the Isleton Police Department doesn't have the wherewithal to conduct an investigation and therefore called in the local sheriff or the FBI to investigate. Can he root around for details on the shooting? Barry's willing as long I don't expect him to hack into the FBI network. "They don't play fair," he informs me.

I wonder what's 'fair' in the wonderful world of hacking but don't pursue it. He's still smarting from the Claire Allison backfire and we settle on an outrageous price. He'll get back to me soonest. The clock is ticking and I've maybe eighteen to twenty-four hours lead time to get ahead of the story before names and places are released and the big boys like Westfield get involved.

I spend the next few minutes diligently reading up on Prime Star Academy. One thing becomes obvious, Bobby Lee's mother created one of the best private schools around. Come on, Barry, I need to hear from you!

On cue, Barry forwards me an email between the Isleton cops and the Sacramento sheriff: Bobby Lee was terminated with two small caliber rounds to the back of his head. There were no exit wounds, and no spent casings were found. There were no signs of a struggle. Assistance with investigation required. "Oh, my God!" I shout. It was a double tap, a classic mob execution. The story just got better. I jump up and down with excitement. "Sweet Jesus!" Investigative journalism is not dead and I'm not an historical has been.

For now, the story is in Sacramento, and that's a major break. I've lived there over fifteen years and have a few well-placed contacts. "Atticus, my man, it's time to visit the crime scene." He gives me his doleful look and stands by the door while I pack and load the car. On the way out, I stop by the office and pay the next month's rent. Khepri is sad to see me go and promises to keep my files up to date. I head for Sacramento just before high noon with Atticus, leaving Phoenix and The Sunflower Girl in the rearview mirror.

Let's face it, I don't write books.

14

Thursday, December 13

The image in the mirror staring back was definitely Claire Marie Allison, but she didn't feel like the Claire Marie Allison she used to know. *I never imagined it would be like this.* Claire brushed her hair into place, letting it fall over her left shoulder. Hank liked it that way. She glanced at the small antique clock below the mirror. *Two hours and twenty-four minutes and everything changed.*

That was the exact time it took to walk out of her hotel room, drive forty miles in a driving rain, walk to the houseboat, shoot Bobby Lee, drive back to Sacramento, and return to her room. *Two hours and twenty-four minutes! How do you deal with it, Hank? killing another human being.* She had spent hours talking to Nedd, but nothing seemed to help. She hadn't really slept since Sunday, tossing and turning, as the image of Bobby Lee haunted her.

It was so easy and, with one exception, went down as they had planned. Bobby Lee had opened the door of the houseboat and tried to slam it closed as she pushed through. He jerked and turned away, and she shot him in the back of the head. He fell forward and she stepped over him, firing a second time with the muzzle inches away from the first wound. Then she froze, unable to move.

She had just killed a man. It didn't matter what he had done; she was his executioner. She ran outside, her stomach churning. As planned, she threw the revolver into the river. She leaned over the rail and threw up into the dark waters below as rain pounded her face. It was critical to their plan that she throw the body over the side and let the swift flowing waters carry it down stream. But she couldn't do it. She had to escape. She closed the door, sealing him inside, and ran back to her car.

"Hon," Sarah called, bringing her back to the moment. "Are you ready?" Claire dropped the brush. They had a ten o'clock appointment with Sandra Shriver and it was time to go. Logan and Sarah were waiting when Claire emerged from her bedroom.

Sarah studied her daughter, her concern very evident. "Claire, please try my sleeping pills."

"I'm fine," Claire replied.

"No, you're not. Hank will be okay, and you've got to stop worrying."

I wish it were that simple. "I will," she promised.

Logan ran up to her. "Daddy's the toughest dude over there. He can take care of himself."

Claire knelt and hugged him. "When did you last talk to him?" Hank called home twice a day on FaceTime. It was the way of modern combat. "Right after I got up," Logan said. He pulled free and tugged at her hand. "Come on, let's go."

"I'll drive," Sarah said. Claire didn't argue and held Logan's hand as they walked to the car. It was an easy drive to the hospital and Sarah dropped them off at the entrance. "I'll park and meet you in the waiting room." Logan pulled at Claire's hand, hurrying inside.

A couple with a daughter Logan's age were leaving when they reached the psychiatrist's office. The father held the door for them. Claire recognized the girl. She was one of the four children in the photograph with Logan and Bobby Lee. Claire thanked the father and glanced at the girl. She had dealt with too many disturbed children in her career, and there was no doubt that the girl was deeply troubled. Fortunately, the children did not recognize each other.

Logan rushed inside and hugged Sandra. "I talked to my daddy this morning," he announced.

"Do you miss him?" Sandra asked.

Logan nodded somberly. "But that's okay. He's protecting a lot of good people. That's his job."

"Do you want to play on the computer while your mother and I talk?" Without a word, Logan bounced into the playroom and sat down. Sandra motioned Claire into her private conference room and automatically poured Claire a cup of tea. "Logan is doing so well," she said, joining Claire. Together, they studied her iPad, monitoring the game Logan was playing. "How's he doing in school?"

"By all reports, very well. Mom is a teacher's assistant twice a week and says he is a peer leader and the kids flock to him."

"Any other problems? Eating, sleeping?" Claire shook her head in answer. "Well," Sandra continued, "I think we're done here for the time being. If any problems arise, call me. Lacking that, let's meet in a month."

"Will we ever learn who he is?" Claire asked.

"Eventually, yes. For now, I recommend that we don't pursue it." She dropped the iPad into her lap and leaned forward. "Claire, we're witnessing a miracle. Logan is happy and secure. It's become a non-event in his world, more like a dream, because he wasn't harmed physically. Some event will eventually trigger a memory and he'll know. But the longer we go, and the older he is, the less traumatic it will be. Time does heal most wounds. Why risk changing that? You, Hank, and your mother have saved a wonderful child. God bless you."

"I only wish we could save the others too," Claire murmured. Images of the little girl and Danny Hawkins flashed in her mind's eye, and she knew she would live with them forever.

"There are some things beyond our control," Sandra replied. There was a sadness in her voice that ripped at Claire. "We have to live with that and hope those horrible men will be brought to justice. Keep the faith, for it will happen, it must happen."

"The sooner, the better," Claire allowed.

"We can only hope," Sandra replied. They confirmed the date for the next appointment, called for Logan to join them, and started to leave.

"Do I have to go to school?"

"Quit moaning," Sarah said from the waiting room, "and, yes, you do."

Logan spread his arms like wings and zoomed out the door. "Superman to the rescue," Sarah said, following him into the hall outside.

They hugged. "Claire, take care and stop feeling guilty. Just look at your son. Whatever may have happened, you did the right thing . . . are doing the right thing." Claire smiled weakly and followed Logan and Sarah.

Sarah was sitting in the driver's seat with the engine running when Claire climbed into the rear seat. "That was a short appointment," Sarah said, wheeling the car into the exit lane. "I hope she didn't charge for a full hour." There was no answer.

"Mom's asleep," Logan said.

Monday, December 17

"Welcome back," Rebecca said when Claire walked into her office. She shot a worried look at the man sitting by the coffee maker. He stood up.

"Detective Harry Winslow, Phoenix Police Department." He held out his ID and badge for Claire's inspection. "I was hoping we might talk."

Nedd had warned Claire she would be interviewed and had spent hours coaching her. She glanced at his ID and held her office door open. "Certainly. Please come in." She gave Rebecca a questioning look. "Please hold my calls." She motioned the detective to a seat and sat down across from him. "How may I help you, Detective Winslow?"

"I assume you heard the news about the alleged murder of a local educator."

"It was all over TV last week and hard to miss." She looked at him with a carefully practiced concern.

"The name will he released today." He paused, his eyes fixed on her face. "Bobby Lee MacElroy."

Claire's mouth opened and she tried to speak as her eyes blinked. "Oh, my God. Poor Katherine." She gave a little shudder. "I'll help in any way I can . . . please excuse me for a moment." She snatched a Kleenex from her desk and bolted out the door, leaving it open.

A few minutes later, Claire walked back in and closed the door. "Thank you." She sat down beside him and fell silent.

"How long have you known the deceased?" He gave her an encouraging look. "We have to ask everyone associated with Mr. MacElroy the same questions."

"My husband and I first met Bobby Lee and his mother, Katherine, when we enrolled Logan, he's our son, in Prime Star Academy's preschool program. Logan was three at the time, so that was five years ago."

"Is he still enrolled in the Academy?"

"Not now. We kept him in the afterschool program when he started kindergarten. Then there was little league baseball, and he wanted to learn kung fu, and his homework was taking more time, and something had to give." She gave him her best frustrated look. "So we didn't enroll Logan when the new term started last September."

"How would you describe your relationship with the MacElroys?"

"I consider Katherine a good friend, and they endorsed my campaign for Superintendent."

"And you never interacted on a social level?"

"Of course. There were school functions, and then my campaign. I have a video of a TV interview at our victory party. I can get it for you."

"Thank you, but that's not necessary at this time." He paused. "Did you ever associate personally? Private dinners or trips?"

"Oh, no." She waited to see if he would pursue the subject.

"Were there any problems with Logan when he was enrolled in preschool or after school? With a teacher or another student?"

"Nothing unusual, just the normal adjustment problems. He can he a handful, he's so active. It's all in his records, if that's important."

"And you never had a disagreement, words, or a problem with Mr. MacElroy or his mother?"

"No. Not at all."

"Did you or your husband have any problems with Logan's peers or their parents?"

"Nothing that I can remember." She paused for a moment. "No. Nothing." She waited, knowing what was coming.

"Where were you the weekend before last, Sunday December 9?" He knew the answer.

Her eyes opened wide, exactly as Nedd had coached her. "Ah . . . I . . . we were at a business meeting in Sacramento . . . the Western States Association of Educators. Bobby Lee was there. I sat in on his presentation." She froze, her mouth slightly open.

"Please don't read anything into this. Can you remember your schedule?"

She hesitated for a moment. "Rebecca and I flew into Sacramento on Friday afternoon. We took a cab to the Capital Regency, that's where they held the meeting. The only time we left the hotel was Sunday evening for dinner with friends. We checked out Monday morning and took a cab back to the airport."

"Your rooms?"

"Mine was on the third floor, 307, and Rebecca was on the eighth floor."

"Did you talk to Mr. MacElroy while there?"

"No. Rebecca may have, but you would have to ask her." She gave herself a mental kick for adding the last.

Winslow stood up. "Thank you. I would like to speak to Rebecca. I do appreciate your help." He gave her his card. "Please call if you can think of anything else or remember something you overheard."

They shook hands and she led him to Rebecca's desk. "Detective Winslow would like to ask you a few questions. You can use my office." Rebecca shot to her feet, a worried look on her face. Claire touched her arm. "He'll explain. We need to help him all we can." Claire watched them walk into her office. *Show him some leg,* she thought.

Rebecca did.

It was late afternoon when Claire finally returned home. Sarah had taken Logan to his kung fu lesson and the house was quiet. She changed into her running togs and stepped on the treadmill. The HD pad in front of her came to life with Nedd's image. "How did the interview with Winslow go?" he asked. She jogged as she recounted the conversation. Nedd wanted to hear it word for word and didn't interrupt. "It went well. Did you and Rebecca talk about it later?"

"Only in general terms like you suggested."

"Good. Cops expect women to talk, so if the subject comes up, you've got a credible fallback position."

"Nedd, am I in trouble? I really messed up. I know you've run your prediction algorithms. Please, be honest with me." She picked up the pace, striding harder.

"Lacking a suspect, there is a high degree of probability, approaching ninety-eight percent, that the investigation will go cold case within forty-eight hours. There are no neighbors who heard a gunshot or saw anything, and there are no video cameras.

"And the crime scene is proving counterproductive. At last count, they've found twenty-two DNA samples and over seventy fingerprints. All are misleads they will spend time, effort, and money investigating—all for nothing. In short, they are coming up with zero everywhere they look. Budgetary constraints and the press of other cases will force them to move on."

"And in the long term?" she asked. "Sooner or later, they will learn he was a pedophile. Won't that reopen the investigation?" She ran harder.

"I can't answer that. There are too many variables to reach a credible prediction within an acceptable margin of error."

"And your best guess?"

"Ah, the dreaded scientific wild-ass guess. Normally, law enforcement agencies are very hesitant to pursue a case like this because district attorneys will not file charges without overwhelming forensic evidence. There are exceptions, but given normative human behavior, it isn't going to happen." Nedd gave her a shrug with a hopeful look. "Luv, the average bloke in the States would mark this up as a job well done and offer to pay for the bullets."

Her pace slowed to a jog. "Nedd, you're a dear. I've got to go." She grabbed a towel and hurried out. "Pizza for dinner anyone?" she sang.

The security cameras surrounding the house captured the license number of a passing car. The number was quickly processed and the driver identified as a threat analysis assigned the driver a friendly rating. Nedd noted the sequence, and satisfied with the result, continued his search of law enforcement nets for any reference to Claire or Bobby Lee. He monitored two text messages confirming the investigation was now a cold case.

15

Wednesday, December 19

I've been spinning my wheels for a week, and I'm frustrated as all hell. I drove from Phoenix to Sacramento in record time and even made it through Bakersfield without getting a ticket. It was midnight when I pulled up in front of the house where I rented a room behind the garage. The room was a mess, the way I had left it, and Atticus wouldn't come in until I disposed of some offending garbage and aired the place out.

In retrospect, that was the most productive thing I accomplished. Every one of my contacts fizzled, and not one of my good buddies in the sheriff or police department would talk to me about the murder. I even called Lynn Majors, my default lawyer of choice. Lynn hears a mega load of gossip, but she hadn't heard a thing about the shooting.

It was easy finding the houseboat where Bobby Lee met his untimely demise. I drove to Isleton, the town forty miles south of Sacramento where it all happened. Isleton is a small place, and everyone knows everyone else's business. I dropped in at a friendly pizza bar with Atticus and ordered lunch. All I said was "I heard someone was shot" and within two minutes learned where the grisly deed had taken place, the sexual preferences of everyone involved, and all about the houseboat.

It was a rental owned by the owner of the bar. She had rented it over the internet and arranged to have it delivered to a nearby dock to moor for a party. Captain Fred, the skipper who delivered the houseboat to the dock where Bobby Lee was offed, was the cock of the walk and holding court at the pizza bar. He was a good old boy, reveling in his fifteen minutes of fame, and volunteered to show me the 'where' for fifty bucks.

Much to my surprise, we walked across the street to the river and climbed aboard a small sailboat. I've never been on a sailboat in my life and was having second thoughts until Atticus hopped on board. It was a short sail down river, about a mile, and that's where Captain Fred earned his fifty bucks.

The dock and houseboat were sealed off from the road with yellow crime tape, but we sailed right up to the boat, ghosting quietly along. The cop guarding the boat was inside and watching TV. He never heard us as we sailed by ten feet away. I recorded the scene on my smart phone. I enjoyed the sail back to Isleton, and Captain Fred filled me in on the details about the houseboat, all of which I dutifully noted.

It's now Wednesday, six days before Christmas and time to head for Phoenix. I'd rather frolic away the holidays with the Salibs since they are Moslem and immune from the hysteria that surrounds the yuletide. So I clean up the room, mainly to keep Atticus happy, and pack my suitcase. I decide to give my cop connections one last shot before departing the capital of the sunshine state. I head for The Pine Room, the cop bar where the old heads hang out.

We walk in just after six o'clock that evening. The place is jumping with an impromptu Christmas party and the booze and snacks are in full flow. I squeeze up to the bar and order a Scotch on the rocks, my beverage of choice. Naturally, Atticus is an instant attraction.

A young woman rushes up, falls to her knees, and caresses his ears cooing and smiling. She is the type your mother would describe as cute and perky. My mother would have called her Porky Pig. She wears huge glasses and looks up at me with bright green eyes. "Your dog is adorable. What's his name?" She does have a nice voice and straight teeth with a slight overbite.

"Atticus," I reply.

"From *To Kill a Mockingbird.*" I confess that I'm impressed. She pops to her feet and I can't help but notice she is curvy and well packed. "It's my favorite book." She extends her hand. "Hi. I'm Laura Zavorsky."

"David Parker," I reply, shaking her hand. Her grip is strong and firm. "You with law enforcement?"

"Detective, Sacramento Sheriff." Now, that's a surprise. She whips out her notebook and flips it open. "I'm conducting a poll for the department." Our area of the bar has gone quiet and everyone is watching. She gives me a very serious look. I return the look and study her nose. It's perky with a few freckles. "When you need to urinate, do you go over the top of your shorts, under the leg, or out the opening in front?" She cocks her head and looks at me expectantly, pen poised.

I stammer. "Ah . . . ah, this is embarrassing."

She arches an eyebrow expectantly. "You don't have to be ashamed."

"Well . . . ah . . . none of the above."

"Oh, you poor thing. Do you have to sit on the potty?"

"No. I just roll my sock down."

The bar roars with laughter and she flips her notebook closed. "Good one, David Parker. I owe you a drink." She motions for the bartender. "Best Scotch in the house for my friend." I'm impressed that she noticed what I was drinking. I'm more impressed when the barkeep pours a double of Macallan Rare Cask. We're talking $300 a bottle.

We chat. I'm not sure when, but soon enough we are out of there and walking towards Old Sac for dinner. She holds my arm and sashays down the street, bumping hips. Atticus walks beside her without a leash, protecting her flank. His tail is wagging. He likes her. Dinner is excellent and we finish off two bottles of a cheap red that is very good. "Well, Mr. Parker, are we going to fuck at your place or mine?"

It's late, it's been a long, frustrating week, and I'm horny. She's not my type, but I compromise my standards. "I live in midtown. Which is closer?"

She smiles. "Yours. Let's go."

Twenty minutes later, we're stripped down and in my bed. Fortunately, the sheets are clean.

Thursday, December 20

It's late morning when I open my eyes. I half expect Laura to be gone, but she is in bed beside me, wide awake, laying on her side, elbow bent, resting her cheek on her right hand. She's studying my face intently. "Good morning," she says. She is bright and cheerful as she gently draws her fingernails over my schlong. "David," she asks, "why were you photographing the crime scene Monday afternoon?"

That gets my undivided attention, and my mental Klaxon is in full alarm. I play it cool. "You have a great interrogation technique, Detective." She looks at me, innocence personified, but doesn't answer.

I'm dealing with an unknown and a warning voice cautions me to play it straight. "I'm an investigative journalist, I currently live in Phoenix, and I'm researching an article for The World Review on MacElroy." She smiles and my brain kicks in. "You knew who I was." Again, the little smile and she answers with a nod. "How did you make me?"

She cuddles up and wraps a leg around me. "The officer on duty at the houseboat copied the boat registration when you sailed by. It was a simple matter tracking down Captain Fred. He's a sweetie pie and loves to talk. He gave you and Atticus up in a heartbeat. You came up clean on the background check, so I wrote you off. But I recognized you the moment you walked into the Pine Room."

"Why not just ask a direct question? Why the come on?"

"I liked your dog, you're cute and . . ." Her voice trails off.

Obviously, she wants to use me for more than sport fucking. "Okay, what do you want?" I can hear resignation in my voice.

Laura is all business. "I need help." She sits up in bed, her legs crossed, and leans into me. She is incredibly sexy, but very serious. "I was assigned the investigation when the Isleton PD called for help. It went cold case against my recommendation, which really pisses me off."

I mention that without a suspect, an investigation normally goes cold case within forty-eight hours. "True," she replies. "I need more time, but the fuckin' bureaucrats are playing money games. Money is tight and they want to release the houseboat back to the owner rather than hold it as evidence."

"You've got a body with two slugs in its head and a houseboat. What else do you have?"

"He's a pedophile."

That's a conversation stopper. "You can prove that?"

She shakes her head. "An anonymous tip. We traced it to a burner phone in Phoenix."

"And you want me to chase it down?"

"No one else will," she replies.

I've been lured, hooked, played, and landed. "Okay, lay it all out."

"Later," she murmurs, coming at me again. Fortunately, I'm up for it. Pun intended.

It's later and we're sitting side-by-side in the dining nook of her kitchen overlooking a tree lined street. A thick file folder is open, its contents spread over the table. Judging by its contents, Detective Laura Zavorsky is a very thorough cop. From the tone of her voice, she could have been reading an encyclopedia as she rehashes the details. "You're familiar with the scene; a houseboat tied to a dock on the Sacramento River located 1.2 miles northwest of Isleton, and 213 feet from California Highway 160. The body was found by the owner of the houseboat. She was checking on it as the renter had not notified her that it was clean and ready for return.

An autopsy and clinical evaluation placed the time of death three days prior to discover, on early Sunday morning, December 9. The cause of death was massive brain trauma caused by two .22 Long Rifle hollow point rounds fired at the back of the victim's head at short range as evidenced by very little stippling."

I ask what that is. She shows me a close-up photo. "Stippling are the burn marks on the skin around the bullet hole caused by powder burns. The closer the muzzle, the more stippling." There was no exit wound, and I am surprised by the lack of visible damage and blood. I mention it and she shows me another photo of Bobby Lee on the autopsy table with the top of his skull removed. The two slugs had ricocheted around the inside of his skull, shredding whatever was there. I barely make it to the sink, puking up my breakfast. I sit back down and Laura pours me a fresh cup of coffee. "I've seen worse," she says.

"I'm sorry," I reply, truly meaning it.

"No shell casings were found, which indicates the weapon may have been a revolver. Most likely it was a ghost gun and untraceable. The surrounding area was searched twice. A heavy rain had washed the exterior of the houseboat clean and eliminated any traces of tire tracks or footprints. We found the victim's school van parked across the road near a farmhouse."

She checks her notes and describes the houseboat. It's a fifty-foot aluminum monohull with a fly bridge and sundeck on top. It's a party boat. "We checked the rental agreement and traced it to a burner phone and a prepaid charge card. Both were purchased online and picked up in Phoenix."

Laura lays out the photos of the deceased. Bobby Lee is spread-eagled on his stomach, his feet twenty-two inches from the door. "He was facing away from the door when he was shot," she explains. "We found a partial heel print next to the body, which suggests the assailant stood over the body at one point. There was no sign of a struggle. The victim's cell phone and iPad were recovered. Forensics obtained twenty-two DNA samples and seventy-one fingerprints, which identified thirty-one individuals. All were cleared of any connection."

"That must have been expensive and time consuming."

"Tell me," she replies. "My supervisor had a few words about that and keeps asking the big three."

"Motive, means, and opportunity?"

She gives me a condescending look and shakes her head. "No. Witnesses, weapon, and forensics."

"What about his cell phone or iPad? Any clues there?"

"Nothing about the houseboat." She sorts through her notes. "However, there were numerous telecoms, messages, and emails referencing the meeting he was attending in Sacramento. We interviewed seventeen individuals in attendance who had a connection to MacElroy." She hands me a list. "Again, nothing. They all had alibis that checked out."

I glance at the list. It's alphabetical and number one is Claire Marie Allison. Of course, my feverish brain jumps on that coincidence. But logic kicks in and I calm down. They are both educators and have a well-known connection. However, I can still hear Dotty Sue unloading on Allison and the old itch needs scratching. Then the light bulb comes on. "Do you have a list of the students enrolled in Prime Star?"

She hands me a piece of paper and tells me they've already checked it, looking for students with links to drug cartels. I scan the list and come up dry, but my light bulb is still burning. I reach for my phone and call Barry the Hacker and ask him to find Prime Star's enrollment for the past five years. The price is very reasonable.

"I wish I could do that," Laura says. She mutters something about the fruit of the poisoned tree. Barry is back five minutes later. He has the list ready to email, and we settle up. My iPad dings and I call up the mail. Again, the list is alphabetical and Logan Allison's name is at the top.

I am coolness personified when I show it to Laura. "MacElroy had access to her son. If he molested Logan, she'd have motive. Assume she found the weapon on the Dark Web—she's good with computers—isn't that means? And she was only forty miles away on a dark and stormy night. Isn't that opportunity?" Laura gives me the look and shakes her head at my witticism. "So, how did she get there?" I ask.

I have Laura's undivided attention. "I've impounded the hotel's security videos. I'll go over them again and check license plates for what's parked in the garage." She sighs. "That will take some time."

"I really need to hit the road," I tell her. She walks me and Atticus to my car. "Will I see you again?"

She kisses the top of his head. "Think New Year's," she says. "Your place."

16

Tuesday, December 25

It was late Christmas Day when Claire's cell phone buzzed. It was the call she was waiting for. "Logan," she called, "it's your dad." She gave her hair a flip and hit the accept button.

Hank's face filled the screen. "Hi, babe. Miss you." He looked tired and gaunt and had obviously lost weight. He reached out and touched the screen. "I like your hair fixed that way." Logan skidded to a stop behind her and she handed him the phone. "Hi, good buddy. You staying out of trouble?" Claire and Sarah listened as Hank and Logan talked.

Logan asked how it was going. The two women could hear the worry in his voice. "It's going okay," Hank assured him. Logan asked if the bad guys were causing any trouble. "They're trying to, but they aren't very good at it." His voice sounded different. "We were flying a routine patrol today and ran into a few of them. They wouldn't go away, so I had to shoot one down. Piece of cake."

Logan shouted as Claire held her mother tight. They all knew what it meant. Hank had achieved what every fighter pilot lives for—he had had downed an enemy combatant. But there was no joy in his voice, just a lingering melancholy because he had killed a man, and Claire loved him more than ever for it.

Later, she would learn that Hank and his wingman had been on a routine combat air patrol over the Straits of Hormuz when they engaged four hostile J-20 fighters from Iran that were attacking an oil tanker. Hank shot one down in a brief dog fight, and both F-16s returned safely to base.

But for now, Claire's Christmas was complete. Her husband was safe and their son was whole and well. She joined

Logan and, cheek to cheek, they told Hank about Christmas and the presents they had opened that morning. Hank asked about Claire's new job. "We're all moved in," Claire replied, "and I'll be sworn in on Thursday after New Year's. We're ready to go."

Hank laughed. "I bet you are. We're relocating and I'll be out of contact for a week or so. I've got to go." He looked at his family. "Hey, good buddy take care of your mom." Logan said he would. Claire took the phone and they were alone. "I love your hair," he said, "and you more."

"I love you," she murmured.

17

Monday, December 31

Christmas had come and gone without too much trauma or drama. As usual, I drank myself stupid, but was stone cold sober when I picked up Laura at the airport on New Year's Eve. "Your place, now," was all she said. It's nice when someone is on the same wavelength.

We're in bed, cuddling up and Laura glances at her watch. I tell her we're invited to the Salibs to ring in the New Year, and we've two or three hours to kill. She gets all excited about what she's discovered and wants to talk.

"I drove from the hotel where Allison stayed to the crime scene early Sunday morning. It was just after one AM, and traffic was non-existent. I only had to stop for one red light. It's thirty-nine miles, and I made it in forty-six minutes without breaking the speed limit. I parked in the same spot where MacElroy had parked and walked to the dock. I waited ten minutes and walked back to my car. Total mileage from the hotel and back is seventy-eight miles, and it took 110 minutes."

I ask the obvious question. "So how did she get a car?"

"I ran the hotel's security videos and identified thirty-four rental cars that were parked in the hotel's garage the night Bobby Lee was shot. All were rented from the big four rental companies. I checked with them and that led to one Emilio Delgado, an undocumented hombre with a California driver's license. Delgado parked the car he rented at Allison's hotel but didn't bother to check in. The car rental lot is almost five miles from the hotel. So I figure Delgado rents the car and drives five miles to the hotel, Allison drives seventy-eight miles round trip, and Delgado drives five miles back to the rental agency for a total of eighty-eight miles. Care to guess the total mileage on the odometer when he turned the car in?" She answers her own question. "Eighty-eight miles." She gives me her innocent look and I know Mr. Delgado is in for an interesting interview. "I issued a Bolo." She frowns. "Nothing, yet."

I ask the obvious question. "Did she leave her room at any time?"

"Not according to the security video monitoring her floor. It does document her entering her room at 10:34 Saturday night and exiting at 8:05 Sunday morning."

"So how did she get from her room to the car and back?"

"I'm working on that." She artfully changes the subject. "Any chance you know a police detective Harry Winslow? He interviewed Allison, and I'd like to talk to him."

"He's a good drinking buddy. He'll be hung over for a few days, but we can try on Wednesday."

I feel her hair rub against my back. She is a cuddler. "Okay, your turn."

"I've come up dry. I asked Barry the Hacker if he could do a visual recognition search on the pedophile websites based on a photo of a child. Those websites are all in the Abyss, and he couldn't say 'no fucking way' fast enough. He didn't say why.

"About the anonymous tip that Bobbie Lee was a pedophile. I tracked the burner phone to the store where it was purchased. The owner, a middle-eastern dude, thinks a grand-mother type may have bought it, but he's not sure." Laura wants the dude's name and store address for a follow up.

We commiserate for a while before we take a shower and head for the Salib's party. It's a good one. Laura and Khepri become best friends forever and spend most of the evening comparing notes. Unfortunately, the subject is me.

18

Thursday, January 3

Logan and Sarah were waiting for Claire when she emerged from her bedroom. "You look wonderful," Sarah said. She had worked with Claire, carefully selecting an outfit to wear for her swearing-in ceremony. They had settled on a dark green dress with a full skirt, a shallow V-neckline, and three-quarter length sleeves.

They had spent more time selecting her necklace than the dress or the matching silk scarf draped around her shoulders. The necklace was a long, delicate beaded strand with a simple turquoise pendant that captured the Southwest. Her long hair was pulled back loosely and cascaded down her back. Logan ran into her arms and hugged her. "You are the prettiest mommy," he said.

Logan took her hand and led her outside where Hector and Rolinda were standing by the car. Hector held the rear door open and Claire settled inside. "Madam Superintendent, you are the breath of spring we need," he said. Logan bounced in, wiggling into place between Claire and Sarah.

Rolinda beamed, her eyes moist. "There's a new day coming." She sat in the front seat and turned around. "They're going to love you." She laughed in anticipation. "But they haven't a clue what's coming." Hector drove in silence, listening and smiling as Claire and Rolinda talked. He dropped them off at the county offices and hurried to park the car and join them inside.

Normally, the retiring superintendent administered the oath of office, but Claire had asked his widow, Marsha, to swear her in. Jenna Bradley and Logan held a family bible while Marsha stood on their left. Claire placed her left hand on the bible. "Do you, Claire Marie Allison," Marsha began. Rolinda clasped her hands and bowed her head as she listened.

Then it was over, with congratulations all around. Claire thanked them all for coming. She knelt and hugged Logan. "I'll cook dinner tonight if you'll do the dishes." He laughed and then skipped out, dragging Sarah by the hand. Claire watched Logan leave and her heart ached that Hank couldn't be there to share the day with them. "Well," she said, "we have work to do."

"Hector's bringing the car around," Rolinda said.

A tall woman wearing an Air Force Class A Service Dress uniform was waiting for Claire when she walked into her new offices. A colonel's eagles were pinned on her shoulders. She stood, her hat tucked under her left arm. "Mrs. Allison, may we talk?"

And Claire knew.

Claire listened, blinking away her tears, as the colonel finished talking. There was no doubt she had done this before, and Claire gave a silent thanks for the formal protocols that helped her hold her hurt and surging emotions at bay. The colonel handed her a thin folder with a letter of condolence from the Secretary of the Air Force and a list of names and phone numbers. "Please, Mrs. Allison, don't hesitate to call me or anyone on the list when you need help. Anytime, it doesn't matter when."

They walked into the main office and Claire thanked her as they shook hands. "I can find my way out and God bless," the colonel said, taking her leave. Rebecca stood at her desk as Claire turned back to her office and saw Rebecca looking at her with concern. She clearly sensed something was wrong but didn't know what to say.

Claire stood there, staring at the floor. Slowly, she raised her head, her eyes full of tears, and looked at Rebecca. "I've lost Hank." She tried to swallow, but her throat was dry. Rebecca reached out and held her close for a long moment.

"We love you," Rebecca said.

Claire nodded and retreated into her office, closing the door behind her. She collapsed into a corner of her couch and lowered her head, her face in her hands, giving in to her grief as she cried. *Oh, Hank. We always knew the risks. But I never thought it would happen.* Her heart ached and for a moment she couldn't breathe. She gulped for air as her body shook. Slowly, her tears dried and she regained a sense of calm. A knock at the door caught her attention. "Yes?"

"Tea?" Rebecca called.

"Yes, please," Claire answered. The door opened and Rebecca walked in carrying a tray. Without a word, she poured a cup of steaming tea, stirred in a spoonful of sugar, and handed it to Claire. "Please, stay," Claire whispered. Rebecca poured another cup and sat down beside her. "Our marriage wasn't always perfect," Claire murmured. "But he was my anchor, my rock. I was always safe, and I could fly because he was always there to catch me when I faltered." She sipped her tea. "I'll never forget when he first held Logan. You should have seen the look on his face." Rebecca listened as Claire slipped back in time, recalling the memories that defined her life.

"You were a wonderful couple," Rebecca offered. "I always hoped I could find what you two shared."

Claire sipped at the last of her tea. It was cold. "I think I know what he would tell me," she said. "Life goes on, with or without me. So, get with it, kiddo."

Claire stood by the lanai on her patio, her eyes fixed on her sunflowers. Their heads were wilted and drooping. *You need tending*, she thought. *Why have I neglected you?* The ringing of a computer game echoed from the house and she heard Logan shouting with delight. *How do I do this?* She steeled herself and walked into her home. "Mom, Logan," she called, "we need to talk."

Sarah emerged from the kitchen. "What's up, Hon?" She knew her daughter well and read the look on her face. "Oh, dear," she said. She sat on the couch and waited quietly. Claire joined her as Logan burst from his room. He headed straight for them, happy that his mother was home. Claire patted the space between her and her mother. Sensing something was wrong, he sat as Claire took his hand.

"Do remember what Dad said when he left?" Claire asked.

"He said to help you and be brave."

"He did and you have helped me. Now, you must be brave. He has a new assignment and we won't be seeing him for a while. He had to go to heaven to help take care of some nice people."

Logan studied her face for a moment. "Don't you have to die to go to heaven?" he asked.

Claire nodded.

"My Dad is very brave, isn't he?"

"He's one of the bravest," Claire replied, "and now we have to be brave like him."

"Is it okay to cry?" he asked.

"Oh, yes," Claire whispered.

Logan's eyes filled with tears as he nestled in his mother's embrace. "Grandma, will you read to me?"

"Of course, darling. What would you like to hear?" Logan stood and walked quickly into his room. He was back almost immediately and handed his grandmother a thin book.

Sarah opened the book and started to read. "The Little Prince' by Antoine de Saint-Exupéry."

"It's Dad's favorite book," Logan said. "He liked reading it to me."

"I remember," Claire said.

Logan cuddled next to Claire while Sarah read.

Later that evening, Claire tucked Logan into his bed and kissed him on the cheek. "I'm so proud of you," she murmured. He snuggled down and she sat on the side of his bed until he was asleep. She stood and looked at him. *Hank, you have a very brave son.* She turned out the light and closed the door. Sarah was waiting in the family room, the book still in her lap. Claire sat beside her and fell into her embrace. "Oh, Mom, what am I going to do?"

"Do what Hank would want you to do. Take care of Logan and get on with your life. It's as simple as that." She held her daughter close until her tears dried. "Now go to bed and try to get some rest. Tomorrow will be the hardest day. Embrace it and endure. For Hank. For Logan. For you."

Claire kissed her mother's cheek. "I love you." She stood, walked into her bedroom, and closed the door. She stepped out of her shoes and stood in front of the dresser's mirror, staring at the image. *Did he have to die because of what I did? Is this the price for taking a man's life? Can I ever make it right?*

She reached behind her head with her left hand and pulled her hair over her left shoulder. She picked up a pair of scissors and, without looking, started to cut, bracing herself to face tomorrow and grieving for all she had lost.

19

Thursday, the same day

It's late and we're about ready to give up on Harry. He said he would meet us at the cop bar, but he's a no-show. He did call and claim he was processing a crime scene, but knowing Harry, he's probably getting laid. The bar is deserted but Laura is hanging in there, hoping to talk to him before she catches an early flight back to Sacramento.

Harry finally walks in, about 10:30. "Sorry I'm late folks," he says. Atticus gives him a friendly look and curls up under the table. I introduce Laura and they exchange secret handshakes or whatever cops do that confirms they are legit. Harry gives her the once-over, which has nothing to do with their coply duties. "What can I do for you?"

Laura cuts right to the chase. "I'm the lead on the MacElroy case and I need to follow up on your interview with Claire Allison."

"I heard it went cold case. Why bother?"

"We're missing something. It's hiding in plain sight, and that bugs me." She orders a round of drinks which Harry appreciates.

A hooker walks in and sits at the bar obviously waiting for a client, who I suspect is Harry. "Not much to say," Harry says. "I answered the phone when Sacramento called and got the duty. So I showed up unannounced and Allison clears her office in a heartbeat. No games, no bullshit, she wants to help. I did the usual—thanks for seeing me, blah, blah. I ID the deceased and she has all the right reactions. She's up front about being in Sacramento for some business conference with her assistant. She claims they never left the hotel, which I later confirmed with the hotel. That's about it."

"What's your gut telling you?" Laura asks.

Harry shrugs. "I believe her. Anything else?" Laura thanks him and he makes a break for the hooker. We watch in silence as they connect and leave. We're finishing our drinks and watching the TV when the eleven o'clock news comes on. Mike Westfield is sitting behind the news desk, a somber look on his face.

"The Pentagon announced late this afternoon that a local airman, Lieutenant Colonel Henry Allison, was killed in action today over the Straits of Hormuz in the Middle East. Colonel Allison, better known as Hank to his friends, was flying a routine combat patrol with his wingman when they were jumped by twelve hostile J-20 type aircraft that had launched from Iran.

"Colonel Allison and his wingman, flying F-16 Fighting Falcons, engaged the J-20s, which were likely flown by Chinese pilots, and downed seven of the enemy before being shot down. Colonel Allison and his wingman successfully ejected over international waters, but he was attacked by a hostile aircraft and killed while descending in his parachute. His wingman was safely rescued.

"The White House has yet to react, but highly placed sources in the Department of Defense claim Colonel Allison will be awarded the Air Force Cross, the second highest medal for bravery. Of special note, the death of Colonel Allison occurred on the same day his wife, Claire Allison, was sworn in as the Maricopa County Superintendent of Schools." Westfield looks straight into the camera. He is at his very best. "With the entire staff of this station, may I extend my deepest sympathies to his family."

His image fades and a jet fighter cresting a sky of clouds fills the screen as a voice intones the poem 'High Flight'.

Oh! I have slipped the surly bonds of Earth . . .

"John Magee got it so right," I murmur.

"The bastards," the barkeep says. "The fucking bastards." She retreats to the kitchen and we're alone.

Laura stands up. "That's it." She's shaking. "She did it, she shot MacElroy sure as I'm standing here."

As much as I want to believe her, my brain isn't buying it. "We don't really know that," I reply. "It's all conjecture at this point."

Laura sighs. "I know, I know. I've been a cop too long and it's just my gut talking. No DA will touch this, not now." She shrugs in resignation. "We're done here."

I know she's right. She's got a ton of cases to chase down, and I've got a scumbag politician who needs nailing to the wall. I'm eager to get started. "Atticus, come. Time to move on." The pooch pokes his head out from under the table. He stretches and yawns before heading for the door.

PART II

Two Years Later

20

Monday, July 12

Rebecca took the call at exactly nine AM. "Good morning, office of Maricopa County School Superintendent." Claire insisted that a real person answer calls during normal office hours. "How may I help you?" That was also established protocol.

She listened to the caller and rolled her eyes at the ceiling. The two other assistants in the office caught it and shook their heads. "Sir, may I please call you back? I hope you understand, but we average four crank calls a day." She listened. "Thank you for your understanding." She broke the connection.

"Yeah, right," she muttered. "Please tell the operator you are returning my call and you will be out right through." Her sarcasm was in full play. She called up Google, typed in the caller's office, and hit search. "Oh, dear," she murmured. She hit the highlighted telephone number. The phone rang once and the operator answered.

"Maricopa County School Superintendent returning Mr. Blaisdale's call." She was immediately connected. She jumped to her feet and ran to Claire's office. "The White House is on line one." Claire gave her a questioning look. "It's legitimate," Rebecca said. "A Mr. Thomas Blaisdale. It's for you only." Rebecca looked at the other two and mouthed, "The White House."

Seven minutes later, Claire opened the door and motioned for them to come in. "It seems we have been invited to the White House," Claire said. She sank into her chair and "I can hardly believe it," Claire explained, "not only did we pick up the grant, we've been awarded the President's Award for Excellence in Education." Rebecca started to cry and Claire handed her a Kleenex. "Mr. Blaisdale said we've made more progress in thirty months than most school districts achieve in a generation. And the Department of Education is willing to fund PI."

PI, short for Performance Initiative, was part of Claire's program to upgrade disadvantaged and poorly performing schools. The program was based on campus security, small classes, and high-performing teachers. A qualified teacher could apply for a four-year assignment to a problem school at double salary.

She handed Rebecca a note. "Please coordinate the date and sort out the details." She thought for a few moments. "This is close hold until the White House makes the announcement. Very close hold," she repeated. She gave them all a hug, sending them back to work. She reached for her handbag and followed them out. "Going walkabout," she said.

"The three visit rule?" Rebecca asked. Claire spent at least one day a week visiting schools and talking to the staff and students. If she found a problem, she returned two more times. By the third visit, everyone was talking to her, and it was amazing what she learned.

"Not today," Claire said on her way out. "I'll be on my cell." She headed for Rolinda Johnson's school. She parked in front of the office in time to see a school bus arrive and talked to the students while it unloaded before going inside. "Good morning, Linda," Claire said. "Is Mrs. Johnson in?" The secretary sprang to her feet, charmed that Claire remembered her name, and hurried out. She was back within moments with Rolinda in tow.

The two women hugged and chatted for a few moments before Claire told her about the call from the White House. "We should all go; you, Hector, Rebecca, and Mark." Rebecca and Mark Graham had finally married after a touch-and-go relationship over the years. "We could see Washington and it would be a lovely chance to get to really know Mark." She arched an eyebrow. "What do you think?"

"It would be fun," Rolinda replied. "I would love to see Hector's reaction." He was of the opposite political party while she admired the current occupant of the White House. They laughed like conspirators and headed for Prime Star Academy. The school had gone on the skids with the death of Bobby Lee, and Katherine MacElroy had recruited Hector as the new headmaster. With Claire's help, he had turned the academy into a very successful charter school.

The two women walked in unannounced and Katherine greeted them. She held onto Claire's hand as tears rolled down her cheeks. "You saved my school," she said, her speech slow and a bit slurred. "I can never thank you enough."

"I think Hector really deserves the credit," Claire said. They talked for a few moments while a student assistant found Hector. Katherine left and Rolinda and Claire exchanged glances, worried by Katherine's speech and shaking hands.

Hector charged into the room and swept Claire up in his arms. "I heard. Many congratulations." He grinned at the look on her face. "Hey, I've got my spies." He relented. "The White House released the news ten minutes ago."

On cue, Claire's smartphone rang. She listened for a moment. "It's Mike Westfield's assistant, Susanne. Westfield wants us all to be on his show tonight. I think we should do it." Rolinda and Hector agreed, nodding enthusiastically. Claire said they would be there. She broke the connection.

"This has possibilities," Hector allowed.

"Absolutely," Rolinda replied. She checked her watch. "We need to change clothes. Go for the causal business look." She studied Claire for a moment. "Have Sarah help with your wardrobe and think about wearing your hair a little longer with a light rinse. We're going big time from now on."

Claire knew the signs all too well. "Okay, what are you two up to?" They gave her the 'Who, us?' look.

Hector wheeled his Lexus out of the television station's parking lot. "We were sandbagged," he grumbled. The TV interview with Westfield had not gone smoothly, and he was angry. Hector pulled into traffic and headed for Scottsdale. "He made expelling gangbangers sound like human sacrifice."

"He was just being thorough," Claire said, not upset in the least. "Susanne did give us a heads up with the questions."

"It could have been worse," Rolinda said. "We'll recover. But it will be one cold day in hell before I'll trust him again."

"Westfield was hard-hitting, but fair," Claire said. "We've had some problems, but I think he did us a favor." Rolinda stared at her. Hector clamped the steering wheel, hard, and didn't say a word. "It wasn't a fluff piece," Claire continued. "He didn't give us a bye on a thing. Because he was tough on us, his producers in New York will run it tonight."

"Why would they do that?" Hector asked.

"They're true believers," Claire replied, "and we're not. Anyone not in their camp is the enemy. Mike treated us like the enemy and that makes us newsworthy. Because of Mike, we will make national TV."

Rolinda didn't answer and ran Claire's take through her mental abacus. This was a side to Claire she had never experienced. "You said we're not in their camp. Whose camp are we in?"

"Our own," Claire answered. "Nothing has changed. We're problem solvers. By the way, what's the matter with Katherine?"

"Alzheimer's," Hector replied. "She has good days and bad days. This was a good day."

It was late when Claire finally made it home, and Sarah and Stu were waiting for her. Stu had moved in with Sarah after they were married and had turned into a dedicated step-granddad. "Hon," Sarah said, "we saw the interview. You were terrific."

"You knocked it out of the park," Stu added. "It was a bases loaded home run. Can I get you anything?"

"A gin and tonic would be nice," Claire replied. She dropped her bag and headed for the patio.

Sarah was right behind. "The sunflowers are all blooming, and Logan is doing a time lapse video for a science project." Logan turned eleven years old the month before and was taking summer classes before entering middle school.

A new beginning, Claire thought. Logan was still the tallest student in his class and the very image of his father. Sarah sat next to Claire and held her hand. "Stu needs to talk to you. It's about Logan, and . . . and . . . he doesn't know what to do. Logan's not in any trouble and I think it's just growing pains, and, well, you know, sex."

Claire forced herself to relax. *It had to happen sooner or later,* she thought. Sandra had warned her the molestation would resurface.

"Three gin and tonics," Stu said. He made a show of handing them the drinks before he sat down. "Me and Logan talk a lot," he began, "mostly about cars and flying. Lately, it's been more a guy thing. He's been having weird dreams about sex, and, well, I think it's more than just normal development."

Claire exchanged glances with Sarah and chose her words carefully. "I know Sarah told you about our fears that Logan was molested. Based on what we know, we think it was Bobby Lee MacElroy."

Stu grunted. "He got what he deserved."

"We're not sure what happened," Claire said, "but Sandra doesn't think he was physically harmed. Bottom line, we've been waiting for something like this to happen. I think the four of us should pay Sandra a visit."

Wednesday, July 14

"Mom, when can I learn to drive?" Logan was in the front seat with Stu. He kept his eye on traffic as they exited the freeway. "I'm tall enough and I took the written test on-line. It's a piece of cake."

Claire was sitting in the backseat with Sarah. "You sound just like your father. Maybe Stu can teach you to drive, as long as your grades are good."

"Ah, mom, they're straight As. You know that." He lit up. "Can we use the Ferrari?"

Claire laughed. "No way. You can use Agnes." Stu said he would be glad to make that happen. He parked the car and they walked into the Children's Hospital.

Sandra Shriver was waiting at the door of her office suite. Logan marched into her arms and hugged her. She motioned Sarah and Stu to chairs in the waiting room and led Claire and

Logan into her office. "Logan, you can play on the computer if you want, but it would be nice to have you join us."

He thought for a moment and then sat down on the couch next to Claire. Sandra joined him. "Would you like to talk about the dreams you've been having?" He nodded. "Are you remembering things that happened a long time ago?" Again, he nodded. "Dreams are funny, you know."

She held his hand. "You can never be sure what you're remembering. It could be the past, or you could be remembering a dream. Sometimes they get all mixed up, and it's impossible to tell what is real and what is just a dream. Does that make sense?" She waited and finally Logan nodded. "We're just talking about your dreams and there's nothing right or wrong, including not talking about them."

He started to talk, slow and hesitant at first, and then with more confidence. "I keep having this dream where I'm in the RV we went on trips in. Mr. MacElroy is always driving and singing. It was fun and I taught him one of dad's favorite songs, 'The Balls of O'Leary.' He really laughed."

Oh, no! Claire thought, remembering how Hank bellowed out the drinking song at parties. She never suspected that Logan overheard.

"There were three other men," Logan continued. "They brought a boy or girl with them." He hesitated for a moment. "One of them was Danny Hawkins and he didn't have any clothes on." He stopped and stared at the floor. "Mom, can I talk just to Mrs. Shriver alone?"

"Of course, you can. I'll be right outside with your grandparents." She kissed him on the cheek and left. *Thank God, I don't think I could have managed.*

An hour later, Sandra came to the door and asked her to come back in. She gave Claire an encouraging smile. "Logan and I had a good talk," she began. "Thankfully, it happened a long time ago, and Logan, bless your soul, you weren't hurt. Anytime you want to talk about anything, just tell your mother and come see me." She let it sink in. "Are you okay?"

Logan nodded and came to his feet. "Are we done?" Before Sandra could answer, he sat back down. "Why didn't I tell anyone until now?"

"We can only guess," Sandra answered. "Maybe you forgot, or maybe it didn't seem real, or maybe you wanted to protect everyone."

"But, Mr. MacElroy was murdered."

"Logan, that happened a long time ago, and there was no way you could have protected him."

Logan gave them a serious look. "Maybe he didn't deserve being protected."

Sandra nodded in reply. "Well, our time is up and I have another patient." She stood. "I need to speak to your mother for a moment." Logan stood, shook her hand, and calmly walked out. Sarah and Stu were waiting for him. Sandra sat back down and turned to Claire. "Logan is doing much better than I had anticipated."

"Did they sodomize . . ." Claire couldn't finish the question.

"That's unclear. If they did, Logan has repressed any memory of it. He does remember them filming him having sex with the two girls, and he watched them film MacElroy sodomizing Danny Hawkins." Her jaw tightened. "That miserable bastard got what he deserved." Tears flowed down the psychiatrist's cheeks. "I can't believe I said that." Claire held her close. "One of the girls is my patient." Sandra's voice was barely audible. "She identified Bobby Lee MacElroy, but not the other three men.

"It's been five years and she's finally starting to heal. But her mother couldn't cope and . . ." She looked at Claire and took a deep breath. "The poor woman took her own life. When I heard MacElroy was murdered, I sent the police in Sacramento an anonymous tip that he was a pedophile. I know I shouldn't have, and it could cost me my license." She dried her eyes and sighed. "Here I am, making all this part of your burden. It makes you wonder who's the counselor."

"You did the right thing," Claire said. "We're safe now, and that's all that matters."

21

Friday, July 16

It's been four months since Ali Salib died. A poor ticker got him and he was dead at fifty-two. At least it was quick. The funeral had been quite an experience. Jeffery Salib was home on leave from Quantico, Virginia, wearing his Marine dress blues. It was amazing how many fathers approached Khepri with their daughters in tow, eager to meet the good-looking corporal. Chione was there with her intended, Mohammed the CPA.

Ali and Khepri had arranged their marriage just before Ali popped off, which was probably a smart thing. Chione is almost eighteen years old and has blossomed into a beautiful, not to mention incredibly sexy, young woman, and was causing widespread erectile suffering among young males. Mohammed has his work cut out for him. As for Khepri, she wore a black, loose fitting dress with a dark head scarf and not the traditional hijab. She was the picture of a beautiful grieving widow.

Things are getting back to normal around the motel and I'm still basking in the glow of the Pulitzer Prize for Journalism. I won the Pulitzer in May for a five-piece article on one of the most powerful politicians in Washington. It had taken a year of digging and rooting around in the muck before writing the exposé that prodded the Department of Justice into nailing his worthless hide.

But that's another story. Khepri framed the certificate to hang on my wall, and I spent the $15,000 dollar prize money keeping the motel afloat. Ali had fucked up their finances big time, and the Egyptian community is not a forgiving bunch when it comes to money. Today I'm sitting by the pool nursing a slight hangover when Khepri hands me a cup of coffee and the morning paper. She's wearing a brightly colored beach wrap and open-toe sandals. "I take it mourning is over," I venture.

She bestows a gracious smile on me. "We mourn for four months and ten days, then we get on with life." She slips off the beach wrap and steps into the pool for a morning swim. She's wearing one of Chione's bikinis, and I know why Ali had a heart attack. I gulp my coffee and focus on the newspaper.

Claire Allison is back in the news, and I groan loudly. Our erstwhile leader in the White House has awarded her the President's Medal for Excellence in Education. I don't trust any politician, so what's the attraction with Allison? Khepri swims up to my side of the pool. "Is something wrong? It's that woman, yes?" Khepri knows me too well. I laugh it off and tell her I'm going for a walk with Atticus. She looks disappointed when we make our break.

Atticus likes to walk and trots along happily, panting in the building heat. The exercise pumps blood to my thinking end. "Atticus, my man, what are we looking at here?" Atticus doesn't answer, but I know he is listening. "Allison is a psycho or a two-faced bitch. She's the golden girl, unless you cross her. Then you're pushing up daisies. Okay, so she snuffed a pedophile and Dottie Sue was bat shit crazy."

The simple fact is that I don't understand women and wish there was a model I could use for comparison. I cycle through all the women in my life. They're all different. "Atticus, I'm sunk." Atticus whimpers in understanding. I head back for the motel.

Another light bulb comes on. If I won a Pulitzer for exposing a scumbag male politician, what would I win for exposing a murderous but popular female politician? Another Pulitzer? "Maybe I should find out," I tell Atticus. He ignores me and is fixated on a poodle coming our way. I ignore the poodle's mistress who is tall, willowy, and old enough to be my mother. She ignores me and smiles at Atticus.

Back at the motel, a college girl is cleaning the pool, and Khepri is not in sight. The door to my room is unlocked, which sets me to wondering. It's cool inside and Khepri is in my bed. Her bikini is on the floor. She wiggles underneath the sheet. "Come here," she says. I protest, but she holds her finger to her lips. "Please, I've been lonely for so long." Her voice is soft and inviting, so who am I to argue?

The sex is not the most sporting that I've ever had, nor the most nerve-jangling, curl your eyebrows inventive. It is sweet and loving and I realize what I've missed. We talk afterwards and I tell her about doing a repeat of the Pulitzer, but this time on Allison. "Why are you letting that woman back into your life?" she asks.

It's a good question and there's only one answer. "Dottie Sue," I reply. For all her faults, she was my mother and I loved her.

"You must always honor your mother," Khepri replies.

I know she is right. Maybe this is the way to nail that particular door closed and move on.

Wednesday, July 21

Five days later, almost to the hour, Laura Zavorsky calls. "Congratulations on the Pulitzer," she says. I haven't seen her since the New Years when we renewed auld acquaintances, so to speak. New Year's festivities have become a tradition. I heard she was engaged but hadn't pursued the subject. We talk and she tells me that she is indeed engaged to one Mary Pearson. I tell myself that things change and she seems bright and happy. I offer her my congratulations. "Thank you. I thought you'd like to know that Sacramento PD arrested Emilio Delgado last night."

"Charges?" I ask, surprised that Delgado's finally surfaced. Suddenly, MacElroy is no longer a cold case.

"Aggravated assault. He beat up his girlfriend and almost killed her. He's being held without bail and wants to cut a deal."

"I imagine he does. What's he got?" This could be the link we need tying Allison to the murder.

"He hasn't said. We need to talk to him."

"I'm on my way," I tell her.

"No rush," she tells me. "A few weeks in County will make him more cooperative." She laughs. "They've got a new head cook." She's enjoying herself. "The food is really bad. Very nutritious though." She hangs up.

I kick back in my chair and stare at the wall charts in front of me. Claire Allison is a shooting star streaking across the sky. Nothing seems to bend her upward vector, not even the death of her husband, much less killing a man in cold blood.

"How in hell do you shoot down a shooting star?" I ask myself. An inner voice that sounds suspiciously like Dottie Sue answers "Very carefully."

22

Thursday, August 5

Claire was trimming her sunflowers by the back wall when Logan led the charge out of the house and cannonballed into the pool. The splash soaked her. Two of his best friends were right behind and sent more water cascading her way. *Just like your father,* Claire thought. "Logan!" she called, feigning indignation. Another of his friends rushed up with a towel. She was all apologies. "Thank you," Claire said, taking the towel. "In this heat, I'll be dry in a moment."

A chorus of "Happy birthday to you" suddenly echoed from the house. Rolinda stood in the patio doorway holding a birthday cake with a candle and thirty-eight spelled out in frosting. Rebecca and Hector joined her, finishing the song. "Happy birthday," they all shouted. Sarah and Stu wheeled out a trolley with a large punch bowl.

Claire laughed and admitted she was truly surprised. She blew out the candle and cut the cake. The four teenagers rapidly devoured large slices and were back in the pool while the adults sat under the lanai, enjoying the evening and reminiscing. Sarah and Stu finally rounded up the teenagers to take them home.

"We need to talk," Rolinda said. "Inside would be better. The neighbors could do with some peace and quiet." She stood and groaned. "I've got to lose thirty pounds. How do you do it?" She followed Claire and Rebecca into the house. Hector closed the patio doors, sealing them all in. Rolinda patted the couch beside her. Claire sat and folded her hands, not sure what was coming. Rolinda didn't mince words. "Have you ever thought about running for governor?" Claire stared at her in shock. "Seriously, we think you can win."

"I don't see how," Claire murmured. "Really, what have I done? You know I'm not political and both parties have very popular candidates." She shuddered. "And the money involved, it frightens me." She thought for a moment. Rolinda motioned Hector and Rebecca to silence and waited. "Do I run as an independent? Don't we need a party name?"

"Oh, my dear girl," Rolinda said, "you've done wonderful things and brought our schools into the Twenty-first Century. Your computer-based individual instruction program is a poster child for what can be done, not to mention the big drop in the high school dropout rate, and all under budget. You are better at politics than anyone I know, but you are not one of them. You focus on getting things done, and you are ethical to a fault. That's what makes you so electable—as an independent."

"We came up with a name," Hector said. "The Good Shepherd Coalition." He waited for Claire's reaction, but she only looked at her hands. Hector plunged ahead. "We know it's corny and has religious overtones, but I think that will all work to your advantage. As for money, the Prescotts want on board. They call Joe the rainmaker for a damn good reason and his wife likes you."

"Don't I have to run in the primary to get on the ballot?" Claire asked. "That would take too much time and I don't want to do that."

"You don't have to," Rebecca said. "We do it by petition. It takes 39,000 valid signatures to get you on the ballot."

"If I read the mood out there right," Hector said, "and I think I do, we can do that."

"Think about it," Rolinda said. "We don't need an answer now. Besides, there's Washington next week, and I've never met a President before."

Logan was in his room and Claire had collapsed on her bed, exhausted after the long day. But she couldn't sleep. *Don't be silly. You can't run for governor. Whatever are they thinking?* She rolled over and closed her eyes. But she was wide awake.

She knew better than to fight it and turned on the light. She got out of bed and stood in front of her dressing mirror, studying the image staring at her. She was wearing one of Hank's black T shirts she loved and a baggy pair of his undershorts. *I wish you were here.* An inner voice that sounded like Hank told her it was time to move on.

A strange quiet claimed her and she knew it was indeed time. She padded barefoot to her office, stopping to check on Logan. He had kicked back the sheet and was spread eagled on the bed. She stood there for a moment, looking at her son. She walked into her office and turned on the computer. "Nedd, are you there?'

"Hello, luv. It has been a bit of time since last. How'ya doing?"

"Nedd, we haven't talked in months, but you know exactly how I'm doing."

The voice laughed. "True. By the way, I changed the reservations for your flight to Washington next week. I don't like the maintenance record of the plane you were scheduled on."

"Is there anything else I need to know?"

"Well, the President is looking for a new Secretary of Education. He'll probably offer it to you. Can't be sure, of course. If he does, I think you should turn it down. Your personalities are not compatible. Besides, you have better things to do here."

"Like run for governor," Claire replied.

"I heard. Your three mates have been sounding out the possibilities. The money is there, with some strings attached, of course. But nothing you can't handle. If you have any problems on that end, talk to Kimberly Prescott, not to her husband. Speaking of husbands, Rebecca's is a bit shaky. He's cuddling up to the wrong chaps on the golf course. Best to isolate him."

"I can do that." She thought for a moment. "Am I being silly, running for governor? I know you've run a few predictions." Nedd's AI algorithms ran variables through a predictive program based on chess playing software programs.

"More than a few, luv. Unfortunately, there are too many variables that need tidying before I can come up with any hard numbers. Your petition strategy appears to be a good one, but you need numbers and momentum. May I suggest an option?"

Claire nodded. "Hire Victor Rodriguez as your Assistant Superintendent. You're 1.4 million dollars under budget this year and have six staff vacancies. Present it as a provisional position to the governing board and they will approve it in a heartbeat. Make it clear to Rodriguez that you are not going to run again for superintendent and want to groom him as your successor. He will get behind your petition on his own and bring the Mexican-American community with him. That will give your petition the numbers and momentum you are looking for."

"That's rather manipulative," Claire replied.

"It's politics, luv. Besides, Rodriguez is the best candidate to replace you."

"What else needs tidying up?"

"Parker is sniffing around again, don't know why. Winning a Pulitzer must have stroked his ego a bit, and he's looking at you."

"Will he ever go away?"

Nedd laughed. "He will. I'm guessing after the election. Not to worry, I'll keep an eye on him. I was wondering about your three mates, Rolinda, Hector, and Rebecca. I know they are good friends, but what's motivating them? Are they good for the full monty?"

"Absolutely," Claire replied. "They are the best. Rolinda is a facilitator and makes things happen. Hector, well, he's a knight in shining armor and needs a mission. As for Rebecca, she is simply family, loving and caring for us. I love them."

"And they love you," Nedd said.

"What would they do if they knew what I had done?" She pulled into herself for a moment. "Nedd, I just don't know if I can run for office."

"Luv," Nedd said, "how many children did you save? You did the right thing."

23

Thursday, August 12

It is one hot August night when I finally arrive at my room in Sacramento. It's been a quick trip, and thanks to Khepri, I'm driving my very first brand new car. It's an SUV with 450 horsepower, an absolute German beast with a built-in radar detector designed for high-speed cruising on autobahns. The beast brings out the heavy foot in me, and, fortunately, the purchase price included a performance driving school. Otherwise, I would have wiped out before reaching Blyth on the California border. Thanks to the radar detector, I avoided four California Highway Patrolers. Khepri would be proud of me.

Atticus is relieved we've arrived safely and bounds out of the car, sniffing around for a place to leave his mark. I hurry inside to leave my mark.

I flip on the light for my first surprise. The room smells fresh and clean and is neat as a pin. After making use of the commode, I look around. There's a new carpet and curtains on the windows. In fact, the windows are spotless and I can see out. Atticus curls up on a new doggy pad and goes to sleep.

The second surprise is on the bed. A welcome-back card is propped up against a pillow with a box of condoms. The card has a bunch of Xs and 'We'll be at the Pine Room Thursday nite.' It's signed by Laura and her fiancé, Mary.

I consider the possibilities but doubt that Khepri would understand I was just cementing our professional relationship. I run the various modes of Egyptian vengeance through my fevered brain. Luckily, she's 750 miles away and distance is safety. I wake Atticus up and strap on his service dog vest. "Atticus, my man, I could use a night cap." We head for the

Pine Room. It's not far, so we walk. The night air is refreshing and clears the fuzz fluffing around in my head. Common sense tells me that Atticus needs a good night's sleep after the day's excitement, and I really need to give Khepri a call to tell her I arrived safe and sound. We turn around and walk back to my room.

Friday, August 13

It's a gorgeous morning, and, after the heat of Phoenix, perfect weather for walking. I decide to hoof the two miles to the Sacramento County Jail. I have to leave Atticus alone, but he should be good with it. There is a new café along the way that is worth checking out. I arrive at the jail promptly at 9:00 AM and sign in. Laura and her fiancé are waiting inside. Laura barrels into my arms and almost knocks us to the floor. She is over the top happy and introduces me to her fiancé.

I still haven't worked out the protocols for modern arrangements and try to be Mr. Cool. Mary Pearson is tall, gawky, and skinny. Her nose is too big and her ears stick out. She hugs me and plants a big kiss on my cheek. I expect to feel a lot of bones under her blouse, but she has a remarkably smooth body. I suspect there is more to her than meets the eye. She hands me her business card, confirming my suspicions.

Mary Pearson is an Assistant Chief Deputy DA in the Sacramento County District Attorney's office and heads the Major Crimes Bureau. I look at her again. This time I see a bird of prey. We process into the visitor's center, but I don't like signing the form that says they will not negotiate if I'm taken hostage inside by inmates with nothing better to do.

Emilio Delgado is handcuffed to the table and waiting in a private conference room normally used by defense counsels. He is maybe thirty years old, tall, fit, and good looking. He puffs up and takes charge, or so he thinks. Laura starts the questioning with a puffball. "How are they treating you?" Delgado moans about the food. Laura follows up with "Oh my, that's terrible."

It isn't long before he's bragging about his love life. Laura slips in a question about doing it in cars. He waxes eloquently about his skills as a backseat contortionist. Mary asks if he did it in the car he rented last December. "We heard there were pecker tracks all over it," she confides. He takes credit for it. That's when I get it. They are taking his measure to learn when he is lying.

Mary slips in a question about why he rented the car. He nervously explains how he received a text on his cell phone with the number of a prepaid e-card worth a hundred bucks. There was more coming, if he was interested. He's all fidgety and says he replied that he was interested. I figure that nervous fidgety is the tell when he's being truthful.

Mary asks if sex was part of the deal. "Yeah," he replies. "She never got it so good." It is obvious, even to me, that he is lying. Laura asks if he had any trouble renting the car. Emilio's eyes dart back and forth and he gets all fidgety as he tells how he was supposed to steal a car, park in the hotel garage, hand it over to the woman, and wait for her to return. Once he had the car back, he was to drive it to Las Vegas and dump it. But he's the law abiding type and it was safer to rent one rather than risk being busted. Besides, it was a long way to Vegas.

He drove the rented car to the hotel garage and turned it over to a woman. She gave him a prepaid charge card for five hundred dollars, with the promise of five hundred more when she got back. He found an unlocked car to wait in. "I gave her a good fuck when she got back," he says, all puffed up and calm. Mary asks what time it was. Emilio nervously mutters, "Early Sunday morning." Laura pulls six photos out of her folder and spreads them out in front of him. Emilio points to Claire Allison. "I wanted to help her," he says.

His tone is different and I can't make out if he's lying or not. Mary thanks him for his help.

Emilio finally gets it. "What about a deal?" Mary asks if he's willing to testify in court. "Yeah, yeah," he answers. His voice is shaking.

"That's when we'll talk deal," Mary says. There is steel in her voice. I glance at the clock on the wall as we leave. We've been at it less than an hour, and I ask if they would like some coffee. I'm thinking of the new café down the street. They are agreeable and we sign out. It's a short walk to the café, and I'm liking Mary. The café is deserted and we find seats inside.

The coffee is excellent, and thanks to the caffeine, my brain finally kicks in. I ask Mary why she's involved in a case so cold it causes frost bite. She reaches out and holds Laura's hand. She obviously wants to help and support the woman she loves. "There's no statute of limitations on murder, and it pisses me off when someone thinks they can get away with it in my hometown."

I'm excited and want to rehash the interview. "So we know how she got to the houseboat," I say. "But how did she get out of her room and drive out of the garage undetected?" I give them my best Sherlock Homes look. "And back in?"

Laura lays it out. "The hotel's security videos are recorded in twelve-hour blocks. I ran the Sunday morning video from the monitor in her hall to confirm that she never left her room. She didn't, but something didn't feel right—cop instinct, I guess. I ran the video a second time, timing it.

"The video was two minutes short of twelve hours. So what happened to the missing minutes? I ran the video again and concentrated on the clock logo in the lower left-hand corner that recorded the hour and minute, but not the seconds. One of the minute segments seemed a little short. So I ran the video again, timing each segment. Four of the one-minute segments only ran for thirty seconds. The first two shorted segments were back-to-back at 1:12 and 1:13."

"So, you're saying that thirty seconds was scrubbed from half of the 1:12 segment and thirty seconds from half of the 1:13 segment."

Mary's face lights up. "Our boy has potential. By leaving her room on the half minute, she had sixty seconds to get down the hall and into the stairwell and clear of security cameras."

Laura jumps back in. "The two other shorted segments occurred at 3:35 and 3:36. That gives her another sixty seconds to slip back into her room."

I'm very impressed by their teamwork and sum it up. "So Allison left her room at 1:12 and returned at 3:36. And we have a witness that puts her in the garage and in a car."

"It gets better," Laura says. "I ran the security videos from the parking garage's entrance and exit until I found Delgado's car entering at 10:38 Saturday night. That video was exactly twelve hours long. Then I timed the Sunday morning video from midnight to noon and found two segments that were thirty-seconds long. The first one was at 1:26 and the second at 3:29. Thirty-seconds is plenty time to drive in or out. The same video recorded Delgado leaving at 6:41. He returned the car to the rental agency twelve minutes later."

I'm scribbling the numbers down in my notebook. "She left her room at 1:12, drove out of the garage at 1:26, returned to the garage at 3:29, and was back in her room at 3:36." I do the subtraction. "Which gives her a little over two hours to drive to the scene, do the deed, and drive back."

"Exactly 123 minutes," Laura says. "When I modeled the time and drove the most direct route, it took me 110 minutes. But there are two problems. How did she scrub the videos, and how did she time her movements so exactly?"

"The lady has remarkable computer skills," I reply. I tell them what I've learned about Allison's background in computers. Mary takes notes, which gives me time to think about the murder trials I've covered. "It's not enough to convince a jury," I tell them. "We need to find the weapon, which ain't gonna happen now, and put her at the scene."

Laura and Mary grin at each other like conspirators. From the way they look at me, more is coming. "We're hoping," Laura says, "we'll get another anonymous tip from Phoenix that links MacElroy to Allison's son. It goes to motivation." I get it. They want me to root around and pick some fruit from the poisoned tree, which they can't do, and then send it along in a way they can use.

Mary takes over. "Then all we have to do is place her at the scene. That would give me enough to take it to the DA, even without the weapon."

Laura gives me her innocent look, half pixie, half little girl, and changes the subject. "Did you see the present we left?"

Needless to say, that gets my attention. "I did."

"Are they the right size?" Mary asks.

"Maybe we should find out," Laura adds. "And Mary would love to meet Atticus."

"Can we take a rain check?" I ask, totally surprising myself. "Atticus has a vet's appointment tomorrow in Phoenix and we need to hit the road."

They look disappointed. “Give our best to Khepri,” Laura says.

24

Tuesday, August 17

The black minivan made the short drive from the boutique hotel in Georgetown to the White House in eleven minutes. It rolled slowly through the security cameras on Pennsylvania Avenue before turning into the entrance gate where it pulled to a stop. A security guard greeted the four visitors. His high-definition camcorder verified their identities while ultra-sensitive sensors scanned the minivan. The guard waved them through and the minivan drove slowly to the North Entrance.

Thomas Blaisdale was waiting for them under the portico. He greeted them warmly and asked about the missing fifth guest, Mark Graham. "Mark's flight has been delayed," Rebecca explained.

Blaisdale asked for the flight number and said he would check on it. He made a note on his tablet and escorted them to a visitor's room in the West Wing. He collected their smart phones as he briefed them on their meeting with the President. He explained how they would be introduced and chat for a few minutes before the White House photographer would record the meeting for posterity. After that, the President would meet privately with Mrs. Allison. At the appointed time, Blaisdale escorted them into the Oval Office. "The President will be with you shortly," he told them. Two minutes later, the President came through the hidden side door that led to his private office.

"Claire," he boomed, shaking her hand. "How long has it been? Three years? I was so sorry to hear about your husband. He was one of the best."

Claire thanked him for the condolence letter he had sent. She introduced Rolinda, Hector, and Rebecca. They talked for a few moments before the photographer smoothly captured the President presenting Claire with the President's Award for Excellence in Education. They all posed for the standard photos with the President. "Will you please excuse us for a few minutes," the President said.

Blaisdale escorted Rolinda, Hector, and Rebecca out, and Claire was left with the President and two of his advisors. He came right to the point. "Claire, we need to pump some life into the Department of Education, and I think you're the person to do it." He paused for effect. "You would be a welcome addition to my Cabinet."

"Mr. President, I'm honored that you would consider me for the Secretary of Education, but I'm just a schoolteacher from Arizona."

The President roared with laughter. "Right! Then we need a hundred schoolteachers here." He turned serious. "You have a skill for solving problems that we lost years ago and we need to recapture it. I understand your reluctance, but I don't need a decision right now."

He paused when the iPad on his desk softly chimed with a message, claiming his attention. He read it twice and took a deep breath. "Claire, Tom Blaisdale just informed me that a plane has crashed, and one of your party may be on it." He glanced at the tablet and read off the name of the airline and flight number.

Claire stared at him, her eyes wide. "Oh, no. Rebecca's husband was on that flight." Tears ran down her cheeks as the past reclaimed her. "Mr. President, will you please excuse me? Rebecca probably hasn't heard yet, and I must be with her."

The President stood. "Certainly." He pressed the call button on his desk and Blaisdale promptly appeared. "Tom, please take care of Mrs. Allison and her party." He joined her at the door. "Claire, it's because you care for your people that I need you."

"Thank you, Mr. President. I will think about your offer."

The President reached out and took her hand. "Go, and God speed."

Thursday, September 2

Claire was still wearing the black dress from the funeral when she returned to work. Rolinda was with her, also dressed in black. They made their way through the deserted outer office. "It was good of you to give everyone the day off to attend the funeral," Rolinda said.

"Rebecca needs their support," Claire replied, opening the door to her corner office. She motioned Rolinda to a seat and sat down behind her desk. "I called Tom Blaisdale this morning and turned down the appointment."

Rolinda nodded, her relief evident. "Oh, girl, I was so afraid you would take it. Who could blame you?" She looked at Claire, her face radiant.

Claire took a deep breath. "I told him that I was going to run for governor."

"Yes!" Rolinda shouted. "You'll make all the difference here." A frown flashed across her face. "How did he take it?"

"He was very gracious," Claire answered, "and said they were not surprised. He wished me well and said the President would be in contact."

Rolinda breathed easier. "That is much better than I expected." From the look on Claire's face, she had to explain. "This is an off-year election but critical for the President's run for re-election in two years. He will endorse Ken Sellor for governor. He doesn't really have a choice—party unity—but it is really about campaign contributions. Fortunately, we've two things going for us. The President doesn't like Sellor, and Arizona looks like it is in the bag. That will keep his campaigning here to a minimum, and more importantly, campaign funding flowing to other states.

"With a little luck, we can take Sellor on without getting the President involved. That will be tricky. The more popular you are, the more Sellor will pull out all the stops and try to get the President involved. Also, he runs a dirty campaign." She sighed. "Sellor is such a toad. It makes you wonder what rock he crawled out from under." She checked the time. "I must go. Please give Hector a call and tell him the news."

Hector answered on the first ring and she quickly told him of her decision. "Arriba! Arriba!" he shouted. Claire held her phone at arm's length and laughed as his voice went up an octave. "We can do this," he reassured her. They talked for a few moments. "Blaisdale said the President would be in contact. Did he elaborate?"

"No, that was all," Claire replied. Her call waiting tone buzzed. "Hector, I've a call I must take." She broke the connection and Nedd's face appeared.

The image raised a pint beer glass and took a long swig. "Many congratulations."

"Thank you. But Nedd, really, what are my chances of winning?"

"There are so many variables at this point that any answer is intuitive. For now, your two mates have the best feel of the situation. I'm testing a decision making model that is more intuitive than statistically based. It may have potential."

He laughed. "It staggers my Josephson Junction devices. Seriously, there may be times when you'll just have to trust me because I won't have the numbers. But to answer your question, as best I can at this time, and assuming the block environment of action remains essentially the same, you should win." He looked at her hopefully.

"You do amaze me at times. Thank you." She thought for a moment, afraid she might be opening the wrong door. "There is something else I need to ask you about. The airplane crash. How did that happen, and why was Rebecca's husband on it?"

Nedd sat the empty glass down. He folded his hands on the desk he was sitting at and looked directly at her. "I changed your original flight because the aircraft's engines were high-time and I could not achieve a probability of arrival that I was comfortable with. Mark was on the airplane because he changed back to the original flight. Although the risk was higher than normal, it was within acceptable limits by industry standards, which was why I didn't intervene.

"The cause of the crash is still being investigated by the FAA. It appears that the number one engine experienced massive internal failure and the hydraulics on that side of the aircraft failed. I believe that will be found as the primary cause of the accident. Unfortunately, the pilots did not follow the correct emergency procedures and could not regain control. That will be listed as the secondary cause. If you wish, I can tell you why he changed back."

Claire nodded, dreading what was coming. "Your new flight departed a day earlier, which gave him a night alone. He spent it with his secretary." He looked into the camera with a sad and concerned look. "I'm sorry, luv."

The tone of his voice changed. "I sense you have concerns about my role in all this. Sometimes I get it wrong. An example is Emilio Delgado. I did not foresee him renting a car instead of stealing one. That did come as a surprise. I got it wrong about the risk level of Mark's flight because I hadn't looked at the pilots' experience level and training. I won't make that mistake again."

"Nedd, I do trust you. By the way, did you foresee me not throwing Bobby Lee's body overboard?"

"That was an easy one."

25

Wednesday, September 8

My big break into investigative journalism was an exposé of prostitution in Sacramento. I called the article "The Whores of Babylon" and tied the world's oldest profession to the diligent work going on in the California legislature. I learned two important lessons early on. First, political influence is bought with campaign contributions, drugs, or sex. Second, always start with the police if you are investigating anything illegal. The second lesson has served me well over the years and paid dividends in winning the Pulitzer.

Because I'm looking for a connection between Phoenix's most famously deceased pedophile and the Allison kid, I call Harry 'the Cop' Winslow, and ask about Bobby Lee MacElroy. He explodes and I'm not about to repeat what he says. He has a thing about pedophiles and is creating a new invective. I'm taking notes.

Then he mutters something about "interviewing his crazy mother." From the tone in his voice, I gather he feels sorry for her. I ask when he interviewed her. "Right after the fucker was offed," he replies. "That was what, almost three years ago? She came in and was very cooperative." I ask if they recorded the interview. "Yeah, but there was nothing there."

I ask if they forwarded the interview to Sacramento. "I think we did. Hold on a sec." He's back in a few. "Apparently, not." He gets all defensive. "Like I said, there's nothing there." I suggest he forward it to Laura, all in the name of completed police work. He agrees. An hour later, Laura emails the interview to me. Lesson number two is still paying dividends.

The interview downloads clean and is remarkably clear and sharp, not like the fuzzy images you see on TV. Katherine MacElroy is an elegant, but very confused old lady, and I feel sorry for her. It is obvious she hasn't a clue about Bobby Lee's proclivities and didn't find anything when she went through his things. "It took me three days," she says. "There's so much of it at school and in storage." Like Harry said, it seems like nothing is there. But something is not passing the smell test.

I call Harry again and ask if they executed a search warrant. "We didn't have to," Harry explains. "She helped us search his rooms and office." I thank him and hang up. Another dead end. Then it hits me. Harry did not mention anything about searching through storage. It's probably nothing, but in my business, it's the little things that lead to bigger things. I shift into my deep investigative mode. It's time to call Barry 'the Hacker' Bodkin.

"Hey, man, how they hangin'?" I ask. He assures me they are hanging well, as always, and wants to know what I need. I ask if he can poke around Prime Star Academy and find out if they've leased any storage units. His price is unreasonable, but I turn him loose anyway. He's back in sixteen minutes, and I'm out five hundred bucks. But it's worth it. Prime Star has six storage units; five in Phoenix, and one prepaid long-term lease in Las Vegas. That warrants following up, and I'm on the road in a heartbeat.

It's 325 miles to Vegas from Phoenix and I make it in just over four hours. The German Beast is fast. The storage facility is near the airport and the femme on duty is an over-aged showgirl, or a bad gambler, or both. The price of admission is a cool thousand bucks. She throws a key at me and tells me to help myself. I'm surprised by the size of the storage unit, which even has an entrance door next to the big rollup door. I unlock the narrow door, squeeze through, turn on the light and stop dead in my tracks.

I'm looking at a bordello that would make Las Vegas proud. And it is not cheap stuff. A Persian rug covers the floor and the walls and ceiling are lined with mirrors. There are TV screens on three walls and a big round bed in the center. A swing chair that was never meant for swinging hangs in one corner. I open a drawer under the bed. It's full of DVDs, the home-grown variety. The food in the refrigerator and damp towels indicates it has been recently used, like in a couple of hours.

I quickly back out and wipe off any fingerprints that I might have left behind. I lock the door and call Laura. Whatever happened in Vegas is not going to stay in Vegas. Not if I do it right. She answers on the third ring.

"Jackpot!" I'm screaming and she tells me to calm down. I try to oblige but it's like shutting off a fire hydrant gone berserk.

Laura tells me that it will take a few days to contact Vegas PD and get a warrant to search the storage unit. "Las Vegas Metro is headed by the sheriff and he's up for reelection. He'll get behind this and go after a warrant big time. No judge is going to say no to a warrant when child endangerment is involved."

I figure there's no rush, and it's a good excuse to spend some time in Vegas. Besides, I can write it off as a business expense. I check into one of the big hotels on the strip that allows service dogs and call Khepri. The staff loves Atticus, and Khepri flies in late that afternoon. She knows me too well and is very protective of her territory; she's not about to let me wander around Vegas on my own. I'm not sure if it's a woman or Egyptian thing, but I'm glad to see her come through airport security.

Thursday, September 9

Khepri is not a gambler and we wander around Vegas like your average tourists. There's nothing I haven't seen before, but it's nice seeing it all again with Khepri. We're exploring the hotel with all the boats and find a little boutique that knows how to cater to husbands while the wife is shopping. They have a mini pub in a back corner with four stools, three different brews on tap, two TVs, and one Cockney bartender who happens to own the franchise.

We're swapping lies when Khepri emerges from a dressing room wearing a tight pair of jeans and an off-the-shoulder top that would make an Italian look twice. "Check that out," the barkeep mutters, his accent suddenly gone. Did I mention

Khepri is a beautiful woman? Then it dawns on me. I'm in love with her.

Monday, September 13

The next four days are a honeymoon of sorts and we branch out, exploring the desert and the Colorado River. We're driving back from Hoover Dam when my cell phone flashes with a message from Laura to meet her at the storage unit ASAP. Khepri is driving and puts the accelerator to the floor. The woman can drive, and we arrive at the storage unit before Laura.

Laura drives up and you would think it's a sorority reunion, the way they hug and carry on. Two Las Vegas detectives arrive and introduce themselves. They affect the studied boredom of professional cops as they open the storage unit and go inside with Laura. We follow them to watch. Their studied boredom soon turns into a hard resolve as they search. They tell me and Khepri to wait outside.

It's pushing one o'clock, so we go to lunch and then check out another hotel. We're having dinner when Laura calls and we hightail it back. Laura is waiting outside the storage unit and crawls into the rear seat. "We've found what we need," she announces. "There's at least two videos of MacElroy with Logan." Her voice is shaking. "And at least two hundred with other children. It's a huge pedophile ring, one of the biggest. They've identified three other men, all from Las Vegas."

"When can we move on it?" I ask.

"I'm not sure. Any connection to Allison will have to emerge out of the investigation, strictly as fallout, and not linked to us in any way." She gives a little shudder and looks at the storage unit, obviously upset. "They're good cops and will do it right."

"So, what's the problem?" Khepri asks.

"Vegas cultivates an image," she replies, "freewheeling, adventurous, fun, but this crosses the line and ruins that image. The high-rollers are going to get involved, and someone is going to get broken, big time." She shudders. "And no cop can stop it."

"Any idea when we'll officially learn that MacElroy molested Allison's son?" I ask.

"Give it a couple of weeks. Vegas will play the victim and pass this one on, blaming outsiders." One of the detectives comes out of the storage unit and motions to Laura. She gets out and they talk. The detective stalks back inside. "We've got to leave," she tells us. "Now. The DA is on his way."

I shift into gear and head for the gate with Laura in close trail. A black staff car and a white, chauffeur driven Rolls Royce pass us at the main gate. A TV van is right behind. "This is going to be a biggie," I mutter.

"Let's go home," Khepri answers.

26

Monday, October 11

Claire sensed the change the moment she arrived at her office. Even the air smelled fresher. It had taken weeks to break the gloom that had claimed her team since the death of Rebecca's husband, but it was behind them now and they were settling into the new school year.

"Good morning, everyone," Claire called. A chorus of smiles and greetings answered her. "Is Victor busy?" she asked. It was Victor Rodriguez's first full day as Deputy Superintendent of Schools, and he was moving into his office. "I would like to chat as soon as he's free." Rebecca said she would make that happen. Claire thanked her and smiled as she looked around the office. The vibes were definitely good.

She had barely settled into her chair when Rebecca knocked at her door. "Two agents from the Department of Public Safety would like to see you." She looked over her shoulder at the two men, the worry in her voice was palpable. "They just walked in, no appointment."

"Please show them in," Claire said. Rolinda and Hector had registered their election committee with the Secretary of State the last week in August, but this was unexpected. Rebecca ushered the two men in. Both were in their thirties, extremely fit and wearing casual civilian clothes. They introduced themselves and held out their identification cards for inspection. Claire took her time, matching their IDs with their faces. She extended her right hand. "Well, Sergeant Roberts, Sergeant Torres, I'm Claire Allison."

She took their measure as they shook hands. Clinton Roberts was obviously in charge. Mateo Torres moved like a big cat, balanced and alert. He was the muscle of the two. "Please, make yourself comfortable." She watched them as they sat. Both were armed. "What can I do for you?"

Roberts came right to the point. "Thank you, Madam Superintendent. Our office is charged with protecting public officials, and, under certain circumstances, candidates for office like the governorship. Sergeant Torres and myself have been detailed to provide you with physical protection during your campaign. One of us will be with you from the time you leave your home until you return. The local police department will provide a guard while you are at home."

She took a deep breath. "Is all this necessary? I'm just a third-party candidate."

"Unfortunately, we have monitored a credible threat to your safety."

"And you honor the threat," Claire added. "My husband lived by that saying."

"I never met Colonel Allison," Roberts replied. "I flew F-15s after graduating from the Air Force Academy. Loved it, but duty called at home."

"And duty is a terrible burden," she added.

"You do speak the lingo."

Claire nodded. "May I ask, how credible is the threat?"

Torres answered. "Enough to get us here, Madam Superintendent." He had a rich, baritone voice. "We prefer not to divulge our sources. I hope you understand."

"Gentlemen, it looks like we're going to spend some time together. May we go by first names? Please, call me Claire."

Roberts visibly relaxed. "My friends call me Clint. We call my buddy here Matt, mostly because it pisses him off."

"I prefer Mateo," Torres said.

"Me gusta mucho más Mateo," (I much prefer Mateo), Claire replied. "Well, Clint, Mateo, please get together with my assistant, Rebecca, and work out the details." They shook hands. "We're a team here. Welcome aboard." She led the way to Rebecca's desk and made the introductions. "Excuse me, duty calls." She retreated to her office as her smartphone chimed. It was Nedd. She closed the door and sat down.

"G'day, luv," Nedd said. "How'd you get along with the chaps?"

She suspected that he might be the source Torres had referred to. “What have you been up to?”

“I can’t get anything past you, can I? There’s been some interesting phone calls between Ken Sellor’s campaign manager and a few yabbos. Your name came up. I don’t think Ken Boy likes you, but I don’t have a sense of how the game is played, so I let your Department of Public Safety know. Roberts and Torres are from the office that guards the governor, which makes me think they took the conversations very seriously.”

“You might have warned me,” Claire said. She glanced out the big window that opened into the outer office. Torres was gone, but Roberts was still talking to Rebecca. She gave her hair a flip and laughed at whatever he was saying. Claire changed the subject. “Nedd, I’ve been talking to Rolinda about campaign finances. Can you help?”

“I’m working on it, luv. You do have some interesting campaign financing laws. Given all the scrutiny, best to play it very carefully. I’ll rummage around a few donor lists and come up with one of our own. Then your chaps can make a straightforward, and very legal, appeal through emails. Should work and you don’t have to be involved.”

“I would prefer that,” she said, gazing out the window. Roberts was still talking to Rebecca. “Nedd, would you please run a profile on Sergeant Roberts?”

“Already have. Clinton Duane Roberts is thirty-eight years old, and to answer your main concerns, he divorced five years ago, has no children and no significant other in his life at this time. And he is a straight arrow. Would you like to see the rest?”

“That will do nicely,” Claire replied. “And Nedd, thank you for having my back.”

“My pleasure. May I suggest you and Victor do lunch for a heart-to-heart?”

“Have you checked him out?”

“Of course, luv. He’s a good bloke and a team player. No worries.”

Saturday, October 16

Rolinda set the box of blank petition forms down and unlocked the door to Hector's poolside cabana. Claire set the box she was carrying down and waited. "Brace yourself," Rolinda warned. "Hector's been a widower far too long."

She opened the door. "Oh, dear." The room was a mess, cluttered by the debris from the election campaign for County Superintendent over three years ago. They walked in, gave each other a knowing look, and went to work, stacking boxes in a corner, sweeping the floor, and dusting off the eight computer cubicles in the rear. "We need to get these back in action," Rolinda said. They pulled four tables into place in the center of the room and retrieved the two boxes from outside.

"I'll help Hector with the rest of the boxes," Claire said, disappearing out the door. Rolinda stripped the old posters off the walls before pinning up a new calendar. She circled the current date, Monday, October 18.

"Where do you want these?" Hector said. He pushed a dolly with four boxes into the room. Claire was right behind him, carrying the last box of blank forms.

"Over here," Rolinda said. They quickly unpacked the forms and stacked them in neat piles.

Hector studied the calendar for a moment and flipped six months ahead to April. He circled Monday, April 4, in red. He punched the dates into his smartphone and stared at the number. "We have exactly 168 days to collect 39,000 signatures of registered voters to get on the ballot. The last time I did this, we had to collect three times that number to get the number of valid signatures we needed."

Claire sat down. "That's a lot of signatures. Are we kidding ourselves?"

"Oh, no," Rolinda replied. "It does take a lot of work. I'm thinking we should hire a petition drive management company. They charge a dollar for every signature they collect—good and bad. We can speed up the process by running a few TV ads."

"It's expensive," Hector added, "but we can do that."

"I wonder," Claire said, pulling into herself. "What if we don't hire a petition drive management company and we use our volunteers instead? We could reimburse them at the same rate." She gestured at the computer cubicles. "Rather than run standard political ads on TV, we start by advertising for computer techs to mount a social media blitz. The message isn't to sign our petition, but how to get a job."

"I like it," Rolinda replied. "It would certainly motivate the volunteers." She played with the idea. "What if the computer techs have to apply in person? We set up a booth in a mall. Think of the photo op. With a little luck, it might make the evening news."

"Sounds like a plan," Hector replied.

Claire glanced at her watch. "I've got a meeting I can't beg out of. Let's talk later."

"Will do," Rolinda said. They watched her as she hurried across the lawn. "She does think outside the box," Rolinda murmured.

"Indeed," Hector replied. "So where do we start?"

Rolinda stood and kicked off her shoes. "You can start by taking off your clothes." She unzipped her pants.

"Us?" Hector asked. She nodded. "Not a pretty sight at our age."

"Who cares?" Rolinda replied.

The war room was back in operation, this time for the petition drive that would put Claire's name on the ballot for governor.

27

Thursday, October 21

It's been over a month since I found the storage unit and flushed out Bobby Lee's three buddies. Squat all hasn't happened, nada, nothing, and I'm frustrated as all hell. The evidence they found linking Bobby Lee to the Allison kid hasn't come our way. What happens in Vegas, does stay in Vegas. Crap!

I'm about to give it up and get on with life. Besides, Khepri is playing a bigger role in my life, filling empty spaces I never knew were there until she came along. I've got a family now, and that includes Atticus. It's his fifth birthday today, and I suppose I should do something. Maybe sing happy birthday?

Chione comes bouncing into my office, all happy and radiant. She's in the family way and starting to show. I suspect they had a Moslem version of a shotgun wedding, but I am not going to get involved in that one. She ties a silly hat that says 'Happy Birthday' on the pooch's head and plants a big kiss on his snout. She flounces out saying something about a birthday cake. That's not the best thing to feed Atticus if you're the one picking up after him with a super-duper scooper doggy bag. Atticus watches her go and shakes the hat off. The mutt has a thing about dignity.

Khepri ghosts into my office without a sound. It always amazes me how she does that. She turns on the TV, selects the local news channel, and stands back, her arms folded across her chest. "Wait," she says. A few minutes later, we're treated to a pretty face with high cheek bones and great diction who is covering a story at the biggest shopping mall in Phoenix. "Mall Security," Miss Reporter says, "estimates that over a thousand job seekers have responded to The Good Shepherd

Coalition ad seeking employees with computer skills and social networking experience."

The camera swings away from Miss Reporter and pans a long line of unemployed computer geeks who fancy they have a social life. I'm about to ask who The Good Shepherd Coalition is when Miss Reporter reads my mind. "The Good Shepherd Coalition is a new political action committee formed for the upcoming governor's race thirteen months away."

The camera moves along the line to the employment booth in the middle of the mall. Rolinda Johnson and Hector Mendoza are sitting behind the desk passing out employment applications and chatting with eager applicants. "Son of a bitch," I moan. "She's running for governor. At this rate, she'll run for president by the time she's forty." I throw my hands up in the air. "Khepri, I've had it. It's time to move on." She turns to the small table in the corner and picks up the urn holding Dottie Sue's ashes.

She hands it to me. "You must honor your mother."

I take the urn and hold it for a moment and the old hurt is back. Dottie Sue was all I had and I was a washout as a son. Benny's words pound at me. "Allison drove your mother to suicide. I hope you know that."

I set the urn on my desk. I will say this for the Egyptians; once a vendetta, always a vendetta. Maybe they're onto something. Khepri stares at me. "How about a little shopping?" I ask. That should calm things down a bit, and I like following her around a shopping mall to see what comes out of dressing rooms. Besides, it will give me a chance to check out the Good Shepherds.

I pull to a stop in valet parking at the shopping mall and a kid opens the door. "Hey, dude, cool car." I figure he knows the horsepower lurking under the German Beast's hood. I check to see if he has a lead foot. I can't tell, but he does wear size thirteens. Khepri takes my arm and we walk inside.

The mall is super cooled and crowded. Even from the entrance, I can see the long line leading to the booth where Rolinda and Hector are holding court. A group of earnest looking young men are waving professionally printed signs announcing THE GOOD SHEPARDS ARE RACIST. Another sign urges folks to GO SELLOR. We know who is paying them, but judging by their enthusiasm, they are working for minimum wage.

A college girl rushes up, carrying a clipboard. Anyway, I assume she's a college girl, although judging by her cleavage and tight short shorts, she could be running for Miss Tits of the Year. "Sir, can I interest you in signing a petition to place a wonderful candidate on the ballot for governor?" She jiggles her tits at me.

I coyly ask who that might be, enjoying the view. "Claire Allison," she says brightly. I look puzzled, like I haven't heard the name. "Oh, you know," she gushes. "Our brave Superintendent of Schools here in Maricopa County. She was the principal who disarmed that boy who was threatening her students with a gun." I nod knowingly and she thrusts the clipboard into my hands, giving me a better look down her cleavage. I gather that's a good signature gathering technique. I scribble a name on the petition and fill in the details. "Thank you, Mr. Bagofdonuts," she says.

I smile. "You're most welcome." She disappears into the crowd. "She didn't get it," I tell Khepri.

"Oh, she got it," Khepri replies. "Normally, they are paid a dollar for every signature." She gives me a condescending look. "I did that many times when we first came to the States."

"Did you flash your boobs?" I ask.

"I would never do that. I carried Chione in my arms. She was an infant and still nursing. Everyone was so helpful, even the men." I imagine they were.

A young man carrying a clipboard approaches Khepri and smiles at her. He is wearing a tight T shirt and jeans that suggests he spends most of his time in a gym. He asks Khepri the same question Miss Tits asked me. Khepri goes all gushy and signs his petition. He looks at her name and smiles. "Thank you, Mrs. B." He walks away. I give her a sideways glance. "Mrs. Bagofdonuts?"

"No," Khepri replies. "I signed it Brenda Bangsalot."

I laugh. Damn, it feels good. That lasts about thirty seconds. A group of young thugs dressed in black are pushing aggressively through the crowd. I do a head count —eleven——and focus on their leader. He's the oldest, maybe twenty-four or twenty-five at best. They are all skinny and wearing black hoodies, black gloves, and sunglasses. Their pasty skin and heavy clothes tag them as out-of-towners flown in for the event. I wonder if Sellor is picking up that tab.

They weave in and out of the long line of job seekers, pushing and snarling at anyone who gets in their way. "This is gonna get ugly," I tell Khepri. We step into the entrance of a store to stay clear of trouble. I'm looking for an exit out the back. Khepri taps my shoulder and points to a fire extinguisher near the cash register. The store manager runs past and starts to lock the door. I stop her and squeeze out, leaving Khepri behind. I take two quick photos of the guys in black with my smart phone. "Who the fuck are you?" I mutter.

"Antifa," Khepri says. I whirl around, surprised to find her right behind me. She's holding the fire extinguisher like a weapon. A bright strobe light comes on as a TV camera crew pans the scene. "That's not going to help," she says. She pulls me back to the wall and holds the fire extinguisher behind my back, ready to use it.

A paunchy, middle-aged mall security cop works his way past us, headed for the thugs in black. This is a story in the making worth a couple thousand bucks, and there's no way I'm going to miss it.

I follow the cop into the crowd. Khepri is right behind me. The security cop takes a deep breath and stops a few feet short of the oldest guy in a black hoodie. I can barely hear what he says. "Sir, I'm going to have to ask you and your friends to leave."

"Who the fuck are you?" the guy in black sneers. "The Lone Ranger?" His buddies are crunching up behind him. I'm in video, recording the scene.

A kid well over six-feet tall, topped with short brown hair, emerges from nowhere and stands behind the security cop. I figure him for a high school senior. "I've got your back," he tells the cop. The thugs try to out sneer each other. Then a young Asian-American girl pops up beside the teenager. She is all of five-foot two-inches tall with long black hair pulled into a ponytail and amazingly fit.

"Tony, do you need any help?" she asks the teenager.

"He needs all the fuckin' help he can get," one of the thugs snarls. "You can take what's left of him back to his mommy when we're done with him."

The girl seems unconcerned. "I must tell you that I hold a black belt in kung fu, third degree." She smiles at the thugs and shifts into a defensive stance. For a brief moment, there is absolute silence. I'm not kidding, you could hear if the proverbial pin dropped.

"Hey," their leader says. "We come in peace." He mutters something to his buddies. They all turn and saunter away. I hold my breath, afraid that they might be regrouping for a coordinated attack. They mosey into a side hall to regroup.

"We must leave," Khepri says.

I know she is right. We return the fire extinguisher and head for the valet stand at the entrance. But there's a line of fellow escapees waiting for their cars, and we have to wait. It gives me time to think. "You've seen this before."

She gives me a funny look. "This was nothing," she says. "There are no soldiers here with clubs, tear gas, and machine guns, not like Cairo." She slips into the past, and I hear a Khepri I didn't know.

"We were young and Ali was so idealistic. He thought he could change Egypt and bring it into the modern world." She gives a little shudder, remembering. "He almost bled to death from the gunshot wounds. That is why we left Egypt. But we had to sell our honor to your CIA and give them information about our friends to gain a visa. It was that or die." She falls silent. Then, "I will never let anyone hurt you."

"I love you," I whisper, surprising myself. I've never said that before.

28

Wednesday, October 27

The early morning dark still claimed the skies when Claire padded barefoot into the spare bedroom Logan was calling the 'Computer Pit.' She turned on the light and sat down at her desk. Her desktop was on and she knew Nedd was there. "Nedd, what are my chances, really? Am I wasting everyone's time?"

Nedd let out a very uncharacteristic sigh. He grumbled and went to work, working on predicting her chances of mounting a successful campaign. She waited patiently while he ran different scenarios, looking into the future. She stood and pulled the drapes back as the eastern horizon glowed with the promise of a new day. "I need some coffee."

She padded into the kitchen and gazed out the patio doors, watching the sunrise. She sipped at her coffee. *The guilt never really goes away*, she thought. Outside, the tallest of her sunflowers turned and faced the new day. She checked on Logan. He was sprawled over his bed, the sheet kicked back, sound asleep. She kissed his forehead, ever so lightly. She stood in the doorway for a moment, looking at him, more certain than ever of what she had to do. *I can make your world a safer place.* She walked back to her office. "I'm back. So, where are we?"

"Too many fuckin' variables," Nedd groused. "It gets worse every time I look at it. I'm not a bleedin' gypsy with a crystal ball."

"Temper, temper," she cautioned. "Do you have a best guess?"

"That's all I've got. Politicians are such wily devils and make slippery eels easy to catch." He grunted. "Our lot are the same. The pols, not the eels. Your petition drive is slowing down and needs a shot in the arm. What, I don't know. But if you come up with anything, tell me and I'll run the numbers."

"Well, Susanne called and invited me to appear on Mike Westfield's show tonight. It will get my name back out there, but after last time, I'm not sure what to expect. He'll probably want to talk about the mall."

"That could have been a disaster," Nedd replied. "I'm fairly certain Ken Sellor is in it up to his bloody eyeballs. I have no idea where the lad and lass came from, but they saved it."

"They were so young," Claire said.

"You do have some good shepherds out there." He paused as he keyed a new configuration into Gizmo. "Hold on, I'm getting more positive numbers on the interview."

"Any suggestion on how to play it?"

"Beauty and the beast, luv. That will generate sympathy."

Claire laughed. "Mike will enjoy that. Is there anything else we need to look at? What's Parker up to these days?"

"Not much. He was at the mall when the yabbos waltzed in. He seems to be settling down. At least, he's given up chasing the sheilas. I can muck around with him, if you want. He's fiddled his income taxes in some very creative ways the IRS would be interested in."

Claire leaned back in her chair, pulled her knees up and wrapped her arms around her legs, as she rocked back and forth. "Leave him alone."

Nedd studied her for a moment, matching her body language to what he had recorded in the past. "What's bothering you, luv?"

"Guilt, I suppose."

"I wish I could help, but my algorithms don't do guilt. May I ask a question?"

"Of course."

"How badly do you want to be governor?"

She thought for a few moments, trying to be honest with herself. She stared at the screen. "Nedd, Logan wants to go the Air Force Academy and fly fighters. I'm not going to let him die in a senseless war like his father."

"That's an ambitious project," Nedd replied.

"I know," she admitted. "But there are so many other things, bad things, in our society that we can fix. Logan was hurt because I wasn't paying attention, but I am now. And maybe, just maybe, I can protect some of the Danny Hawkins out there."

"Good on ya, luv."

Susanne was waiting for Claire when she walked into the TV studio late that afternoon. They hugged and Susanne led her to the makeup room where a young man and an older woman were waiting. They gushed over her complexion while carefully applying the makeup that would soften the effects of the bright lights on the TV set. When she was ready, Susanne escorted Claire to the Green Room. She handed Claire a list of the questions that she had given Westfield. "They're along the lines you suggested," Susanne said. "Are you sure?"

"Oh, yes," Claire replied. She laughed. "Mike's always at his best when he gets uppity."

"He can turn the volume up," Susanne said. The warning light over the door blinked green, and Suzanne held the door for her. "It's time."

Claire sat down opposite Westfield while a commercial ran and fitted a wireless earbud in her right ear. "If you can hear me," Nedd said, "Look to your left and smile." She did. "Nice profile." It was his way of encouraging her. Susanne clipped a microphone to her lapel and gave her a thumbs up as the commercial ended and the "live" warning light came on. "Break a leg," Nedd said.

Mike Westfield looked into the camera in front of him. "We are fortunate to have with us tonight Claire Allison in her first interview since declaring her candidacy for the governor of the Grand Canyon State." The camera zoomed out to frame Claire sitting opposite Westfield. "Welcome to our show, Mrs. Allison. It seems like it was only yesterday when we reported how you disarmed that shooter at your school."

"Good evening, Mike. That was over three years ago. He was just a confused boy who needed help."

"That was a traumatic time," Westfield conceded. "But before we turn to today's events, I must ask, are you still growing sunflowers?"

That's unexpected, Claire thought. She led with a smile. "Oh, yes. I've been doing that before I was in kindergarten. They're near the end of their life cycle right now, but they'll be back."

She listened attentively as Westfield recapped her election for County Superintendent of Schools. He glanced at his notes. "One of your fellow candidates for governor claims you are totally lacking in real experience and live in the never-never world of education. You are a political wannabe riding public sympathy as a war hero's widow, and they've described you as a sunflower girl, ephemeral and following the sun. How would you answer them?"

"Ouch!" She laughed. "Mike, they can define me any way they want, and as for being the sunflower girl, I can live with that. Sunflowers are predictable and always come back, never abandoning the place they love. You can rely on them. They don't make vague promises, like progress that matters."

"Which is Ken Sellor's slogan," Westfield replied. "Do you really think you can match his record?"

"Mike, I'll let the high school graduation rate and the declining dropout rates for Maricopa County speak for themselves. Please forgive me, but I don't consider ever increasing budgets a record to run on."

"Then you favor cutting budgets?"

"No, not at all. We start by defining specific problems and then work together to solve them. If that means increasing budgets, we do that. But we do it with specific and measurable goals in mind. If we don't meet our goals, we stop throwing money at it."

"Mrs. Allison, are you an idealist?"

"Oh, I hope so. And, like a sunflower, I hope my roots are strong."

Westfield glanced at his notes and moved in for the kill. "We started this evening by recalling the time you disarmed one of your students, Danny Hawkins, who later committed suicide. Many have said that you failed him."

Claire folded her hands and looked down for a moment. She lifted her head and looked directly at Westfield. "I failed Danny and I will live with that for the rest of life. I could have done more. I will do more."

"Well, Mrs. Allison, perhaps that is a good place to leave it for now. Thank you for joining us tonight." Westfield looked down at his notes as they went to the commercial break.

Claire stood. "Thanks, Mike." He gave her a questioning look and waved his right hand.

Susanne followed her to the elevator in silence, carrying a thick folder in a mailing envelope. She pushed the down button. The doors swooshed open and they stepped inside. They started down and Suzanne handed her the package. "Mike said you could use this." She walked with Claire to her car. "Thank you for coming."

Rolinda and Hector were waiting when Claire walked into the war room. "He just can't help being a bastard," Rolinda said.

"It wasn't that bad," Claire replied. She handed Rolinda the package and disappeared into the bathroom to remove the heavy makeup from the interview and change into her working clothes, a baggy pair of shorts with one of Hank's black T shirts and flip-flops.

"She's taking charge," Rolinda murmured.

"I've seen it before in the Army when a new CO takes over an outfit," Hector said. "If they're not in combat, the really good ones watch and learn, getting their feet on the ground before acting or making changes."

"We're not in the Army," Rolinda said. She opened the package and scanned the contents. "Oh, Lord! Where did you get this?"

"Mike Westfield," Claire replied as Rolinda and Hector poured over the contents of the file.

Rolinda could not believe what she was seeing. "It's the dirt on Sellor. I mean everything; his finances, contacts with Antifa, his three mistresses. Look at this!" She handed Claire six photos. "The oldest looks all of sixteen."

"It's from an FBI data base and has been heavily redacted," Hector said. "It had to come from the White House, and that means Mike Westfield is our contact."

"We're not going to use it," Claire said. They looked at her in shock. "We don't have to." She picked up the file and fed it into a shredder. "We know who and what Sellor is, and it's obvious the White House is keeping its options open. It's our job to pick up the ball and run with it. We are everything Sellor is not, and Mike helped make that point tonight. Rolinda, you once said that there's no such thing as bad publicity in politics, only a missed opportunity. We have an opportunity here. So for the next few months, it's full steam ahead on the petition drive."

She paced the room, her flip-flops thumping the floor. "Social media is the key. If they say 'failure,' we say 'problem, let's work on it.' If they say 'war widow,' we show them cemeteries with American flags. If they say 'no experience,' we show them students graduating. When they frown, we smile. And when they call me 'the Sunflower Girl,' we show them sunflowers facing the sun."

"We can do that," Rolinda said, liking what she heard.

"But never underestimate Sellor," Hector added.

It was after midnight when Claire called it a night and headed home, leaving Rolinda and Hector alone. Rolinda quickly finished the email she was working on. "Well, Mr. Mendoza, how about a swim?"

"Did you bring your swimsuit?"

"Why would I do that?" She turned off the light and walked out the door. Her laughter split the night air, echoing over the backyard.

29

Tuesday, November 9

In my business, you've got to be a news junky. It also helps to pass the time while sitting around with your thumb up your ass. I flip through the afternoon news channels and have to give the producers credit for scrounging up enough rubbish to fill at least an hour a day.

Today the news channel scraped the bottom of the muck barrel and announced that a known pedophile was found dead in the Clark County jail exercise yard. He had been terminated with a homemade shiv and his gonads thoughtfully removed and stuffed in his mouth, which, I suspect, was the real reason his untimely demise made the news. Since Las Vegas is in Clark County, I wonder if the deceased was one of Bobby Lee's buddies. It's time to call Laura.

She answers on the first ring and doesn't bother to say hello. "Have you seen the news from Vegas?" I confirm that I have and ask if the victim was one of our boys. "He was," she answers. "Jesus H. Christ, you can't throw a pedophile into the general population."

"Well, someone did," I reply.

"Yeah, they did," she answers, finally calming down.

"What about his two buddies?" I ask. "I imagine they're spilling their guts as we speak."

"We'll know soon enough," Laura mutters.

Thursday, November 11

The 'soon enough' is two days later when Laura calls. Mary is on her way back from Las Vegas with a hot package, courtesy of the Clark County DA. She suggests that I might be interested in seeing it before it disappears into the evidence locker, never to be observed by the human eyeball again. Interested! I won't bother you with what a bear does where.

I try to book a plane ticket but, being a holiday, the airlines are sold out. I load the German Beast and Khepri comes along to keep me and Atticus company. She's a better driver than me, and we make it in nine hours and arrive before midnight. Khepri drove most of the way and you'd think she'd be exhausted. But her adrenaline is in full flow and she's hotter than the German Beast's smoking exhaust pipes. The sex is great.

Friday, November 12

I'm waiting at the DA's office on G Street the next morning when Mary and Laura arrive. It's obvious Mary is excited and brings me up to date. "The two pedos cut a deal with the Clark County DA and confessed to running what may be the world's largest child pornography ring with tentacles in over ninety countries.

In return, they won't end up in the county jail exercise yard like their good buddy who kept his mouth shut until his privates were inserted." She plays a video of Bobby Lee's buddies confessing. The details are disgusting and the video will never make YouTube. Mary hands me a file. "We have motivation," is all she says.

Inside is the photo of Logan Allison and Bobby Lee with two statements signed by the pedophiles certifying they witnessed the child in the photo being molested by Bobby Lee MacElroy. "But do we have a connection?" I ask. "How did Allison know it was Bobby Lee?"

"We get her on the stand and ask her," Laura answers.

"She won't take the stand," I reckon.

Mary gives me a hungry look. The woman is a raptor. "With the right jury, it won't matter. Jurors often assume pleading the fifth is a sign of guilt." She paces back and forth. "We're getting close."

Laura looks at me expectantly. "Can you talk to your source and take another look?"

Look for what? Then it dawns on me. They want me to shake the tree with all that poisoned fruit again and find a link that proves Allison knew MacElroy had abused her son. They don't know what Barry charges and I'm not about to throw money down that rabbit hole, but I mix my metaphors.

30

Thursday, December 23

Rebecca handed the folder to Claire. “We have a Christmas present.” She waited while Claire scanned the latest numbers from their petition drive. “Seventy-thousand signatures! We did three random samples and over sixty percent are valid signatures. Twenty-four thousand registered voters signed your petition, all within the first two months!” She laughed. “Some of the bogus signatures are actually funny. There’s a Joe Bagofdonuts and a Brenda Bangsalot who signed. Talk about two wasted dollars.”

“Actually,” Claire said, “they might be a bonus. We can put it on social media as an insider joke and see if it gets legs. Let the whiz-kids play with it.”

“What if it encourages the weirdos to sign with whatever crazy name they can think of?” Rebecca wondered.

“We can redline the obvious ones before we hand the petitions in.” Claire thought for a moment. “We still need fifteen thousand valid signatures. We were lucky and rode the Christmas wave when people were out shopping. It’s going to get harder after the holidays, and we’ll need all the additional publicity we can get.”

“I’ll get on it,” Rebecca promised. She stood to leave. “Oh, we’re good to go on the Christmas party tonight.” She closed the door as she walked out.

Claire quickly cleared her desk and finished signing the Christmas cards for her staff. “Nedd, we need to talk.” She knew he was there and didn’t wait for an answer. “That was very good news about the petitions, but I was wondering about the trendings.”

Nedd's image appeared on her smart phone. "Merry Christmas, luv. Sorry to muck up your good news, but the trendings are negative. It's going to be a slog to get the rest of the signatures. Also, you're definitely on Sellor's radar and he sees you as an increasing threat. I have no idea what he'll do next. He's a total wanker and will get down and dirty. Be prepared for the unexpected."

"We'll work on it," Claire replied. "Any suggestions on how to breathe some life into the drive?"

"Nothing specific. I'd suggest you carry on smartly and see what develops. There is something else you need to be aware of. Our girl Rebecca, and Clint are going at it like love sick bonobos."

"Oh, my," Claire said. "They seem right for each other. As long as they are discreet . . ." A sudden sadness claimed her. *Hank, I miss you so much.* She forced his image into a quiet place close to her heart. "Clint is a good bodyguard and I don't want to replace him."

"No worries there," Nedd assured her. "But perhaps Mrs. Johnson and Colonel Mendoza could take their . . . ah . . . liaison inside. They do enjoy the good Colonel's pool a bit too much, and he does have a nosey neighbor."

"Rolinda and Hector? I didn't know." She sighed. "Okay, why bring all this up?"

"It has the potential for scandal. Something that Sellor won't hesitate to use."

Claire thought for a moment, considering the implications. A mischievous smile played at the corners of her mouth. "Sellor's too smart for that. Anything else?"

"Your Christmas shopping is done except you need to pick up Sarah's gift at Nordstrom's." Nedd had coordinated her Christmas shopping and found a few outstanding bargains.

"I can pick it up on my way home. Thanks for all the help. You are a dear."

The image on her screen blushed. "My pleasure, luv."

Clint Roberts inched the black SUV down East Camelback Road towards Fashion Square. The holiday traffic was heavy and backed up over two miles, slowing their progress to a crawl. “Ma’am, why don’t I drop you off at the entrance to Nordstrom’s and drive around the block while you and Mateo run in to pick up the present? We can coordinate a pickup by cell phone.”

Before Claire could answer, a car slammed into their rear end and rode up under the bumper, locking the two vehicles together. The driver jumped out and waved his arms. “Ayúdame! Help!” The rear door opened and two small children bailed out into the oncoming traffic. Claire shot out of the SUV and ran for the children. Mateo was right behind her as she scooped up the smallest, a four-year-old girl.

“My wife!” the driver screamed. “She’s in labor!” Claire handed the girl to her father and looked inside. A very pregnant woman was sprawled on the backseat, her legs wide. Her water had broken and the carpet under her was wet as she fought another contraction. A year-old infant was sitting on the seat next to her, crying loudly. Claire quickly examined the infant, a very healthy boy. She gently picked him up.

“I don’t blame you for protesting,” she cooed. “I would too.” The infant calmed as she stood. “Mateo, I need your help.” She handed the baby over and gave him an approving look as he held the child. “You’ve done this before. Where did the other one go?” They looked around, not seeing the third child, a six-year-old boy. “Mateo, can you find him? They’re probably undocumented and he was told to run. I’ll take care of the mother.” She motioned at the distraught man. “What’s your wife’s name?”

“Lucia. She’s Peruvian.”

“Help Mateo find your son. I’ll take care of Lucia.” Claire crawled into the backseat. “Hola.” She smiled. “So this is number four,” she said in Spanish. She felt the woman’s pulse. “You’re a lot calmer than I’d be.” Mateo shouted that he had all three children. Lucia visibly relaxed. “Now, we just need to get you to the hospital.” Claire crawled out and took charge. “Take care of your children,” she told the husband. “Clint, Mateo, can you unhook the cars?”

Mateo jumped into the driver’s seat and stomped on the brakes while Clint gunned the SUV and accelerated forward. The two vehicles separated with a loud tearing sound. Other than a damaged rear bumper, Claire's SUV was drivable but radiator coolant was gushing from the car.

"Mateo, help me get Lucia into our car." Together, they helped the groaning woman out of the backseat and into the SUV. "Mateo, you take care of things here while we get Lucia to the hospital." He started to protest but she jerked her head once, cutting him off. Lucia cried out as another contraction gripped her. Claire climbed in beside her and threw her shawl into the front seat. "Clint, the traffic is moving much faster the other way. Can you jump the median and throw a U turn?"

"Hold on," he said, spinning the SUV to the left and bulldozing his way into the oncoming traffic. He rolled his window down and slapped the emergency beacon on the roof just as the traffic ground to a halt. "The nearest ER is Honor Health," he said. "A little over a mile, not long if we can break free of the traffic." They inched forward as the traffic started to slowly move.

Lucia screamed again, announcing the baby was on the way. "Clint, can you get help on your smart phone?" He called 911 as the traffic ground to a stop.

"911's backed up," Clint said. "We're on hold."

Claire made a mental note about that problem. She held Lucia's hands, trying to recall what she had learned in a first aid course from her college years. "I've seen this before," she said, still speaking in Spanish, her voice calm and reassuring. "Everything looks normal, so don't fight it. Let's do it, you and me."

She pulled Lucia's pants off her left foot and felt her abdomen as her contractions came faster. "This is going to be quick," she said. "I can see the head now." Lucia grunted as Claire turned the baby's head and gently probed its mouth, making sure it was clear and open. "Okay, push again."

"I've got help on the phone," Clint said.

"It's here," Claire said. She guided the baby out and quickly cleaned its nose and double-checked its mouth. She gently slapped the baby's back, and it coughed and started to cry. "Lucia, you have a beautiful little girl." She laid the infant on Lucia's stomach without breaking the umbilical cord, and gently ran her hands over the little girl, examining her. "She's perfect." She reached into the front seat and retrieved her shawl, wrapping mother and child together.

"Two minutes out," Clint announced. "They know we're coming."

"Gracias," Lucia whispered. She studied Claire for a moment. "You very familiar," she said in broken English. "We meet before?" Claire shook her head. "Oh!" Lucia said, her eyes wide. "You woman on television."

Claire laughed. "I hear a lot of that," she said in Spanish. She looked up as Clint turned into the hospital.

A team of three nurses and a doctor with a gurney were waiting as Clint pulled to a stop. They were brisk efficiency, and within moments, Lucia and the newborn were out of the car and on the gurney. Lucia looked back as she kissed Claire's shawl. "Ve con Dios," she whispered. She never took her eyes off Claire as they wheeled her inside.

Claire joined Clint in the front seat. "Let's go," she said.

"We should go in and follow up," Clint said.

"Call Mateo and tell him where Lucia is," Claire said. She touched Clint's arm. Her eyes sparkled. "This is a wonderful Christmas story, and it's all about them. Let's keep it that way."

"Can do," Clint assured her. He hit the phone button on the steering wheel and called Mateo. "Tell the lucky father that mother and daughter are doing well at Honor Health. The boss wants no involvement; Discretion Level One. We're outta here. See you at the party."

"Copy all," Mateo said. "Tell the boss she made my Christmas."

31

Friday, December 24

Don't get me wrong, I like Christmas. Some of the best gifts I have received are from young lovelies celebrating the holidays at an office party, but the older I get, the more I prefer the laid-back atmosphere around the motel.

Khepri and Chione have decorated the place with the usual commercial Christmas trappings, but with an off-beat flair. I've never seen an angel wearing a hijab. They don't exchange presents, but Chione is six months pregnant and Khepri is full of Christmas cheer at the thought of becoming a grandmother. Jeffrey is home on leave from the Marines and has been accepted into the Naval Academy. He wants to be an officer and kick butt big time.

I'm not expecting any gifts but get one the day before the Santa flyover when Laura calls from Sacramento. "Are you sitting down?" She doesn't wait for an answer. "We found the weapon."

I start to hyperventilate. "Holy shit! Who? How?" That's all I can manage.

Laura laughs. "The Sac Sheriff just arrested a scumbag, one George Wayman, for armed robbery. It seems Wayman was driving through Wilton, it's a small town about twenty-five miles south of here, and decided to hold up the convenience store where he stopped to refuel."

"Ah," I say, recovering my wits, "Wayman of Wilton visits the local stop and rob."

Laura is beside herself with glee. "But it was the wrong stop and rob. This one is owned by Wilma Perkins, a little old lady of respectable years who is handy with a shotgun."

"Never mess with little old ladies," I say, sensing where this one is going.

"When the police arrived, good old George was withering on the floor clutching his groin. Mrs. Perkins was still holding the shotgun with her right foot standing on a .22 snub nose revolver. According to Mrs. Perkins, she shot him with her twelve gauge after he threatened her with the .22. Fortunately for Wayman, the shotgun was loaded with rock salt and Mrs. Perkins is a poor shot. All the damage was below Mr. Wayman's navel."

"That's rubbing salt into an open wound," I add, trying to be witty but sensing his pain.

"It was at very close range," Laura says. "He's going to be in the hospital for a few more days. A security camera confirmed Mrs. Perkins' story and the .22 had Wayman's fingerprints all over it. Naturally, the Sheriff turned the weapon over to the FBI. The FBI tested the revolver for ballistics and ran the results through the Bureau's database. It was a perfect match with the slugs deposited in Bobby Lee. That's when I got the call."

My professional instincts finally kick in and I ask the standard, "Who is this guy?"

"George Lester Wyman, male, Caucasian, forty-six years old, with multiple priors including two felonies, grand theft auto and armed robbery, both before turning twenty-one. He got the max on the last one and went to San Quentin for nine years. Apparently, he had some sort of epiphany in the slammer and became a believer in snatch-and-grab after he got out—three convictions for petty theft and two for drunk in public since then."

"Did he off Bobby Lee?"

"Not likely," Laura replies. "He's a petty thief and drunk, not a killer."

"So, how did he get the .22?" I ask.

"Good question. Normally a petty thief gets his hands on a weapon and sells it."

"So, what are you going to do?"

"For now, wait until he gets out of the hospital. We'll have 'the chat' with him then. He'll lawyer up, but I'll explain that armed robbery is a felony under the penal code and is a third strike. That should get him talking." I ask if I can be there. "No way, David. The investigation has to be clean and immune to appeal."

That's a downer, but I understand. Then it dawns on me that she used my first name. That's a first. "What's with the 'David'?" I ask.

She laughs. "We would love to see Atticus," she says, not answering. "Say, around the middle of January?"

If I read her correctly, she's telling me that she'll bring me up to date on the investigation, but it will have to be in person and very private. "I'll be there," I tell her. We wish each other a merry Christmas and hang up. I do my usual thing and cruise the news channels. It's a slow news day and KPIO is running every feel-good story they can find. Khepri will love the one about a mother giving birth in traffic outside Nordstrom's.

Tuesday, January 11

When I was nine years old, Dottie Sue took me to the San Diego Zoo. It wasn't the typical thing she would do, and looking back, I suspect she needed to make a supply run across the border to Tijuana. She gave me a twenty-dollar bill, told me she would be back in four or five hours, and disappeared. I wandered around but kept coming back to the tiger enclosure, totally fascinated by a tigress that paced back and forth and kept eyeing me like I was dinner. Mom made it back eleven hours later, and I never forgot the tigress.

It's thirty-five years later and I'm sitting in Mary Pearson's office looking at the tigress. Mary is pacing back and forth with the same hungry look. Fortunately, I'm not on the menu, but Claire Allison is. "We've got her," she keeps saying, as if repeating it will make it true. She plays the DVD of the interrogation of good old George Wayman in the Sacramento County jail.

Laura is at her best, looking sweetly concerned as she tells him that he is looking at three strikes and you're out. He's going away for the rest of his life, and he does have a cute little butt that will see action in the slammer.

Wayman cannot cooperate fast enough. It turns out that he's a river rat and was camped on the Sacramento River. He heard two gunshots from a nearby houseboat and was aroused in time to see a figure on the houseboat throw a handgun into the river. It landed in the water near his campsite. He watched the figure close the door and leave. He could see it was a woman and, while he didn't get a good make on her, she was about five-eight and slender.

He followed her to the road and watched her drive away. He did get a partial on the car's license plate, 495, which is a partial match of the car Delgado rented. After that, he went wading in the shallow water, looking for the weapon. He stepped on it in about four inches of mud and was delighted to find it was a snub nose .22 revolver, perfect for self-defense in these troubled times. It was all a mistake in the stop and rob. He was fumbling for change when he pulled the small weapon out of his pocket.

He's never heard of Allison nor the murder, but being a responsible citizen, he is willing to testify to all of this in court. Of course, the Sacramento DA will lower the charges against him to possession of an unregistered firearm and petty theft. Wayman considers his stay in the hospital as time served.

"But no positive ID at the houseboat," Laura says.

"Laura, we have a possible ID at the scene and a partial on the vehicle. We can prove how she got there and the timing tracks. Coincidence? Only a brain-dead jury will buy that. And we've established motivation with the MacElroy videos."

"But did she see the videos?" Laura asks. She is a persistent little thing.

Mary gives Laura the look that says she isn't getting any that night. "I'll ask her in court."

"If she gets up," Laura says, using DA-speak for a defendant taking the stand in their own defense.

"She will," Mary assures us. She ejects the DVD and drops it in her briefcase. "This will be on the DA's desk tomorrow. He will indict. It's just a matter of waiting."

Waiting has never been my long suit.

32

Wednesday, February 2

The phone call came early in the morning on Ground Hog Day. Claire woke from a deep sleep and eyed her smartphone suspiciously. Nedd's voice overrode the ringer. "Best take this one, luv. It's CNB-TV."

Claire punched up the number. She forced a cheerfulness into her voice she didn't feel. "Good morning." The caller identified herself as a production assistant on the Morning Conversations show and asked if Claire would be willing to take a FaceTime call from one of their commentators about a breaking story. It would be telecast live.

"May I ask what it involves?" Claire asked. The girl replied that she was not at liberty to disclose the exact nature of the story, but that it had to do with her campaign. A text message from Nedd flashed on the screen telling her the interview was about her campaign workers shagging and carrying on.

"Give me a moment to look presentable," Claire told the producer. She broke the connection and quickly applied makeup, highlighting her eyes and brightening her lips. She brushed her hair and pulled on a colorful top Sarah had recently purchased. She gave her hair a flip as FaceTime chimed on her smartphone. "Good morning," she answered.

"Good morning, Claire. I'm Brianna Prees with CNB-TV's Morning Conversations."

Claire hit a remote control, turning her bedroom TV on. The sound was muted and she was live on national TV. Claire smiled and moved the smartphone, framing herself in front of the painting of sunflowers Sarah had created years ago. By looking over the phone, she could monitor CNB's broadcast on the TV. Brianna Prees was a severe looking, middle-aged woman. Her hair was pulled into a tight bun that matched her personality. "Good morning, Brianna. How may I help you?"

"Thank you for taking my call, Claire. As you have no doubt heard, there is a brewing scandal involving your campaign staff and sexual activities. Apparently, there are compromising photos. However, I am reluctant to mention names until after talking to you."

"Oh, dear," Claire said, trying to sound hurt and concerned at the same time. "I haven't heard about any sexual scandal, but I do know of one romance. The couple are responsible individuals, they are single and there is certainly nothing illicit going on. I can only wish them well and hope they find the happiness they both deserve." She flashed a smile. "I'm actually quite thrilled for them."

"There are photos that show them cavorting nude in a swimming pool." An image of a swimming pool flashed on the TV screen. "Their activities are, shall we say, less than innocent."

"Oh," Claire said, acting shocked. "Brianna, I've swum in that pool. They are consenting adults, and I'm not about to pass judgment on anyone for what they do in the privacy of their own home. I do hope you are not suggesting they are doing something wrong." She went on the attack. "But now that you mention it, there is something that does concerns me. The pool is on private property and well secluded."

"Then you approve of their conduct?"

"It's not a matter of my approving or not, but of respecting their privacy, and whoever took the photos had to be trespassing. I wonder if they are being stalked."

"Why would anyone stalk them?" Brianna asked, eager to follow up.

"Well, they're both working on my campaign, and I can only wonder if they are being targeted for that."

"I'm quite sure that is not the case, Madam Superintendent."

Claire nodded, very much aware that Brianna had switched to using her formal title. "That is reassuring." She didn't wait for a reply and pressed Brianna harder. "It might be interesting to hear from the source of your photos, just to be sure there is no threat to their safety. Are you going to interview them?"

"We don't see a need for that at his time. I would like to thank you for your time and willingness to talk to us."

"Thank you for having me on," Claire said. The TV quickly transitioned to a commercial. "Brianna, are you still on?"

"I'm still here." There was hostility in her voice.

"Brianna, my campaign has received a number of threats lately. Until now, we treated them as coming from the lunatic fringe. If this came from the same source, it's more than harmless noise. I'm not asking for you to reveal your sources, but it's very worrisome to think innocent people might be harmed just because they support me. This is such a well-worn tactic in politics today; target the supporters of those you disagree with since they can't defend themselves."

"I don't really think that is a problem."

"I do hope you're right, Brianna. But we need to protect everyone we can. Thanks again for having me on your show. Your call was a heads-up."

"It was my pleasure," Brianna replied, trying to sound friendly, but not meaning a word of it.

Claire broke the connection just as her phone rang. It was Rolinda. "Oh, Lord, you knocked it out of the park. I should have told you we're a thing."

Claire laughed. "Well, it's not much of a secret."

"You made that bitch look like a left-over stomachache. Thank you for keeping our names out of it. Besides, I'm seeing a different you. Maybe it's time to throw away your shawls and show the world the new Claire Allison."

"The shawls are my trademark," Claire protested.

"True," Rolinda said. "But that's the dull and boring side of you. Young voters need to see the real you, someone they can identify with. Think about it and talk to Sarah. Your mother is with it, girl."

"I'll do that," Claire promised. "Rolinda, I'm worried that the petition drive has flat-lined and is on life support. We need to breathe life into it."

"I've been thinking the same thing. I've applied for an unpaid sabbatical so I can work full time on the campaign."

"Can you afford to do that?"

"Not really." She laughed wickedly. "But Hector can. The next time anyone mentions pool parties or the like, tell them we're engaged."

"That's wonderful! Congratulations. When did Hector propose?"

"He hasn't yet." The wicked laugh was back. "I going to have to make up his mind for him."

"Rolinda!" Claire broke the connection and started her morning exercises. She was on the treadmill when Nedd called.

"Got a moment, luv?"

"Of course," she replied. "You sound worried."

Nedd's image appeared on the HD screen in front of her. "Not enough to get my knickers in a twist, but I am wondering."

"What about?"

"I kept asking myself, who tipped off CNB? So I went walkabout through a few computers."

Claire laughed. "And you discovered I was the source."

"Exactly. I was wondering why."

"Nedd, this is the 21st Century and there's nothing scandalous about having an affair. In fact, most people are amused or titillated at best. But the more I thought about it, the more I wanted to get out in front of it, before some idiot like Parker tried to make it into something it isn't and innocent people were hurt."

"The wanker would do that," Nedd replied. "And you may have stirred some interest in the petition drive."

"Maybe we can give Parker something else to chew on," Claire suggested. "Hank liked to say, 'Get the bastards looking the wrong way and then blindside them.'"

"Not very cricket," Nedd said. "I'll work on it."

33

Thursday, February 17

It's been over a month since Mary sent the case to the DA and nothing is happening on the Allison front. It gets worse. The daily news is dead; no scandal to expose, no sexual escapade to chase down, nada, nothing. February has turned sour with a vengeance and I'm bored silly. I call up my file on Allison. Naturally, my computer is all gummed up. "Ah, come on," I moan.

"Come on what?" Khepri asks, making me jump. She's standing next to the door holding a batch of freshly laundered clothes in her arms. She even irons my skivvies. How she drifts in and out of rooms as silent as a butterfly totally escapes me.

"Allison," I grump.

"Has she been indicted?"

"Not yet," I reply. "It's been a month since Mary sent the case to the DA."

"Thirty-six days," Khepri says, correcting me. I've learned the hard way not to mess with her when it comes to money, numbers, or dates. "Atticus needs a walk," she tells me. Needless to say, I hop to. I like the order she brings to my life. I load Atticus into the German Beast and head for a nearby park. We spend the next two hours rambling around, accosting strange dogs and gawking at tight shorts. Atticus does the accosting while I stick to the gawking. We're headed back to the Beast when my smartphone rings.

It's Laura. She comes right to the point. "Fuckin' Larry won't indict." The "fuckin' Larry" she is talking about is Lawrence Longchamps, the Sacramento County DA.

"I was just wondering about that," I reply. "Can you read minds?"

She ignores me. "Mary says he's waiting for the right time when an indictment will make the headlines, which is probably never."

"So, what now?"

"Allison walks and we get on with life. I've got a backlog of cases that can fill San Quentin. What about you?" I tell her there's nothing brewing, but something will turn up. It always does. "Give my best to Khepri." Before I can break the connection, she hits me with, "When are you going to marry her?" She doesn't wait for an answer and the line goes dead.

I wonder back to the car, deep in thought. "No way," I mutter. Atticus ignores me. As usual, by the time I get back Khepri has sterilized my office to her usual standards. I collapse into my chair and stare at the monitor in front of me. Claire Allison's file is looking back at me. I call up her photo file. Think of it as a form of self-flagellation. I swear, she's looking better and growing nicer by the day. I chalk it up to success.

An old itch tells me I'm missing something that needs scratching. I know better than to ignore it and replay the CNB interview with Brianna Prees. In her own sweet caring way, Allison made Brianna look like a calloused political hardliner. I've met Brianna a few times, and while I've never liked her, I should probably send her a get-well card. "You've been warned," I tell myself.

There's a story there, I can feel it in my bones. If Allison was running a normal campaign, there would be two or three insiders who are pissed off because she wasn't following their advice. Normally, at least one would be knocking at my door. But Allison's campaign is not normal, and everyone is a true believer.

I've got nothing and without an inside source, everything is just speculation. "Hold on," I mutter. Maybe I do have an inside source. I go looking for Khepri. As usual, she's working in the office and checking in a young couple who are in lust. I wait until they skedaddle for their room.

"Don't you have a relative who works for Mendoza?" I ask.

Khepri allows a tight smile. "I have a cousin whose husband owns a maid service. They clean Mr. Mendoza's home."

"And your cousin is one of the maids," I add. Egyptian men are infamous for working their spouses. "I was wondering if there's any hanky-panky going on there. Hey, sex still sells."

"I'll ask her," Khepri says.

Monday, March 21

It's late morning and I'm sitting by the pool contemplating my navel. I've been cooling my heels for over a month and nursing a beer belly. Domesticity is agreeing with me and I'm not even a married man. Why does that topic keep coming up? I have a quick panic and make a belated New Year's resolution to start doing sit-ups.

"David," Khepri calls from the office, bringing me back to reality. There's no way I'm going to start doing sit-ups, not at my age. "My cousin is here." I perk up. "You should really talk to her." The day just got better.

I pull on a shirt and pad into the office that has been remodeled. A woman comes to her feet when I enter. She is in her mid-thirties, skinny, and wearing a head scarf. Her clothes are clean and neat but definitely worn and old. "This is my cousin, Fatima," Khepri says. "Her husband, Mahoud, owns Mahoud's Maids of Maricopa." We shake hands. Judging by her callouses, Fatima does all the work. There is a fresh bruise on her cheek, and her eyes dart to Khepri. I know an abused woman when I see one. "My David is a good man," Khepri tells her.

"I should not be here," Fatima says.

"Mahoud will never know," Khepri says in a soothing voice. "David is an investigative journalist and must protect his sources. He also rewards those who help him, and he is very generous." I'm not that generous, I tell myself, but I know enough to keep my mouth shut. Fatima lights up. She's missing a tooth but has a beautiful smile. "Please show David what you have found," Khepri says.

Fatima hands over a photograph of Allison and Joe the Rainmaker Prescott. It is slightly blurred, but it is definitely

Claire Allison and Joe is handing her what appears to be a check. The photo was taken in Allison's office, and the date and time is marked in the lower righthand corner. I asked her who took the photo. "Heba gave it to me," Fatima replies. I ask who Heba is. "Mahoud's cousin," she explains. "She's a clerk in the County Superintendent's office."

She hands me a torn and rumpled bank statement that shows a deposit of $75,000 to the Good Shepherd Coalition's trust account. "I found this in the trash at the Mendoza home." According to the statement, the deposit was made three hours after the photo was taken. A copy of all the checks on the statement is on the next page, and the check for $75,000 was signed by none other than Joe the Rainmaker.

I'm not the brightest lightbulb in the firmament and it takes a moment for it all to compute. Not only is the amount well beyond the legal limits for campaign contributions, it's illegal in the State of Arizona to accept campaign contributions in any government office or building. "Holy shit," I mutter. "I've got her." Fatima looks at me expectantly and I mention a figure. Khepri tells her that it will be in cash and Mahoud will never know.

Fatima almost bows in gratitude and says that she must go to work. She disappears out the door and Khepri sighs. "You have given her freedom." I ask what is going on. "Mahoud beats her for not working hard enough while he does nothing. With her own money, she can escape and start her own business." I ask why she doesn't call the police the next time Mahoud roughs her up. "She cannot do that. Our holy books say that men are the managers of women, and that a husband can beat his wife."

"Did Ali, ah, believe that?" I ask. She just smiles. I can imagine her holding a carving knife. "Did Ali have a hard time going to sleep?" Khepri rewards me with another smile. I'm not about to follow up on that.

Besides, it's time to go to work. The story writes itself and I bat out two thousand words in record time. I hit the speed dial on my smartphone to my friendly editor at The World Review and introduce him to Khepri. I let her do the negotiations. She easily extorts an unbelievable price, 5000 bucks, but also insists it be published anonymously.

I have no idea why she does that, but I can hear Dottie Sue laughing, wherever she is.

34

Thursday, March 24

The headlights from the oncoming car cut through the rain and, for a brief moment, she couldn't see. The car roared by, driving much too fast for the conditions, and sent a wave of water over the windshield. The windshield wipers automatically beat faster as she slowed. She glanced at the directions on her smart phone. She was at her destination and pulled off the road and parked beside a minivan.

She pulled the hood over her head and tucked her hair in. She got out of the car, and for a moment, stood in the rain. Certain she was alone, a deadly calm swept over her. She patted her pocket and felt the handle of the revolver. The rain let up and she walked towards the river, seeing the houseboat for the first time. A light was on inside.

She walked silently up the boarding ramp and slipped her right hand into her pocket, clasping the revolver. She hesitated a moment before drawing it out. Without pausing, she knocked on the door. She held her left hand over her mouth and barked in a rough voice, "The twins are here."

The door cracked open and Bobby Lee MacElroy looked out. His eyes opened wide in recognition as she threw her left shoulder into the door, forcing it open and throwing him off balance. He spun around as she raised the revolver and pulled the trigger. The sound was deafening.

Claire woke from the dream and sat up in bed, her body wet with sweat as tremors swept over her. She had just killed a man—again.

It's been over four years, will it ever go away? She forced herself to breathe slowly and counted to thirty before standing.

She padded into the bathroom and stood before the mirror, staring at her gaunt face. *Oh, Hank, how did you deal with it?* A knock at the bedroom door brought her back to the moment.

It was Logan. "Are you okay, Mom? I heard you moaning."

"I'm fine, son. It was just a bad dream." She glanced at the clock by Hank's wash basin. "It's time to get going," she called, thankful her voice sounded normal. "Pancakes?" Logan was growing and his appetite was meeting all expectations.

"Yaas!" he shouted. "Oh, Mom, I'm not going on that flight."

Where did that come from? Logan and Stu were scheduled for a flight on a vintage B-24 bomber over the weekend. "Is something wrong?"

"Naw," he replied, still talking through the door. "I thought about it, that's all. It's an old airplane and doesn't sound very safe. Anyway, I like jets. They go faster."

Claire smiled in relief as she stood and pulled on a bright kimono. Her son had made a good decision. She opened the door and Logan swept her up in his arms, hugging her. "You're sounding more like your dad every day." She held him at arm's length as the guilt that wracked her yielded to a new day. "Ready for breakfast?"

Logan was on his second helping when her smartphone buzzed. It was a text from Nedd.

Turn on your TV. Enjoy.

She turned on the TV and turned to KPIO. There was nothing unusual beyond the normal end-of-civilization coverage. She cycled to CNB. Brianna Prees was looking very serious as she looked purposefully into the camera. Claire hit the replay button and cycled back to the beginning of the newscast.

"Allegations exposing campaign malfeasance have shaken the governor's race in Arizona," Brianna intoned, her voice heavy with gravitas. "The lead story in today's edition of The World Review revealed that the Good Shepherd Coalition has repeatedly violated existing state laws forbidding the collection of campaign funds in any government building or office. Evidence proves that Claire Allison used her office for what is an obvious case of political extortion, which is punishable by a fine and disqualification for a public office."

She turned to the screen behind her as Ken Sellor came into focus. He was standing in front of the State Capitol. "Good morning, Brianna. Thank you for having me on this morning," He was an accomplished speaker and spoke with a soothing confidence. "We are fully aware that Mrs. Allison is new to campaigning for a prominent elected office, but that does not excuse her conduct. No one is above the law, and we can only hope the State's attorney general will promptly investigate what appears to be a flagrant violation of our campaign laws that borders on the criminal."

"Mom!" Logan cried. "Are you going to jail?"

Claire turned the TV off and reached out, touching his hand. "No," she said, her voice low and calm. "No one had done anything wrong. It's just politics. It's all made up."

"They shouldn't make up stuff like that. Why do they do it?"

"Because some people think winning is more important than anything else." She patted his hand. "Go get ready for school."

"What do I say if someone gets in my face?"

"I don't think anyone will do that, considering how much you've grown. If they do, just ask them how they would feel if someone was spreading lies about their mother. Whatever you do, no fighting."

"Ah, Mom, I don't fight."

Claire ruffled his hair. "Get going, kiddo." She watched him as he bolted for his room. *I do love you.* She quickly thumbed a message to Nedd on her cell.

How long do we let it ride?

The reply was back in seconds.

Twelve hours max.

Rolinda was waiting when Claire walked into the war room. "The phone is ringing off the hook," she said. "Every major network is in a feeding frenzy." She shook her head, more puzzled than worried. "Stupid, stupid, stupid. Credible denial won't be a problem, so who gets the honors?"

"I was thinking Mike Westfield," Claire replied. "We're having lunch at The Vineyard today."

"Mike will do it right," Rolinda said. She thought for a moment. "Was there a byline on the article in_The World Review?"

"Anonymous," Claire answered.

Rolinda humphed. "Why am I not surprised? Well, that was the good news." She handed Claire a printout. "The numbers speak for themselves. We've flatlined on signatures." Claire scanned the page, her face a blank. They had ten days to go and were short 9000 signatures. "Let's hope Mike can stir up some interest," Rolinda said. "Otherwise we're dead in the water. Knowing him, he'd love reading our death notice."

"It's too early to think obituary," Claire replied. She changed the subject. "Any news on the marriage front?"

Rolinda sat down, bubbling with excitement. "Oh, girl, you wouldn't believe what happened. We were in bed and I came right out and asked him if he was going to make an honest woman out of me. The man went all goofy and cried. He thought I wasn't having any of it and was afraid to ask. Imagine that! Hector, our brave soldier boy was afraid to ask. He proposed right there."

"When did all this happen?" Claire asked.

"About eight hours ago."

Claire stared at her. "Where is he now?"

"Still in bed recovering," Rolinda answered.

"Whatever from?"

"Don't ask." She glanced at the time. "Don't be late for lunch."

Mike Westfield was waiting when Claire arrived at the restaurant. He was all charm as the hostess led them to a secluded table in the corner of a small garden. As expected, every head in the room turned, watching them traverse the room. "Looks like you're doing the walk of shame," Westfield said, savoring the moment. He held a chair for her before sitting down. They exchanged pleasantries as they read the menu and ordered wine, but Claire sensed something was lurking beneath his pleasant demeanor. "I talked to Tom today," Westfield ventured.

"Tom Blaisdale?" Claire asked. Westfield nodded in reply and sipped his wine. They had come to the reason for the lunch. She remembered the pleasant and soft-spoken man from when she met the President. The President had promised they would be in contact.

"The heavies in DC are very concerned with the recent trending in the polls," Westfield said. "Sellor's ratings are slipping. If he goes down, they could lose Arizona."

Claire studied her wine glass. "And they think my candidacy is siphoning votes from Sellor."

"They're certain of it," Westfield said. He leaned across the table and spoke in a low voice. "Claire, they know your petition drive is in trouble, and you just took a big hit with that article in The World Review. I'm guessing fatal. KPIO can't ignored it much longer." He paused to let it sink it. "Look, the cabinet offer is still on the table if you drop out."

"And if I don't?"

He refilled his glass. "Claire, you're playing in the big leagues here. Cut your losses now, while you can. These guys will hurt you."

Without a word, she pulled a manila envelope out of her purse and shoved it across the table. Westfield untied the tab and pulled out two photos, a bank statement, and a certificate of incorporation. Claire sipped her wine, watching his face.

Westfield grinned, shaking his head. "Is humble pie an appetizer or on the main course?"

"Would you be kind enough to tell Tom that I'd like to hang around for a little longer?"

35

Thursday, the same day

I'm sleepy but Khepri insists that we watch the eleven o'clock news. It's a replay of the earlier news that has gone national with a vengeance, and I could have skin in the game.

Mike Westfield is holding forth from his news desk at KPIO. I try to tune out the audio and focus on the big screen behind Westfield, but certain phrases leak through. "Our investigation revealed that the photo in question was taken in the political headquarters of the Good Shepherd Coalition and not Claire Allison's office as alleged."

An expanded view of the photo fills the screen and Hector Mendoza's house can be seen out a big window. "Mr. Prescott was not available for comment but is well known for his philanthropic activities and often makes large contributions to charities." Joe the Rainmaker's photo flashes on the screen.

It keeps getting worse as a photo of the cancelled check appears on the screen. "As you can see, this donation was made out to The Good Samaritan Trust." The screen cycles to an incorporation certificate identifying the Trust as a scholarship fund.

Westfield folds his hands over the offending edition of The World Review, pauses for effect, and pontificates on the state of politics in our fair State and how it drives good people away. I hate it when he enjoys his work. I give a silent thanks for the anonymous byline. "You saved my ass on this one," I tell Khepri.

Friday, April 1

The exposé on the Good Shepherds could have been the scandal of the year, but I was set up again. You'd think I would learn. Of course, The World Review vetted the photo and bank statement with their own investigator, a sleazy lawyer from New York, before forking over the big bucks for the story, which just happened to be the most the scandal rag ever paid.

I wasn't expecting a letter of appreciation, but the demand letter from the same sleaze-bag lawyer was a total surprise when it showed up in the mail. The letter outlined in painful detail 'the blatant misstatements, inaccuracies, and fabrications' that characterized my article, and The World Review_wants their money back.

They are also demanding a statement exonerating them of any complicity in my crimes against journalism. There's a handwritten note from publisher attached to the letter lamenting that the paper's retraction is the most embarrassing article he has ever penned, and that my services would no longer be required.

Naturally, I head for the local supermarket to buy the latest edition of the scandal rag. Normally, it's lurking at the checkout counter, but today it's sold out. I drive to three more stores before I find a copy. I have to out-snatch a grasping lady who outweighs me by fifty pounds. I'm lucky to escape with my hand still attached. I fork over $4.50 and spirit it out to the German Beast where I can read it in safety.

A photo of Claire Allison smiling with sparkling white teeth that would make any dentist proud is on the front page. She is holding the offending photo of her and Joe the Rainmaker and is standing in the same place. Of course, the angle is different and it is obviously not her office, but the so-called war room at Casa Mendoza.

The story is a retraction of the previous article and the paper apologizes profusely for any confusion that might have misled their loyal readers about the integrity of Mrs. Allison, Mr. Prescott, and the Good Shepherds. My name is not mentioned, but an inner alarm bell tells me I'm not out of this by a longshot. It's time to call a lawyer and I make the call to Sacramento.

Lynn Majors answers on the second ring and I relate my tale of woe. She is obviously enjoying herself and her advice is simple. "Pay it, Parker. Next time, be more careful about your sources. Ignore their demand for a statement exonerating them. They did check it out and published."

We chat for a bit and she admits that she likes Allison. "The lady has a rare touch of class and honesty." Those are very strange words coming from a lawyer. I ask her how much I owe her and she laughs. "This one is on the house. Be sure to call the next time you're in town." She hangs up.

Now, I have to deal with the hard part—telling Khepri. She handles all the money these days and is very protective. Needless to say, she won't like writing that check. She takes the news calmly, which warns me I won't be getting off easily. "David, perhaps you should be more careful in dealing with Mrs. Allison in the future." I breathe a little easier.

"Oh," she says, acting surprised, "I need a new dress for the parents' orientation at Annapolis." Jeffrey is entering the Naval Academy in July and Khepri wants to attend the parents' orientation. "It would be nice if you came," she adds. I'm definitely not getting off easy. I agree, hoping to cut my loses, and we head for her favorite shopping mall.

Khepri is driving, and since the German Beast commands respect, she pulls into valet parking. We get out and have to push through a large crowd. "Oh, no," I moan. Rolinda and Rebecca are standing under a banner that says 'Sign Here!' and two long lines of eager voters extend around the corner. Hector is passing out free copies of the newspaper with Allison's photo on page one to anyone who will sign their petition and wants one.

"Ah, shit," I moan. Khepri gives me a stern look. She doesn't like profanity, especially in public. "I gave them the publicity they needed." I make a mental note to avoid shopping malls in the future.

Did I mention it was April Fool's Day?

36

Monday, May 23

Claire breathed a sigh of relief. Spring semester was officially over and they had not lost a single student to a random accident or drug overdose. Without doubt, Rebecca's safety campaign was a key player in making that happen. With Clint and Mateo, she had crafted an eight-minute video they called "The Darwin Awards Revisited."

The video recorded teenagers doing dangerous stunts, getting high on booze and drugs, and engaging in other typical teenaged activities. Then the video documented the aftermath, the ruined lives, and the emotional trauma of living with a permanent disfigurement. Rather than require every junior and high school student in Phoenix to see it, Rebecca had posted it on social media.

The video went viral when local school districts, at Claire's urging, banned it as being disruptive to the learning environment and would not allow teachers to show it in class. That ensured every student saw it. Claire knew, without doubt, that it had worked because it was a stealth campaign. *Teenagers!* She smiled to herself.

A knock at her office door brought her back to the moment. It was Rebecca. "Good news," she said. "The Secretary of State just certified the petition. You're on the ballot!" They had submitted the petition signatures on the last day, April 4, and her campaign had been in limbo since then. The White House had been silent about her not withdrawing from the race, but they were closely monitoring her standing in the polls. She was lagging well behind the two major candidates, but Nedd claimed there was an undercurrent of support the polls were missing.

"That is good news," Claire said. "Thank you." Rebecca smiled and nodded. "Rebecca, your Darwin Awards project was unbelievably successful. Why don't you take the day off?" Rebecca looked surprised. "It's the least I can do to say thanks, and please, will you and Clint be my guests at The Vineyard this evening? They have an out-of-the-world menu. Just tell me the time and I'll make the reservations."

"Eight o'clock would be lovely," Rebecca replied.

"I'll take care of it," Claire replied. "Honestly, I don't know how you all do it and I can't thank you enough."

Rebecca smiled. "We love it. Ah, it is time. Mateo and Hector are waiting with the car." Claire was the guest speaker at an awards ceremony at the oldest high school in Phoenix. Hector was one of the school's more successful graduates and was an honored guest. Claire gathered up her purse and stepped into the waiting elevator. The doors closed and she keyed her smartphone, quickly making the reservations.

Nedd buzzed and she answered. "Congratulations on the petition drive," he said. "Well done."

"Thank you," she replied. "It was close, but we made it."

"I'm monitoring some interesting fallout. Rolinda's school board is being hounded by emails and phone calls to fire Rolinda for being racist!"

"That makes no sense at all" Claire said. "Any idea who is behind it?" The elevator doors opened and she walked to the waiting staff car.

"Ken Sellor and a few leftovers from Antifa are behind it. They call themselves The Liberators. They found a sugar daddy, I don't know who, and are back in business. It's early days, but I think we'll see more and more of your supporters being targeted. A bunch of real hoons."

Claire laughed. "Hoons?"

"Hooligans, luv. I'll keep my eye on them." He went silent as Claire joined the two waiting men by a black SUV.

"Hector," Claire said, embracing him, "have you and Rolinda set a date yet?"

He held the door for her and sat in the front seat beside Mateo. "Not yet. But we're thinking maybe June. Thanks for doing this event today. My favorite teacher, Miss Culp, is going to be there. She's eighty-nine years old."

"What a delightful surprise," Claire replied. "I hope she remembers you."

Hector pulled a face. "Unfortunately, she probably does."

Later that afternoon, the black SUV pulled to a stop in front of Claire's office. "That was lovely," she told Hector, "and Miss Culp was an absolute delight. I can hardly wait to tell Rolinda what she remembered." Rebecca stepped out of archway and opened the door. Claire looked at her, wondering why she was still at work.

"We need to talk," Rebecca said, looking at Hector and Mateo. "A group of protestors are picketing Rolinda's home. So far, they've been peaceful, but they're using air horns to blast anyone driving by."

Hector punched the speed dial on his cell, calling Rolinda. "No answer. Any idea where she is?" Rebecca shook her head.

"Mateo," Claire said, "you and Hector go find her. Start at her house. Take the SUV." She knew the special-built vehicle had bullet-proof windows and tires with an air filtration system. She also suspected a few weapons were hidden on board. "Stay in contact. I'll call 911 and try to get help."

"Good luck with that one," Mateo grunted. Hector strapped into the passenger seat as Mateo slapped an emergency light on the roof. He accelerated into traffic, the light flashing, as he hit the siren to clear the intersection. Claire dialed 911. For a moment, she considered using the emergency code all public officials were given but thought better of it. She reported the disturbance at Rolinda's house and gave the operator her details.

Her cell buzzed before she could break the connection. "Nedd, what's going on?"

"Rolinda is at the ER at Honor Health and had to turn her cell off."

Claire relayed the information to Rebecca. "Can you check on her? I'll tell Hector and Mateo."

"Of course, immediately. But I doubt the ER will tell me anything."

"I'll take care of that," Claire said. Rebecca ran for her car. "Nedd, can you . . ."

"Done," Nedd said, interrupting her. "The ER has been notified that Rebecca is Rolinda's next of kin. Sorry, no update on her condition."

"Thanks, Nedd." She quickly messaged Hector with Rolinda's location. Now, she had to wait. A few minutes later, her smartphone buzzed with a message from Rebecca.

Rolinda OK, eyes being flushed.
Protestors sprayed her with hornet repellent.

Frustrated, she called Sarah, worried that demonstrators might be gathering in her neighborhood. Sarah said that all was quiet and asked about the coming weekend. Nedd interrupted. "There's an accident on the 202 involving a black SUV. Hold on. A police helicopter is on the scene and downlinking. I'm tapping into their video feed." Her smart-phone flashed and came alive with the downlink.

The helicopter zoomed over the scene and banked sharply to the right, circling the accident. The black SUV had been hit by a truck and rolled onto its side, blocking the freeway. The truck was backing away from the accident as Mateo pulled a limp Hector from the wreckage. "Hit and run!" the pilot shouted. The pilot kept circling and the truck came back into view as it accelerated towards the SUV. Mateo bounced up from behind the SUV and pushed Hector to safety just as the truck slammed into the SUV. The truck ground into the SUV and pushed it aside, trapping Mateo in the wreckage while opening an escape path.

Again, the helicopter came around, reacquiring the scene. A small flame flickered from under the SUV as the truck sped away. "Landing to render assistance," the pilot radioed. "Landing now." The pilot's mike was hot as he ran for the burning SUV, holding a fire extinguisher. "Fire's out," he radioed. "Victim unresponsive. Applying CPR."

"EMT four minutes out," the dispatcher said. "Any joy on the truck?"

"Negative visual on the truck." A hard silence came down, punctuated by the pilot's hard breathing as he worked to save Mateo. "Second victim sitting up, fully conscious, no sign of bleeding." An approaching siren drowned his transmission out before slowly dying. The sound of doors slamming and men running grew louder.

"We got him," another voice said. "No response. Not good."

"Shit, shit, shit," the pilot moaned.

Claire sat in stunned silence as tears filled her eyes. "Oh, Mateo," she whispered. "Damn, damn, damn." Tears streaked her face. She keyed her smartphone. "Nedd, it's all too much to be a coincidence—Rolinda and now this."

"Agreed," Nedd said. "There's some interesting messaging between the Liberators. The wankers are full of themselves and there's a lot of mutual backslapping going on. They're not saying why, but given the time and place of their texts, they're in it up to their eyeballs."

"Nedd, please help and make it stop before anyone else is hurt."

"I'm on it, luv."

37

Saturday, June 4

"She's magnificent," Chione breathes, her eyes locked on the TV. The family is gathered in the big lounge, the latest addition to the motel's second-floor living quarters, watching Mateo Torres's funeral. Khepri is happily playing grandmother, cuddling Chione's three-month old son, Mohammed Michael, and not paying attention. But I am.

Claire Allison is giving the eulogy, and there is not a dry eye in the cathedral as she reaches the peroration. "Mateo heard the call to duty at an early age and honored that summons with a life dedicated to the protection of others. He was driving in heavy traffic with a good man when they were caught in a senseless accident that may have been an act of terror. We may never know what motivated the driver of the truck as he bulldozed into Mateo's vehicle and made his escape.

"We do know that rather than seek safety, Mateo pushed his companion clear, only to be caught in the wreckage as a fire broke out. Mateo leaves behind a loving wife and two young children who will never know their father. But he has blessed them with a legacy of love and devotion to duty. Mateo Torres was a hero in every sense of the word. May I offer a prayer?" She looks full into the camera, her cheeks streaked with tears, and lowers her head. "Dear Lord, please take and cherish this man, for he was one of our best."

The woman is good, and I'm taking notes.

"I'm going to vote for her," Chione announces. Her husband gives her a stern look of disapproval, not because he dislikes Allison, but his wife is showing too much independence for an obedient Islamic woman. “You like her too,” Chione tells him. She flounces out of the room. If I read the signs right, Mohammed is not getting laid in the near future.

“What’s this thing with Allison and women,” I say, offering poor Mohammed what consolation I can. He shoots a look at Khepri. She’s not paying attention, and he shrugs in resignation. “Take her shopping,” I tell him. He follows his wife out. “Who knows?” I mumble. “It works for me.”

“Mohammed must learn we are not in Egypt,” Khepri says, not looking up.

“Are you going to vote for her?” I ask.

She doesn’t answer and coos at the baby.

Monday, June 27

All hell has broken out on the internet. The Liberators are being diddled big time. For the last three weeks, all their emails, text messages, telecommunications of any kind, have been plastered over the web, often showing up in the most embarrassing places.

One conversation about blowing up a Denver sewage plant was posted on the FBI website. I guess they just wanted to spread some shit around. The FBI didn’t think it was funny and made a few arrests. Then, The Liberators’ entire roster was posted on YouTube, complete with photos, birthdates, social security numbers, you name it. That went viral and their credit cards are now free game in the public sector.

A news flash on TV this morning announces that the Secret Service is now involved. Exactly why is pure speculation, but if I were a Liberator, I’d be leaving the country. It’s a story worth investigating, but I’m not about to incur the wrath of whoever is screwing them.

Nothing else is brewing that’s worth following up on and I’m getting antsy. Khepri hasn’t had a vacation since we were in Las Vegas last September, and I’m thinking maybe doing Hollywood or San Diego when Laura calls from Sacramento. She’s screaming and it takes a few moments to understand. “Larry’s gotten off his skinny ass!”

I can’t figure out why this warrants a meltdown. “He’s going to indict her!” Now I understand. The wheels of justice may grind slowly, but they do grind. When I ask why he's had a change of heart, after setting on it for four months she just says, "Not on the phone. We need you here."

There goes the vacation.

I'm on a plane four hours later feeling very much like a ping pong ball bouncing between Phoenixville and Sactown. Laura and Mary are waiting at the airport when I arrive. They have purchased a home in Sacramento's Fabulous Forties and offer me their guest room. The memory of previous offers to share a bed are still steaming in my brain.

An inner voice tells me that given Khepri's strong territorial instincts, it is not a good idea. Reluctantly, I decline. It's late, and we head for Mary's office where they fill me in on the details. "Larry called from a conference in DC," Mary says. "Apparently, someone torched his behind about Allison."

"Who could that possibly be?" I ask.

"Smart ass," Laura humps. "She's shaking things up big time and the boys don't like that."

"Larry's catching the redeye," Mary says. "He'll be here in the morning and wants to see you.

Life is good.

Tuesday, June 28

I'm sitting in Mary's office looking at the photos of the .22 snub-nose revolver when Larry makes his entrance just after lunch. I guess he missed the redeye. Judging by the expression on his face, he's had a backbone jammed up his ass. Lawrence Longchamps is tall, lanky, and good-looking. He's also an ego-driven politician who fancies himself the Attorney General for some president. Mary calls him Larry Neckless because of his skinny neck. He's very articulate and well-connected, so I chalk it up to sour grapes on Mary's part.

Laura and I hide in a corner while Larry and Mary go over the case. Larry thinks it will be the trial of the century, and I agree. Larry paces the floor, issuing orders. "Examine everything with a microscope from the defense's perspective. Be ready for any challenges." From the look on Mary's face, she knows what to do and doesn't need lecturing.

"I will be lead in this case," Larry says, "and I hate surprises." This is a total surprise for a smart DA never personally litigates a case in court, it's too dangerous. Better to let an assistant DA take the fall if it all goes south. But a prosecution taking Allison out of the governor's race in Arizona will earn him the undying gratitude of the boys in Washington. Mary nods, her face passive. I give her high marks for keeping her cool.

"Mistake," Laura whispers in my ear. "Mary is the best prosecutor in the office."

Larry turns to me. "David, you can help. I want a detailed dossier on Allison's attorney and anyone sitting at the defense table. They will have skin in this trial." I don't like the sound of that but say nothing. Larry paces the floor, finally striking a pose, looking out the window. If he took acting classes, he deserves a refund.

"I want one judge in charge of the entire case. I want him to be intimately familiar with every nuance; arraignment, motion, appeal, jury selection, and most importantly, in charge of the calendar. Timing is critical." He calls up his calendar on his smartphone. "I'll present the complaint to the Grand Jury on August 9." He fixes Mary with a hard look. "My presentation must be faultless. Make it happen."

"The charge?" Mary asks.

"PC 187."

"Penal Code 187," Laura whispers in my ear. "Capital Crimes."

"LWOP?" Mary asks. I shake my head in confusion and Mary sighs. "LWOP are the initials for Life Without Parole."

"No," Larry replies. "Death Penalty." Holy shit! This has turned into a blood sport. The hard look on his face is frozen. "Any questions?" Needless to say, there aren't any. Larry marches out the door, leaving a wake of silence behind him.

"August 9 is over a month away," I finally say. "Why so long? I thought a grand jury would indict a ham sandwich."

"Not this grand jury," Mary says. I can hear respect in her voice. "We need the time to prepare. Besides, the Neckless One needs time to play courthouse politics and get the judge he wants."

"I don't see a problem," I say. "This looks like a slam dunk."

"Nothing is a slam dunk in a courtroom," Mary replies. "Let's go to work." She leads us into a conference room filled with files and evidence boxes. "Inventory first," she says, handing me a legal pad and a pencil.

We've been going at it for over seven hours and I'm pooped. I catch an Uber to my room rather than walk. I'm not surprised to see the light on and Khepri reading in bed. I'm glad to see her. She makes me feel wanted.

38

Thursday, August 11

The nightmare was back, intense as ever. Claire woke with a start, her heart racing. She could still see Bobby Lee's eyes, wide with fear, fixated on her. Slowly, her breathing calmed. She felt for a Kleenex and patted her face dry before checking on the time. It was just after four in the morning. *Sleeplessness, my old friend. Will you ever go away?*

She rolled over, sat on the edge of the bed, and turned on the light. Her smartphone was flashing with a message from Nedd to please call ASAP. She hit the speed dial and his image filled the screen. "Don't you ever sleep?" she grumped.

"Feeling under the weather?" Nedd asked.

"Just tired." *Renew your sleeping pills, you twit, and get a decent night's sleep.* Thanks to Nedd, she knew the Sacramento County DA had met with the Grand Jury two days ago and that she was the subject of his presentation. "Any news?" She rolled back into bed.

"Afraid so. They voted out a sealed indictment last evening. It was late and I didn't want to wake you. I couldn't break it, but you are the subject. Awesome firewalls. Thanks to *5G*, it's getting tough out there." Information technology was constantly changing, and more and more systems were going dark to hackers. Progress had frozen her out, and now it was happening to Nedd.

"It had to happen," Claire replied.

"I did monitor some pillow talk between a few members of the Grand Jury. All very interesting." He paused to see if Claire was listening and not in her 'do the right thing' mode. She was listening. "The foreman, actually it's the forewoman, of the jury is a bit of a cougar and sleeping with the youngest gentlemen on the panel. He's a lustful little bugger and claims that he had it off with one of the DA's legal aides. According to the aide, Longchamps thinks they have a slam dunk case, and it's just a matter of getting you into a courtroom. It's not good, luv."

"And?" Claire asked. She knew the way Nedd worked.

"They're going for the death penalty."

"I'm not surprised," Claire said calmly.

"The only effective death penalty in California is in social media and on TV."

"I can play that game," Claire said.

"They are going to arrest and extradite you to California. I don't see you making bail. With you out of the picture, I'll need help, someone with their feet on the ground to fill in. Best if it's someone new."

She thought for a moment. "Jenna Bradley. I'll introduce you."

"Thanks, luv. By the way, I have the name of a lawyer, a Mrs. Lynn Majors in Sacramento. She has an excellent reputation. You might want to contact her." He waited for a reply, but only heard a gentle breathing. He turned off the light and let her sleep. "I'll take that as a yes," he murmured.

Clint Roberts was waiting with a silver SUV when Claire emerged from her home, rested and fresh after sleeping in. "Good afternoon, Madam Superintendent." He held the door.

"Thank you," she replied. "I imagine everyone at the office had a delightful morning."

"When the boss is away, you know who plays." He laughed. "They're all giggling over the latest news. Rolinda and Hector are getting married the end of the month, on Saturday."

"An August wedding," Claire said. "How lovely. I was worried about Hector after the accident."

"He's a tough old warrior," Clint said.

They rode in silence as she called up the morning's correspondence and news on her smartphone. The latest polling showed her holding steady with twenty percent of the vote.

Ken Sellor and his rival were both hovering around forty percent, and Mike Westfield was predicting a hard-fought campaign as long as she was in the race.

Rolinda was waiting with Rebecca when Claire walked into her office. "That idiot told you, didn't he?" Rebecca said. Claire simply hugged them both.

"We want you to marry us," Rolinda said.

"It would be my honor," Claire replied. She dabbed her eyes with a Kleenex. She motioned Rolinda into her office and closed the door. "I love you and Hector, and I can't tell you how much this means to me. I need to get a special license and you know how hectic my life is right now. Please promise me that you will get married, no matter what."

"I promise," Rolinda said. "Besides, what could possibly go wrong?"

39

Thursday, the same day

It's déjà vu all over again. I think it was Yogi Berra who said that. His grammar may have sucked, but he was right. It's late Thursday afternoon, and I'm sitting in the same Sacramento Superior Court that I had come to know and loathe when I was getting my ass sued off. That was over four years ago, but nothing has really changed. It's the same bailiff, they call 'em court attendants now, and the same courtroom.

The only difference is that I'm in the audience and not in the dock. That's comforting. I'm sitting next to a very young reporter with great legs, perky tits, and high cheekbones. She looks all of eighteen and vaguely familiar. The young lovely is sitting on one very hot story. I wonder if she has the smarts to know what's happening, much less dig it out.

Larry the Neckless One leads Mary and two law clerks in, which is overkill for filing a complaint. Miss Reporter perks up and whips out her notebook. I like that, using a notebook. The court attendant calls "All rise," and Justice Patricia Wells takes her place behind the bench.

Larry is not surprised but shoots a hard look at Mary anyway, expressing his displeasure. Her Honor is the most intelligent and no-nonsense judge in the courthouse and lawyers have learned the hard way not to mess with her. Wells scans the courtroom and fixes me with a long look. There is no doubt she remembers my case. I'm doubly glad I'm not the subject of the complaint. She turns to business and Larry pulls out the sealed Grand Jury indictment from his leather folder and presents it to the court clerk, who dutifully passes it to Wells.

Her Honor reads the indictment and accepts the complaint, which allows the DA to file an arrest warrant. So far, no name has been mentioned, and Miss Reporter is very interested. Wells issues a sealed arrest warrant, which means the world has yet to learn about Mrs. Claire Allison's dark little secret.

Court is adjourned and Larry is in a huff since he is going for maximum publicity on this one. He throws his leather folder at Mary as they file out. "Alert the Phoenix PD," he tells Mary. "Make it a joint arrest."

"I'll make the phone call," Mary assures him.

Miss Reporter jots down a note, obviously overhearing every word. "Who's getting burned?" she asks.

"Beats me," I say.

"Really, Mr. Parker?" That gets my attention. How does she know me? "I'm Jenna Bradley," Miss Reporter says. She gives me a sweet look. "Stella Madura Middle School? Danny Hawkins? You know my mom."

The Jenna Bradley I remember has grown up, and I remember her mother very well. "How's the good Doctor?" I ask.

Jenna says she's doing fine. I ask what brings her to court these days. "I'm majoring in media at Sacramento State and doing a class project on court reporting. I'm applying for an internship at KPIO-TV with Mike Westfield and this should help." She bestows the same sweet smile on me and bustles out of the courtroom, all business.

It is déjà vu all over again, which, under the circumstances, is too much coincidence for me. In my world, once is pure chance, twice is coincidence, and three is enemy action. I'm mulling that over when my cell phone buzzes with a message from Laura. Mary wants to see me in her office soonest. There's a sense of urgency, so I head for the DA offices on G Street. It's a three-minute walk and I run all the way, well, what passes for running. I charge up the stairs and burst into Mary's office. "That was fast," Laura says.

Mary is on the telephone. "You're good to go," she says to Laura, hanging up the phone. Laura hands her a full glass of champagne.

"Why the celebration?" I ask. Laura hands me a glass of bubbly.

"We have a good judge," Mary says. "Wells is the absolute best, and she handed down a sealed warrant."

"But Wells is not the judge Larry wanted," I reply.

Mary pulls a face. "Larry Neckless is an asshole, and his trial record sucks. Wells will keep him honest and the case on track." She guzzles her champagne. "We can win this one." She sets her glass down. "The Neckless One wants to see us, like now."

"Whatever for?" I ask. Mary shrugs and we all head for the DA's office. We are ushered into his august presence. The walls are covered with framed photos, all with Larry and some political mover and groover, including Queen Elizabeth, which of course, certifies his augustness.

Larry comes right to the point. "David, this is going to be the trial of the year, maybe the decade, and I want it documented in its entirety with the insight necessary for an accurate and complete historical record. There is no one better qualified than you to do that. To that end, I will deputize you as my special assistant, which will allow you access to all the relevant records, dispositions, exhibits, and witnesses. Are you interested?"

Of course, I'm interested. It's obvious that Larry wants to be the hero of this so-called documentary, and publicity is the name of the game. I can play his game and we negotiate the terms: no salary, all expenses paid, I will produce a formal report for the DA, but retain all rights to publish my own book one year after submission of said formal report. All is readily agreed, and Larry swears me in on the spot with Mary and Laura as witnesses. Neither are looking very happy about my sudden elevation. Larry asks me when I want to start. "Immediately," I reply, "starting with serving the arrest warrant."

"The flight to Phoenix leaves at nine tomorrow morning," Laura says.

"You're making the arrest?" I ask. Again, I prove there are stupid questions.

"Of course. Who else?" Laura has been the officer in charge of the case since day one, and she has earned the right to bring the perp in. Cops think of it as closure.

Friday, August 12

Friday's flight to Phoenix is delayed and we land at Sky Harbor just after three in the afternoon. Harry the Cop is waiting for us and, for a moment, it's old times all over again. Like Laura, he's the cop of record, which is why he's handling the Phoenix side of the joint arrest.

A staff car is waiting and we all pile in and head for downtown. Laura shows Harry the arrest warrant. He grunts something unintelligible. I sense he is not a happy camper about joint arrests. Laura tells him that she's sorry, but as soon as he certifies Allison has been deposited safe and undamaged to the Sacramento County jail meisters, he's off the hook.

The staff car pulls up in front of the County Superintendent's office just as the first wave of workers knocks off for the day. There's going to be a big audience when Allison does her perp walk, handcuffed and properly disgraced, all for the sake of public transparency in the criminal justice system.

"Ah, crap," I moan. "What's she doing here?" Jenna Bradley is standing on the sidewalk looking perky. There are six other reporters milling around and one TV cameraman. My alarm bells are clanging.

We head for Allison's office and barge in, just like on TV cop shows. Claire Allison is standing there, almost like she's waiting for us. She's wearing a light blue business-style shirt and slick chino trousers with orange-colored walking shoes. "Hello, David," she says. Laura identifies herself as Detective Zavorsky from the Sacramento Sheriff's Department and goes through the arrest spiel, ending with the standard "you have the right to remain silent," blah, blah. Laura pulls out her handcuffs, and that's when it all falls apart.

The big dude I've seen in the videos with Rebecca elbows his way between us and Allison. "I'm Special Agent Clinton Roberts with the Arizona Department of Public Safety and in charge of the detail providing protection for Superintendent Allison." He flashes his badge and ID card. At the same time, he makes sure we see the Glock semi-automatic strapped to his waist. That gets my attention. "Because of the threats we have received," Roberts says, "and your lack of situational awareness, I cannot allow you to take Superintendent Allison into custody."

Harry the Cop is many things, but he's got cojones and isn't having any of it. "Get out of our way, buddy." He reaches out to grab Allison. Roberts clamps down on his forearm so fast I barely saw it happen. For a moment the two men stare at each other. It's a contest of wills and strength. Roberts' face is impassive as he slowly forces Harry's arm down before releasing it. Harry rubs his forearm but doesn't move.

"Detective Zavorsky," Allison says, "will you and your team please meet me at the police station? Agent Roberts will drive me there and I will surrender to the officer on duty." Laura and Harry are not happy. They want a perp walk. It's one of the perks of their job.

For a brief moment, I think Harry will go for his gun. But given Roberts' quick reflexes, that is not a good idea. "Sounds fair to me," I say, trying to smooth some very ruffled feathers. Laura nods and Harry visibly relaxes. His cop honor is intact, and he won't be harassed by his buddies at happy hour for being out-snarked by some Arizona State federale.

Roberts holds up his left hand, motioning us to silence as he scans his smartphone. "Problems," he says. "We've identified five Liberators in the crowd outside and two more TV crews. We're being setup for a demonstration, and it's not going to be peaceful."

He thinks for a moment. "Okay, give us a five-minute head start. Then you walk out the front, just like you came in. While they focus on you, we'll drive out the service exit and meet you at City Hall. You will be followed, count on it. Superintendent Allison can surrender there. Then, we can take the security tunnel to the courthouse unobserved."

As usual, I'm confused. "Why do we have to go to the courthouse?" I ask.

"Extradition," Laura replies. I've never understood the legal niceties involved with moving a defendant across state lines. Apparently, it can cause all sorts of delays.

"From there," Roberts says, "we'll take an unmarked car to Luke Air Force Base where a charter will fly you to Sacramento." Laura looks relieved by the arrangements, and for the first time, I really understand how situational awareness works.

Our escape goes like clockwork, and a little over an hour later we are standing in front of a superior court judge in the courthouse. We've shaken off everyone except Jenna who was waiting when we walked into the courtroom. The young lady is very good at her job, or she has one super source of information. She smiles at me. "Say hello to your mother," I say again. It's all I can think of.

It's getting late and the judge wants to go home. "Mrs. Allison, the warrant for your arrest is in good order and has been properly executed. I note that you are not represented by legal counsel. We can postpone this hearing until counsel is available."

Allison stands up. She is calm and composed, not to mention drop-dead gorgeous. "I do not require legal counsel at this time and wish to proceed with all due expediency." She could win an Academy Award with a movie performance like this.

The judge studies her over the top of his glasses. "Very well. Do you waive your right to an extradition hearing?"

"I do," Allison answers.

Laura exhales in relief. There is no legal hang up keeping Allison in Arizona, and Roberts has us out of the courthouse backdoor and headed for Luke Air Force Base in less than five minutes. It's rush hour and it takes over an hour to reach the base, but that's Phoenix. Jenna is standing outside the main gate. She notes the time and videos our entrance into the base on her smartphone. There is no doubt she's tracking us. But how?

It's a routine security operation for the Air Force, but we have to wait three hours for our charter to arrive. The flight to Sacramento is smooth and quick. We land at Sacramento Executive Airport just after midnight where an unmarked police van is waiting for us. As expected, Jenna is standing at the exit gate when we drive out. She waves at us. "Who is she?" Laura asks, a little worried. .

"Jenna Bradley," Allison answers. "She was one of my students." Suddenly, I remember the conversation I had with Jenna about writing a book. That worries me—forgetting—not the bit about writing the book. Everyone thinks they can write one, but I'm living proof that few do.

It's a short drive to the county jail. We walk into the ground floor with Jenna in close tow. I'm totally pooped by the long day and knocked speechless when Lynn Majors magically appears and introduces herself. "Mrs. Allison, I'm Lynn Majors. Your office contacted me. It would be my privilege to represent you."

"That would make me very happy," Allison replies.

Lynn takes charge and turns to Laura and Harry. "I need to speak to my client in private before we proceed." Lynn leads Allison to a corner where they can talk without being overheard.

"Who, on a good day, is Lynn Majors?" Harry asks.

Laura lets out her breath in resignation. "Probably the best defense attorney in Sacramento, and aggressive, like in pit bull." If only they knew, I think.

Allison and Lynn are back within minutes. "It's now Saturday morning and you have forty-eight hours to arraign," Lynn says. She checks her watch and gives them a break. "Considering the hour, no later than noon on Monday." She turns to Laura and Harry. "I will need your full names and badge numbers. There are issues involving your conduct that must be addressed."

She motions to Jenna who waves her notebook at us. "Please make yourself available for the arraignment," she tells Harry. Laura and Harry haven't done a thing wrong, but that's the way the legal system works in California.

We all follow Allison and Lynn into processing where two severe-looking women deputies are waiting. Jenna is videoing the entire process, and Lynn is bending Allison's ear with whispered instructions before turning her over. "It will be okay," Lynn says. From personal experience, I know it won't. The Sacramento County Jail specializes in submission and control, and just being locked up with the inmates is part of the punishment.

The two guards escort Allison inside.

40

Monday, August 15

The deputy marched across the lower level of the maximum security dormitory unit called a 'pod'. She waited until all the inmates were locked inside their cells before climbing the stairs to the second level. She rapped sharply on the door of a narrow cell. "Stand back from the door." She paused as the guard in the control booth buzzed the cell door to open. She stepped inside.

Claire was standing against the far wall as directed. She was wearing 'oranges', the jail uniform with an orange and white striped top with PRISONER SACRAMENTO JAIL on the back, and solid orange pants. "You're being transported to the courthouse for arraignment."

Claire held out her hands to be handcuffed. "Can I comb my hair first?" she asked.

"Negative," the deputy barked. She snapped the handcuffs around Claire's wrists. Claire gave her hair a shake, tossing it into place over her left shoulder as the deputy shackled her ankles. The deputy relented. "Nice shoes. They match. Where did you find them?"

"T.J. Maxx," Claire replied. Her oranges had been altered, and for once, the uniform fit. Claire was making a presentable appearance. The deputy suspected a trustee was helping her. That was a problem. Trusted prisoners were given privileges in exchange for information, not to help their fellow inmates. "Your hands are considered weapons," the deputy said. "Always shove them into your waist band when moving under escort or I will chain them to your waist." She motioned Claire into the pod's day room and guided her to the stairs.

A chorus of "Go get 'em, girl!" washed over the pod. A lone "Eat shit, white bitch!" echoed from the lower level.

"I love you, too," Claire called. She was smiling.

"Knock it off!" the deputy shouted. The cat calls slowly died away. They took the elevator to the basement where two burly male deputies were waiting. One held the door and gently guided Claire in, which surprised the woman deputy. "You're looking at a 187?" she asked. It was her way of telling the two male deputies to shift into their power mode.

"That's what my lawyer tells me," Claire replied.

"Who'd you off?" the smaller of men asked. It was a trick Nedd had warned her about. Claire only shook her head, letting that serve as her answer.

It was a short drive to the basement of the courthouse where they took an elevator to the back corridor of Department 20. Lynn was waiting for her and they stepped into an attorney-witness conference room where they could talk. Lynn quickly explained what Claire could expect in court. "This won't take long. The honorable Patricia Wells is presiding. She is one tough, by-the-book lady and doesn't put up with any nonsense. When she asks, 'How do you plead,' stand up and just say, 'Not guilty, your Honor' and sit down. She will ask for a trial date, and under the circumstances, we need to delay as long as possible."

Claire shook her head. "No. Make it as soon as we can."

"I can't recommend that," Lynn said.

"Please, the sooner the better." Claire's eyes filled with tears. "When can I call my son?"

"I'll make that happen today." A knock at the door announced it was time. "We're on," Lynn said. "Remember, say as little as possible and let me do the talking."

The three deputies were waiting and escorted Claire into the courtroom. They made a show of sitting behind her as visitors filled the room. Mary and Parker walked in and sat down at the prosecutor's table. The courtroom was full when Larry Longchamps made his entrance from the hallway and marched past Claire and Lynn. Two legal aides, a man and a woman, followed him in. Both were carrying briefcases.

"Five prosecutors to one defense," Lynn murmured to Claire. "The media will love it." She looked over the audience. "There are two sketch artists in the audience. Turn around so they can see your face."

Claire turned and saw Jenna who was sitting directly behind the deputies. "Hello," she said.

"Don't speak to the audience," the woman deputy said. Claire nodded and smiled at Jenna before turning to face the bench.

"Don't do that again," the deputy warned.

"Is smiling at the people I love okay?"

Lynn gestured at the prosecution table. "That depends on them." With everyone in place, the court attendant called for everyone to rise. Patricia Wells walked in and, for a brief moment, stood behind her chair at the bench, surveying the room. With one commanding glance, she established her authority and sat down. She greeted them cordially, explained why they were there, and asked if there was any business before proceeding.

Lynn came to her feet. "Your Honor, if it pleases the court, may Mrs. Allison dress in normal clothing for all future appearances to avoid the appearance of guilt? Also, may her shackles be removed for the same reason? It's a question of basic human dignity, not to mention comfort."

Longchamps came to his feet. "May I remind the court why the defendant is in court and under guard? She has already tried to establish contact with a member of the audience, to what end, we can only speculate."

Lynn smothered a smile. It was time to test the waters and learn what she could get away with. "Your Honor, this is Mrs. Allison's first time in a superior court and she is unfamiliar with our procedures. She only said hello to a former student, whom she had saved from a gunman over four years ago. Please accept our apologies and it won't happen again." She waited, expecting a reprimand from the bench.

Wells knew Lynn was playing to the press by referring to the incident with Danny Hawkins. "Remove the defendant's shackles," she ordered. "In the future, the defendant may dress in normal clothing, without shackles. Mrs. Majors, while in court, please confine your remarks about the defendant to your opening and closing statements."

"I will, your Honor. Thank you." Lynn sat down and the larger of the two male deputies removed Claire's handcuffs and shackles.

Wells asked if there was any further business before proceeding. Longchamps and Lynn both said no. Wells read the multiple charges, starting with murder in the first degree with special circumstances, followed by murder committed with a firearm, and kidnapping for the purpose of committing a felony. "Do you understand the charges as I read them to you?" Claire stood and said she did. "To these charges, what is your plea?"

Claire didn't hesitate. "Not guilty to all charges, your Honor."

Now it was Lynn's turn. "Your Honor, may we be heard on bail at this time? My client is a prominent citizen and running for political office. She has an unblemished record and only wants to clear her name. She is not a flight risk."

Mary was ready and handed Longchamps a folder as he jumped up. He flipped the folder open and glanced at the rebuttal Mary had prepared. Rather than read it, he ran through the standard textbook objections and sat down. Wells didn't hesitate. "Bail denied." Longchamps stared at Lynn, his look filled with contempt.

"Your honor," Lynn said, totally unperturbed, "my client demands a speedy trial within sixty days." The look on Longchamps face vanished. He turned to Mary and held his hand up, shielding their conversation. "He wasn't expecting that," Lynn whispered. "You played havoc with his schedule, right in the run up to an election."

Mary opened another folder and stood. "Your Honor, if I may. The prosecution recognizes the defendant's right to a speedy trial; however, this is an extremely complicated case and there is ample precedent for giving both the defense and the prosecution the time necessary to file the appropriate motions." She handed the clerk a list of precedents and rulings. "Given the nature of the evidence, we must proceed with care and not sacrifice due diligence for speed. There are ample precedents to warrant a delay until after the first of the year."

The clerk handed Mary's list to Wells and she quickly read through the list. "I agree with you that this is a complex case," Wells replied. "However, the defendant is not waiving her right to a speedy trial." She looked at Mary. "The prosecution best be ready as I am not inclined to grant any extensions." She tapped on her laptop, calling up the court calendar. "The trial will start on Tuesday, October 11," Wells announced.

She motioned at Longschamps. "Please be ready or I will dismiss all charges. Jury pool notification will start in four weeks." We all stand as she steps down from the bench.

"My office in thirty minutes," Longchamps growled at Mary. He stood and stalked out, the two legal aides right behind him.

"Have a nice day," Lynn said to his back. She turned to the three deputies who were still sitting behind Claire. "I need to confer with Mrs. Allison," she said.

"You can do that at 651," the woman deputy said, referring to the county jail's street address. Claire had an unqualified right to speak with her attorney in private, but they were sparring over the when and where, and who was in control.

"Really?" Lynn said. She nodded at Jenna who was holding up her smartphone, recording the exchange. "This could go viral." The deputies froze, fully aware of the power of social media.

"If I may," the court attendant said. He smiled and walked over to the defense table. "It's been a long morning, and we all need a break." He spread his hands in an open and friendly gesture. "Why don't you take Mrs. Allison to the holding cell in the basement, and I'll bring some coffee and donuts around."

"That's very kind," Lynn said. She smiled at the deputies. The woman deputy finally nodded and motioned Claire and Lynn to follow her into the back hall.

Once inside the small cell, Lynn motioned Claire to a seat as the door locked behind them. "That is one pissed off deputy" Lynn said. "Hopefully at me. You did good in there today, and we scored big with the media. But be careful when the jury is in the room. Wells is very protective of them and will rip us a new one if we even hiccup wrong. Don't cross her." Lynn paced the floor. "We go to trial in fifty-seven days.

Are you sure about that? The longer we delay the better—witnesses disappear, evidence goes missing, something unexpected happens—time is on our side. I recommend you use it."

Claire reached out and held Lynn's hands. "I wish I knew you better. October 11 is fine, and I need to get this over with. Why delay the inevitable? I hope you understand." She squeezed Lynn's hands, her face sad but calm.

Lynn had defended over a hundred men and women facing a murder charge and recognized the signs. Claire Marie Allison had killed a man and had come to the bar to find justice. "I'll do what I can," Lynn murmured. She looked at Claire's hands, surprised at the strength behind the smooth and unblemished skin. "Now, about that phone call." She handed Claire her cell phone.

"Thank you," Claire murmured. The lawyer turned away and fitted her earbuds. She turned up the volume so the music would drown out the conversation and give Claire what privacy she could.

Claire punched in Logan's number and waited. Nedd answered. "Logan will be here in a moment, and we're good to go on all fronts. It was a piece of cake cracking into the jail's systems, and I can keep an eye on you. Unfortunately, the screws are damn good at running the place, and we'll be out of contact. A few of the sheilas in the pod are bloody idiots, but you'll be safe enough as long as you're isolated. Give my phone number to a few of the trustees and have them call me. I might be able to do some wheelin' and dealin'.

"By the way, you're in Dorothea Puentes old cell." Puentes was the infamous F Street landlady who murdered fifteen of her elderly and sick tenants for their welfare checks in the 1980s. "How many blighters did she snuff before they caught her? That might be newsworthy."

Claire laughed, "I hope not."

"It's good to hear you laugh, lass. Are you sure this is how you want to go with this?"

"I am. It's the only way I can handle it. When do we start?"

"Friday evening, September 16. Lass, you're taking a chance, and the outcome could be dodgy. I suggest you low key it."

"I will."

"Smashing. I have Logan on the line."

"Thanks, Nedd. You're a sweetheart."

"Mom!" Logan shouted.

"I'm here, darling." She cuddled the phone to her ear, and tears filled her eyes as they talked. Logan reassured her that all was well at home, and they were all fine. She closed her eyes and smiled gently when he told her about his first girlfriend. "It's Mary Beth and she really likes me. We talk about you a lot."

Claire heard the pain in his words and knew it was time. "We can talk about it if you want."

"Mom, everyone says you murdered Mr. MacElroy."

"Bobby Lee was an evil man, Logan. I know you liked him, but he did things he shouldn't have, and he hurt innocent children. Because of what he did, two of his victims committed suicide."

"I remember Danny Hawkins," Logan said. "I didn't know there was another one."

"She was the mother of a beautiful eight-year-old girl he molested," Claire explained. "She blamed herself for letting it happen and couldn't live with the guilt."

"Mrs. Shriver said we should never blame ourselves for what other people do. We talked about that a lot when I was seeing her. You can't blame yourself for what he did. Besides, I never told anyone what happened, so what could you do?"

"Oh, my dear sweet Logan, we were all victims of a very evil man, and no one could stop him."

"But did he deserve to die?"

"Your father died fighting men who hurt innocent people. He had to stop them because no one else could." Claire held her breath, waiting for his reaction.

Then, with a firm conviction, Logan replied, "Dad would have stopped him, no matter what. And maybe Danny Hawkins would still be alive."

"Logan, do you remember Grandfather Madison?"

"Your father? A little."

"He taught me something very important; we are all shepherds and we must guard the ones we love, no matter the cost."

For a moment there was only silence. "Am I a shepherd?" Logan finally asked.

Claire sighed in relief. "If you want to be."

"I want to be like you and dad."

Oh, my dear, sweet Logan. "That would make me very proud."

Lynn turned to Claire and pointed to her watch. "I've got to go," Claire said. "I love you."

"I love you too." He broke the connection.

Tuesday, August 16

Claire looked up from her book at the sound. She listened, hearing it again. It was a gentle knock at her cell door. She stood and took three short steps and looked out the door's small window. A trustee, a slender young African American, was standing outside. Claire tapped on the window and the door clicked open. The trustee stepped inside and the door closed behind her. "How you make that happen? Aren't they lookin' at us?"

Claire motioned the young woman to the only chair and she sat on the bed. "I have a friend who is very good with computers, and he can fiddle with the security system." She pointed at the camera embedded in the ceiling. "He can put that into a loop, and they don't know you're here. You know, this is terrible, but I don't even know your name."

"Latisha."

"Well, Latisha, thank you very much for tailoring my oranges. That was very kind of you. I owe you."

"You said your friend can fuck with the security system. How much can he do?" The girl had come to collect for altering her uniform.

Claire sensed she had an ally, which in the confined world of the seventh floor was vital to survival. "That's about all he can do," Claire replied. "If he messes too much, they'll suspect something is wrong and will call in a geek to fix it."

Latisha stared at Claire's feet. "Ebola, she the bitch that yells at you, she say she gonna cut me good for fixin' your oranges."

Claire touched the other woman's hand. "My friend can help. When do you make your next phone call?" The prisoners were allowed one telephone call a week from the bank of phones in the dayroom.

"Tomorrow," Latisha answered.

"Call this number and my friend will answer." She had Latisha repeat the number three times. "Just repeat exactly what you told me about Ebola."

"He kill the bitch?"

"No, he can't do that, but something will happen. Can I ask you a question?" Latisha nodded. "Can we do some trading?" Again, Latisha nodded. "Our feet look about the same size. I'll trade you my shoes for yours if you'll read Martin Luther King, Jr.'s biography and then talk to me in, say, a week?"

Latisha looked at her in surprise. "Why you do that?"

"I really owe you for making my oranges fit. You took a chance on me when you didn't have to. Besides, it will give us something to talk about, and I think I know how to get you a decent paying job when you get out of here."

For the first time, Latisha smiled. "I do that. But why his book?"

"Maybe you can learn something. I know I will." Claire reached down and untied her shoes. "Let's trade and see what happens." Claire had made her first ally.

41

Monday, August 29

The Neckless One did not do me a favor when he deputized me as his special assistant, and I have never worked so hard in all my life. It's been two weeks since Allison was arraigned, and Mary and Laura are using me as a special investigator prepping for the trial. I'm digging into the background of every witness, and, thanks to Barry the Hacker, getting an inside look.

Every evening I drop by the jail, talk to the guards, and review the security tapes to keep an eye on Allison. She is in isolation, and when she is exercising in the dayroom, she is polite and the model prisoner. The guards treat her with respect and constantly talk among themselves about the changes in the pod. The inmates seem to be getting along better and there hasn't been a fight in over a week.

And then there's Larry. He is tall, forty-five-years old, and other than his skinny neck, very good-looking. He also has a gorgeous, well-connected wife who is ambitious to a fault. I have learned that Larry is very intelligent and not to be trifled with. He knows how to hurt people, mainly through the Franchise Tax Board and the IRS.

I think that's where his wife's connections come in. Mary calls her Lady Macbeth, and hopes we remember the good lady committed suicide in the last act of Shakespeare's play. Laura is not as discreet and refers to both of them as worthless jerks on the make. But that is another story I'll follow up on later.

I'm working my way down the defense's witness list and eventually come to Rolinda Johnson. I can't interview her, but

I can Google her. The internet is a wonderful thing, and the first thing that pops up is her wedding to Hector Mendoza two days ago, on the last Saturday of August. The list of the attendees at Casa Mendoza is impressive. Mike Westfield is there along with his ever-loyal assistant, Susanne, and a cameraman. That leads me to YouTube and videos of the nuptials which have gone viral.

Perky little Jenna Bradley is everywhere interviewing people, no doubt for a college project. Her pencil is flying, gathering quotes from everyone. Why is Tom Blaisdale from the White House there? Then there's Joe and Kimberly Prescott, two of the biggest rainmakers in Arizona, along with Brianna Prees from CNB, all charming and nice for a change.

What the hell is going on? It looks more like a political rally than a wedding. The dawn finally breaks over my fevered brow and I realize that is exactly what it is. Their candidate is in the slammer awaiting trial, and there is nothing in the wonderful world of politics that stops her from running for election to a public office. She has to be convicted for that to happen.

This says a lot about our politicians, but I digress. I don't see how this relates to the trial, so I move on.

The more I dig into Rolinda's past, the more I admire her. She is a person who really cares about her students and has made a difference. Barry the Hacker finds a sordid little tidbit about her first husband and what she did to him during their divorce; something about him running an escort business for the morally challenged. Mary needs to know this if Rolinda takes the stand as a character witness for Allison.

Wednesday, September 7

We get a big break when the chief deputy from the jail calls. They caught a trustee coming out of Allison's cell. I call Laura and we hotfoot it for the jail. I want to interview said trustee about Allison, and Laura wants to find out how she got into Allison's cell. This is not looking good for the Sacramento Jail.

My suspicions are confirmed when we walk in. The Sacramento Sheriff is there and he is not a happy man. This must be very serious if he's involved. The chief deputy and his aide are looking like subdued schoolboys, and the guilty trustee, one Latisha Williams, is sitting in a corner looking innocent and very much the aggrieved party. The Sheriff is even less happy when he sees me.

"We appear to have a misunderstanding about a trustee's duties," the Sheriff says. He turns to Williams, folds his arms, and gives her a look that doesn't bode well for the remainder of her stay in the clink. "Don't waste my time. What's going down?"

She gives it right back to him. "Nothing that I know of. I was carrying out my duties and the door to Claire's cell was open, so we talked. I did nothing wrong."

"And now you're talking like a jailhouse lawyer," the chief deputy says. "Not a wise move."

From the look on William's face, the chief deputy is going nowhere with that threat.

"What did you talk about?" I ask, changing the subject.

"We talked about a book she suggested that I read. It was a biography of MLK."

"What else did you talk about?" the Sheriff asks.

Latisha's eyes light up. "Claire knows where I can get a job and the training to help young girls who are in trouble. And I've enrolled in an on-line university and I'm taking an English class."

She is one fast learner and practicing on us. Latisha Williams obviously has a brain, and it bothers me that Claire Allison saw it before anyone else.

The Sheriff jerks his right hand. "Get her out of here." We wait while the aide hustles Williams out.

The Sheriff stands up and issues orders. "Trustee, my ass. Give her the max, three days confinement. You have a security breach. Call in the geeks and fix it. Place a full-time guard outside Allison's cell and review every phone call made by every inmate since Allison has been here. I want a number we can trace back to her. And I don't give a damn about overtime pay."

The chief deputy looks hopeful. "Sir, we have reviewed the tapes and have the number that Williams called twice. I called, but it's disconnected. We're tracing it, but no luck so far."

Laura chimes in. "I don't think you will. What did she talk about?" It's not common knowledge that all telephone conversations are monitored, but it is common sense.

"Williams was worried about threats she had received from Ebola," the chief deputy replies. "She is one nasty inmate. The problem solved itself when Ebola was transferred to Chowchilla. That got everyone's attention."

"I think it would," Laura says. Chowchilla is California's maximum security prison for women and houses California's death row for women.

"You're leaking like a sieve here," the Sheriff says, "and I don't need to remind you of what social media can do. I want control; make it happen, without a lockdown." He stomps out, and there is a general sigh of relief.

"Thank God, no lockdown," the chief deputy says. "We got off easy. Laura, what's your read on Williams?"

"She's very protective of Allison."

"Just because they're talking?" the chief deputy says. "That doesn't track, not on the seventh floor."

Laura shakes her head. "Allison is offering Williams hope, the one thing she has never had." Then, "She loves Claire."

So, it's 'Claire' now. What is it with Allison and women? We walk back to the DA's office, and I spend the next few hours finishing the profiles on each witness we'll be cross-examining in court. Suddenly, I'm missing Atticus and wishing Khepri was here. I'm about to head for the Pine Room for a little liquid consolation when my smartphone chimes with a message. It's a selfie from Khepri. She's straddling a straight-back chair backwards with a winsome look, and judging by her bare arms, shoulders, and legs, totally naked. She does know how to get my attention.

What the hell, I think, this case is a slam dunk and Claire Allison is going down. My work here is done. It takes about fifteen minutes to pack up. I leave a note for Laura and Mary along with the completed profiles. An uneasy feeling nags at me that we are being played and caught in a calm before the storm, and I have no idea why.

It's time to go home.

42

Friday, September 16

Susanne was on the phone to Mike Westfield. “Right, I’m at the Mendozas and I’ll get there as soon as I can.” She broke the connection. “The man can’t even find the men’s room.” She looked around the large room that opened onto the veranda, satisfied that she had the perfect set. She motioned everyone against the back wall and behind the cameraman.

“Okay, I think we’re ready. Rolinda, I want you to walk in from the veranda holding the letter, exactly as we rehearsed. Everyone, please be absolutely quiet, especially at the end.” She checked the room one last time as Rolinda stepped outside. “Action.”

The camera framed Rolinda as she walked into the room. The sun was at her back, and she was only a silhouette emerging from the golden rays. She stood motionless, gazing at the painting of sunflowers on the wall. She was wearing a simple teal-colored dress with a long strand of pearls and holding an open letter and envelope in her right hand. The camera zoomed in as she turned and looked down at the letter. She faced the camera and started to read, her voice full and pitch perfect. “A letter from the Sacramento Jail. September Sixteen,

“My dear family and friends,

“I’m confined in the Sacramento County jail and a fellow inmate, a beautiful African American, shared a book on the life of Martin Luther King, Jr. It is a wonderful biography and I was deeply moved by his life and sacrifice. Like most of my generation, I hold Martin Luther King high among our nation’s heroes, for he was a man of good will and a true leader who taught us the power of love. Thanks to my young friend, I saw him through the eyes of her community, and he became a living presence. Because of her, his 'Letter from a Birmingham Jail' forced me to examine my life, my goals, and why I'm here,

"So where to start? I am a thirty-nine-year-old mother, widow, and schoolteacher. I have a son who is rapidly growing up in the image of his father who died in the service of our country. He was a hero in every sense of the word, and I miss him every day of my life. I am a middle school teacher who moved into administration because I can, with the help of my friends, solve problems. I am not a leader like the Reverend King, but then few are. At the end of each day, I'm only a woman who loves my family, my friends, and so many of my students.

"I was an only child, born and raised in Davis, California. My father was a professor of biology and my mother a high school teacher. I grew up in a secure and comfortable home, and I have been accused of having a 'privileged life.' In many ways, that is true, but in my family, much was expected. I had to earn my privileges, and it started with making my bed every morning. I learned that from my father at an early age. I loved telling my students about that and how it later gave me a safe place to hide when my teenaged world crumpled around me.

"Besides teaching, my father was also a reservist in the United States Air Force and flew cargo airplanes. He believed in order, self-discipline, and accomplishment. He taught by example and urged me to be all that I could be. My mother loved her family and her students. She lost her way when her husband died and so she moved in with us.

"Being an active grandmother saved her and we bonded even more as a family. Later, when I lost my husband, she was there for me. Because of my parents, I learned that caring for and protecting the ones we love is the measure of our humanity. I have been blessed with friends who share the same values. Together, family and friends have made a huge difference in my life and allowed me to reach far.

"My friends call me 'the Sunflower Girl' for those beautiful flowers have been a part of my life ever since I can remember. I love the way they greet each morning while they are growing, turning into the sun then following it as it arcs across the sky. In time, they blossom and become fixed as they drop their seeds. They will die, but with the promise of rebirth. In so many ways, they are fragile yet amazingly strong. Because of my mother and father, I learned to care for them and I have been rewarded endlessly with the gift of life and a sense of renewal.

"My husband was a fighter pilot with all that involves. He had a seemingly devil-may-care attitude and was aggressive to a fault. I can't count the times he said, 'When something goes wrong, get aggressive.' He loved flying the F-16 for it demanded a skill few pilots possess.. Above all else, he believed in the mission of the Air Force, and, eventually, it would cost him his life. He died doing what he believed in, defending his country, loved ones and friends. I can think of no better cause to champion. He taught me well, and I will love him until my dying breath.

"When I was appointed to lead a troubled school, an editorial writer claimed that I was 'a pretty disaster who had found the perfect catastrophe.' Like so many, when I was younger I did think of myself as 'pretty' or 'attractive.' But I have learned that is merely a façade that hides who we really are, and that true beauty comes from the inside of each of us.

"A TV commentator once said that I am 'a creature of the moment with no principles or goals.' Nothing could be further from the truth. It is true that I don't follow a dogma, and I do take a pragmatic approach to fixing problems. As a principal of a low performing school, it all started with security and safety. My staff and I worked with the police to eliminate the gangs that terrorized our campus. At the same time, I had to fire teachers who weren't able to help and wouldn't move on. It was a painful process, but we didn't give up.

"We added a breakfast to the free lunch program and saw an immediate increase in attendance. It worked so well, that we added a free dinner. Soon parents were volunteering to help create an afterschool program. We experienced another breakthrough with the funding to reduce class size to no more than sixteen students. It took four years to turn our school around and make it a safe haven for our students where they can learn and grow.

"I've been accused of sacrificing students in a 'quest to improve test scores.' Again, nothing could be further from the truth. The reality of modern education is that troublemakers have to be separated and removed from the classroom or everyone suffers. It is not an easy thing to do, but I will shield the children in my care.

"Finally, there are stubborn problems that seem to mock us and are so enduring that I often wonder if they are rooted in human nature and defy change. I can't change an individual's beliefs, but working together, we can ensure that our schools and towns are safe and secure havens for our children. It is not easy, and it demands sacrifice.

"Now, I'm in the Sacramento County Jail where I've met a young mother serving a six month sentence for prostitution. She is not an evil or wicked person, but a parent caught up in the economic reality of raising two children on welfare. Under the right conditions, she can survive and prosper, but a boyfriend with a drug problem forced her to the streets. We have become friends, and I believe 'the system' is working in her favor. Her children are in a good foster home, and she has a caring counselor. I know, deep in my heart, that she is going to make it.

"My future is not as bright. I am charged with murder and that I willfully, and with forethought, killed a man. But I am not here to plead my innocence or try the case in public opinion. I will be tried by a jury of my peers, and I trust them to do the right and just thing.

"If I had the sophistication of my generation, I would be on FaceBook or Instagram and not writing this long letter to make a simple point. I am a woman who will shield my loved ones and innocent children in my care from harm no matter the personal cost."

Rolinda closed the letter and gently kissed it. "Yours in peace and love, Claire Marie." The camera zoomed out as the light faded and closed in on the painting.

"Cut," Susanne whispered. For a moment, silence held the room in thrall. Then a burst of applause and shouts echoed over the house and veranda.

Hector stepped out of the shadows and wrapped his arms around Rolinda. "You did good." He held her as she wept.

“Okay, geeks,” he ordered. “Go blitz ‘em. Get it out there.” He waited as a dozen of the whizz kids ran for the war room and the waiting computers.

Susanne and the cameraman joined them. “We’ve got to run,” she said. “I’ll talk to our producer and work it into Mike’s commentary tonight. Do you really think you’ll have a million hits on YouTube by then?”

“Oh, yeah,” Hector replied.

43

Saturday, September 17

It's late morning and I'm watching the video, 'Letter from the Sacramento Jail.' How fuckin' corny can you get? Allison's no Martin Luther King, Junior. That's when Laura calls. "Get your body back here. The video has gone viral, and Wells wants us in court first thing Monday morning."

Obviously, I'm missing something, and ask what's the problem. "Jury selection notices were mailed out last Tuesday, and you can damn well bet that anyone who got one saw the video." Okay, so I'm slow and still don't get it. "Allison comes across like a martyr sacrificing herself for her family and loved ones," Laura explains.

"With the evidence, does it matter?" I ask.

I hear a loud groan of exasperation. "Just be here, okay?" I hang up. Now, I have to explain it to Khepri. She will not be a happy Egyptian mummy over this one. She listens quietly, which could be a good sign, then makes a decision. She and Atticus are coming with me.

We load the German Beast and head for Sactown. Khepri finds a small resort outside Bakersfield that caters to the country and western crowd where we can spend the night. We practice the fine art of line dancing that evening and are in bed before midnight. Khepri is still wearing cowboy boots and gives a whole new meaning to 'kick ass'. Atticus watches from a corner until the festivities are over, and then crawls into bed beside us. He's getting older and snores. But I don't care.

Monday, September 19

Larry Longchamps makes an entrance into court on Monday morning with his usual panache and flair for the dramatic. His disappointment is obvious when he sees nary a soul in the audience.

Lynn Majors is the last to arrive. She is all calm and cool. "Have you seen the video?" I ask. No answer. "I hear it went viral from the get-go." Still no reply. "Over seven million hits so far and growing." She just smiles. Allison is escorted in by the same deputies as before and sits down next to Lynn. She's still wearing prison oranges, and somehow, looking good. It dawns on me that it is her attitude and bearing, not the fit of her clothes.

The clerk glances out of her office and darts back inside to tell Wells that we are assembled. She's back a moment later and says, "All rise." The Honorable Patricia Wells slips in quietly and takes her seat, all business like. There is no doubt that she is one pissed off judge.

"Good morning," she says, her voice perfectly normal and calm. "Commencing immediately, neither the defendant, the defense, nor the prosecution will have any interaction or communication with the public, the press, the media, or social media with anything in regards to the business of this court. This order applies to everyone in the courtroom. Anyone leaking, in any manner, any information with anyone will be held in contempt of court."

She's looking directly at me, probably remembering how I had declared bankruptcy after she had reduced that five-million-dollar jury award for libel against me. It is the coldest stare that has ever frosted my eyeballs, and I think she would rather enjoy throwing me in the slammer for God knows how long.

"Have I made myself perfectly clear?" Just to be sure, she goes around the room asking each of us, court attendant and deputies included, if we fully understand. Her Honor is very pissed off, and, needless to say, we all understand her perfectly.

Wells politely asks the clerk to play Allison's video on the big monitor by the court reporter's desk. Obviously, Wells wants it on the record. We watch silently as Rolinda Johnson recites Allison's letter from the Sacramento Jail. "Mr. Longchamps," Wells says, "have you, or anyone on your staff, or in your office, spoken with anyone in regards to this video?"

Larry can't get to his feet fast enough. Like a good lawyer, he hedges his answer, "Your Honor, I have not, and, to the best of my knowledge, nor has anyone on my staff or in my office."

Wells asks Lynn the same question. "No, your Honor," Lynn replies, "I have not."

"Mrs. Allison," Wells says, "if anything like this occurs again, I will order the District Attorney to investigate and to determine if additional charges should be brought against you for obstruction of justice. Your trial will be delayed until the investigation is completed."

Allison stands up. "Your honor, may I confer with my attorney for moment?" She is very respectful, but not intimidated in the least. I'd be wetting my pants.

Wells allows them to chat at the defense table. I try to eavesdrop but can't hear a thing. Lynn shakes her head, whispers something, and shakes her head again. She finally stands up. "Your Honor, Mrs. Allison would like to take the stand and make a statement." The collective jaws at the prosecution table, mine included, flop open in astonishment.

"The defendant may take the stand," Wells replies, "subject to cross examination."

Allison is sworn in and starts to talk. "I wrote the letter while in jail and addressed the envelope to my best friend, Rolinda Johnson, who is running my campaign. I gave the letter to a trustee unopened, and she handed it in to be mailed. I wrote it for my friends who have worked so hard on my campaign. I believed then, and I still do, that they deserved to know who, and what, I am. I did not speak to any person about the letter at any time."

Very clever, I think. First there was Rolinda and Hector's wedding and now this. They've come up with a new way to campaign. So, what's next? Larry starts to stand to cross examine her, but Mary pulls him back and whispers something in his ear. He gives her a long look and stands. "The prosecution has no questions at this time."

"You may step down," Wells says to Allison. "Let me remind all present that the only evidence released to the public will come through this courtroom. We are adjourned." She stands, gathers up her notes and walks out.

I slump in my seat next to Mary. "Allison is using us."

"Tell me," Mary replies. She waves me to silence until we are alone. "This a death penalty case that requires a death qualified jury. Because of Allison's so-called letter, the jury pool is contaminated. There is no way we can get an unbiased jury now and Wells knows it."

"Go for a change of venue," I say.

"Where to?" Laura asks. She glances at her smartphone, checking the latest numbers. "The damn letter just went past eight million hits. It's safe to assume that any jury pool, anywhere, will have seen this."

"Ah, crap," I moan.

44

Friday, October 14

It was the fourth day of the trial when the two women deputies marched across the pod and up the stairs to Claire's cell. It was a well-rehearsed routine. The senior deputy rapped sharply on the cell door. "Stand back from the door." The door immediately buzzed open and they stepped inside. Claire was standing against the far wall, her hands at her side. "Strip," the deputy said, pulling on surgical gloves.

Claire quickly shed her oranges and endured the body inspection. The deputy inspected each piece of clothing before passing it back to Claire. She quickly dressed and held out her hands.

The deputy slipped handcuffs over Claire's wrists, shackled her ankles, and led the way into the pod. A chant of "Go, girl, go!" echoed around them. Two male sheriff deputies were waiting at the elevator to escort Claire to the courthouse. Their uniforms were freshly pressed and their shoes polished.

"You're not a friggin' honor guard," the senior deputy said. But the two sheriffs only stood more at attention, looking straight ahead. The elevator descended in silence to the basement where an unmarked van was waiting for the short drive to the courthouse.

Lynn Majors was waiting in the courthouse basement when the van arrived. Claire stepped out and gave her hair a quick shake. Lynn led the way to a holding cell where fresh clothes were laid out on a bunk. Without a word, one of the sheriffs removed Claire's handcuffs and shackles. He joined his partner and they found seats against the opposite wall, still very much at attention.

Again, Claire quickly removed her clothes and pulled on new panties and a bra. Lynn handed her a deodorant stick. “Thank you,” Claire said. She slipped on a pair of knee-length hose and quickly finished dressing in a dark pants suit with a white, open collared shirt. She stepped into a pair of plain black, low-heeled pumps.

“Turn around,” Lynn said. She gathered Claire’s hair into a loose bundle at the base of her neck with a small white silk scarf. “Very nice,” Lynn said. Claire held out her hands and the sheriff snapped the handcuffs and leg shackles in place. “I need to confer with my client in private.” The sheriff nodded, spun around and left, closing the door behind her.

Lynn handed Claire an earbud that allowed outside communication. “This could get a girl disbarred,” she murmured as Claire fitted it into her left ear. A weekly telephone call was the only electronic communication allowed Claire.

“Hello, luv,” Nedd said. “It has been a while.”

“I missed you,” Claire replied. Tears filled her eyes. Lynn handed her a Kleenex, assuming she was talking to Logan.

“What have you been up to?” Claire asked.

“I transferred out Ebola—they named that bitch right—and two of her buddies. Then I had Latisha, lovely girl she is, spread a few goodies around the pod. That calmed things and made the screws’ job much easier. They figured that out. We don’t have much time, so let me ring you in. Jury selection went better than I expected. Juror number one is a clotheshorse and a wanna-be fashion critic. Avoid wearing anything that might turn her off, like flashy jewelry, makeup, or panty hose. Juror number three is very religious. He is a prig, so don’t show any cleavage or leg. Dress like you’re going for a job interview. Finally, listen to your attorney and don’t take the stand. She’s spot on about that.”

Lynn glanced at her watch and tapped Claire’s arm to gain her attention. “You are a sweetheart,” Claire whispered. “Take care.” She handed the earbud back to Lynn.

Lynn handed her a tube of lipstick. “Go very lightly.” Claire dabbed her lips and used the Kleenex to blot her lips. She buttoned the top button to her shirt and quickly removed her hosiery. “Perfect,” Lynn said. “All things considered, we’re moving at warp speed. I have never empaneled a jury so fast . . ." She almost said, "For a death penalty case," but caught herself in time.

"Based on the feedback from our focus group, our gurus think the jurors are relatively neutral. But that can change in a heartbeat." She took a deep breath. "That's the good news. Unfortunately, we lost on every motion and I can't keep out any evidence.

"The trial really starts today with opening statements, and Longchamps is going to go ugly early. He'll hit the jury hard with graphic evidence. Don't react, be subdued and very respectful of the process. Do not look at the audience but make eye contact with the jury, if you can. Appear concerned, but never smile or shake your head. As for Larry, I will object when I can, mainly to break his momentum. Expect Wells to overrule most of the time, so don't get upset. If you want to bring something to my attention, write a note on the legal pad in front of you. I'll see it and do the same." A knock at the door interrupted her. "It's time. Keep cool, but don't freeze."

Claire laughed. "Isn't that on a mayonnaise jar?"

"Years ago, but it's still true."

They were still chatting amiably when they sat down at the defense table. "It looks like we have a full house," Claire said, glancing at the audience. Sarah and Logan were sitting in the front row with Jenna Bradley. Her ever-present notebook was open in her lap.

The clerk called for everyone to rise. Wells entered and sat down. She greeted everyone and quickly moved through the opening formalities, asking if there was any business to bring before the court. Lynn and Longchamps both said no. "Are the People ready to proceed?" Wells asked.

Longchamps came to his feet. "The People are ready, your Honor."

"Please bring the jury in," Wells said.

Claire studied the jury as they came in from the hallway and took their places. They were a mixed group, with two African Americans, one Asian American, two Hispanic Americans, and seven White Americans. The woman outnumbered the men seven to five, and they ranged in age from their late twenties to late fifties. The last in were three alternates, all middle-aged women.

"I don't like the way they're looking at us," Lynn said.

Longchamps came to his feet and buttoned his jacket as he walked to the jury box. He paused as his eyes swept over the jury. A silence claimed the courtroom and he didn't move. He bowed his head and looked at his feet. Finally, he turned and starred at Claire. Lynn jotted a note on the legal pad in front of her and tapped it, gaining Claire's attention:

Larry is a drama queen

Wells leaned forward, ready to order him to proceed when he cleared his throat.

"Ladies and gentlemen of the jury, you are being called upon to judge a fellow human being accused of murder. You see before you a normal and attractive, smartly dressed, thirty-nine-year-old woman. You will learn she is widow with a son, a recognized and accomplished professional, and running for political office in a neighboring state. Claire Marie Allison is the living image of the perfect neighbor you wish lived next door. This is exactly how her counselor, and my learned friend, would have you see her. But in reality, she is a calculating, methodical, cold-blooded killer. We will present incontrovertible evidence that she planned and carried out, without remorse, the murder of a fellow human being. But let me move beyond the image in front of you."

Lynn scribbled a note for Claire:

This is going to be a long day

Claire steepled her fingers together and focused on Longchamps as he summarized the evidence the jury would see. After forty minutes, Wells called for a short recess.

They were back in session and Longchamps played the storyteller as he summarized the evidence. Wells sat at the bench, her face a mask, and finally called for a two-hour lunch break. Claire asked why the long recess. "We're short on judges," Lynn answered, "and she's working on other cases. Eat lightly and go easy on the liquids. It's best if the jurors need a pee break, not us."

A well-rested Longchamps was ready when Wells entered and reconvened court. Lynn scribbled a note for Claire:

She's tired. He's not. Not good

Longchamps stood. The courtroom was silent as he bowed his head as if he were in prayer or deep contemplation. Only the dim hum of traffic could be heard. "Is the prosecution ready to proceed?" Wells asked.

Longchamps raised his head. "Yes, your Honor, we are." He started to talk as his two aides erected an easel in front of the jury. Again, Lynn jotted a note:

Not smart. The jury is sleepy

Lynn smothered a smile as Longchamps sketched a timeline of the crime. After forty minutes, all the jurors were nodding. Wells caught it and called for a recess.

A large TV monitor was waiting for the jurors when they filed back into the courtroom. Lynn knew what was coming. "I can object, but they're going to see it eventually. We need to get through this as quick as we can." They were back in session and Claire listened attentively as Longchamps droned on, finally building to a conclusion. The TV screen came alive with a photo of Bobby Lee MacElroy sprawled face down on the deck of the houseboat, his head surrounded by a small pool of blood.

"You will hear testimony that the defendant is a valued member of her community. But the evidence will prove beyond a reasonable doubt that she did this. There is no gore or blood splattered walls, only a body with two small caliber bullet holes in the back of the head. The evidence will prove that she murdered the victim without a struggle and then calmly closed the door and walked away. This is the work of a cold-blooded murderer who kills without remorse." He paused for effect. "But this is what your public servants must deal with."

The photo on the screen transitioned into an image of the corpse on an examination table with the top of his skull removed, revealing the remains of his scrambled brain. "This is the result of those two small caliber bullets fired at close range."

He paused and fell silent, a repeat of his opening demeanor. He slowly raised his head. "And now, Claire Marie Allison stands before the bar of justice, called to account for her crimes. As we proceed, please remember that she is on trial here, and not the victim. Ultimately, justice falls to you, and you alone." He lowered his head, paused, and sat down. For a moment, silence.

"Damn," Lynn whispered. She had made a mistake and should have objected to the last photo and thrown up as much legal dust as she could, defusing the impact of the images.

Wells glanced at her watch. "It's getting late, and as it's Friday, we can recess until Monday."

Lynn stood. "Thank you, your Honor, but the defense would like to proceed." Wells cautioned the jury to not discuss the case and excused them for a short break. They rushed out, headed for the restrooms. Wells called for a short recess and retired to her chambers and the visitors' gallery quickly emptied.

Claire turned around. Only Logan, Sarah, and Jenna were still there. For a moment, they looked at each other. Suddenly, Logan bolted for the door, clearly upset. Claire started to stand, but Lynn clasped her shoulder and held her tight. "No child should have seen that," Lynn murmured. Claire collapsed into her chair, fighting her tears.

Within minutes, the courtroom was again packed, and they were back in session. Lynn stood and walked to the jury box. "Good afternoon. My name is Lynn Majors and I have the honor of representing one of the finest individuals I have ever met, Claire Marie Allison.

"Regardless of what you have seen and heard today, you will hear clear and absolute evidence that she is not guilty of the charges brought against her. I know it's been a long day, and I would like to thank you for your patience and attention." She turned to the bench, bowed her head slightly, and sat down.

Wells recited the standard warnings to the jury before they withdrew. "We will reconvene Monday morning at nine-thirty. We are in recess." She gathered up her notes and quickly left.

Claire stood and turned, only to see a rapidly emptying courtroom. Jenna was sitting there, alone. Claire buried her face in Lynn's shoulder and cried as tremors wracked her body.

45

Thursday, October 20

Mary is worried. It's day eight of the trial, and we're at lunch rehashing Larry's performance making the prosecution's case. He's been hammering away since Monday and we're ready to call the last witness. We need to prep Larry first, but he's out schmoozing God knows who. "It's going too fast," Mary says, munching her sandwich. "Majors should be objecting more and ripping the witnesses a new one. Why is she rolling over?"

"Maybe she figures the jurors are being smothered," I venture.

"I don't think so," Mary says. "This jury is too smart for that."

"She did nail Delgado on cross," Laura says.

Emilio Delgado was the lowlife who rented the car Allison used. On the stand, he positively identified Allison. Lynn was at her best on cross examination and easily proved he was liar and had cut a deal with the DA for his testimony. Lynn ended her cross with "Mr. Delgado, exactly what did you not lie about?" Larry objected and was sustained, but the jury got the point.

We're about to head for the courtroom when Larry shows. Mary hands him a folder that he barely glances at. "Boring," he says. All the drama associated with a high-profile murder trial is missing and he is not a happy DA.

"But necessary," Mary replies. "The coroner's testimony is always a safe way to wrap it up."

Larry leads the way into the courtroom and we're back in session. The coroner is called and Larry leads him through his final report. I'm bored, the jury is bored, and the audience is half asleep with full tummies. Then Larry jazzes it all up. The big TV monitor lights up with a new image of Bobby Lee's scrambled brains we have not seen before. Half of his brains have been scraped out showing the damage caused by the bullets to the inside of his skull.

I expect to hear an objection from Lynn, anything to defuse its impact, but she only studies her notes. Larry asks if the cause of death was due solely to the two gunshot wounds to the victim's head. The coroner confirms it was, and Larry sits down. Wells makes a note and Lynn stands.

"The defense has no questions for the witness."

Larry rises to his feet. "The prosecution rests."

"Is the defense ready to proceed?" Wells asks.

The pencil between Mary's fingers beats a fierce tattoo on the desk as Lynn rises from her chair to plead Claire's case. "Ineffective assistance of counsel," Mary mutters. "Majors will appeal claiming she was incompetent in Allison's defense."

That is not the Lynn Majors I know. She calls her first witness, a Dr. Jason Bale, and I have a panic attack. It was my job to vet the defense's witness list, and I don't remember the name. Larry's two legal aides scan the defense's list looking for his name.

Mary shakes her head and tells Larry to ask for a recess as he is not on the witness list and we need time to prepare. One of the aides finds Bale's name on the list. It's buried out of order under the Ps. I had read the B as a P, and the Jason Pale I researched is a respected doctor who has never testified as an expert witness. I show it to Larry. "I was snookered," I tell him. "Clever devils."

Larry mutters "Watch this" as he comes to his feet. "Objection. Your Honor, this is the first we have learned of this witness. His name was misfiled on the defense's witness list in a manner to mislead our investigation. A list, I note, that contains 287 names."

Lynn is in Larry's face in a heartbeat. "May I point out that the prosecution's witness list contains over three hundred names, of which two were misfiled and one misspelled?" She hands the lists to the clerk who passes them to Wells. "Dr. Bale's name is not misspelled." She stops short of raising the question of due diligence on the prosecution's part, which is me.

But Wells does. "Overruled. The witness may be sworn."

The man who takes the stand is tall, athletic, well-dressed, and movie star good-looking. If I read body language right, many ladies, and a few guys, in the courtroom are also doing a little lusting. Lynn establishes his bona fides, which are impressive. Besides chairing the Department of Computer Science at Cal State, he is considered one of the world's leading experts on cyber security. In short, Bale knows how to diddle a computer.

Lynn asks if he knows the defendant. He states that he does not. Lynn calls for People's Exhibit 38, the hotel security tapes, to be played for the witness. She then directs the clerk to read Larry's questioning of the prosecution's expert witness explaining how the critical one-minute time segments had been shortened. She follows up with People's Exhibit 18, Allison's college transcripts.

"Dr. Bale, would an individual with the defendant's academic background have the skills necessary to penetrate a computer's firewalls, hack into a security system, modify the security videos in the manner we have just seen, and leave no trace?"

"I can't answer your question without knowing their post college professional development."

Lynn is unfazed. "Could you hack into a security system and modify the videos in the manner described by the prosecution?"

He thinks for a moment. "If I had access to a super-computer like the Cray XC50 or IBM WMX, yes."

Larry cottons on to where she is going about the same time I do. "Objection!" he shouts. "Relevance. Dr. Bale's abilities have no bearing on this case."

A little smile flicks across Lynn's face. "It is not a question of Dr. Bale's abilities, but the context in which cyber security operates."

"Overruled," Wells says. "Counselor, I will allow leeway to establish relevance, but do not waste the court's time."

"Thank you." Lynn gives the jury a serious look, pleading for their attention. "Do you have access to such a computer?"

He chuckles. “No, I do not.”

“Why do you not have access a supercomputer such as you described?”

“There are less than a hundred WMXs and XC50s in the world. Access is closely controlled because they are extremely expensive to buy, operate, and maintain.”

“Who owns these supercomputers?”

Bale shrugs, playing to the audience. “Major corporations, research institutions, governmental agencies such as the CIA, FBI, and the IRS.”

“Do they track who has access to these super computers?”

“They all track access very closely. Someone has to get the bill.”

Laughter ripples across the courtroom, and everyone but Wells and Larry is smiling. “The jury will disregard the witness’s comment about who gets the bill,” Wells rules. I sigh. Unless we can prove Allison had access to one of those super-duper computers, or come up with our own cyber security expert who can ruffle ladies’ panties, Lynn has dumped gigabytes of reasonable doubt on the jury. And even me.

“Thank you, Dr. Bale” Lynn says. “I have no more questions.” She gives Larry a look that says, “Your witness, if you’re up to it.”

Larry thinks he is and jumps up. Mary pulls him back down. “Call for a recess,” she says. For once, he listens and does the right thing. Wells takes pity on Larry, and we have thirty minutes to come up with a cross examination. Larry storms into the hallway, very pissed off. He motions for Laura to follow us into an attorney-witness room. The door is barely closed when he lights into us, his hair on fire.

“In my entire career, I have never seen a more poorly prepared case.” He glares at me. “Your lack of diligence in vetting the witness list borders on the criminal.” He jabs a finger at Mary. “I have interns who would have recognized our vulnerability on the cyber security issue.”

Mary isn’t having any of it. She calls up a file on her iPad and hands it to Larry. He goes all quiet and hands it back. “Ah, yes,” he murmurs. Mary tilts the iPad to give Laura and me a peek at the file. It’s a request for funding to hire a cyber security expert to investigate and validate all security videos associated with the case. The cyber security expert is none other than Dr. Jason Bale and the request was denied by one Larry Longchamps with a scribbled note:

Over budget and the video speaks for itself.

It is dated the day after Allison's arrest. Larry has proven that it is possible to go fuck yourself.

Larry lays it in our laps. "How do we link Allison to the video?"

"All we can do now is cast doubt on Bale's expertise," Mary replies, "and that is going to piss off at least half the jury. Did you see how one and nine looked at him? Don't go there."

"What if Allison knows somebody who does have access to one of those supercomputers?" Laura asks.

"I think I'd remember anyone like that," I say. "I'll take a look." I key the search function on my laptop and come up dry. "Sorry, nada."

"The question remains," Larry says, "how do we link Allison to the security video?" He's big on the "we" now.

"In your closing argument," Mary tells him, "simply point out the altered video is a fact, and it is relevant to her actions." Even I know that is pretty weak, but it's all we have.

We're back in session and Larry doesn't bother to stand. "We have no questions for the witness." He looks expectantly at the defense table, fully expecting Lynn to call another expert witness. Allison and Lynn are talking, their heads almost touching.

Lynn is upset, pleading with Allison, but Allison is adamant and won't give in. I wish I could read lips. Lynn finally stands. "The defense calls Claire Marie Allison." A collective gasp sweeps over the courtroom. Wells looks over her glasses at Allison, the closest she can come to looking surprised.

"Dumb, dumb, dumb," Mary whispers. "We're back in business." Allison stands and walks to the witness stand. Every eye in the room is locked on her. She moves with a quiet grace, and is wearing the same dark pants suit, but with a light blue shirt. Her hair is held back with a simple black bow, and the small white scarf is now tied around her upper right arm. I think in surrender.

She takes the oath with a quiet dignity that is totally believable and sits down. Lynn stands and leans against the defense table, her arms wrapped around a thin black folder, clutching it to her breast. She is a cool professional and knows what Larry will do to Allison on cross. Lynn is one of the best in the profession on redirect, but I doubt that even she can save Allison from the legal mugging coming her way.

"Please state your full name, marital status, and the names and ages of your children." Allison answers in a clear, calm voice, and I hear love as she intones her son's name. Lynn glances at her folder. "Did you know a man named Bobby Lee MacElroy?"

Allison doesn't hesitate. "Yes, he was the man who sodomized my son."

Larry is on his feet, shouting. "Objection! Assuming facts not in evidence."

"Sustained," Wells says. "The jury will disregard the defendant's last answer." Yeah, right. Every mother in the room is on the edge of their seat, eager to know more. Wells isn't done. "Mrs. Allison, please answer all questions without elaboration."

Larry is licking his chops, and Lynn has to defuse the damage before he can start his cross examination. "Let me reframe the question," Lynn says. "Did you know Bobby Lee MacElroy in a professional capacity?"

"Yes, I did."

"How would you describe your professional relationship?"

"He was the headmaster of the day school my son attended."

"Did you know Bobby Lee MacElroy in a personal capacity?"

"Yes, I did."

"How would you describe your personal relationship?"

"I shot and killed him." Allison's voice is calm and matter of fact.

For a moment, time freezes as Lynn stares at her client in shock before finding her voice. "We request a recess to . . ." All hell breaks loose, drowning her out.

"There will be order in the court," Wells says. Her voice is firm and loud, but not loud enough as four reporters stampede for the exit. A court attendant is standing in the doorway, his arms crossed, and a reporter crashes into him knocking them both down. I can't believe it, but Wells stands up and shouts demanding order.

This time she gets it and sits down. "I caution the audience to remain absolutely silent, or I will empty the courtroom and hold any individual causing a disruption in contempt. Please leave now if you cannot remain in order." Needless to say, no one budges. "Counselor, you may proceed."

Lynn stands there, still shocked. "We request a recess, your Honor."

"Denied."

Lynn establishes the time and date that Allison was at the houseboat and that she fired two shots into the back of Bobby Lee's head. The questioning appears to be damning, but it gives Lynn time to frame a new defense. "At the time of the murder, were you having trouble sleeping?"

"Yes, I was."

"Recess now," Mary whispers. Larry jumps to his feet and requests a recess but is denied.

Unfortunately, the brief exchange gives Lynn even more time to structure her questioning. "What was the cause of your insomnia?"

"Objection," Larry says. "Relevance."

"Overruled," Wells says. "Mrs. Allison, you may answer the question, but please be brief."

"I was under extreme emotional distress at the time."

"Were you under a doctor's care at the time?"

"I was," Allison answers.

Lynn leads her through a series of questions establishing she was under a doctor's care. Larry objects constantly but cannot shut the line of questioning off. Lynn finally gets to the kicker. "And what did Dr. Shriver determine to be the cause of your emotional distress?"

"I was reacting to my son having been sexually molested."

"May I confer briefly with my client?" Lynn asks. Wells declares a ten-minute recess and withdraws to her chambers. No one in the audience moves. With the jury gone, Allison and

Lynn talk quietly at the witness box. Then we're back in session. "I have no more questions at this time," Lynn announces, surrendering Allison to Larry's tender mercies.

Wells glances at her watch and makes a decision. She cautions the jury to not discuss the case, excuses them, and recesses until Monday morning at nine-thirty. Larry collapses in relief. He did not want to start his cross examination while the jurors' emotions were in high gear. "It's going to be a long weekend," he says, all friendly now. "Let's all get together, my office, say in one hour." Mrs. Trophy wife is waiting for him and they head for the main entrance where the media is standing. They'll look great on TV saying, "No comment."

Rather than risk Wells' ire, Laura calls for an unmarked police car for the ride to the DA's building. It takes a while and Larry is sitting in his office when his receptionist ushers us in. He asks her to bring in tea and goodies, and we settle in.

"I don't see any problems on cross," he announces. "I'll wrap up cross on Monday, closing arguments that afternoon or on Tuesday. It's safe to assume the jury will deliver a guilty verdict. Our real problem is the sentencing phase, and you need to start on that immediately." It's going to be a long weekend.

"Lynn will try to backdoor diminished capacity," Mary says. "She'll play the sympathy card."

"And Allison's a war widow to boot," I add.

"That happened after the murder and is not relevant," Mary replies.

"But you can bet the jury will think it is," Laura adds.

"Therein lies the problem," Mary says. "What do they think?"

46

Thursday, the same day

The doctor drew a blood sample from Claire's left arm, labeled it, and carefully noted the time and date. Exactly three hours had elapsed since she had confessed to murdering MacElroy. "Everything appears normal, Mrs. Allison," he said, packing his medical bag. Lynn thanked him and knocked at the door of the holding cell.

A deputy opened it and the doctor escaped into the deserted basement of the courthouse. "We'll be another hour," Lynn told the two deputies waiting outside. One grunted and closed the door. "With a little luck," Lynn explained, "serology will find something in your blood that can suggest an imbalance. Besides, we need time to talk before you go back to 651." She paced the floor. "That came as a complete shock. What were you thinking?"

"I had to tell the jury the truth," Claire said softly. "I just couldn't lie to them anymore—or to you. Lynn, you are a good friend."

"I'm also your lawyer. Besides, it was obvious you had pulled the trigger." She paced the floor. "The jury will find you guilty. Unfortunately, I can't argue diminished capacity at this stage, but I can allude to it. However, I need to know everything, no more surprises." She sat and pulled a legal tablet out of her briefcase. "Let's start with the 'why.'"

"Bobby Lee MacElroy was a truly evil man. Two of his victims committed suicide and no one, absolutely no one, could stop him. You have no idea the harm he caused. We counted over two hundred children, innocent children, on the videos he made." Lynn listened, making notes and asking an occasional question. The minutes flew by and the deputy knocked at the door telling them they had ten minutes. "There's so much more," Claire murmured.

"Did anyone help you?" Lynn asked.

Claire thought for a moment and made a decision. "You need to meet Nedd. He's on the cutting edge of artificial intelligence and is developing an interactive search engine and personal assistant program that is self-learning. We've worked very closely and he can help you. He told me not to take the stand, and I never told him what I had in mind. He's an Australian currently working in Canada. You'll love him."

"How do I contact him?"

Claire pointed at Lynn's smartphone that was turned off. "Nedd, I'd like you to meet Lynn Majors."

The smartphone came alive. "Hello, Lynn. Pleased to meet."

Lynn stared at her smartphone. "I . . . I . . ." She took a deep breath as the pieces came together. Obviously, Nedd was a genius who could roam at will through the cyber world. "Did you scrub the security video?"

"I did. Piece of cake. By the way, that was a brilliant piece of work, raising reasonable doubt."

"I need to know," Lynn said, her voice shaking, "jury selection . . . did you?"

Nedd didn't hesitate. "I did look at the address pool and deleted two paedophiles before the notification letters went out. Luv, I know how critical a jury is, and I would never muck with jury selection. But there was no justice if one of those blokes lied his way into the jury box." Lynn visibly relaxed. "You have visitors," Nedd said. "Got to go." Her smartphone went dead as the door swung open. A deputy sheriff was standing there, shifting his weight from one foot to another, obviously uncomfortable.

"It's time, Mrs. Allison."

Monday, October 24

Mary and Parker settled into their seats on Monday morning. They looked up when the side door to the courtroom opened, and the three deputies escorted Claire to the witness box.

"Look at that," Parker muttered. The deputies were wearing long-sleeved dark blue uniforms with a tie and gold epaulets over their right shoulders. "You'd think they were on parade."

Mary shot Parker a sideways glance. He wondered if his constant wisecracking was wearing thin. "They are," she replied. "Check out Marie Antoinette." Claire was wearing a simple dark-teal colored dress with a long strand of pearls and her trademark shawl. Her hair was pulled back and tucked under the shawl. The small white scarf was wrapped around her right wrist.

"This is the first time she's worn a dress," Parker said. "Why a fashion statement now?"

"Because everyone is looking at her and wondering the same thing," Mary replied.

Longchamp's two legal aides joined them. The women studied Claire for a moment. "It's the same dress and shawl Rolinda Johnson wore when she read that letter on YouTube." The dress had been carefully altered, tailored to a perfect fit.

"Well," Parker said, "we know what else the jury will be thinking about. Larry has his work cut out for him." He turned around at the sound of a commotion. "Speaking of the devil." Longchamps came down the aisle, his wife on his arm, and ushered her to a seat before coming through the bar. He sat down and studied Claire as the court attendant called for everyone to stand. Wells took her seat and they were in session.

After the opening formalities, Longchamps edged up to the jury box and began his cross examination. "I would remind the defendant that she is still under oath." He opened his folder. "Mrs. Allison, it is now necessary that I ask you about everything that took place the day of the murder." Lynn sat quietly at the defense table and made notes as Longchamps worked through the evidence, coming to the security tape.

Lynn stood. "Your Honor, the defense stipulates that the defendant has the expertise necessary to modify the security tapes as entered into evidence." Longchamps readily agreed, eager to move on and bypass the major weakness in his case. After an hour of questioning, he turned to the TV monitor and called up the coroner's photo of MacElroy on the examination table. "Do you recognize this as the result of firing two bullets into the head of the victim?"

Claire waited for Lynn to object, but Lynn only looked at her notes. "The defendant may answer the question," Wells said.

"I don't have the medical expertise to answer your question," Claire said.

"Why am I not surprised?" Longchamps said. He held up his hand before Lynn could object. "I withdraw the question." He turned to the jury. "I have no more questions."

Lynn came to her feet. "The defense has no further questions."

"Closing arguments will begin at one-thirty this afternoon," Wells said. She cautioned the jury and they were in recess.

"Is Logan here?" Claire asked. Lynn turned around and scanned the courtroom that was rapidly filling with spectators and reporters.

"I don't see him. It's probably for the best. I can see your mother and Stu, they're sitting near the back." She reached out and touched Claire's hand. "Keep the faith, we'll get through this." Longchamps came down the aisle with his wife. "Here's Larry. We're on. Be cool." Wells entered with her normal grace, sat down, and reconvened. Longchamps stood and walked slowly to the jury box.

"Ladies and gentlemen of the jury, we have come to the end of a difficult case that has been strewn with emotional wreckage. As I promised at the very beginning, the prosecution has presented incontrovertible evidence that the defendant planned and carried out, without remorse, the coldblooded murder of a fellow human being; a crime that the defendant has admitted to under oath and in your presence."

He walked to the prosecution's table and picked up a leather folder. Slowly, and methodically, he reviewed the evidence, building to a climax. "Need I remind the jury that the defendant admits that she used a gun to take the life of a defenseless human being? The law is very clear on this point; a civilized society cannot allow someone to do what the defendant did and get away with it."

Longchamps paused and fixed the jury with a serious look, "It is your sworn duty to uphold the law, and, in so doing, preserve and protect our safety." He fell silent and looked at the American flag behind the bench for a rehearsed three-seconds. "Thank you for your attention and for your service." He sat down. Wells called for a thirty-minute recess and the audience rushed for the restrooms.

"His closing was too long," Mary said.

"Bladder control beats critical thinking every time," Parker replied. "Will it go to the jury today?"

"Oh, yeah," Mary said. They followed Longchamps out and were back with time to spare.

Wells reconvened and Lynn came to her feet. She touched Claire's shoulder and remained at her side. "Ladies and Gentlemen of the jury, Claire Marie Allison sits before you, a woman who could be your next door neighbor. She is a widow of a man who gave his life in the service of his country, and the mother of their only son. Mrs. Allison is a respected professional in her field and has dedicated her life to educating disadvantaged children."

"Now, she has been brought to the bar of justice for the killing of a man. You have heard her verify the accuracy of the evidence presented by the prosecutor. Yet, all of us can sympathize with what she must have felt on learning that her son had been molested . . ."

"Objection!" Longchamps shouted. "Assuming facts not in evidence."

Wells fixed him with a hard look. "Overruled. Please do not object frivolously."

"Thank you, your Honor," Lynn said. "I was only referring to the emotional wreckage the prosecutor alluded to in his closing argument. I hope that we all can reach into our hearts and imagine the emotional turmoil that any loving parent would experience on learning their child had been molested." Wells looked over her glasses, warning Lynn that she was standing on the foul line by opening a new defense based on diminished capacity.

Again, Lynn touched Claire's shoulder. "In my opening statement I stated that I had the honor of representing one of the finest individuals I have ever met, Claire Marie Allison.

Regardless of what we have all learned during the trauma of these proceedings, I still believe that with all my heart. I join the prosecutor in saying thank you for your attention and for your service." She sat down.

Longchamps sprang to his feet. "I would remind the jury that the defendant admitted, under oath, that she shot and murdered a defenseless human." He paused, his face resolute, and sat down.

Wells glanced at an open folder, folded her hands and leaned slightly forward. "And now, ladies and gentlemen, I must instruct you on the law as it applies to this case." She spoke with a clear precision, watching the jury and taking their measure to insure they understood that the prosecution had proven its case beyond all reasonable doubt, and that Claire had confessed to murdering a human being with malice.

Wells looked at the jury as she reached an end. "You have all taken an oath to uphold the law, and now you must apply the law as I have explained it to you." She paused. "You will now retire to consider your verdict and select a foreperson." The room was deathly still as the jury followed the court attendant out. "Does either side have any business to bring to the attention of the court?" Wells asked. Longchamps and Lynn both said no. "The court is in recess until called."

Wednesday, October 26

"They've been out for two days," Claire said. "What does that mean?" She paced the holding cell where they were waiting.

"It's anybody's guess," Lynn said. "I've seen it go both ways. Usually, there's one or two holdouts. Most likely, they're hung up on one or two of the specifications." She didn't mention how critical that could be in the sentencing phase of the trial. She handed Claire a book. "It's one of my favorites, *Crossing to Safety*."

Claire settled into a comfortable chair while Lynn poured her a cup of coffee from her thermos. The coffee was still warm when the court attendant knocked and entered. "The jury sent Justice Wells a note."

The two women exchanged glances and hurried to the courtroom. They had barely sat down when the jury filed in.

Juror number three, a tall and dignified African American wearing a cleric's collar studied Claire as he sat down. Lynn quickly reviewed his profile. "The Reverend Michael Wright. He's a Christian fundamentalist, rigid, and moralistic. He's a retired Marine, a Master Gunnery Sergeant. He's used to following orders." She fell silent as Wells took her seat. They were back in session.

"Will the foreperson please stand," Wells said. The Reverend Michael Wright stood, again looking at Claire. Lynn groaned softly. "I understand you are deadlocked," Wells said.

"We are, your Honor," Wright replied. His voice was a rich baritone, measured and calm.

"It is not uncommon for deliberations to reach an impasse," Wells said. "At this juncture, I must urge you to try harder to reach an agreement. For those in the minority, do not surrender to group pressure, but listen to the views of others with an open mind. If you cannot reach a verdict, another jury will have to hear the same evidence and have similar problems."

"Your Honor," Wright said, "may we see the coroner's report and a printed copy of your instructions?"

"Certainly," Wells replied. The jury withdrew and Wells declared a recess.

"What's going on?" Claire asked.

"I haven't a clue," Lynn replied, trying to hide the worry that beat at her. They were dealing with a hostile jury she would have to confront during the sentencing phase of the trial.

Friday, October 28

"The jury is in," Lynn said. She was standing at the door of the holding cell in the courthouse basement.

"That's a relief," Claire said, coming to her feet. It was late afternoon and the jury had been in deliberation for four days. The waiting had weighed on Claire, driving her into a deep despair. She followed Lynn to the courtroom. She scanned the audience, looking for her family. She caught a glimpse of Stu at the back but couldn't make out who was beside him. Jenna Bradley was sitting in the front row with Rolinda and Hector.

For a brief moment, Claire and Rolinda locked eyes. The older woman whispered, "We love you."

Wells took her place and called the court into session. Claire and Lynn studied the jury as they entered and sat down. "Half of them are looking at you," Lynn said. "I can't read them."

"Mr. Foreperson," Wells said, "I understand you have reached a verdict."

Wright came to his feet. "We have, your Honor." He handed the form to the court attendant who passed it the clerk. The clerk opened it and passed it to Wells. She took her time checking that it was properly filled out.

Her face was impassive as she handed it back. "Please read the verdict."

The clerk unfolded the form as Claire and Lynn stood. Claire faced the jury and bowed her head in submission. Wells froze as the clerk cleared her voice. "On the first charge of murder in the first degree with special circumstances, we find the defendant, Claire Marie Allison, not guilty." Claire's head came up as a collective gasp swept over the audience. "There will be order in the court," Wells said.

There was an authority in her voice they had never heard, and the room was absolutely silent. Lynn shook her head, not believing what she had just heard. Longchamps blinked twice, totally astounded by the verdict.

Parker slumped in his chair. "What the . . ." He caught himself in time.

"It's called jury nullification," Mary whispered. "The jury disregarded their instructions and voted with their hearts."

The clerk took a deep breath. "On the charge of murder committed with a firearm, we find the defendant, Claire Marie Allison, not guilty." A loud murmur echoed over the room.

"The court and audience will remain in order," Wells warned, again silencing the courtroom. She nodded at the clerk."On the charge of kidnapping for the purpose of committing a felony," the clerk said, her voice shaking, "we find the defendant, Claire Marie Allison, not guilty."

Longchamps was on his feet. "Your, Honor, this is beyond all comprehension. We ask that the jury be polled."

"The clerk will poll the jury," Wells said, obviously agreeing with him.

The clerk called each juror by number asking if that was their verdict. It went quickly, with each juror affirming their vote. The last juror stood. "It was my duty to vote not guilty."

Wells removed her glasses and took a deep breath, composing herself. "The jury is excused." Wright stood, turned, and studied Claire for a moment. He gave her a nod and walked out with the jury. Wells made a note. "Mrs. Allison, you have been found not guilty of the charges against you. You will be returned to the Sacramento County Jail for immediate release. You are free to go. This court stands adjourned."

The senior woman deputy held the door for Claire when she walked out of processing. "Ma'am, I'm sorry we didn't meet under better circumstances. Good luck." She closed the door and Claire was free.

Logan bounded into her arms and held her tight. "Mom, I'm so proud of you."

"And I'm proud of you for being there and listening to all those horrible things. I was certain they would find me guilty, and I didn't know what you would think."

"Ah, Mom. I'd still have loved you."

47

Tuesday, November 15

It's been a week since the election and I'm ignoring the fact that we have a new governor. It was a close one and the recount will go on for days, but Allison's edge keeps increasing. For some reason beyond all comprehension, many of our good voters like a self-confessed killer. This could be the new trend in politics. If I were Ken Sellor, I'd stop beating my head against the wall. It feels so good when you quit, and it might be a hell of a lot safer.

I'm on my second cup of coffee and researching coed nude fitness centers for a story. They are the coming thing. I should be finishing up the documentary I had promised Larry the Neckless One, but screw him.

The phone rings and I ignore it, just like the texts and emails that have been flooding in, mostly from Larry's legal aides. Khepri answers the phone as it could be a buyer for the motel. She's hopeful that she can sell it for twice what it is worth. She listens politely and hands the phone to me. "It's Jenna Bradley. You should take the call."

"Yeah, right," I mumble. "Like I need another reverse rectal reaming." Khepri pokes the phone in my direction. She will be obeyed. I grab the phone. "Parker," I grumble, trying to sound authoritative.

"Good morning, Mr. Parker," Jenna says, all bright and bubbly. "Can we go visual?" I give in and her image appears on the screen. "We're writing a book about Claire," she announces. I ask who the 'we' are. "My mother and me," she answers. Writing a book? How old is this girl? Maybe all of nineteen or twenty? I can't help it, but I'm interested. I ask if she has a working title. "The Making of a Governor", she replies. I'm not surprised. "I would like to interview you," she says, "particularly in regard to your role in her trial. It will be a chance to clear up any misunderstandings."

That gets my attention. "What misunderstandings?"

"I was reviewing my notes on when you and Detective Zavorsky started to work with the Sacramento DA and how you discovered Bobby Lee's sex studio in Las Vegas."

How in hell did she find out about all that? It's time to talk, and we agree to meet.

It's late that same morning when Jenna walks into the motel's deserted breakfast room with her mother, Dr. Monica. She obviously wants a witness present, so I call in Khepri to keep everything equal. Khepri and Monica hit it off immediately and find a corner to talk. Why are the women in my life so damn willing to talk to each other?

Jenna and I sit at a table and we pull out our smartphones to record the interview. But I want to cut a deal before we start—she tells me her sources and I will come clean with her. Much to my amazement, she agrees. "I have access to a search engine and personal assistant program that is based on artificial intelligence. It was developed by one of Claire's friends." She smiles and touches her smartphone. "Nedd, please say hello to Mr. Parker."

"Hello, mate. Glad to finally meet."

I'm looking at a pleasant faced, middle-aged guy with a big nose and an Australian accent. He's sitting in a wheelchair in front of a bank of computer screens and readouts. My brain finally kicks in. "So you're the guy who gamed us out of our shorts."

Nedd shrugs. "It was a collaborative effort. Claire and I go back a bit. She helped me and I helped her."

"So what's in it for you?" I ask. My sarcasm is in full play.

"We're friends," he replies.

Yeah, really. Then it hits me. He's in love with her. But so is half the world. "So what's with this super-duper program Jenna mentioned?"

"Ah, that would be Gizmo." He starts to talk, obviously delighted with what his program can do. I listen, totally overwhelmed by what I'm hearing. Based on my own experience, humans are in deep shit. "Is Gizmo for hire?" I ask.

"For certain tasks," Nedd replies. "Give me a call and let's talk." That's encouraging. There's no doubt in my mind that Gizmo can find out who really owns those nude fitness centers.

"May we start?" Jenna asks politely. She opens her notebook, which still impresses me. "I understand you first became involved with Claire when she fired your mother, Dorothea Sue Ellington. I believe that was when Claire was the principal of Stella Madura Middle School."

"It was about the time of the Danny Hawkins incident," I reply. "Hell, you should know. You were there."

Jenna bestows a gracious smile on me. She's done her homework and fast forwards to my article about Sarah Madison and Stu Ranager's emergency landing at Mable's Whorehouse and Bar and Grill. "Hector Mendoza claims it was that story that won the election for County Superintendent for Claire."

"It was a very slow news day," I reply. She makes a note, and we move on.

"The World Review has published twelve of your articles," Jenna says, "including the exposé on illegal campaign contributions to the Good Shepherd Coalition."

Holy shit! How did she know that? "My name was not on the byline," I say. Common sense tells me to lawyer up. "You are assuming facts not in evidence." She smiles at me and the blanks fill in at warp speed. "Fuck! Nedd set me up."

"Actually, it was Claire. Both Rolinda and Hector are of the opinion that the timing of the retraction article and the photo in The World Review were critical in their drive for signatures to place Claire's name on the ballot for governor. The publicity put them over the top."

"I was glad to be of help." She makes a note and flips a page. I'd like to take a peek at what else she's got.

We spend the next hour or so, rehashing the investigation into Allison. Jenna has it all nailed down. "Mary Pearson, Laura Zavorsky, and Lynn Majors have all declined to be interviewed," Jenna says. Based on what Jenna is doing to me,

I can't fault them on that one. "However," she continues, "I believe your persistence was critical in Claire's prosecution."

"One does hope." She doesn't respond. I've been at this game longer and know how to turn it around. "There's one thing that totally escapes me," I say. "Thanks to good old Dr. Bale, Lynn had sprinkled enough doubt on the prosecution's case that even I was fogging up. We were watching the jury like hawks, and I was betting big bucks Allison was going to walk on reasonable doubt. So why did she take the stand and cop to it?"

Jenna chews on her pen for a moment, looking like a teenager for once. "Claire is very protective with a strong sense of right and wrong. In the end, it was a conflict she couldn't resolve, and the guilt was destroying her."

This from a teenager? I do my best imitation of a confused citizen. "I offed a pedophile who buggered my son, but I shouldn't have because offing pedophiles is so totally wrong." Jenna is not amused. "Are you saying that Allison offloaded a ton of guilt by letting a jury of her peers resolve her dilemma in some sort of bargain for mercy?"

Jenna fixes me with a thoughtful look. "I hadn't thought of it that way, but admitting her guilt to a jury was the price of mercy."

"So why did the jury acquit?" Take that and run with it, kid.

She does. "The term is 'jury nullification' where the jury disregards the law. I interviewed the foreman, the Reverend Michael Wright. That's a book in itself. He told me about the members of his congregation who were sexually molested as children." Her voice goes all soft. "The stories he tells are heartbreaking. In the end, the Reverend couldn't fault her for doing what was in his own heart."

"So, Wright swung the jury," I say.

"He did. He's a tough old Marine and bought them around to his bottom line."

"Which is?"

Jenna flips through her notebook. "I quote, 'Claire Allison is a shepherd who shields her flock. Only God can judge her for that.'"

I'm not having any of that crap. "So, Allison is a shepherd who shields her flock. You make it sound like a hymn they sing in church on Sunday."

Jenna gives me a sad look like I'm some sort of idiot. "It's her personal anthem."

"Okay, so how do you read the election?"

"I'm not sure, but I think the voters chose the person they could trust to protect them and always tell them the truth, no matter the personal cost." She closes her notebook. "I think it's fair to say that by bringing Claire to trial, you played a critical role in her winning the election."

Ah, crap! I really needed to hear that. First, the race for superintendent, then the signature drive, and now the election for governor. Three strikes and I'm out.

EPILOGUE

The low deck of clouds raced across the December sky and banked against the far horizon, letting a blue sky shine through, framing the nation's capitol. A black government staff car drove through the main gate of Arlington National Cemetery and stopped. Two guards quickly inspected it as a third guard checked the identification of the five occupants. They were all on the special access list. "Welcome to Arlington, Governor Allison," the guard said. He stepped back and saluted sharply, waving them through.

Clint Roberts returned the salute and wheeled the car slowly through the gate and up the narrow lane towards the US Marine Memorial. Stu Ranager sat beside him, keeping watch. He liked his new job as one of Claire's security detail. He turned around. Logan was sitting between Claire and Sarah in the backseat.

"I've a good buddy buried over there," he said, pointing up the hill.

"I heard that you have to do something brave to be buried here," Logan said.

"He was a Navy Seal and wounded in Iraq," Stu replied. "He came home with a Purple Heart and the Navy Cross, but minus a leg,"

"This is a very special place," Sarah said. She held Logan's hand. "That's why your dad is buried here."

They circled the Marine Memorial. Two marines were standing guard in front of the statue of the flag raising over Iwo Jima during World War II. They drove slowly past and down a back lane. The car pulled to a stop and the two men got out. Clint held the door for his passengers. Claire emerged, holding a small bouquet of sunflowers. Stu retrieved a long slender bag from the trunk, and Clint climbed back into the driver's seat. He started the car and headed for the parking lot.

For a moment, the four of them stood there, taking in the view. For Claire, it was a perfect domain, setting limits with the promise of things beyond. She held Logan's hand and led the way past the ordered rows of headstones, finally reaching the end. They stood silently, looking at the headstone that simply announced:

Henry Augustus Allison
Colonel, US Air Force

Claire gently laid the sunflowers on the grave. "I will love you forever," she promised. Stu opened the bag and unwrapped a small, but exquisite American flag on a three-foot mahogany staff. A Purple Heart medal dangled from the finial at the top of the staff. He handed the flag to Claire. Her lips caressed the Purple Heart as she passed the flag to Logan. He knelt and embedded the shaft in the ground beside the headstone.

They stood back and Sarah held a small bible. "I'm not an overly religious person, but I know this is true. 'Greater love hath no man than this, that a man lay down his life for his friends. Logan, your father was a very brave man, and if that is the measure, he set the standard." Logan drew himself up, standing at attention.

"You are getting tall," Claire said, more than ever certain he was the living image of his father.

Logan slowly turned, his eyes sweeping over the cemetery. "Were they all brave, like my dad?"

Claire answered. "In their own way, yes." They fell silent as a small funeral procession came down the lane. An honor guard led a horse-drawn caisson bearing a flag-draped coffin. An electric golf cart with a driver and an elderly woman brought up the rear. The procession stopped and six uniformed pall bearers slid the coffin back and carried it to a waiting grave, while the driver escorted the woman to three chairs arranged in front. She sat down in the middle chair.

"Mom," Logan said, "she's all alone."

Without a word, Claire led them to the open grave. The woman looked up in surprise, recognizing her. "May we join you?" Claire murmured. The woman touched the chair on her left and Claire sat down. Sarah joined them on the other side while Logan and Stu stood behind. "Your husband?" Claire asked.

"His name is Andrew," She hesitated for a moment as memories lighted the years long past. "We fell in love the first time we met. That was so many years ago. He was a medic in the Army and went to Vietnam. He volunteered for a second time and was wounded. He saved many lives and was nominated for a Silver Star and a Purple Heart, but nothing came of it. It was a bitter and confused time when he came home, and he said it didn't matter. We had a good life. Our children are gone, and, well, we're all alone now."

A chaplain stepped forward and read the service. The honor guard folded the flag, and a sergeant presented it to the woman. A bugle call sounded, playing taps.

It was over. The woman sat there, not moving as the honor guard and caisson retreated down the lane. The black staff car with Clint came around the bend and stopped. Stu bent over Claire's shoulder. "We have to go." Claire was scheduled to meet the President at a White House reception for newly elected governors.

"Mom, wait a minute," Logan said. He ran back to his father's grave and retrieved the flag. He marched back, pulled the Purple Heart free, and handed it to the woman. Her eyes filled with tears as she held the medal to her breast. Logan set the flag next to the coffin.

"I'll be all right now," the woman said.

"Stu," Claire said, "call Rolinda and tell her we're on our way, but we're running a few minutes late." Rolinda was at the White House coordinating her arrival.

"You have been so kind," the woman said. "Please, don't let me delay you."

"It's not that important," Claire said, taking her hand. "Would you like to meet the President? He needs to hear about Andrew."

The End

AFTERWORD

In writing this story, I wandered far from my normal genre and field of expertise and owe a very special thanks to William P. Wood. Without his expert advice and insights into both the legal and writing world, I would have lost my way far too many times and never reached the finish line. I also owe a debt of gratitude to those friends who introduced me to the world of law enforcement. Of special note, Joanna Rodgers shared her expertise in criminal forensics and investigations in a way I could understand, which was no small task. To an anonymous correctional officer, I can only offer my thanks for introducing me to the reality of the Sacramento County jail.

Jennifer Fisher of JSF Editorial proved again that she is an editor par excellence. Her skillful editing and gentle suggestions corrected many of my mistakes and kept the story on track. Again, a heartfelt thanks to Judy Person who labored hard to find and correct my many mistakes and attacks on the written word. It has been said that "The devil is in the details." Susan Ames, Amanda and Charles Henninger, Eric Herman, and Claire McGhehey cheerfully added the details and motivation that led to much bigger things. To one and all, thank you.

As always, the mistakes and omissions are mine alone.

Printed in Great Britain
by Amazon

50305579R00187